SELENA

Books by Ernest Brawley

SELENA   (1979)

THE RAP   (1974)

SELENA

Ernest Brawley

NEW YORK   1979   **ATHENEUM**

For Chiara, with love . . .

Lyrics from the following songs were quoted by permission:

"When Sunny Gets Blue"
Lyric by Jack Segal
Music by Marvin Fisher
© Copyright 1956 by Marvin Music Company
International Copyright Secured. All Rights Reserved.

"Do You Wanna Dance"
By Bobby Freedman
Copyright © 1958 by Clockus Music, Inc.
All Rights Reserved.

"(Sittin' on) the Dock of the Bay"
Words and Music by Steve Cropper and Otis Redding
© 1968 & 1975 East Memphis Music and Time Music Co., Inc.
International Copyright Secured. All Rights Reserved.

"Kansas City"
Words and Music by Mike Stoller and Jerry Leiber
Copyright 1952 and renewed 1958 by Halnat Publishing Co.
Permission granted by Saul Halper. All Rights Reserved.

Library of Congress Cataloging in Publication Data

Brawley, Ernest.
  Selena.
  I. Title.
PZ4.B8264Se 1979 [PS3552.R356] 813'.5'4 78-65199
ISBN 0-689-10951-2

PART I

One

EVERYTHING STARTS WITH little girls.

This little girl was walking down a white dirt farm road one day in June 1954. Her slender shadow was just twice her height. And it crossed the road in a westerly direction, reaching out nearly to the irrigation ditch that ran alongside. A single thick braid was bouncing up and down on her back. The braid was stiff and damp, for the little girl had just been swimming at the big Vanducci house on the hill. *Plomp, plomp, plomp* went her bare brown feet in the warm soft dirt, little puffs of dust blowing up in her track to settle slowly in the windless air.

Cradled in her long skinny arms she had a big nervous fighting cock with beady eyes. She had found him by the side of the road just a moment before. And she was very happy to have met him there, for she'd had no idea that he had escaped from his pen in her mama's backyard. The cock was brown and gold and purple. His feathers shone in the sun. He was turning his head all the time, fast and jerky from side to side. Her eyes were like the bird's eyes, black and darting. She turned her head like him too, looking everywhere.

Surrounding her were vast fields of alfalfa, tomatoes, and sugar beets. The fields were cut through with irrigation canals and county roads, sliced like adobe cakes into gigantic squares. The valley was green where it was planted, brown where it was fallow, and very wide, running fifty miles from the yellow Diablo Range, which rose up directly behind her, to the blue Sierras on the horizon. Lengthwise its dimensions were beyond her imagination: five hundred miles from Red Bluff in the north to Bakersfield in the south.

This was farm country, but there were no weathervanes or silos or split-rail fences or quaint barns with hex signs painted on them. Barns were great sheet-metal buildings resembling factories. Farmhouses were suburban tract homes. The landscape was cooking with mechanical energy, crawling with trucks, tractors, cars, and freight trains. The skyline was punctuated with the smokestacks of fertilizer factories, cement plants, canneries, and sugar mills, all of them spewing out yellow exhaust. Above the ground smog the sky was hard, white, opaque.

The girl loved her hot yellow and green valley, her white sky, her fiery western sun. On the other hand, sometimes she preferred the clouds and rain. Her mama always said, "*Muchacha*, you jus' don' know you own min'!" And it was true. One instant she was happy, the next she was sad. One second she was shivering, the next she was fever-ish. One minute she was screaming with rage, the next she was cooing like a dove. Some days she was sweet as cactus candy, other days she was mean as could be. Sometimes she was calm and reasonable, the medi-ator of all family squabbles, and other times she was crazy and irrational and did nothing but instigate trouble. In her heart she knew why this was so. The Virgin had told her. It happened in the field one day behind her mama's house. She was picking tomatoes out there alone, and all of a sudden the field seemed too . . . big . . . for her and the work too hard and long. She went fuzzy in the head. She fell to her knees in the dirt, overwhelmed by the immensity of nature all around her, the huge flat expanse of valley stretching away north and south and east as far as the eye could see, the great brutal brown mountains which seemed to loom over her from the southwest, threatening her personally. There was an electrical storm raging over the Diablos, the Devil Mountains. Thunderheads rose above them, black as ink, higher than the air force bombers that flew by. She felt that the lightning would come down and strike her dead. She felt a swirling dust devil would come down and sweep her up and carry her away. She felt a flash flood would come hurtling out of the canyons and drown her. They would find her a week later in a tree with flood debris—highchairs and tin cans and old shoes—ten feet above the ground.

"Oh, please, Holy Mother, help me!" she cried out in despair, with her lips pressed to the warm fragrant earth.

And then in her mind's eye she saw a great presence, female, rise up out of the heart of the storm. And she shrank even closer to the ground in fear.

"Hey-now-you-just-get-on-up-off-of-your-knees, girl!" said the appari-tion. "Get-up-off-of-your-kneeeeees!"

And it was not a harsh voice, but kind and gently scolding, like a mother who wants her daughter to do something, but quick, for her own good.

Trembling, the girl opened her eyes and looked up. There, way off down the tomato row, over the mountains, was a real-life vision of the Blessed Virgin, Madre de Dios. Yet, she was nothing like the Virgin that old Father Murray had described during catechism at Saint Ber-nard's. A dark Virgin, this Lady was, arrayed in silver and turquoise vestments. And her features were those of a beautiful Aztec maiden, a mirror image of oneself at a later age.

"Fear not the storm," said the Virgin, in a breathy, rhythmic, slightly Mexican-accented voice (a magically compelling voice that the little girl would never forget, would even imitate one day to great political success), "for you are the rain. Fear not the wind, for you shall tame it with a word. Fear not the great valley, for it is but made of clay, which you shall trample beneath your feet. Be not dismayed by your own nature, for you are the bird, and the bird is the rain and the fire in one.

Now-come-on-girl-and-just-get-on-up-off-of-your-knees! Get-up-off-of-your-kneeeeees!"

Then, after the Virgin disappeared, the little girl obliged her. She went right ahead and . . . got-up-off-of-her-knees.

And at that moment she began to scheme.

She would scheme for the rest of her life. And, through her clever scheming, she would someday become a remarkable person.

Already she felt herself to be remarkable in certain ways. Unlike anyone else in all this great valley.

And under her tattered frock her brown slim legs were swishing one against the other. And her breasts were budding already, changing color. She looked at them in the bathroom mirror all the time. And every day at school the boys chased her around the monkeybars, shouting *"Bonita, bonita!"* And every night in her dreams there was a little brown garbanzo under her mattress, growing and growing.

Her name was Selena Cruz.

Ahead of her now, a mile or more to the north, she could make out the bent backs of stoop laborers, her mother, brother, uncle, and cousins, working in the fields of Mr. Tony Vanducci & Son. Behind her, on the first yellow rise of the Diablos, loomed the Vanducci big house. Old Tony had built his first one-room shack there thirty years before, above his first precious irrigable fifty acres. He had planted a pair of date palm trees at the same time, out in front of his house. Now the shack had turned into a slapdash twelve-room home thrown together in different styles, different materials, different odd-shaped rooms. And his little date palms had grown into scruffy brown umbrella-shaped monsters that dominated the southern skyline. And his land stretched out in a patchwork pattern from the hills to the San Joaquin River, miles away.

Selena had spoken to old Tony only twice in her life: once when her mama's goat got loose in his tomato field and once when her father died. Tony was a tiny, ruddy, bald-headed man with huge round pop eyes and a square jaw. And he bore an amazing resemblance to his countryman Mussolini, whom he had supported with fervor till America entered the war. He spoke in a thick Sicilian accent. His voice was very high and completely unmodulated, and it carried an incredible distance across the fields.

"The Dootch," they called him in town. It had started out as a joke. But the nickname had stuck. In the country he was called "Patroncito," or "Meester Banducci." And no one made jokes. And yet the old man still possessed only one Sunday suit to his name, still drove his beat-out old '47 Ford station wagon . . . and him the Rico of Calmento, liege lord over a hundred permanent men and a thousand peons at picking time.

Selena had just left the patroncito's place a few minutes before. Left there every morning at about this time.

Out on the patio by the pool the patroncito's daughter-in-law, Angie

Vanducci, ran an informal summer school for all the "most promising" children on the nearby ranches. This morning her lecture had been the one on natural history. It was Selena's favorite. "In the beginning," it began. She knew it by heart.

"In the beginning," Angie had begun this morning, pointing a long red fingernail at the blank blackboard while her boy, Jay Jay, and her godson, Big Johnny Ammiratti, and his little sister, Rose Mary Ammiratti, counted their toes and Selena and her brother, Rudy, and her cousin Connie Pescadero and all the other Mexican kids looked up at Angie openmouthed at her eloquence, smitten with her elegance and *belleza:* her short, bouncy black poodle cut that curled down her forehead, her pert little titties that jiggled in their loose-fitting halter, her long tan legs in their tight white short-shorts.

"In the beginning what happened?" Angie demanded, pointing at one kid after another. But none of them would answer her. For Jay Jay and Big Johnny and Rose Mary were too bored to bother. And the Mexican kids, awaiting those sublime lines that only Angie could deliver so well, would not break the spell.

"In the beginning," Angie said again, smiling, teasing, hesitating. And then as a great double-edged sigh swept over the patio she launched at last into her lecture.

"In the beginning this valley was nothing more than a great flat plain at the bottom of an immense sea that covered all the West. Then fires burnt out of the molten core of the earth, pushing up a great mountain range," Angie said, drawing with amazingly quick and skillful strokes of colored chalk an enormous lifelike volcano boiling up out of the sea. "Then the waters retreated," she said, having won with pictures what she could not win with words: Jay Jay and the white kids had hunkered down on the tile now and were gazing up at her just as enthralled as the others.

"The mountains captured moisture off the Pacific Ocean and it fell as snow on the peaks. In spring the snow melted and raced for lower ground, carving deep canyons, depositing rich sediments on the valley floor," Angie said, drawing with wondrous art and precision each conception, animal, vegetable, or mineral, as it came to mind.

"And upon this deep, well-watered topsoil there grew up a great savanna. Herbivorous animals—elk, deer, and antelope—spread over the valley in their multitudes. Then predators came to eat the ones who ate of the grass: bear, cougar, wildcat, coyote, eagle.

"The next predator to invade the valley was man. He came from the north and settled in small independent villages at great distances from his fellows. A fisher, a hunter, a gatherer of acorns, he barely disturbed the land. It is now difficult to tell he was ever here. Only his names remain. Tubatalubal, Yokut, MiWuk, Wintin, Yano, Yolo, Maidu, Nisenan. . . .

"The following invader came from the south, and he lasted only half a century as ruler of the land. Timidly he clung to the Pacific seaboard, only venturing into the valley to hunt. He hunted in moderation, and the animals still ranged freely in their numbers.

"The last invader came from the east. He was white," Angie said, drawing a little white man with a Davy Crockett fur cap as she had drawn a little red man with colored feathers in his hair, and a little brown man with a sombrero on his head. "He was white and he brought progress—and destruction. In twenty-five years of his rule all the animals herbivorous and carnivorous and all the northern men were dead and buried in the ground. And out of their bones, out 'of their blood and flesh, there grew up the richest agricultural valley on the face of the earth!"

Angie terminated her lecture with a little flurry of chalk—a peaceful, productive modern farm scene—and a tone of voice that was charged with a powerful emotion. This emotion was impossible to describe. It was lost somewhere between exultance and nostalgia. Vague though it was at its source, its effect was profound: Selena would never forget it. And part of her would never forgive it. And it would influence her feelings toward her native valley for the rest of her life.

Then to dispel the pall that invariably fell over the patio when her lecture was done, Angie laughed loudly and shouted, "Last one in's a rotten egg!" And, followed closely by the children white and brown, she leapt into the swimming pool.

To Selena this dip in the pool was a rare and marvelous treat, served up only in summer, and only after Angie's lectures, which (on her knees in the Vanducci tomato fields, under the blazing tin roof of their packing shed) she would forever associate in her Hispanic mind with cool water and the coming of quick physical pleasure.

Now, a ways down the white road, halfway to her mother and the other stoop laborers, Selena saw a car parked by the irrigation canal. It was an ancient two-tone gray and green Cheeby sedan, rusted, battered, with old tires and boxes tied on top. In a moment she could make out a bundle of rags in the shape of a human form, lying in the coarse green grass on the bank. Closer, she determined that it was, in fact, a man, a large dark man sleeping with his arms thrown back behind his head. He was very dirty. His long black hair was matted with hay, oil, and dust. His toes were peeping out of his workboots.

And yet, she was not afraid of this man. If he had been older, toothless, bearded, oafish, like the tramps she often saw under the Southern Pacific bridge, he might have frightened her and she would have hastened by him to her mama. But there was something different about this one, something . . . open. He lay on his back, head thrown back, body abandoned to the sky. It was a well-proportioned body, tall and muscular in its dirty denim pants and jacket, with long legs, long thick arms, great shoulders, a tough sinewy neck. And under its coat of dust his face was beautiful, copper-colored, eagle-nosed, severe, like an Aztec god in a Mexican calendar from the Mi Ranchito Tortilla Factory. Yet he was not a stern god. He was smiling in his sleep. His teeth were bared, enormous. Now he was laughing. His chest heaved up with laughter. He kicked his legs in the grass. "It's a joke in his dream," she said to herself, as she dawdled near him on the road, holding her fretful rooster in her arms.

She just could not take her eyes off that man.

All of a sudden he stopped laughing. Turned over on his side. Curled up and slept soundly, snoring loudly, lady bugs crawling around in his hair, flies lighting in his ears and nose.

She carried on down the road toward her mama, meandering, squeezing dust between her toes, taking in the sights around her: a John Deere tractor straddling the furrows in the tomato field, a flock of red-winged blackbirds sitting on a telephone wire, the contrail of a B-47 in the sky, a dead field mouse floating in the muddy canal, tules growing in the shallows.

The sun rode up higher in the east. Heat waves rose off the blue alfalfa. The ground smog got yellower. The sky grew whiter, brighter, harder.

The next time Selena looked back down the road the Mexican was standing up. He was a huge man. The biggest Chicano she'd ever seen. Stood out against the horizon like a tree.

He did not appear to have noticed her yet. She stood transfixed, watching him squat down to wash his face in the canal, watching him stumble down the embankment to the field.

Holding her rooster tightly to her breast, she began to move quietly back up the road. The cock started clucking nervously in her arms, trying to flap his wings and fly away. She held him tighter. She petted his head. She toyed with his coxcomb and wattles. He shushed right down.

Up there ahead of her now the man had unbuttoned his pants.

Peering out of the deep grotto that was the inside of her head, looking through the two peepholes cut in the granite that were her eyes, excluding in this manner all the periphery of field and sky and mountains from her sight, she narrowed in on that big greaser. This was what she called her tunnel vision. In all her family, in all of South School, in all of Calmento, nobody had her gift. It was a gift of the great.

The man pulled out a dark big penis and urinated suddenly. A wide strong stream of pee, bright yellow, arcing spectacularly in the sun, falling indiscriminately on plants, fruits, weeds, cactus plants, splattering on the black-yellow San Joaquin clay. She was dumbfounded by his action. It stopped her in her tracks. That penis seemed to her the largest human appendage she'd ever seen. And it was so stiff and hard, jutting into the air like a great black cannon, firing a solid barrage of peepee into the field, killing things with it. And the most remarkable thing was, the longer he peed, the less and less stiff it became, till when he was finished it was quite limp, hanging down the front of his dirty pants between his legs.

Then he stuck it back in his pants. Buttoned up. Started back toward the road. Then he stopped and picked a big vine-ripened tomato. Wiped it with his hand. Bit into it. The juice ran down the black stubble on his chin, fell onto his denim jacket. She watched his teeth, his jaw grinding, the red tomato color on his tongue, his huge mouth. A horsefly buzzed around his head. A cobweb flew from his jacket sleeve.

He did not appear to have seen her yet, though she couldn't imagine why not. She felt a need to signal her presence. It was getting embarrassing, standing there unnoticed so long.

The rooster was fretting in her arms again. She threw him into the air. He squawked loudly, beat the air frantically with his wings, and settled down on the grass by the canal.

Out in the field, chewing steadily at his tomato, the man took no notice. In this way she came to know that he'd been aware of her all along and was ignoring her on purpose. Rather piqued by this slight, she chased her gamecock down in the grass, gathered him up, and stalked off again down the road toward her mama.

"Hey, *chavalita!* Where you get that rooster?"

She spun in her tracks. "Ain't a rooster, it's a fighting cock!"

"Where you get that bird?"

"Belong to my papa."

"Where he at?"

"Dead."

"Whew! Filipino down in Chowchilla, he give plenty for a *gallo* like that."

He was laughing now. The same nice open laugh she saw when he was asleep. Laughing and talking, he came across the field toward her through the tomato plants, his eyes sharp and dancing, like a bird, like her.

"Hey, what is your name? What you doing? Where you headed?"

All of a sudden he stopped, tensed up. Spotted something under a cactus plant on the embankment. Backed off real slow. Reached down for a rock, one rock, two rocks. Threw them at something down there, with all his might. *Bam, bam!* Got some more. Threw them too. Harder. Harder. Then he stomped down on something. Ground it down into the dirt with his heel. Took out a pocket knife. Opened it up. Slashed down at something. Again, again. Then he reached down and picked up a big headless snake by the tail. Blood was dripping out of the open neck. The body was jerking, jerking all around, coiling on his arm, coiling fast, letting go, coiling. He came climbing up the embankment toward her.

"That a rattler?"

"Look like it."

"He dead?"

"Yep."

"Don't seem like it."

"Takes 'em awhile," he said, and went right past her. Went over by the car. She trailed along behind him, fascinated.

"Here, take ahold of that," he said, and gave her the tail. She grabbed it, felt the scaly rattles in her small hand.

"With both."

"Huh?"

"*Dos manos, chavalita.*"

She released her rooster automatically. It dropped to the road at her feet and strutted off down to the canal.

"All right now, hold tight."

She clamped down hard on the snake. The Mexican took out his knife and slit it down its white belly, skinning it neatly with two strokes.

"Okay now, *déjalo caer.*"

She opened her hand and let it fall into the white dirt. The man cut the rattles off on the ground and threw the bloody corpse into the field. Then he hung the skin on the aerial of the Cheeby to dry.

"*Chale, ese,* where you goin', *rucita?*" he wanted to know, towering over her in the road, tall as a hill.

"Going down the road," she said, looking right up at him, unafraid.

"That your people down there?"

"Yep."

"Where you stay, anyway?"

"Over there," she said, pointing north toward the low white and green profile of the town, the metal water tower with CALMENTO WHERE EVERYTHING GROWS written around it jutting into the sky.

"That one?"

"Yep."

"*Casita* on the edge of town there?"

"Yep."

"*Oye,*" he said, "I won' tell you no lie. I am starving. You got somethin' to eat?"

"Where at?"

"Over home."

"Mama says, '*Don't you ever let no strangers in,*' " she said, imitating her mother's adult voice.

"Why's that?"

"Don't know."

"Well, she won' mind me," he said, whooping with laughter, slapping his knee. "Not *too* much, anyway!"

She liked the way he said that. He had an accent in English, very heavy. "*Not too moch,*" he said. Probably some kind of *cholo*, wetback from across the border.

"Ho ho ho!" she said, nodding her head.

"Ho ho ho!" And they had a nice little laugh together, just the two of them, about nothing special.

"Mama gonna beat my bottom!" she hollered carelessly, turning to catch her rooster in the grass.

The Mexican's car was hot, stuffy, and incredibly filthy, with open cans of food lying around, overturned, spoiling, and old dirty rags lying all over. The springs were coming through the seat. The windows were shattered. Felt from the ceiling hung down in her face. Under her feet she could see white road going by. But there was a lit plastic Virgin on the dashboard, and green, white, and orange tassels hanging from the window frames, and a decal reading MEXICO running all the way across the bottom of the windshield.

"Quite a short, eh?" he said. The way he said it was funny. "*Chort,*" he said.

"Seen better," she said flatly, holding back a grin.

"I bet," he said, laughing at himself, his car, laughing at her.

And the rooster clucking contentedly on her lap, her short torn dress, her long brown legs with no hair.

Cholo could not keep his eyes off that bird.

"Filipino give a *fortuna* for that rooster, *te juro!*"

"Ain't a rooster, it's a gamecock!"

They rode bouncing down the road, kicking up a cloud of white dust behind them, the snakeskin flying from the aerial.

Selena ducked when they drove past the stoop laborers in the field.

At a line of juniper windbreak she beckoned the *cholo* to slow down. Stopped him at her mailbox, which said MRS. DELIA CRUZ, 358 SOUTH "C" STREET, CALMENTO, CA. Directed him down her bumpy dirt driveway to the house. It was a little unpainted wooden house, with a green tarpaper roof. Cactus, oleander, roses, peach trees, and a small pepper tree grew in the dusty front yard. Chickens were plucking around in the dirt and corncobs and yellow wild oats. Next door, over a tall patch of corn, an irrigation ditch, and a high wire fence, Mrs. Alvarez could be heard running a miniature rototiller tractor, cultivating her beans.

Selena ran up the front steps, opened the screen door, and let the stranger into her mama's house. It was a poor but clean house, as he could see for himself. The living room was small and neat, with swept green linoleum floors, a big old moth-eaten davenport covered with a gay-colored serape, and a TV set on an overturned tomato lug. A cheap gold crucifix, a Mexican poncho, and a large black tourist's sombrero from Tijuana hung on the wall. A cage with two gray cooing lovebirds dangled from the ceiling.

"*Bueno, bueno,*" said the man, his eyes dancing. "Say, my name is

Aguilar. What is your name? Who is your mama? How long she be gone? This here is nice. What you got to eat? *Estoy casi muerto de hambre.*"

"Come on in here, Mr. Aguilar," she said, and he followed her into the little unpainted wooden kitchen. She motioned him to sit down at her mama's red formica table. She let her clucking big cock down on the floor and set about heating up some beans and rice on the gas stove. There were a dozen tortillas in the refrigerator. She took them out, heated them in the oven, wrapped them up in a clean white rag, and served them with a heap of beans and rice and red chile sauce. He gobbled it up like some kind of giant steam shovel. It was gone in thirty seconds, all of it. She just stood there staring at him. She had never seen anyone eat so fast in her life.

"Whew! *Mil gracias. Muy amable.* Say, you got somethin' else? I am starving, *de verdad!*"

She heated him up a pan full of Menudo tripe soup. He ate that right down too. Sucked it down like a vacuum cleaner.

"Anything else? I am still hungry," he said, *steel hongry*, touching his belly, throwing his head back, rolling his eyes comically, like Cantinflas in a movie she saw once. The more this *cholo* ate, the hungrier he seemed to get. The only thing left was to go out and pick some vegetables. It was harvest time so the garden was loaded. A lot of it would have just gone to waste anyway.

"Come on out here and help me then," she said. He followed her out to the backyard, helped her chop a head of lettuce, pick five big tomatoes, two garlics, a cucumber, a mess of dandelion greens, and four red peppers. Back inside she made him a big salad, smothered it in olive oil and chile sauce, tossed it, and served it with a can of her mama's ice cold beer. He gulped that down too. She sat across the table from him and watched him tear into it. The salad disappeared before her eyes, going into that great maw of his with those huge teeth, one of them solid gold, grinding, chopping it, crunching it up like an enormous bird. She loved the sound the roughage made while he chewed it up. She imagined him as a great brown eagle with fierce black eyes and gigantic black wings. She would ride him if she could, tucked wide-legged up behind his thick feathery neck, right across the sky! In her dreams she often flew, sometimes with her own wings, wings of a dove, like her middle name: Paloma. Sometimes even when she was awake she felt sure that all she really had to do was run and spread her arms and she would glide away over the valley, above the clouds. She would pet this great bird, this Mr. Aguilar, if she could. She would ruffle his soft plumage with her long-fingered little hands. She would keep him, if she could, right here in this house. She was not like other little girls and she knew it. She was always scheming.

"My mama ain't married," she said when he was finally done and a six-pack of beer was down his gullet, rumbling in his belly.

"That a fack?" he said, belching loudly, contentedly.

"My daddy died on the Vanducci ranch," she said, her heart going up into her mouth. Something was at stake here, all of a sudden. "Papa died last year. Got run over by a Cat D-1. He was still talking till they rolled off him."

"Hey now, that is too bad."

"Boss give us some money. Mama got it in the bank."

"No me diga."

"Yeah. Hey, you're dirty!" she said, laughing, slapping his big rough talon across the table. "Come on out back. We got a hose. I'll show you."

Dragged him around in back by the side of the house where her mama had a wooden shower stall with a hose and sprinkler attachment. It was rigged up behind a line of oleander shrubs and young eucalyptus trees for privacy.

"Go on now," she said, "get in there. Boy, do you need it! Pee you!"

"Hey, what you mean? I smell sweet. *Dulce, dulce!*"

"Like shit you do," she said.

Cholo started taking off his clothes right away. "Goddamn, *baño, baño!*" He kept shouting, *"Baño, baño!"* slapping his shoulders, jumping up and down. Took off his denim shirt and his T-shirt. He was a strong man in his thirties. Body just rippling with brown muscles. There was a scar on his belly, not too long, his belly with no hair, like an Indian, like her.

When he started unbuttoning his blue jeans she giggled and ran into the house.

In the house, though, she peeked.

In her father's closet there was a clean white shirt, a pair of clean suntan pants, starched and carefully ironed. There were fresh boxer shorts, an undershirt, socks, and a pair of polished high-top workboots. She took care of all this stuff by herself. She loved men's things and taking care of them. She loved to feel them and fold them and sniff them to make sure they were clean, and she liked to put them away neatly in their proper place, a way no man ever would. "Stop spoiling your papa," Mama used to say when he was alive. "Now you leave my girl alone," he would reply. "She is just a regular little *mujer!*"

She gathered up all those clothes of her father's now, her beloved gentle *papacito* from Mexico, grabbed a towel from the linen closet. . . . She was sweating now, down her brow, under her arms, between her bare legs. The day was heating up. Soon it would be up there in the nineties, or higher, and her mama would be home for lunch. Got to hurry, girl!

Out at the shower the man was already starting to get back into his filthy old clothes.

"Sucio, sucio!" she yelled, in horror. "No, no, wear these. What's a

matter with you, anyway? Huh? You crazy or something? You can't wear them nasty things. Dirty, dirty, *sucio!* Here, take these."

"Whose are these?" he wanted to know, real persnickety. But his face was lit with pleasure, and he fingered them like they were made of gold cloth.

"Beggars can't be choosy," she said fussily, as her mama would have said it before she went goofy-eyed with grief. Selena preferred her mama fussy to goofy. Goofy she was often embarrassing, babbling to relatives for hours on end, crying out in the middle of South Central Avenue in front of perfect strangers: *"Mi marido! Mi marido!"* Seemed like it would never end. *Mama Loca* they called her at school, *Crazy Mama,* and teased her poor daughter unmercifully. . . . "Come on, Mr. Aguilar, gimme them damn dirty things!"

"Eh, my walleta, my walleta!" he hollered, jumping up and down with one foot in the leg of his pants, and one foot out.

She got his "walleta" out and took it back to him.

"I'll give you a better one," she said.

For some reason he was truly moved by her offer. With tears of gratitude in his eyes, he said, "You are my guardian angel, *angelita de merced.*"

Then she got some kerosene in the shed and lit the incinerator. When his clothes burned they smelled sweet, like burning flesh . . . *dulce,* just like he said.

"Ay *simón,* do I feel better!" he said when he was all dressed and his black hair was shiny and slicked back on his head.

"You look better," she said, though actually he looked ridiculous. His pants were riding up to his shins. And the sleeves of his shirt only reached a little below his elbow.

"Here, take that cuff down. That's better. Now roll your sleeves up. All right, that's nice."

"No lie, no lie!" he said; he was bursting with happiness to be so clean, to be treated so kindly.

"Now lookit," she said, in a lecturing tone of voice, a tone she had sometimes used on her father, to his secret delight. "My mama's gonna be home now any minute. And she's gonna be real mad if she catches you here. But if you say you're *familia,* she ain't gonna mind."

"Familia?"

"Sure. Daddy come from Old Mexico. We don't know nothing about them, down there. You just say you're his *primo.*"

"Primo?" he said, almost a little embarrassed.

"Yeah."

"Where they from?"

"Cuautemoc."

"What state is that?"

"Colima, my papa said."

"Then what?" he asked doubtfully, then ran ahead with a barrage of more questions before she could reply: "What is your name, *rucita?* How old are you? When your mama comin' home?"

"Mama be home in no time," she said.

"*No me importa.*"

"Huh?"

"I can't stay anyway," he said slyly.

"My name is Selena Cruz and I am nine years old."

"Oh yeah?" he said, standing in the yard, squinting away into the sun. "Well, I tell you what. I think I gotta be goin' now. You know what I mean?"

"We have something."

"*Como?*"

"We have . . . something, in my mama's bedroom."

"What's that?"

"Come and see, come and see!" Selena said, standing on one leg in the dirt, crossing her little bare brown feet, hopping around, hop, hop, like a little bird, looking as cute as could be.

And led that big *cholo* back into the house. Into her mama's bedroom with its blond Goodwill bedroom set, its pictures of palm trees and lonesome Indians and sleeping Mexicans on the wall, its altar to the Virgin on the bed table, its crucifix above the bedstead. The rooster was in there too, pecking around on the green linoleum between her legs.

"Here it is!" she said, and showed him a blue Bank of America bankbook in which was folded a letter on Vanducci & Son stationery:

> Dear Mrs. Cruz:
> In view of your husband's tragic and untimely accidental death and his long years of service I am prepared to offer you a consideration of $500.00 in cash if you will kindly sign and return the enclosed statement to the effect that you will make no further claims on me or my heirs. Please accept my family's deepest condolences on your recent bereavement.
>   Sincerely,
>   Anthony V. Vanducci

"*Bueno, bueno,*" said Mr. Aguilar. But he was barely looking at it. He was looking at Selena.

She slipped through his big fingers like a bee through a butterfly net.

"Mama be home any minute now," she said confidentially, turning to face him, pursing her small pink lips that she knew were pretty, touching a single copper-colored finger to them.

Cholo let out his breath like he'd been holding it in a long time.

"*Señorita,*" he said, "you ain't nothing but trouble."

"Come with me now, Mr. Aguilar."

"What do you want from me?"

"I want you to be my daddy," she said. And she reached down and

scooped up her rooster in one easy motion and she laughed a triumph-
ant little laugh and let it hang in the air between them, and she led
him back to the front room where she placed him and herself formally
at opposite ends of the room to await the return of her widowed mama.

"Sure is a pretty rooster."

"Ain't a rooster; it's a fighting cock."

"Filipino give—"

"You want him? You want him? Here, he's yours!"

Two

O n a c o l d February morning a few months after Mrs. Cruz's sudden remarriage to Victorino Aguilar, little Delano Range was lying in his bed listening to the wind in the juniper trees out in back of his daddy's house. And to the rain pattering on the tarpaper roof. And to his sister Debbie in the twin bed beside him, sleeping deep. And to the steam engines in the Southern Pacific yard four blocks away, hooting and puffing to get traction on the wet iron rails.

Then Delano's daddy got up. Dad in the bathroom now, shaving at the sink. You could hear the razor scraping over his skin.

Then Mama got up and followed him in, bashing into things: the door, the dirty clothes hamper, the towel rack. She banged down the toilet seat and took a loud pee. You could hear it sizzling in the bowl. Then she flushed. Dragged her slippers over the tiles to the tap. The scraping stopped. Not a word between them. She turned the water on. Turned it off. Slammed the door when she left the room. The scraping started up again.

Now there was gray light coming in through Delano's window. Never would he look out of that window, no more. When he was in the second grade he seen a man there, late at night. Had a face like the moon. And he was laughing, laughing.

In the kitchen now, in a pink kimono and dirty red slippers, there was Del's fat little Mexican mama, standing at the stove. She was puffing a cigarette, scowling, scowling.

Then Dad came in. A tall, sandy-haired gringo, he wore black Frisco jeans and a denim shirt with his longjohn top showing at the throat. Plopped down long-legged at the table and started scarfing up his huevos rancheros.

Mama slid a plate of eggs in Del's direction. Slid it clean across the formica table. Del laughed. She didn't.

Debbie stumbled in, cranky, rubbing her slanty little eyes. She was only six. Built like Mama. Dark like Mama, with a voice like an angel.

Like Mama, she would be a singer someday, maybe, and go on the road.

Like his daddy, Del would be a railroad man someday, maybe, a rambler and a gambler, a teller of tall tales.

"I don't want no eggs!" Debbie whined. Even when she whined it sounded like an angel.

"Don't want no eggs!" she said again. Couldn't get a rise out of any-one. So she just shut her little face and plunked down at the table. Mama slid a plate at her. She ate. She'd got the drift by now. About time. Been going on for months now like this.

Dad gobbled his breakfast right down. Sopped the plate with his last tortilla. Got up and started for the door. He was wearing black rubber rain boots. Around his thick belt a switch key and a brass caboose key were jangling.

Mama just standing there doing her dishes, staring into the suds.

"Can I go with you, Daddy?"

"Little early for school, ain't it, Del?"

"I wanna go with you. I don't like it here."

"All right, *honcho*. Can't say I blame you."

Mama, she didn't say a word.

"Oh boy! Oh boy!"

Nothing Delano rather do than hang out at that old caboose with his dad.

Out on the back porch the windows were all steamed up. Dad got into his rubber overpants, his yellow slicker, and his black Stetson hat, a hat like no one else on the Southern Pacific ever wore. Got his lan-tern and brake club off the wall and opened the back door.

"I gave you everything," Mama said in the kitchen, "and look what I get back."

"You ain't the only one that gave."

"You got no idea what other people feel. All you think of is yourself."

"Don't know what's got into you here lately," he said, and went down the back steps.

Out in the yard it was howling wind, pissing rain. The junipers were bent over double. The dog was droopy-tailed. The chickens looked mis-erable. The lawn like a tule bog. Over the back fence old Tony Van-ducci's plowed-over tomato field was squishy and black as a bean turd. And beyond that were the foothills of the Diablos, cold winter green.

Del had his jacket on now, and a ball cap. Ran down those back steps with his daddy.

"Fuck you, Jack," Mama hollered out behind them, "and your little brat too!"

His father's name was not Jack.

Running with his old dad to the car. Running with old Eddie Range. Hunching his shoulders like him. Splashing in the puddles. Laughing out loud. Hopping up and down like a couple of baboons. Running from mean old Mama.

The car was sitting out in the driveway. A light green 1950 Ford sedan with whitewall tires and bright blue plastic seat covers. Blue was Del's favorite color.

Jumped in that car, slammed them doors!

Dad pulled out the choke. Started her right up. Just the two of them out there in that cold automobile. Every time Eddie wound her out she rocked back and forth. An old flathead V8 Ford. That's the way they would rock when you revved them.

The windows were fogging up, so he turned on the defroster and the windshield wipers and cracked a window. Backed down the driveway fast, splashing through the gutter.

Across the lawn there was Delano's house in the wind and rain. A low, flat-top house with a bay window. The grass needed cutting. The gray paint was peeling. A light was on in the side kitchen window.

Driving down Mount Diablo Avenue with his daddy now. All the houses on this street were just like Del's. This was where all the labor contractors had built. You could walk from one house to the other across the lawns.

Left onto West Street. Here the houses were smaller, made out of cinder block, painted funny colors: pink, yellow, purple, turquoise. No lawns here. Everyone had a wood fence. In summertime they all grew a vegetable garden in the front yard. Sometimes the corn got so high you couldn't see the house. Lots of trees here. Pepper trees. Cottonwoods. Weeping willows. This was where the railroad men lived: hostlers, roundhouse helpers, section hands. . . . Mexicans, they were not allowed on the train crews. That's what Delano's mama said. And his dad was the only conductor on this side of the tracks.

Right on Third Street. Here there was nothing but clapboard shacks. Belonged to farm workers, tomato packers, people on relief. All it was here was just cactus, junipers, oleanders, goats tied to the broken-down wood fences, ducks and chickens wandering in the dirt yards. This was where Del's Grandma Robles lived, before she died.

Down Third Street to South Central Avenue, the main street of Southside. Cantinas. Marquetas. The Mi Ranchito Tortilla Factory. When Del was little, his mama used to bring him here. *"Güero, güero!"* the ladies all hollered, petting his sharp little handsome face, his curly black hair, smooching him icky wet on his soft olive-skinned cheek. They always made a lot of him at the Mi Ranchito. *Güero* means light-colored. *Moreno* means dark.

The storm blew the trees. Bent them right to the roofs. Wet leaves flying. Rain coming down on the roof of the car. Harder. Harder. *Druuuuuum!* The street filled with water. The water blistered and bubbled. Mexicans on the dirt walkways, splashing in the mud, running for cover, hiding in doorways, laughing, yelling, *"Ah qué viento, no? Qué lluvia, caaaaaabrón!"* Almost never rained in Calmento, California. April to November it was dry as a bone. And a storm like today didn't come but once a year.

Left on South Central. Up the embankment to the Calmento yard, bouncing over the fifty-seven lines of track, splashing water every time they bumped. Switch engines out there in the wind and rain, blowing smoke and steam. Big iron wheels slipping round and round in one place, till the engineer sprayed the track with sand. Boxcars and tankers all around, standing still and running fast. Switchmen riding the slippery tops, their black and yellow rain slickers flapping out behind them. They were twisting the brake wheels with their long wooden clubs, humping them into other lines of cars, cattle cars, gondolas, reefers, flats, hoppers with funny names on them: Lackawanna, Phoebe Snow, Ferrocarril del Pacífico, Santa Fe.

On the way out to the caboose park they ran into a friend of Dad's. He was a little freckle-faced guy with a funny accent.

"Ello, Mistah Range."

"How they hangin', Mike?"

"Where's he from, Dad?" Del asked, as they headed over the gleaming tracks.

"He's Irish."

"What are we?"

"You mean what nationality? Well, lemme see. On my side of the famliy we are—"

"Can I be a conductor when I grow up, Dad?"

"You don't want to work for the railroad, son. No future in it."

"There's old forty-three thirty-seven," Del said.

Forty-three thirty-seven was a big red and yellow animal-cracker box on wheels, with a cupola on top. SPRR it said on the side. Inside the caboose the air was cold and clammy. Two long benches ran alongside the wall. In the middle of the car, under the ladder to the cupola, were a desk, a big captain's chair, a potbellied stove, and a sheet-metal coal bin.

Dad set out his marker lanterns, made himself up a pot of coffee, and sat down at his desk. He hoisted his legs up, laid his muddy boots up on the ink blotter, and leaned back in his chair. He pulled his Stetson down over his eyes and folded his hands in his lap.

"Now," he said. "What was that you wanted to know, son?"

"About what?"

"Oh, yeah, I remember now. Well, I tell you. On my side of the family we are one hundred percent Anglo-Saxon. Didn't I ever tell you the story of old Randall Range? He was one of the first white men in this valley."

"Nope," Del said. But, come to think of it, maybe he had heard it, a time or two before. Nothing old Eddie'd rather do than sling the bull.

"Well, sir," Dad said, in his funny story-telling voice that he'd copied from Okie guys on the railroad and perfected in barrooms and poker parlors all along the SP line. "Well, sir," he said again, shifting to a more comfortable position in his chair, "your great-great-grandfather, Del, was a gentleman from the county of Yorkshire, England, by the name of Randall Range. He graduated from Oxford College in the year 1834, and set out for America to seek his fortune. But at first things didn't go too well for him over here. In New Orleans he got into a duel and killed a man. In St. Louis he opened a dry goods store which failed. In Minnesota Territory he got himself thrown into the calaboose for selling arms and whiskey to the Indians. In Santa Fe he got the alcalde's daughter into trouble and was lucky to escape with his scalp. On the Gila River he was robbed and abandoned by a party of half-breed French traders and left to die in the desert. He wandered for weeks, living on cactus apples and horned toads till a wandering Spanish priest found him and nursed him back to health.

"All the way up and down and across the continent, Del, old Randall just ran into nothing but trouble. Till in the year 1838 he found himself marooned in the remote Mexican pueblo of Los Angeles, Alta California, with nothing but the buckskin on his back. At the point of desperation, he went to the local authorities and applied for a license to practice medicine. As proof of his learning, he showed his Oxford diploma, which was written in an ornate Latin script that none of them, not even the village priest, could read. Soon after, though he didn't know a scalpel from a paring knife, he became L.A.'s first doc. People rode in from miles around to see him, all the way from Berdoo and Dago, afflicted with everything from gout to consumption to brain fever. Within a year old Randall had made himself a small fortune, without doing overmuch harm to his patients. He introduced a friend of his, another itinerant gringo, as his 'worthy successor,' and rode north, looking for a piece of land where he could plant his roots.

"Well, son, eventually he settled on seven square Spanish leagues of prime bottomland between Mount Diablo and the San Joaquin River, sixty-five miles east of the little village of San Francisco de Asis. There he built himself an adobe hut and put in wheat, corn, kitchen vegetables, and fruit trees. The local MiWuk Indians heard he was a great medicine man and came to him in droves, looking for quinine for their malaria, which was rampant around here at the time. When Randall cured the MiWuks of malaria they were so grateful they volunteered to work on his ranch for nothing, just food and quinine. They didn't need clothes or lodgings, they said, 'cause they were so used to running around naked and sleeping on the ground.

"So, anyway, Del, to make a long story short, Randall's enterprise prospered quite well. With the help of his MiWuks he planted olive trees, nut trees, and even cotton. He rounded up wild cattle and slaughtered them for their hides, which were legal tender in these parts at the time. After a few months he took a wife for himself, a pretty Indian gal of fourteen by the name of Astera Chacón. Astera kept his house and bore his kids and lived with him for several years, till the Gold Rush came along and changed everything and reminded him all of a sudden that he was a white man. Now, it was in the Gold Rush that old Randall finally made the fortune of his dreams. Actually, son, he made two fortunes. The first one he made when he took Astera and his vaqueros and rode up to the Feather River and in one incredible afternoon picked up forty thousand dollars in gold nuggets from the sand at Bidwell Bar. His second and greater fortune he made when he had the sense to take his winnings and head back to the rancho and start selling hides and foodstuff to the forty-niners in the Mother Lode.

"Well, son, I'm sorry to say that in the year 1856 Randall got rid of poor Astera Chacón. Gave her the adobe hut, built himself a ginger-bread mansion by the river, and rode to the city to find a white woman to take to wife. Four months later he married Miss Maude Catlin, a fugitive from penal servitude in Queensland, Australia, and built her a formal French garden that people came from miles around to see. Maude lived like a lady for a year and a half, and died giving birth to James Catlin Range, who later in life got famous for bribing the Southern Pacific Railroad to come ten miles out of its way just to run through his property.

"Now, James, he married Miss Tracy Calmento Parker in 1878, and named the town he'd just laid out by the side of the SP tracks in her mother's honor. James sired five girls and a boy, William, who managed to squander most of the Range fortune on gambling, land speculation, and bad investments in the Comstock Lode. My dad, Hardy, who was William's only son, he sold off the rest of the property to old Tony Vanducci piece by piece to support his divorce habit and his four wives and four sets of kids. And by the time I was old enough to figure out what was going on, Del, there was nothing left, not a lousy crumb. Me and my sister Mary, we were born land-poor and raised real poor, and in the year 1943 I went to work as a brakeman on the SP and counted myself goddamn lucky to have a job, and a draft-proof job at that. In 1944 I met a pretty young lady named Rita Robles, who was singing at a roadhouse just outside of town. And I courted her and married her against my mother's express wishes (my dad, he was gone by then), and moved with her across the tracks, just to show the old bag, and the circle was complete. Because (and I want you to remember this, Del), because your mama Rita is the daughter of Juana Chacón de Robles, who was the daughter of Ignacio Chacón, who was the son of Octavio Chacón, who was the son of Carlos Chacón, who was the first child of the union of Astera Chacón and old Randall Range, a hundred and some-odd years ago."

Dad finished up his story with a great slow wave of his arm, and a big shit-eating grin.

"Aw, I don't believe that story, Daddy," Del said, laughing.

"That story is just as true, son, as I am setting here now. And if you don't believe me, when you grow up I want you to go into the San Joaquin County Bureau of Records and the Weber Museum in Stockton and then you'll see. And you'll be sorry you called your old daddy a liar."

"I didn't mean it."

"Yes, you did."

"No, I didn't."

"You promise?"

"Yes."

"You promise you'll go up there, when you grow up?"

"I promise!"

"All right then, I'm gonna hold you to that," Dad said. Then he hauled his boots off the ink blotter, wheeled his chair up close to his desk, and started sorting through a great big pile of waybills, adding up long columns of numbers on a sheet of lined paper with SPRR written across the top. "Shit," he said every once in a while. Then he had to erase and start all over. Dad never was any good at figures.

A few minutes later Del felt a shock and the caboose started moving. In railroad talk a train was called a "man." In the Calmento yard they had Fresno men, Firebaugh men, Roseville men, and a fast Frisco man. That was his daddy's man. Diesel engine dragging them over to tie them onto the ass-end of him right now. Del always felt a great thrill when he heard them rails going by, *clackety-clack.*

After a while, he started poking around in all the crannies and corners of the caboose. "Now come on, kid, quit fooling with my stuff!" Dad said. But Delano just kept right on doing it, anyway. He peeked in the closet where Dad kept his extra pressed suit that he wore when he laid over in the city, his shiny black cowboy boots, his clean white shirt and black string tie. Looked under the benches where he kept blankets, fusees, torpedoes, light globes, placards, time slips, accident forms, and other railroad stuff. Looked at the naked magazine pinup girls that he had pasted up on his walls. Just loved poking around that old caboose. It was his daddy's secret world. And Del was the only one who got a peek. In the closet there was a guitar and a bottle of whiskey, against company rules. On his desk was a picture of a pretty blond woman who was no relation.

Boom! they hit. Switch engine backed off. Dad went out and clamped on the air hose. *Sssssssssss.*

Then he pulled out his pocket watch and said, "Okay, *honcho,* time to go to school."

On the way across the yard they ran into the little Irishman again.

"Go on in and dry off, Mike," Dad said. "Water's on if you want a cup."

"Does he work with you, Dad?" Del asked.

"Yep."

"What's he do?"

"He's the rear brakeman."

"Where's the other brakeman?"

"He's up at the head end."

"Can I be a brakeman when I grow up?"

"I keep telling you, son. Wouldn't want no boy of mine on the railroad. It's a dying enterprise. By the time you grow up, Del, the truckers are gonna have all the trade. And people like me, hell, we're gonna be as extinct as the dodo bird. Just wait and see. Now, you hurry on up and get to school, before you get too wet. . . ."

Walking across East Sixth Street alone in the storm, going up the Anglo end of Central Avenue, past the Tom McCann shoe store, J. C. Penney's, Lerner's, Monkey Ward's, Safeway, Midas Muffler, Western Auto, the Ford garage, Delano played a game with himself. When the cars came splashing up the street he tried to see how close he could get to the curb without getting wet. After a while he got pretty good at it. He stood right at the edge of a deep puddle. And when the cars came through, he ran like the dickens, laughing when the water hit the pavement behind him. Pretended like he was a soldier in the war and the drops of water were shrapnel flying after him. By the time he got to West Eleventh Street, though, he was getting pretty wet. Then a lady came along in a brand new Ford pickup truck and drenched him from head to foot. Water came up in a solid wall. Hit him in the chest and face. Knocked him down in the gutter. "*Aaaiiieee, they got me!*" Water, smelling of dirt and grease, running all down his face and neck, into his eyes and nose. He was coughing and blowing, sloshing around in his tennis shoes, sopping wet.

Now, pretend like the water is blood: "*You guys go on back without me. I'm done for, boys. . . .*"

Lady pulled up to the curb ahead. Got out holding a newspaper over her black poodle-cut hairdo.

"Did I get you wet, honey?" she said, drawling it out. She was a slim, dark, pretty lady in a clean white raincoat. Looked like a rich Portagee lady, off a dairy ranch.

"That's all right, ma'am, it ain't nothin'," Del said. And then he tried and he started to sniffle a little bit, like he might be catching cold.

"Why, you poor little thing. Where are you going?"

"Going to school, ma'am."

"Here then, dear," she said. "Let me give you a ride. You look like some kind of drowned little rat."

In the pickup she had the heater and defroster going full blast. Felt fabulous. The inside of the cab was immaculate. Leather seats. Padded dash. FM. Radiotelephone. Dual spotlights. It was a brand new machine. And it rode like a dream. Machine set Delano to dreaming.

"Is that better now?"

"Yes, ma'am."

"And what's your name?"

"Delano Range."

"That's a nice name. And what grade are you in?"

"Fifth."

"My little boy's in the fifth."

'What's his name?"

"Jay Jay Vanducci. Do you know him?"

"Yes, ma'am. But we call him 'Tiger.'"

"Why is that? I hope he doesn't get into fights."

"No, ma'am. It's just cause . . . cause he's so big and . . . sleepy-eyed, with blond hair."

"Jay Jay won't be in school today. He's had tonsillitis."

"What's that?"

"It's something you get in your throat. You have an operation for it."

"Oh."

"He's in the hospital getting well. I'm going to see him now. It's just a minor thing. But I worry. You see, Del, I can't have any more children. And I lost my other little boy not too long ago. He died at birth. During what they call a cesarean operation. So, ever since then I have been a little bit . . . nervous," she said. Then she pulled up in front of North School.

"Thanks a lot for the ride, ma'am, and I'm sorry about your little boy."

"Why, thank you, Del. What a polite child you are," she said, petting his head. "Now, here's a dollar, honey. And you run along and get dry before you catch your death of cold."

On his way across the schoolyard Delano couldn't resist taking a quick swing on the jungle bars. He had long strong arms for his age and short little bandy legs. At recess all the kids laughed and called him "Ape Man." But they were just jealous. On the jungle bars he was champ of North School. He jumped now for the first crossbar, swung, wrapped his legs around the second wet cold bar, swung, let go, did a neat little flip, and landed on his feet in the soggy sand. Across the playground, in the lit-up classrooms, he could see all the gringo kids turn at their desks to watch.

In the classroom Mrs. Wallace was furious with him.

"What in the world have you done to yourself?"

"Lady come speeding by in a pickup truck. Splashed me and run off."

"You are going straight to the nurse, young man."

Delano liked it at the nurse's. Made up excuses to go there all the time. She knew he was nothing but a big fake. But she didn't seem to mind. Her name was Mrs. Pine. Had a face like a white valentine.

"What's wrong with you this time, Pancho? Aside from being soaked to the skin?"

"Teacher says I got tonsillitis."

"Okay, let's see. Take off your clothes and put 'em up on that radiator. Then wrap yourself up in this and lay down on the couch."

She threw him a blanket, hard. He started to laugh. He liked the way she handled him. She handled him rough. Under the blanket he let a poop and sniffed. It smelled good.

"Pee you!" said Nurse. "Who cut the cheese?"

Then she looked down his throat and stuck a thermometer in his mouth.

"Nothing wrong with you that a good licking wouldn't fix," she said, when she'd read his temperature. "But no use taking chances. You stay under that cover till your clothes are dry. Then I'm gonna drive you home."

"Don't wanna go home!"

"You should've thought of that before you started playing in mud puddles," she said. In a little while she took him out to her car and drove him back to Southside. He looked for his dad when they crossed over the tracks, but his train was already gone.

"You know, young man, you're supposed to go to South School."

"Principal says it's okay. They put down my grandma's address."

"Don't know why you ought to get special privileges," she said, but she was only kidding. She was always doing that.

At home there was a strange pickup in the driveway, a white Chevy, with mud tires in back.

Mama was mad because they let Del come home early. She was all dressed up to go out and she hollered at the nurse.

"What you bringin' that boy home for? He ain't sick. Anybody can see that!"

Nurse, she didn't say a word. Just turned around and skedaddled back out to her car.

Then Mama calmed down. Petted him on the cheek. Gave him a great big wet sloppy kiss on the mouth.

"Yuck!"

"Now what what what is supposed to be wrong with you?"

Del wouldn't talk.

"What's a matter, Delano? Huh? Huh? Huh?"

"You're talkin' funny."

"How's that? How's that? How's that?"

"Naw," he said, "I'm just kiddin', Mom."

Truth was, she really was talking funny.

"All right, damnit damnit damnit, you little monkey," she said, laughing. "How'd you like to drive over to the city with me? Surprise Daddy at the other end of the line. Been a little rough on him lately. Take him out on the town and make it up to him. How 'bout that? How 'bout it? How 'bout it?"

"Where's Debbie?"

"Over at Mrs. Alvarez's. She let me borrow the pickup."

"Okay."

He was starting to laugh. He'd never been to Frisco in his life. It was sixty-five miles away.

So his mama bundled him up in nice warm clothes. And they piled into the pickup truck, and headed down Mount Diablo Avenue to

Calmento Boulevard and over the tracks. A mile out of town they picked up Highway 50. And now they were heading west to the city. And the radio was on, playing Latino music. And Mama looked kind of nice, all dressed up in a green suit, white blouse, and green high-heeled shoes. Tapping her foot to the beat. Laughing, singing real loud, going "Ay ay ay!" at the end. Acting up, playing games like she used to.

Used to be she would take Delano out in the backyard and wrestle with him. Used to squirt water at him with the hose. Used to let him and Debbie help her feed the chickens, the rabbits, the gamecocks in their pen by the back fence. One time she had a mud fight with him. Rubbed it in his hair. He got her back. Splattered her all over. Rolling around in the mud. Then she hosed him off. Hosed herself off too. And the dog, Prince. Squirted him off while he ran away yelping with his tail between his legs. Then she picked Del up and carried him bouncing into the house. Across the blue linoleum floor, tracking water. Put him in the hot shower bath naked behind the blue shower curtain with her naked and washed him down all over. Washed him down. Washed herself all over too. She used to be so slim and pretty, then.

Over the Altamont Pass to Livermore Valley with his mommy in the rain. Laughing and cutting up all the way. Laughing maybe too much.

Past the Alameda County Jail at Santa Rita. Past Parks Air Force Base and Dublin Y. Over the East Bay hills to Castro Valley, Hayward, Oakland. Across the Bay Bridge to Yerba Buena Island and the city.

She took him to a movie matinee on Mission Street. 'Too early for Daddy," she said, "he's still out on the line." It was a Mexican movie, with Dolores Del Rio and Pedro Armendariz, and it was sad. Pedro died at the end. But Mama wasn't watching.

"Darling," she said, "long as you take care of home, I don't care what you do."

"What?" said Del.

"You know that, baby."

"Huh?"

"Believe me, I'm willing to forgive and forget."

"Mama . . ."

"We'll make a fresh start."

"Mama, I'm trying to watch the movie," Del said, but she wouldn't listen. Kept talking all the way through, right out loud. Cleared a circle ten seats wide around them.

Afterwards she drove him to a restaurant on Twenty-fourth Street. Guadalajara de Noche it was called. Del had a chile relleno. Mama drank wine and talked. Talked with the waitress and a Mexican man at the next table. Talked to everyone in the place. None of it made any sense. But they didn't seem to care.

"Time to go get Daddy," he had to tell her finally, pointing to the clock on the wall. "Now's when he pulls into Bayshore yard."

She drove down to Third and Townsend. Parked in the SP employees parking lot, right in the middle of a big mud puddle, and waited for Dad to come out of the yard office. She was fidgeting in her seat, lighting one cigarette off the other, getting lipstick all over the filter tips. Acted like Delano wasn't even in the cab with her.

Del was looking out the window. Across the parking lot a new gray Oldsmobile was parked in the rain. Inside was a pretty gringa with yellow-streaked hair and a sharp little nose. Del had seen her picture before. She was no relation. Had two little kids in there with her. Two boys.

Dad, he came out of the yard office pretty soon. But he didn't see Mama or Delano. Looked right at them, but didn't seem to recognize them in that white pickup. Del and his mom were both holding their breath. It was like they already knew what was gonna happen. Like they'd already figured out he wouldn't notice them. Would head straight on across the muddy parking lot, smiling and waving with his black Stetson hat, splashing through the puddles in his cowboy boots. In his clean pressed tan western suit and string tie. With his rain slicker over his shoulders like a cape. Going over there toward that brand new Olds. There he went! He was laughing now. Dragged one of them squirming little towheaded kids out the window. Threw him way up in the air. Yellow cape fell down on the wet blacktop at his feet. Blond mother smiling. Thin white mouth smiling at him, wide. The kid going up, up.

Mama, she cranked up the truck. Backed around. Goosed her in neutral: Vroooooom, vroooooom! like she might want to run them down.

But Dad and the kid, they didn't seem to notice, they were having so much fun.

Mama dropped her in low and crept out of the lot.

Then, as soon as she was out of sight, she hollered out, "I'll kill him! I'll kill him!" and started to drive crazy. Drove all over the road. Up on the sidewalk, even. Speeding up and then slamming on the brakes for no reason. Del fell down on the floor. He could see her green high-heeled shoe pressing on the gas pedal, clomping down on the brake. He was rolling all over the floorboards, banging his head on the heater and the door, feeling hurt and dizzy, feeling like he was gonna throw up.

"I'll kill him, I'll kill him!" she kept saying. But you could tell she was talking shit. It was like, since Dad hadn't taken any notice of her, she was too embarrassed.

Yet, on the way home to Calmento she was just as nice as pie. Stopped and bought candy and soda pop for Delano and a bottle of muscatel for herself. And all the way home she was sipping at that bottle, getting her lips all red. Talking real sweet. But too fast. . . .

Late that same night Del awakened to hear the pickup truck screech out of the driveway. He climbed out of bed and crept barefoot to the door. Fire! He ran to the window. But it wouldn't open. Ran to the closet. Got his baseball bat. Hit it, hit it. It shattered, struck the screen, fell back into the room. Cut him on the wrist, on the forehead and neck. He got up into the window frame and butted the screen with his head. The smoke started getting to him. But the screen would not give. He groped for the latch. Pulled. He couldn't breath. Pulled, pulled. The screen flew open and clattered into the flower bed below the window.

Damp rainy air came in, cooling his face and hair.

The wind had stopped. Down in the yard, in the flickering light of the fire, the juniper stood still and straight and tall.

A man was standing on the back lawn, his face like a winter moon. What was Del to do?

Behind him all he could hear was the fire going *crack crack*. In front of him all he could hear was the rain going *plink plink*.

He jumped. He jumped. He jumped.

Even before he hit the ground the specter had disappeared into the trees.

Del landed on the lawn, cushioning the fall with his hands. He sprang to his feet. He ran across the yard and through the side gate. Then, guided by the light of the fire, he set off purposefully across Mexican Town, making for the house of Mrs. Alvarez, the house where his little sister Debbie was staying.

ABANDONED BOY SAVES SELF
FROM SOUTHSIDE INFERNO

Six days later, while he was still at Mrs. Alvarez' place, Father Murray from Saint Bernard's came to call. He took Del aside, out on the screen porch, out of hearing of little Debbie and the rest of the household, and said, "My son, a lady in our parish has read all about you in the newspaper. And she remembers giving you a ride to school on the day of the fire. Now, she recently lost a child of her own. And she thought you were such a nice, well-behaved little chap. So, she spoke to her husband and got his agreement and they looked into your case . . ."

Father Murray was a thin, bald, elderly little man with smooth gray skin and bulbous blue eyes. When he spoke, saliva formed at the corners of his tiny white mouth. And his body odor was oddly sweet, like candied ham. He moved very slowly and softly and he was always sweating and opening his mouth to yawn. And when he talked you could barely hear a word he said. Acted like it was just too much trouble to speak, like it was all he could do just to get the phrases out of his mouth. At Mass on Sunday he always put Del to sleep.

". . . Now, you and your sister, Del, you are going to be wards of the county, you know," Father Murray continued. "Mrs. Alvarez hasn't the means to keep you here, of course, with her five children. And, as I'm sure you know, she was never a very close friend of your mother's. . . . She left your sister here on the . . . spur of the moment. So, this lady—Mrs. Angela Vanducci—and a very kind lady she is, would like to have a talk with you, Del. She would like to come over here and meet with you again and introduce you to her husband. And then, if you are willing, they would go down to the county welfare department and fill out a formal application to make a home for you as a foster child."

"Well, thank you very much, Father," Del said. "But my sister Debbie and me, if you don't mind, we would like to go back with our mom and dad, if we could."

"Your mom and dad?" Father Murray said, with some surprise. He was smoking a cigarette when he said it, holding it in his trembly little thin yellow fingers. When, later in life, Del tried to recall the scene, all he would remember was that smoking butt of a cigarette. It was a roll-your-own cigarette, wrinkled, wilted, and stained at the tip. Out of the tip a brownish liquid was forming, falling on Mrs. Alvarez' green linoleum. "But haven't you been told yet, Del?"

"Told what?" Del said. Though, the fact was, he had been told several times, by several different people, in two languages. He had even read about it in the newspaper.

"Why, your mother is gone, Del, and your—"

"Gone where?"

"Well, she has disappeared. You see, she has committed a crime."

"Then I tell you, Father, we want to go with our dad."

"My son, the police and the welfare people and the Southern Pacific Railroad have tried and tried, but unfortunately they haven't been able to locate your father. He hasn't appeared at his job in over a week. Now, I'm sorry, Del. But I'm trying to be as frank with you as I can. You're a big boy now. Aren't you?"

"Sure," Del said. "I guess we will go with our grandma, then, Father."

"Well, that is another problem area, I'm afraid. Mrs. Range has refused to accept responsibility."

"Then it would be awful nice," Del said, "if Mrs. Vanducci could take us in, Father."

"Mrs. Vanducci can't take both of you in, my son. But I'm sure that your little sister will find another home."

"Oh," Del said. And he thought for a long, long moment and then he said, "Gee, Father, I'd just love to stay out at the Vanducci place!"

"Angela was right about you, I believe," Father Murray said, smiling, smoking his cigarette. "What a polite little boy you are!"

Three

W H E N S E L E N A C R U Z W A S S E V E N T E E N she ran for queen in
the Calmento Jaycees' Frontier Days contest. Later she would recall the
entire episode as one long sultry afternoon in June 1962. It began in her
bedroom, a room not much larger than a hall closet, which reeked of
three bean-eating women, two of them overweight, all of them doused in
cheap perfume. Selena sat at her vanity while her mother and cousin
dressed her up for the last day of her long campaign.

"*La reina, la reina,*" they called her, lovingly, jealously, as if she were
already elected. And she *was* a teenage queen in her heart. For months
now the people of the barrio had hushed, blushed, held their breaths
in wonder when she strutted by. *Ay ay ay,* they said, she cannot be real.
Southside's own. *No es posible, no puede ser.* So straight, they said, so
long-legged and tall. Taller than any Chicana in town, and still growing. So haughty, so long-necked, and her nose always sticking up in the
air. And she don't even chew gum! Her back like a ramrod, her clicking
heels, her flashing eyes, her profile like an Aztec queen. *Ay qué chava-
lona esa, ay!* they said, leaving her personally rather unimpressed. "La
Palomita," they called her. But she didn't feel much like a dove. She
felt more like a falcon or a hawk.

Ay! Even at home they treated her like a celebrity. Her brother wor-
shiped her. Her mama waited on her hand and foot. Her step-dad
Aguilar would have laid down his life for her without blinking twice.
At her confirmation they dolled her up like a fairy princess, drove all
the way to East Oakland to buy her dress. When she got her first period
it was like the Miracle of Fatima. They walked around the house in a
trance for days, afraid to come nearer than five feet. Oh, that girl, she
was the *favorita,* never anyone like her before. And so smart in school!
Scholastic Honor Role two years in a row, the first Chicana ever. Oh,
they bragged on her all over the barrio, spoiled her rotten, fought for
her attention at the dinner table, would not leave her alone for even a
momentito. . . . Ay, Holy Mother, if they only knew how she hated
their adulation, hated the imperious virgin queen inside her that required it now, demanded it as her due.

Hating it now, precisely now, like a *reina* in her lavender spike-heeled
shoes, her flesh-colored stockings, black garter belt, black lace panties,
black bra, a tiny gold chain and crucifix around her neck, Selenita sat
half naked before her bedroom mirror. Behind her, through the small

window across the room, she could see the weedy backyard, the chicken coop, the dusty juniper windbreak, and a black and white nannygoat tied up to a cactus plant. Under the window frame she could see her baby sister Jovita napping naked on the double bed. Closer, in the middle of the room, she could see her round little pregnant mama, could *hear* her wheezing over the ironing board, pressing her daughter's new lavender dress. And still closer, just over her shoulder, she could see her fat, kinky-haired, pimply cousin Connie Pescadero ("La Trucha," they called her in school—"The Trout"—for her fish face, her funny little pursed mouth, her scaly greenish skin, her unblinking eyes, and her surname, which meant "fishmonger" in Spanish), could *hear* her, *smell* her, *feel* her. Breathing heavily, perspiring heavily under the arms, Connie was brushing Selena's long, shiny black hair. Back-brushing it. Beehiving it. Teasing it into a rat's nest twelve inches high. Selena's hair was rich, thick, very coarse, every strand like a piece of heavy-duty thread. Every stroke *hurt*, pulled at her scalp, the back of her slender neck, her heavy blue eyelids. . . . The queen winced in pain.

"Damnit, can't you sit still a minute?"

"I'm sorry, Connie, but it hurts."

La Trucha's only response was to stroke it all the more roughly.

"Ouch!"

"Aw, shut up, for Christ's sake. You'd think you was made outa glass."

"Connie!" said Mama, wiping the sweat from her low dark brow. "Now you leave that girl alone. Got enough work ahead of us, without you makin' things worse."

"But, Tía—"

"You heard me. *Ya basta.* I had enough of your jealousies."

On the bed Jovita had been awakened by the commotion.

"Wha? Wha?"

"Nothing, *hijita mia,* come 'ere and give Mama *un besito.*"

Jovita was plump and brown as a little bruin. She ignored her mama and, rubbing the sleep from her eyes with her chubby fists, waddled over to Selena to stand between her dimpled knees. Selena la Reina bestowed a kiss upon her baby *carnalita's* bangs of thatchy blue-black hair, on her fat smooth little cheek, cuddled her perfunctorily in the oppressive valley heat, the closeness of the tiny room.

"Stop moving, goddamnit!"

"I'm sorry, Connie. Here, Jovita. You gonna have to go back and sit on the bed. Go on, now. But first give Mama a kiss. Atta girl."

Jovita sniffled with displeasure, resisted for a moment, and finally did as she was told. Within a minute she was fast asleep on the bed again.

Selena devoted all her attention now to just being good. She sat as quietly as she could, knowing this would probably irritate Connie worse than anything else. She took a certain perverse pleasure in this notion.

At the same time she pitied her cousin. Poor Connie. What could a pretty cousin do to please her?

Often La Palomita felt that her beauty must be borne like a cross. By nature she was a shy and retiring girl, she told herself, a lover of shadows, of solitude and study. In her daydreams she saw herself in a tiny cottage in a dark European forest, all alone by a fireplace, in a room lined with books. Yet, in her heart she knew it would never be. *La reina* belonged to *la familia*. *La reina* belonged to all. Consequently, she belonged to no one, not even herself. She had every right, every privilege but the one she held most dear: privacy, the sanctity of self.

Selena understood that her queenship had at once glorified her and cheapened her, in some ineffable way. Her brother and step-dad, for instance. A year ago they would never have dared enter her room, even after knocking. Now they thought nothing of barging right in on her, even when she was half undressed. No longer did even the queen's body belong to herself alone. Sometimes she felt it as a great heavy weight on her, like her full new breasts, and she yearned for that slim quick little sparrow Selena of years gone by. Other times she felt that things were just as they should be, just as the Virgin would have wanted them to be, and loved and pitied her poor hardworking *familia* and *raza* with her whole soul, a soul, she believed, that was big enough for them all.

As for her beauty, the *belleza* that everyone was always raving about, to Selena's mind it had so far brought her little more than trouble. And the trouble, she knew, was just beginning. Yet she suffered in silence while Connie, "beautifying" her for the queen contest, yanked viciously at her hair.

Why did Selena suffer it? In her *corazón* she knew: *Looks is all I got, my only ticket out*.

As if to verify her ticket, her seemingly impossible luck, she regarded herself in the mirror. Coldly, assessively, in the manner of professional pretty girls, she looked at herself from the tip of her lavender-painted toenails that poked out of her lavender spikes to the top of her foot-and-a-half-high hairdo. The ticket was still valid. She *was* beautiful, goddamnit. A beauty by anybody's standards. A beauty just beginning to bloom. An imperishable Andalucian beauty, taut-skinned and severe, that would not fail or fatten or falter at twenty or even forty, that would grow only more beautiful with seasoning. Long-limbed, high-breasted, undulant, her body was perfection. Her skin was smooth, nut-brown, blemishless. Her bone structure was fine . . . divine. She had wide, high cheekbones and a strongly defined jaw line, but her face narrowed down almost to a point at the chin. Her chin had a large dimple down its center. She had a remarkably high forehead for someone of Indian blood, a truly "noble" brow. Her eyes were black as night, large and slanted like a cat's, with little points of yellow and red, and flashed like fire in the light. Her nose was broad and prominent, with wide, flaring nostrils. It was, even more than her eyes and skin color, her most "exotic" characteristic. It ran gently curved and bridgeless and perfectly Mayan from her brow to its rounded tip. Her mouth was very generous, very red, wine-colored, a remarkable natural color: edible. Her teeth were small, straight and white, except for her two front teeth, which overlapped in the cutest way. Her lower lip was quite full, with two little dimples at the corners. Selena's dimples, she knew, were one of the things that made her "pretty." Her upper lip was not as full as the lower, but still not thin. It rocked upward sharply, filled out, then descended to a small pouting kissable valley in the center. From this valley, two defined little ridgelines ran to her flaring nostrils. The indentation was shallow, but pronounced, and was also part of what people looked at when they called her pretty. She had an exceptionally long, forward-slanting neck, which she considered her greatest elegance.

The problem was, this year the Calmento Jaycees had deemed that the queen would not be elected on the basis of mere beauty. Queen would be the young lady who sold the most tickets to the Frontier Days raffle of a new Ford pickup. Her prize would be a two-thousand-dollar scholarship to the college of her choice.

Mama was sure that if there was any justice in the world the prettiest girl would sell the most tickets.

Selena labored under no such illusion.

And yet still before her entrancing mirror La Palomita dreamed. She dreamed of an ivy-covered campus in some cold and clean northern clime. Under enormous elm trees, she imagined it. In autumn, with flaming leaves. Elm trees like those at Napa State Mental Hospital where her Great-aunt Chacón died. She imagined a large clean girls' dorm surrounded by spacious lawns, flower beds, pavilions, benches, lovers' walks, quads where the clean-cut students lingered and gossiped, swinging their books in green Harvard bags. A clean white-painted room with two beds and two desks. A clean blond roommate with a photogenic smile. A neat college wardrobe all her own, paisley print blouses with Peter Pan collars, polished cotton skirts and brown loafer shoes with a penny in each one, and her hair cut short and straight in a university flip . . . ay! And then after college and graduate school she saw herself wearing a white smock over a tweed skirt, working at something very clean and practical and professional, working with the deaf, blind, or mentally retarded, something that would earn her good money, and the respect of the community, and would also give her a "feeling of accomplishment." She saw herself married to a gringo doctor. Ay!

"Okay," said Connie, "you're done."

Selena looked again in the mirror. Her hair stood precariously a full eighteen inches above her forehead.

"Oh, it's lovely, Connie!" she exclaimed, beaming her best smile at her cousin. "Looks almost . . . Egyptian, doesn't it?"

"*Claro que sí,*" said Mama. "Ain't she just gorgeous, Connie?"

Connie shrugged her beefy shoulders. "I better get outa these here jeans," she said, and headed for the door.

"Thank you so much, Connie. You've been a dear!" Selena yelled after her.

"Wait, don't you wanna see what she looks like in the dress?"

"Oh, all right," said Connie peevishly. And turned, and lingered now fatly in the doorway.

Mama held out the dress and Selena the queen rose, half naked in her lavender open-toed spike shoes and stockings, garter belt, panties, bra, crucifix, and strutted her stuff hippily across the room to the oohs and ahs of her female relatives. Stepped into that new dress—a thigh-length lavender sundress with white noodlelike "spaghetti" straps—fastened on her lavender-and-pink cluster-bead earrings that hung down and tickled her neck. She was perspiring now in the fierce San Joaquin heat, under her bristly shaven arms. Between her legs now her stockings were stuck together with sweat. She smelled herself, the sweat, the heavy perfume, the female smell. She smelled her cousin, her mama, even little Jovita. They smelled like her. She. *La reina*, the Indian queen. Our Lady of All Flesh and All Earthly Scents. Her mama took her hand. "Almost forgot!" Beckoned to Connie. Connie came back. She was smitten in spite of herself. Took her other hand. And the two of them now painted *la reina*'s fingernails, the last single item they had forgotten, painted them lavender, lavender, lavender, to match, to match, to match.

Wham! The front door. The sound of two men in heavy workboots, clomping across the wood floors of the little *casita*. *Blam!* They stomped in, violating with impunity their *reina*'s regal boudoir. A poor pair of Mexican stoop laborers, looking humble as hell: Aguilar her step-dad, big as a mountain, but running to unhealthy beer-and-bean fat around the belly and in the jowls, wearing his sweat-stained straw sombrero, his dirty khaki pants, his black Pancho Villa mustache; and brother Rudy, Rudycito, a dark, ferret-faced little pachuco, with an oil smudge of black down on his uneven upper lip . . . and a ducktail, a greasy pimp curl, a tattooed cross on the web of his right hand. And his pathetic self-conscious slouch that made him look like some kind of humpback almost. The *pobrecito, ay!* "La Rata," they used to call him in school.

"*Ay qué belleza, carnalita!*" he said now, croaking it out in his little broken-winded soprano voice.

"Man oh man, lookit *la reina!*" Aguilar bellowed. And both men plopped down and made themselves comfortable on her bed beside Jovita, amid teddy bears and carnival dolls and pastel pillows. Both of them filthy, green-stained, and juice-splattered after a morning's work in the fields of Tony Vanducci & Son.

Six people here in La Palomita's tiny room on a hot day, packed in like *sardinas*, smelling each other, loving it, loving the *intimacía*, six people, *la plebe*, pressing around ever closer to their queen. All eyes on *la reina, la reina,* who now sniffed haughtily, offered them each a brief flickering unfathomable smile, and floated away in a swirl of lavender and perfume to the bathroom, the only place where she would be left alone.

"Blessed art thou among women," she prayed, seated like a queen on the closed toilet cover, "blessed art thou, and bless please poor me for only thee can know, only thee can know."

Then she got up off of her fine ass and set about cleaning herself like a fucked cat for the third time today.

All the time she was washing herself, she was listening to the Alameda jazz station, KJAZ, on her little bathroom transistor, listening to her favorite album, her favorite song, "When Sunny Gets Blue," sung by that sweet-faced young gringo Chet Baker. A face like an *angelito*. You'd never know he was a junkie. And then his beautiful, lyrical trumpet solo at the end. . . . Selena saw herself as Sunny, the girl in the song. She saw herself as basically a "sunny" kind of person, who often got blue, who suffered from extremes of emotion, ups and downs, highs and lows. She saw herself with Chet Baker, in the event that she couldn't get into college. Exiles, traveling around Europe. She would care for him, nurse him back to health. He would be forever grateful. " 'When Sunny gets blue,' " Chet Baker sang, in his tremulous untrained voice, an innocent voice, wounded by life. " 'When Sunny gets blue, her eyes get gray and cloudy, then the rain begins to fall, pitter patter, pitter patter, love is gone, so what can matter . . .' " he sang.

And pitter, patter, Selena's great dark eyes began to cloud up, and she started to cry, and her tears fell on the tiny octagonal white tiles of the bathroom sink, splattering like rain.

It was a heavy delicious shower, and left her renewed and refreshed.

"Selena, Selenita!" her mama called, in her shrill peasant voice. "*Ven a comer!* It's gonna get cold!"

After lunch Aguilar came and knocked on her throne room door and she let him in. He wanted to map out the day's strategy, he said.

"Here is the way I figger it," he said, *feeger eet*, in his thick Mexican accent, leaning in the bathroom doorway, watching her repair her makeup. "The gringo, he make up two-thirds of the *población* of this town. Southside is solid for La Palomita. And we sold every other Mexican town in the north San Joaquin. So I think where we at now, we almost even with that Wop girl. But we gotta put you over the top, *mijita*. So here is what I feeger: Nobody thought about them labor camps yet. Who would think them poor wetbacks would buy a ticket? You know what I mean? But that is *exactamente* what we gonna do. We gonna hit every camp in Calmento. And we going right over the top. . . . What you think, Selenita? Eh?"

Selena, though apparently absorbed in her own reflection, had been listening to him attentively. But she hesitated to answer him now. She puckered her lips close to the mirror, reapplying her lipstick. Then she blotted, capped the stick with a little snap, and turned to regard him in the doorway. He was a huge man, with fierce little slanted brown and yellow eyes and a thick fringe of jet black hair. But he had aged and weathered greatly since that summer day when she wove her spell around him by the irrigation canal. And the weight he had gained, and the puffy black bags under his eyes, were not at all flattering. He had changed into a black charro costume, and his great beer belly hung over his silver-studded belt buckle. He held his wide black sombrero in his hand, swatting it nervously against the thigh of his tight vaquero pants. He was looking at her expectantly, grinding his massive jaw with apprehension, scratching his mustache, his two-day growth of beard. . . . Him. The father she had invented. He who had come out of nowhere to save her mama, Mama Loca, from an insanity of grief. Aguilar. The man who would make her a queen.

All of a sudden La Palomita broke out into her most winning smile, the smile he loved, a true Miss America smile that was at once genuine and affected, personal and professional, sincere and ironic.

"You know what?" she said huskily, approaching him like a woman, swaying her hips.

"No, what?" he said, trembling above her like a great tame *toro* in the doorway.

"Ay, Papacito," she said, "you are truly my tortilla!"

And, grasping his huge shoulders in her hands, standing on tiptoe in her lavender spikes, she impressed a chastely affectionate kiss upon his thick oily lips.

When everyone was dressed and ready, Aguilar and Rudy went around the side of the house and got the throne. *"El Trono,"* they called it, though actually it was just a large platform that Aguilar had built to fit in the bed of the pickup. It consisted of three big coffin-sized wooden boxes, two of which fit together on the bottom, one on top. Sweating in their heavy black charro suits and sombreros, straining in the windless midday heat, they loaded the *trono* on the pickup, covered it with gaudy Mexican blankets, and decorated it with green, white, and reddish-orange streamers and cardboard flags of Mexico. Aguilar had bought all the decorations and costumes at a Mexican outfitters in Modesto, and he'd spared no expense. He and Rudy wore the finest black Mexican boots, bolero jackets with red silk lining, white lacy shirts, red silk sashes and kerchiefs. Mama, Connie, and little Jovita wore long white, red, and green skirts, with embroidered peasant blouses, gold earrings, roses in their hair. . . . Mama wore her skirt high on her waist to hide her swollen belly. These costumes, and the two-piece Norteño band that Aguilar had hired for the day, had cost a small *fortuna.* Selena knew it would be many months before the *familia* recovered financially from her campaign. But she accepted it as her due. Her queenship would honor them all. And then of course La Palomita would work with the rest of them, queen or not, work all summer full-time

and all through the autumn after school and on weekends at the Vanducci packing shed to help pay off the debt.

On the rickety wooden front porch the women stood waiting in their
holiday finery, each with a burden to bear. Connie had a plastic freezer
of beer and soda pop. Mama had Jovita in her arms. And Selena had
her own load, her weight, her freight, her precious beauty, her fate.

There was not a whisper of air, not a sound but the grunting of the
men and the creaking of summer insects. Everything was white around
them—the sky, the truck, the dust in the juniper trees, the sandy yard.

The afternoon smelled of rotting fruit, wilting flowers.

The men finished up, put a sign on both sides of the truck:

SELENA FOR QUEEN
SELENA SERÁ REINA

And, summoning the energy from some deep untapped source, they cried
out, "*Vamos, que nos vamos, ay!*" And then, followed closely by the
women, they leapt aboard the pickup truck in a clatter of leather boot
heels.

Down the sandy driveway they went, the truck bouncing, springs
squeaking, platform teetering precariously, the white dust settling, sticking on their shiny Indian faces. Now up along the hot crackling gravel
of South "C" Street on an afternoon the color of tapioca pudding.
Gnarled pepper trees, trembling cottonwoods, wind-bent junipers, dusty
willow trees growing alongside the rickety wooden fences. Rosetrees,
oleanders, carnations, and tall corn growing in the dirt front yards of
clapboard Mexican shacks. Goats and ducks and chickens wandering by
the side of the road.

Rudy pulled over at Second Street to pick up the musicians. Two slim
young Indio-looking dudes from Chihuahua, they stood bow-legged on
the black melting asphalt, flashing their big stainless steel teeth, cradling their instruments: a fat guitarrón and a battered little concertina.
They were dressed exactly alike in Norteño cowboy gear. They had
identical brackish skin and identical grins and appeared to be twins.
Rudy had barely stopped before they clambered aboard, shouting, "*Ay la
reina, que nos vamos con la reina!*" Immediately they struck up a fast
bouncy polka in the Norteño style.

"'*Concha Perdida*,'" they sang, in their swift keening tenor voices
that were at once comic and tragic, happy and sad, "'*Concha Perdida,
tu de mis ojos, tu de mi peeeeeensamiento . . .*'"

Now the Cruz-Aguilars were caravaning down potholed South Central Avenue, the main street of Southside, waving at all the Chicano
pedestrians, passing by cafes, marquetas, cantinas with foreign names:
Mi Ranchito Tortilla Factory, The Golden Taco Cafe, El Chico's, La
Frontera, El Farolito. From inside the cantinas the usual racket arose:
whoops and war cries and loud braggadocio and scratchy Mexican music

piped out onto the street through loudspeakers set in the cottonwood trees.

" '*Ay Concha Perdida*,' " the Norteños sang, " '*day un besito al hombre que t'llama, para viva contento . . .* ' "

Whole cantinas emptied out as they tooled on by. Selena stood up, waved, smiled, tilted her dignified Egyptian hat (held stiffly in place with two cans of Richard Hudnut's Hairspray). And the drunkards, *borrachos*, sons of the great whore, they raised their glasses and bagged bottles and howled at her: "*Que viva la reina, la niña reina chicana!*"

Then the truck ran up the Southern Pacific embankment to the Calmento rail yard, bumped over fifty-seven lines of track, and glided out onto the smooth asphalt of North Central Avenue. Now as they rode by the Bank of America, Western Auto, the Low Ball Poker Parlor, Midas Muffler, the Norteños' music—their raw voices, the loud fast concertina and guitarrón—seemed rowdy and inappropriate to Selena. The SP tracks might have been the Mandelbaum Gate or Checkpoint Charlie. Suddenly her colorfully costumed *familia* was transformed. They had become loud and gaudy and vulgar. And Selena was deathly afraid that one of the other queen contestants, Clare Pine or Johanna Grierson or Rose Mary Ammiratti, would see her. Rose Mary was so beautifully coiffed always, so perfectly turned out in the latest Frisco fashion. And her daddy, the rich asparagus grower, he got her a new T-Bird convert for her sixteenth birthday.

Rudy stopped for the light at Central and Eleventh. All the Anglo kids were "taking the drag," cruising up and down, checking the action, low-riding, slumped down low and bad in their seats, rapping their pipes for the girls, digging the different Kustom Kars going by: Phil Hough in his loaded black 'vette. Frankie Silveira in his chopped and channeled candy-apple red "88." Delano Range and Jay Jay Vanducci in Jay Jay's raked '53 Ford pickup with chrome cut-out pipes and flicker hubcaps . . . All of them stopped at the light to stare. Some even tittered, or smiled to themselves, at this incredible load of greasers in their beat-out chile wagon.

Selena ignored the stares and repeated to herself, "I am beautiful, *soy bien chula*, I am beautiful, *soy bien chula*," all the way down Eleventh Street, all the way out of Calmento. Finally, just as they were leaving the eastern city limits, and as if to confirm his stepdaughter's dreams, Aguilar shouted to the truck drivers at the World's Largest Truck Stop: "*Ain't she purty?*"

And the gringos, big beefy men in baseball caps and greasy T-shirts, they raised their beer cans in salute.

"Hey, seen-yor-eeda!" they yelled. "Hey, seen-yor-eeda!"

And then they were gone.

Connie passed up some cold brew and soda pop. Everyone cracked a can and settled back for the ride. Selena tried her best to hold her hair

in place against the buffeting of the hot wind. But it was no use. By
the time they reached Carbona, where the labor camp was located, she
was a total mess. But the wind and the smell of the road and fresh-
mown hay had revived her spirits. And she was in high good form when
Rudy pulled off the highway and headed down a little dirt lane toward
the Carbona Canal. About halfway to the canal she could see the labor
camp, a cluster of long khaki-painted wooden barracks in the middle of
a great flat field of tomatoes.

TONY V. VANDUCCI & SON, CAFONE BRAND TOMATOES, a sign said out
front.

Rudy stopped the truck in the center of the camp, an open space of
white dirt between the barracks. The Norteños rose and started up a
new song, in the Corrido style. "*Justicia Ranchera*" it was called:

> Yo soy ya donde
> Que fué sentenciado
> Después libertado
> Porque maté al patrón
> Que me arrobado
> Derecho y libertad
> En un sembrado
> Que supe trabajar
> De ese lazo
> Mi jacalito
> También mi maisito
> Van perdido
> Diez años de labor
> Y sacrificio . . .

For a long moment they were absolutely alone, sitting out there in
the dusty plaza, in the rusty pickup truck, playing for themselves. Then
a small brown head popped out of one of the barracks windows. And
another. And another. Pretty soon a little wetback in Jalisco rubber tire
sandals, bare green feet, white cotton pants, and a low-brimmed Indio
sombrero with a little red tassle, came forward shyly. Soon he was joined
by others of his *carnales*. Then others with the more colorful look of
Nayarit and Michoacán, the austere look of Zacatecas, the American
cowboy look of Sinaloa and Sonora appeared on the scene. All of them
laughing now, shouting and calling out to each other to abolish their
common shyness. They were very excited, and delighted for this diversion in their otherwise hard and monotonous lives, lives for the most
part without women.

Slowly Selena the queen stood up in the truck to receive the homage
that was her due.

"*Mira, mira la reina,*" the braceros whispered among themselves, in
tones of the greatest wonder.

The Norteños finished up their first song with a chorus of ragged yells, "*Ay ay ay aiiiiiii Chihuahua!*"

Aguilar rose in his charro rig and his huge black sombrero and placed his large brown hand on the *reina's* small shoulder.

"*Mira, mira el grande . . .*"

"*Esta chavala,*" Aguilar began, in deep stentorian tones, enunciating every syllable, "*Señores, amigos, compañeros y compatriotas, esta joven-cita aquí, bien chulita como es, será la reina mexicana de Calmento de California, con el ayudo de ustedes. . . .*" And he delivered an extremely artful and rousing speech beseeching them on patriotic grounds to make Selena Paloma Cruz the first Chicana queen of Calmento, California.

Here on this rock-strewn white plaza Selena felt at one with herself at last, all-powerful, all-*raza*. She saw these little brown barefoot men below her as her humble subjects, and loved them with all her *corazón Azteca*.

"*De verdad, de verdad!*" the wetbacks yelled at the end of Aguilar's speech. It was a wonderful, marvelous speech, if a bit ungrammatical, and won them for his *causa*. Mama stood up now, with Jovita in her arms. Connie and Rudy came smiling out of the cab in their costumes. Aguilar beamed with happiness. The Norteños struck up "*Las Mañanitas*." The queen smiled serenely. The wetbacks went wild, tossing their sombreros high into the dry valley air.

Selena *la reina chicana*, feeling the mystery of dominion in her Indian breast, submitted herself to the arms of the *jefe* Aguilar, who lifted her high over the tailgate and down into the crowd. Ten brown arms reached up at once to help her to the ground. She landed like a swallow among them, with a fat roll of Frontier Days tickets wound tightly round her slender wings. She could smell these little Mexican peasants around her. It was the smell of toil. She found it not at all unpleasant. They made a circle around her and gazed at her in frank openmouthed wonder. The moment was suspended in time. Never before and never again would they see such beauty in the flesh. Their hearts would not beat again till she was a mile down the road. To La Palomita it was a feeling that was half-fantasy. She believed that she could if she wanted make them fall down on their knees in homage to her perfection. And . . . she almost did it! She looked at them. They went weak in the knees. You could see it. And then the whispering began.

"*Ay la reina la reina la reina tan bonita . . .*" And the sun above. The hard sky. The wind starting up, blowing sand across the plaza.

"*Quién quiere una boleta?* Who wants a ticket?" she asked, in her most beguiling voice, the tiny voice of the girl-queen.

"*Ay todos, todos, todos!*" they cried as one, besieging her, begging her to sell them just one little favor of her person, just one more little *boletita, por favor.*

All day it went like that, at every labor camp they hit. That evening, when they counted up the tickets, they were amazed. It was their best day yet. Aguilar was certain that nothing could beat them now.

Totally confident of victory, they showed up at the fiesta in Southside's McDonald Park with signs reading: SELENA IS THE QUEEN—SELENA ES LA REINA.

Then word came that old man Tony Vanducci had bought a roll of two thousand tickets in honor of Rose Mary Ammiratti, his only goddaughter.

Four

PLINK. PLINK.

Two o'clock by the luminous hands of his Timex. In his bed in the Vanducci big house, on a moonlit night during that same long summer when Selena ran for queen, seventeen-year-old Delano Range lay stark naked, stark awake, under the hulking poster of his hero, King Kong.

Plink. Plink.

It was Angie again, leaning out of her window on the second floor, dropping pennies into the empty flower box outside the screen. She had discovered an odd acoustical property of this remote corner of the rambling Vanducci house. Sound was squelched, and the plinking carried only a few feet in any direction.

Plink. Plink.

It had been going on all summer like this. Every time her hubby Bruno went out to supervise the irrigating it got worse. She must have raided a piggybank to have so many coins.

Plink. Plink.

Range crawled out of bed finally, breaking wind. Crossed the shadowy wickery porch and opened the creaky screen door. The Vanduccis' whole immense ranch yard—the shiny new pickup trucks and tractors and farm implements, the big new aluminum barns, the beat-out old private cars and junked jalopies, the piled roofing, stacked lumber, bags of cement, the chicken coops and rabbit hutches, the vegetable garden, the unpainted wooden cottages of the section foremen, the high wild oats and mustard weed between, and the yellow hills beyond—all was bathed in a ghostly light.

He could see her now above him, her frizzy hair like a halo round her moonlike skull.

"Shhhhhh, come up here a minute, Del."

She was trying to smile when she said this, but the deadly seriousness of her lust made it come out more like a grimace of pain. The effect was alarming rather than seductive. To Range she looked like some kind of beautiful ghoul up there who would suck his young life out, if she could.

"Come on, Del, really. This is silly. I just want to speak to you for a moment. Come on."

Angie always delivered her provocative appeal in a moderate, reasonable tone of voice. Unlike the rest of the Vanduccis, she was very careful with her diction and prided herself on her intelligence, breeding, and musical talents. She was equally unlike them in her looks. Small, slender, and very dark, with mischievous blue eyes, a Roman nose, and a wide laughing red mouth, she was exceptionally attractive and extraordinarily youthful in appearance. People were always saying she looked more like Jay Jay's elder sister than his mother. Actually, she was older than Bruno by a couple of years. She had been a girl friend of his brother Mike's, before he went off to get killed in the Pacific. Her father, a Manteca winegrower of Tuscan origins, had aristocratic pretensions and held himself above the Sicilian Vanduccis.

Angie held an AA degree from Modesto Junior College, a BA from Fresno State, played the organ at Saint Bernard's, and belonged to the Native Daughters of the Golden West. But she was slovenly in her personal habits and kept a dirty house.

"Come up here for a second, Del. Please. Just for a moment, I promise."

He said nothing, pretended to reflect on the proposition for a second, then smiled politely up at her, shook his head no thanks, shut the screen door, and padded back across the moonlit porch to his bed.

Plink. Plink.

There went them damn pennies again. And yet, Range knew, if he actually succumbed to her wiles, actually sneaked up to her room, kissed her pretty olive-skinned face, entered her thin shapely body, she was capable of reacting in any number of ways, several of which could be to his distinct disadvantage. This was not mere speculation on Range's part. Angie could be thoughtful and thoughtless, constructive and destructive by turns. Seven years ago, from what her boy Jay Jay said, she had moved heaven and earth and bucked everyone in the 'Ducci family to get Del accepted as a foster child. Yet once she'd achieved her desire, she had ignored his existence for months, left him to fend completely for himself. Then suddenly one evening for no particular reason she ran across the living room in front of the whole family and smothered him in wet gooey kisses, the kind that all little boys hate.

It was not that Angie was a cold or calculating person. She behaved this way on impulse. Her nature was passionate. But her passion was exceedingly short-lived.

If Range went up to her room right now, there was a chance she would cry rape once she'd got her rocks off. Or kick him out of the house for good. Send him back to the county. The possibility was remote. But he could not afford the risk.

This was a sad commentary on his relations with the Vanduccis, but all too true. Range had come as a stranger, and a stranger he remained. The 'Duccis treated him more like an employee than a member of the family. Kept him as a house nigger, dishwasher, packing shed slave. Wouldn't even let him work in the field with the men, or trust him with a forklift or tractor. And Bruno and Tony let him know in a million different little ways that he was not a Vanducci, that he was not Italian, that he was not to get any ideas, that he could stick around and eat 'Ducci chow till he was grown, and then he must be on his way. They didn't even try to be subtle about it. Like old Tony said, every time he got the chance: *"Guarda serpe nella casa è subito diviene morso. . . .* Keep a snake in the house and soon you get bit."

And even their boy Jay Jay, he had turned out to be an unsteady friend at best. They were the same age and hung out together at school, but there was never any question of calling each other "brother." "This is Del," Jay Jay would say to strangers. "He lives here with us on the ranch." And he could be real touchy too. One minute he might be nice as pie. And then the next he might haul off and slug you for no reason, or ridicule you in front of his dad. And he was always inventing excuses to touch you in creepy ways, to pinch you in the crotch, slap your cheeks, goose you with his thumb, give you Indian burns.

Therefore, and such as she was, Angie was Range's sole protector on the 'Ducci ranch. And he felt he could take absolutely no chance of alienating her, even through loving her . . . too much.

Still, sometimes he found Angie almost unbearably attractive. Here was a grown woman of forty-one, after all, his own foster mother, who wanted him, wanted *him*. He found her especially seductive when she got herself all dolled up in her long black wig and cowboy outfit to go to do with the fact that she wanted more kids but couldn't have any, on Saturday night. She had the kind of shivery distracted awareness of her own body that many frustrated ladies possess. It all had something to do with the fact that she wanted more kids but couldn't have any, Range figured. For some crazy reason, maybe because she believed that promiscuous sex might somehow make her fertile again, she had convinced herself that she was a wanton woman. And, right or wrong, her conviction was sufficiently strong to tempt the imagination of a horny teenage jack-off artist like Delano Range.

Plink. Plink. All through the night. It was like a little silver bell in his ear with just the tiniest flaw . . . incredibly sweet, incredibly false.

Sitting up on a pile of overturned tomato lugs the next morning, leaning against the hot tin siding of the packing shed, smoking cigarettes and shooting the shit about nothing in particular, Range and his new friends the Cruz kids enjoyed their long break. The gray behemoth above them—a maze of motors, belts, rollers, conveyors, stays, struts, wires, chutes, electrical circuitry, canvas webbing, ball bearings, water tanks, fuel tanks, chains, and gear boxes—the great machine was dead, reeking of squished fruit on a hot day.

Hazy August sunlight splashed through the big sliding doors, through the skylights high on the tin roof. All along the wall the workers sat or lay on the cool green-spattered floor. Old people, young people, Mexicans, Filipinos, niggers, they spoke loudly in their various languages, smoked, spat, chewed gum, laughed, adjusted their straw hats and bandannas, scraped the encrusted tomato gunk off their boots, and sipped at their Mission Orange soda pop.

Though Range bitterly resented the 'Duccis for treating him like a peon—him, Delano Fucking Lee Range, the only white male descendant of the original owners of this goddamn land—the truth was that he enjoyed working at the packing shed. He liked the potpourri of races, colors, lingos, liked the noise of the workers, who laughed and yelled and joked with each other to kill time. He liked their smell, sweaty and sour from the heat. He liked the sound of the machines when they were running full blast. He liked the coffee breaks and noon breaks, when he would work out on the horizontal bars above the conveyor machine, earning loud applause with his incredible feats of gymnastic derring-do, swinging, vaulting, upstarts, giant circles forward and backward without pausing, whirling his entire body round and round like a windmill with changes from left to right handgrips, with bar releases, handstands, uprises, and dismounts with backflips off the bar. . . . And then the sore but good feeling of his body after a hard day's work and a long hot shower. . . .

To tell the truth, Range's highest ambition in life was one day to be a Vanducci foreman. And there was no place in the world he'd rather be right now than right here on these tomato lugs, sitting next to beautiful Selena Cruz. The only discordant note in the whole place was Jay Jay out on the floor, roaring around on his grandaddy's new red Fergy Forklift, showing off for the Chicana girls.

"*Chale, ese,*" said Rudy La Rata, spitting in Jay Jay's direction, "that fuckin' gringo. *Watchalo.*"

Small, wiry and slump-backed, mahogany-colored and slippery as a sidewinder, Rudy wore his cigarettes rolled up in his stained T-shirt. His arms were festooned with home-needled tattoos: "C/S," "Pocho Yo," "Born to Lose," a pair of dice, and a crudely drawn pachuco cross. When he spoke, his tiny pointed tongue darted out to lick the corners of his wet purple mouth. He was never without his bebop shades. Range found him delightfully unsavory.

Though Delano had known Rudy all his life, had even played kick-the-can with him and his sister on the dirt streets of Southside when he was a kid, it was only here on the conveyor line that he had reestablished an acquaintanceship with the Mexican boy. Neither of them had any illusions of its extending beyond the walls of the packing shed. In Calmento the races were rigidly separated by caste, custom, convention, discrimination, and railroad tracks. And Range had long ago crossed the line. Though the two boys had been born in the same town, lived on the same man's property, and went to the same high school (till Rudy got kicked out), they had sometimes gone years without speaking to each other. And there was something absurdly foreign and mysterious about Rudy that Range found utterly charming.

"No lie, *mano*," Delano said, grinning widely, proud of his new rap with Pocho Caló, the Chicano dialect. "Jay Jay's a real *gabacho pendejo*, even if he is *mi carnal*."

"*Ay, simón*," Selena said, laughing, slapping his hand. "You *vatos* are just jealous, that's all."

Selena wore a red and yellow bandanna around her hair in a kind of turban. To Range she looked absolutely bitchin', bewitchin', looked like some kind of fuckin' Cherokee, looked wild as hell.

"Of what?" La Rata said. "Take his bread and the fucker's nothing."

"*Oye*, bro, you better cool it."

"What for?"

"Here is his *compadre*, no?"

"I don't give a sheet."

"Eh?"

"Delanito is our leetle frien'. He ain' gonna tell nobody. Right, *cuñado*?"

"*Consafo, puto*," said Range. "No way, man."

"Ain't it something?" Selena said.

'The way this gringo raps Pocho Caló?"

"Yeah."

"*Nel*. Another month, the *vato* gonna be the king of the baby chooks."

"*Pues claro que sí, cabrón!*" Range yelled, wrapping his tongue around the difficult Spanish syllables. "*Qué loco yo, no? Soy el carnal del Candi y el Ponchi!*"

La Rata hooted with pleasure, slapped the unclean knee of his khaki pants. "*Ese, mano*, I still don't know how you do it. How you do it, *chingado?*"

"Eh, you know, man. *La jefita* was *chicana pura*."

'To be Pocho," Selena said, with some dignity, "you got to have more than just a Pocho mother. You got to pay Pocho dues."

And that shut Range's yap right up. He was nowhere near ready to pay them kind of dues. Sure, he might dig hanging out with the Cruz kids on the job. And it was groovy speaking dialect with them. And Selena turned him on something fierce. But he ate lunch every day with the boss's son. And he wouldn't live in Southside if you paid him.

Ruuuuuum, ruuuuuum! There went Jay Jay now, a great big blond four-eyed fucker with a flat-top haircut and shoulders like a pro full-back, up on his grandaddy's fancy forklift. He wailed down to the end of the shed at twenty per, raising his forks as he went. Slammed on his brakes, skidded into the truck, teetering precariously, and then slipped his forks to the pallet. It was an act of perfect skill, an act of almost sexual beauty. Then he lifted the whole big load of green tomatoes, seven lugs high, lifted it clean off the truck and lowered his forks and spun around in one easy motion, a motion so wonderfully coordinated it was more animal than machine. Barreled down the length of the shed again, *ruuuuuum!* with the tomatoes held high above the concrete on his forks like prey in the claws of tyrannosaurus rex. Spun again on the front wheel, raising his forks at the same time. Laid his burden up nice on top of the huge stacks of pallets and boxes without a jiggle, crack, or bounce, without losing a single tomato out of all those thousands. Jay Jay was a true artist of the forklift. Made no mistakes, no wasted motions. On his broad young face was an expression of total concentration, total exaltation. In five minutes he had the whole truck unloaded and was whipping around the shed feeding conveyor loaders with fresh pallets of tomatoes.

His daddy Bruno looked tickled pink. You could tell the kid was the apple of his eye. But he'd never let that on to Jay Jay. He trained his boy hard, just like old Tony had trained him—still trained him. Thirty-nine years old, for Christ's sake, and still no voice in the ranch business, still living with his wife and kid in his daddy's old wooden house above the tomato fields. And old man Vanducci farming four thousand acres of the richest farmland in all of California.

A stocky, red-faced, hairy blond man with huge arms, great tough hands, Bruno had been standing in the doorway of the office for an hour now, waiting for a fresh load of tomatoes from the field. Fretting and fuming, prodded and nagged by old Tony, who was sitting at his desk behind the office door (old Tony who was losing money, paying his help by the hour to lay around on their asses), Bruno had just about been ready to have a shit-fit when the tomato trucks showed up at last.

"Goddamn you drivers!" he had shouted furiously. "Where in the holy fuckin' hell have you been anyway?"

"It ain't our fault, Mr. Vanducci," one of them had yelled out of his cab, "it's on account of the—"

"Hey!" the Dootch had hollered, appearing suddenly beside his son in the office doorway. "Ask a stupid question and you get a stupid answer."

"Aw, Pop," Bruno had whined. "Now, what do you mean by that?"

"How come you ask them boys where they been? You oughta *know* where they been, for Christ's sake. Whatta you think I pay you for?"

"Come on, Pop, it ain't my fault."

"Not your fault?" the old man had said, shaking a finger at his son, and speaking in a tone of voice that was meant to be heard by the whole packing shed. "Then whose fault is it, huh? Is it mine? Is it? Huh?"

And then, just when things had looked bleakest, and Bruno had stood humiliated in front of all his employees, Jay Jay had saved the day.

Working like a demon, doing the work of ten forklift drivers, unloading the boxes in record time, he had primed the entire packing shed for a long new morning's run.

And how did Bruno show his appreciation? He went at the kid all the harder. Just like his own dad did with him.

"Jay Jay, goddamn you!" Bruno hollered. "Stop speedshifting that thing or I'll have your ass. You're gonna strip them gears for sure!"

All the workers laughed. Everyone in the place was watching Jay Jay perform. Packers, sorters, sweepers, drivers, they all dug his act.

Selena sat there watching with her mouth hanging open till he was done.

"Wow, can he drive!"

Over at the office, Bruno switched on the conveyor belt again.

"About time!" old Tony yelled, and pressed the back-to-work buzzer. Aaaaaawk! Aaaaaawk!

Over on top of the pile of boxes, Range hollered out, "*Arriba cabrones chavalos!*"

Selena laughed and shouted, "*Vamos a jalar*, you lazy bums!"

"Lez go, *esclavos!*" Rudy screamed, and slapped Range on the back.

They sprang off the tomato lugs, horseplaying, doing a little bebop Little Richard shuffle to their places of work: "*Bomp bomp aroo bomp aromp bomp bomp, tutti frutti, awrooty, tutti frutti, awrooty, well abomp bomp aroo bomp aroomp bomp bomp . . .*"

Selena worked across the conveyor belt from Range. She was the glue girl. Her job was to stand at the end of the conveyor belt and glue the label onto each box of packed tomatoes. It was a colorful and rather crudely drawn label, the work of a local sign painter. It pictured a straight-furrowed field of green tomato plants, with farmhouses, irrigation ditches, windmills, yellow hills, and a giant ball of red sun in the background. In the foreground stood a fat Italian peasant woman, smiling rustically. There were wide gaps between her teeth. She looked exactly like Jay Jay's Grandma Letizia, who had died last year speaking not a word of English, though she'd left Sicily over forty years before. She was holding a big ripe beefsteak tomato that gleamed in the light. Under the picture was a sign in large block letters:

CAFONE BRAND
FRESH-PACKED CALIFORNIA TOMATOES
ANTHONY VANDUCCI & SON
CALMENTO, CALIFORNIA

Range's job was set-off man. Selena scooted the sixty-pound boxes down to him on a roller and he picked them up and set them off in neat six-high piles behind him. Then La Rata and the other hand-truck men got under them and pushed them out to the Western Pacific ramp, where they loaded them into refrigerated reefer cars for delivery back east.

They worked fast together, faster than the conveyor belt. That way, every few minutes they usually got a little break. Sometimes Rudy would catch up too and hang out with them. The first words of Pocho slang Range ever learned were on the conveyor line: "*Mi jale es real facil, mucho tiempo para sling the mitote.* . . . My job is real easy, plenty of time to sling the bull."

Range had only had one problem all summer long. And that was he could not keep his eyeballs off Selena.

"Eh, *mijo*, what you looking at?" she asked him one time, when she caught him peeking.

"*Pues nada*," he said, half emboldened, half embarrassed, "just checking the merchandise."

"Well," she said, poking her bro, "*te digo, vato*, don't be getting any ideas about a *producto* you can't afford."

"*Te watcho, cabrón, mirando mi* sister," Rudy said in mock anger, "you better *cuidado*, eh?"

They were always kidding him like that. Range understood that in learning their dialect he had at once gained their favor and forfeited a measure of their respect. Under all their horseplay the Cruz kids were riddled with self-derision.

Now the boxes came hot and heavy. Bruno had the conveyor belt going full speed to make up time. Range worked like a demon, slamming his hard bare hands down on the splintery wood, puffing, grunting, levering with his tense stomach muscles, boosting the boxes up on the stack, turning around quickly again, slamming his hands down hard again, hoisting, lifting, going as hard and fast as he could. . . . But he never seemed to find a moment when he could talk to her alone, and they worked without letup till the buzzer blew for lunch.

Range did notice one thing, though. Every time Jay Jay came wheeling by on his shiny new forklift, Selena had eyes only for him.

At lunchtime Selena always split with her bro in his car. Rudy was what they called in Calmento a "lowrider." He drove a gray-primered '53 Cheeby hardtop with the seats cut down so low you could barely see over the windshield. The idea of lowriding was to sit in your car with only your ducktail, pimp curl, and bebop shades showing. It was supposed to be cool. Every time Selena got in with her brother, she looked embarrassed as hell. It was such a fucking chile wagon, after all, that car he drove. So, anyway, Rudy and Selena always drove over and ate at the Mexican store in the nearby hamlet of Carbona. The lady there always made them up a batch of tortillas and beans, and let them eat in her air-conditioned back room. She was some relative of their mother's. Sometimes they'd take their fat cousin La Trucha Connie along with them.

As for himself, Range always went out back to the shady side of the Dootch's mountainous quarter-mile-long stack of empty tomato lugs. And there in the white dirt he sat down with Jay Jay and, while the wind blew tumbleweeds by and dust blew in his eyes and cement trucks roared out of the gate of the open-pit concrete plant behind the shed, he ate a big sack lunch, drank a thermos full of ice cold milk, and had a good long smoke.

Today the first thing he said to Jay Jay, as soon as he sat down in the dirt, was "I think Selena's got the hots for you."

Jay Jay didn't say a word. Just kept chomping down on that sausage and green pepper sandwich of his, sipping at his orange soda pop. He was a huge, heavy, bizarre-looking fucker. His head was very big and very round and perched on his thick sinewy neck like a great round provolone cheese on a large pedestal. He had an extraordinarily weak chin and jaw. Or rather, because of the smooth and spherical nature of his head, you looked in vain for any definition of feature. Chin, jaw, ears, nose, mouth, all were small, flat, smooth, childlike, vestigial, in vivid contrast to his great masculine physique. His eyes were perfectly circular, milky brown, expressionless, enormous, and owllike behind his horn-rimmed glasses. As for his coloring, people referred to him as a "dishwater blond." But his hair wasn't really blond at all. Nor was it brown or gray, or anything in between. It had no color, not even the bright white of an albino. People only called him blond for lack of a better definition. His skin was the same. It was neither olive nor ruddy nor sallow nor dark nor light. It was neither rough in texture nor especially soft. It was opaque, mysterious, indescribable. Perhaps the one adjective you could use to describe it was "rubbery." Like a baby's skin, it was amazingly elastic. It rarely bruised or bled or got scratched. You knew that when he got older his musculature would run to fat and his skin would stretch comfortably to accommodate his new girth and he would never know a wrinkle in his life.

The fucker looked like he might have come from another planet or direct from the womb. You'd think that even his mother would wonder. When he ate he got it all over himself and you could see the white sandwich dough sticking between his tiny colorless teeth with their large colorless gums. . . . And yet, for all this, Jay Jay had a rep as one of the smartest guys at Calmento High. Straight A's three years in a row. Four years on the Scholastic Honor Roll. Skipped the ninth grade. Range couldn't believe he was really smart, though. In his book, smarts had to do with people, understanding their characters and motives, predicting their future actions, judging them . . . using them. After all, what else was there but people? What else was there that could come walking up to you and look you in the eye and say, "Hey, I'm real; I'm me. I'm a thing, a person." Intelligence could not be determined in a vacuum. It did not relate to things you could read in a book in school. It related to how successful you were with people, out in the world.

By these standards Range was way out in front. And he was quicker, smoother, hipper.

Jay Jay dressed like a fucking clodhopper, and he was always stepping on himself. At high school hops he sat out every dance, even the slow tunes, while Range was out on the floor for every number. Jay Jay wasn't nearly so popular or well-liked as Range, and he hadn't even earned a letter. As far as Range could see, the only talent besides schoolwork that he possessed was driving the forklift. With that he was a magician, granted. But Jesus Christ, it's pretty fucking pathetic if that's all you can say about a guy you've lived with for seven years. . . .

"I think Selena's got the hots for you," Range said again.

Jay Jay just kept gnawing away at his fat sandwich. Finally he said, "Who's Selena?"

"Come on, man. She's lived on your ranch all her life."

"Range," he said, "let me tell you something. Since I was a kid probably two thousand Mexican girls have come through this ranch. I ought to know because my mother tried to educate half of them. Now, am I supposed to remember every one of them?"

"Don't gimme that shit. Selena Cruz. The one who ran for queen against Rose Mary."

"Who's Rose Mary?" he said. This was Jay Jay's idea of a joke. Rose Mary Ammiratti was the granddaughter of Tony's oldest friend. Her family came from the Vanducci home village in Sicily. In Calmento they were second only to the Vanduccis in wealth of land. And her mother already had her eye on Jay Jay as a possible marriage match.

"Very funny."

"What makes you think she likes me, then?"

"Which one?"

"Selena."

"I thought you didn't remember who she was."

"It's coming back now," Jay Jay said. "In the pool after summer school I used to try to feel her up. Eleven years old and she already had nice tits. Then in history class she used to sit in front of me. She was the smartest girl in class. But I wasn't interested in her mind. Used to peek up her sleeveless blouses. What got me was her white bra strap against that brown skin."

"That's the one."

"So?"

"So, she's always checking you out when you go by on the forklift."

"I'd fuck her," Jay Jay said, in his high squeaky adolescent voice, "but I wouldn't be seen with her in public."

Range laughed, as he laughed at everything Jay Jay said, funny or not. Looked on it as a debt, something the Wop would have to repay someday with interest.

Jay Jay finished up his lunch with a wide yawn and a vigorous stretch, stuck a cigarette in the corner of his pale mouth, lit it up, and lay down on his back in the dirt with his hands behind his neck. Range followed suit, and the two of them, one large and light and cheesy and implausibly feline, the other small and dark and sharp and implausibly simian, lay there for a time very quietly, blowing smoke rings up at the hog-white sky. "Tiger" and "Ape Man" the kids had called them in grammar school, with uncanny aptness.

"Want me to line you up?" Range whispered.

"What're you, some kind of Mexican pimp?"

"No, I was just trying to do you a favor, for shit's sake."

"Spare me your favors, man. I can take care of myself."

"Oh, sure, I know you take care of yourself," Range said. "But wouldn't it be fun to try it with a woman for a change?"

Then quick as a spider monkey he leapt up, laughing at his own joke, and scurried off before Jay Jay could gather up his lazy ponderous bod and get after him.

After lunch the first thing he said was, "Say, how 'bout a date tonight, Selena?"

It just popped out. He hadn't even meant to say it. Actually, he'd meant to start trying to line Jay Jay up with her.

"Where we going?"

"The movies?"

"Where?"

"The Hi-Way Drive-In?"

"Okay," she said, and her answer seemed as unrehearsed as his question.

He whizzed through the rest of the day.

Toward quitting time La Rata came by and said, "Eh, *cabrón*, what you so fuckin' *contentito* about?"

And Range had to sing the entire chorus of "I Just Got a Date with an Angel," before he caught on.

Then he got all brotherly and protective and serious. "*Ese*, you be good to her, *cabrón*," he said. "*Te watcho, sabes?*"

"But who's gonna watch meeeee?" Selena teased.

And Range, he just about bust the buttons on his workshirt, he was feeling so fine. Felt like, "Fuck it, I'm gonna do something for myself, this one time."

After work Jay Jay gave him a ride back to the ranch in his pickup truck. Bounced up the packing shed driveway, turned left, and floored it, spinning rubber all through the sleepy hamlet of Carbona. Sixty, seventy, eighty, ninety miles an hour, on the rough blacktop of Valpico Road. Into the sun they went, lickety-split, with the Western Pacific embankment on one side and a row of tall oleanders on the other. Then south at the turquoise-painted general store, one-pump gas station, and Mexican labor camp at Corral Hollow Road. The intersection was full of wetbacks. They were standing around in their sandals, white cotton pants, and sombreros, drinking beer, shooting the breeze, waiting for the after-work bus into Southside.

Now Jay Jay accelerated up the white dirt road, into the shadows of the Diablo Range, up the hill toward the two huge old scraggly date palm trees that marked the Vanducci ranch.

Over the canal bridge he drove, up the sandy driveway along the barbed-wire fence, and into the Vanducci ranch yard. The yard reflected old Tony's continuing priorities: It was lawnless, flowerless, dusty, and chicken-plucked, littered with beat-out old cars, some running, some not. Yet Tony's farm implements were ultramodern, and the yard was full of shiny new tractors and flashy pickup trucks with dual spotlights, gun racks, and radio telephones.

The Dootch had kept his family barefoot and hungry all through the Depression, just to buy up more of his neighbors' cheap land. He was insane about land. "Eh, what else is there but land?" he always said. And he let his house and yard go unkept for years at a time, and tended his fields with meticulous care.

Jay Jay parked in the dirt by Angie's kitchen window, chickens flying out from under his wheels.

"What you doing tonight, Del?"

"Got a date."

"Oh, yeah? Who with?"

"Who you think?"

"What the fuck you up to, you little prick?"

"Thought you weren't interested."

"I said I'd fuck her, didn't I?"

"So?"

"So, ain't that enough?"

"I'm sorry, man. But you're gonna have to be a little more specific than that from now on."

"Listen, shrimp . . ."

"But I already got the date!"

"Cancel it, Range. Or I'll run you off the property. You don't belong here anyway."

"I belong here as much as you do."

"You *what?*" Jay Jay scoffed. "You don't belong nowhere."

"My family was farming this land when yours was still digging rocks in Sicily."

"Hey, you're a little behind the times, Del. And if you're typical of the rest of the Ranges, then they were a pretty sorry fucking lot, if you ask me."

"Then what is it about me that gives you so much trouble, Jay Jay?"

"Maybe I don't like your slinky spick ways."

"Maybe you're just jealous."

Jay Jay sniffed derisively. "Whose car did you think you were gonna borrow tonight?"

"I was intending to ask you," Range said, and climbed down out of the cab.

"Think again, punk," Jay Jay said, and burnt rubber out of the ranch yard, raising up a storm of white dust.

Uh-huh, Range thought. I know where you're at, boy: You dig that Chicana a damn sight better than you let on.

"Hi, Angie," he called, stepping in from the back porch.

"Hi, Del, honey," she said, as he leaned over the living room couch for a kiss. She gave him a motherly peck on the cheek and went back to reading her book, *The True Believer*, by Eric Hoffer. She had her pink terry-cloth bathrobe buttoned primly all the way to the neck and, as usual, she pretended that nothing had passed between them during the night. Range was convinced that she didn't even admit the truth to herself. In the morning she told herself it was all an erotic dream. Sometimes he was afraid he might have made the whole thing up in his head. Every night he waited in his bed, half expecting to hear nothing but the crickets chirping on the hill behind the house. And then, without fail, as if to verify his own sanity in this insane world: *plink, plink.*

"Where's Jay Jay?" she said.

"He went into town. Said he had something to do."

"I wish he wouldn't drive so recklessly. What's the rush?"

"I don't know. But, say, I wonder, could I borrow your car tonight? I got a date."

"I don't know why not," she said, barely shifting her eyes from the book. "There's some macaroni and cheese on the stove, if you want to heat it up."

After a quick dinner, Range ran into the bathroom, showered, brushed his teeth very carefully, and rubbed some Dixie Peach pomade into his curly hair, combing it into a shiny black ducktail with a pimp curl dangling down his low forehead. This was just one of his hairdos. Sometimes he combed it straight back, like Rudolph Valentino. Other times he combed it forward, like Marlon Brando. He was always changing his hairstyle, always changing his mind about which one he liked best. He was like that about a lot of things. Decisions came hard for him. Like in his plans for the future. Sometimes he thought he wanted to be a Vanducci foreman. And sometimes he thought he might like to go into the army, or law enforcement. And still other times he thought he'd like to be an actor. He was dark and green-eyed and suavely handsome, with very regular aquiline features. His eyelashes were the most remarkable thing about his looks. They were extraordinarily long, thick, and black. All the girls said he had "bedroom eyes," and he was known as the "cutest guy at Calmento High." If there was a flaw in his appearance it was perhaps his chin, which might have been a trifle weak and pointy. But you could always get that fixed, he thought.

Range threw on a dark blue button-down shirt with white buttons. Didn't go for that one much. Whipped on another, a green one with a mandarin collar. That was better. Still, he wasn't sure. Maybe he should have put on the new red one. Naw. He loved his different costumes, and getting all duded up. Spent hours in front of the mirror. Blew all his cash on rags. Now he clamped his big silver Saint Christopher medal around his neck. Fastened his ident bracelet around his wrist. Stepped into a pair of charcoal corduroy pants. Naw. Took them off. Got into a pair of tan polished cotton pants with a buckle at the back.

Now, that was more like it! Slipped into some white athletic socks and a pair of brown loafer shoes. Put on a green and tan stretch belt and some teardrop shades. Gave himself a final once-over in the mirror, and he was on his way. Looking cool, looking sharp, bouncing up and down on the balls of his feet as he walked.

Angie didn't even notice him go.

He whipped into town in her big old Buick Roadmaster and pulled up in front of Selena's place in Southside. Jumped out and ran up the steps and knocked at her door. Rudy opened it.

"Look who's here," he said, grinning.

Selena was right behind him. She looked adorable in a white sack dress and leather sandals. She was wearing faint pink lipstick. And her dark hair swung delectably at shoulder level. She took him by the hand to say hello to her mom and step-dad and sister, who were sitting over dinner at the kitchen table. Then with everyone staring and humbly smiling after them, he escorted her decorously out the door and across the white dirt yard to his big old gringo car.

They drove across the SP overpass to the drive-in movie. She let him hold her hand but that was all. She wouldn't take him seriously, no matter how serious he tried to be. Every time he wanted to kiss her she just laughed and said, "Come on, Delanito, can't we just be friends?" The color of her skin and the texture of her hair inflamed him. She was so . . . foreign, so exotic. Her hair was unbelievably thick, and coarse as straw. It astounded him when he remembered that his own mother's hair had been the same: the hair of another race. Utterly astounded him. He had forgotten.

On the way home he stopped to park on a levee above an asparagus field on Roberts Island.

He knew the place well. This was where they had the weekend cockfights. One day when he was just a little guy, and his sister was teeny, his mom and dad brought him out here. Gave him a quarter and he went and bought two strawberry snow cones from a little Filipino with a freezer in the trunk of his car. Went to the river beach with his sister and sat on a cottonwood stump by the water, licking sweet ice. Late spring and the river in flood, very high, very muddy. The smell of decay. He could hear the people at the cockfights downriver, cheering and calling bets. It was hot, so he and Debbie, they took off their tops and tennis shoes and dragged their feet in the water. Debbie, she saw a big fat catfish come up and roll on his belly. Delano saw a green water snake. And dirty white bubbles popping slow in the silted water. A blond lady came waterskiing by. STOCKTON YACHT CLUB the motorboat said on the back. She yelled something at him, but he couldn't make out what it was. She was wearing a green one-piece bathing suit. Had a very good tan for that early in the year. And her wet blond hair flying out behind her. The wake of the boat made big waves. Sent him and his little sister running up the bank. *Woosh*, they hit! Part of the bank caved in. *Splash!* Right into the water. Debbie dropped her snow cone in the sand. Started crying. He gave her some of his. They stayed a long time there on the sand, listening to the frogs croaking, the daytime crickets in the tule reeds, the crows in the willow trees, the meadowlarks on the levee. He heard his mama calling, but he was having such a good time he didn't want to answer. "So this is where you been, you little rascals?" she said, when she found them. And they thought they were going to get a licking, but all she did was smile and kiss them each on the top of the head. Then she led them back to the fight by the hand. She was very dark and voluptuous and pretty then. And she smelled delicious. Smelled like Selena did now. "Your daddy's winning again, Delanito," Mama said. And her eyes were like Selena's eyes, like the river, brown and muddy, with little dancing pools of yellow light.

He told Selena the story, but she didn't listen very well.

"Boy," she said, when he was done, "you sure have got a good memory."

"Just for certain things."

"Poor Delano," she said. Selena knew well the sad tale of Del's boyhood tragedy. For years it had been the talk of Calmento. What really seemed to stir all the interest was the fact that his parents had disappeared simultaneously, but in opposite directions.

At first Range wanted to take advantage of Selena's pity. Then he felt himself getting all creepy and nervous with her, and he tried to kiss her again to hide his trembling. Tried again, And again. Then he just tried to lay his head on her breast.

She moved away from him across the front seat.

"Say," she said, "what do you and Jay Jay do with yourselves on weekends?"

"Aw," he said, "nothing much. Take the drag. Drink beer. Chase girls. Hit a flick, maybe."

"Oh," she said, enunciating her words very carefully. "What other kinds of things is he interested in?"

"Who?"

"Jay Jay, of course."

"Nothing."

"Huh?"

"Nothing. Unless you count farming. He's just like his dad and his grandpa, that way. Never thinks of anything but the ranch. It gets kind of boring."

"I haven't seen his mother in ages," Selena said dreamily. "Still just as pretty as ever, I guess."

"Oh, I don't know. I guess she's kind of good-looking. When you're around a person so much, though, you don't think about that kind of thing," Range said, lying. He felt compelled to lie. He wanted to reveal as little as possible to Selena. Her questions grieved him.

"Has . . . has he got a . . . girl friend?" she asked.

"Not unless you count Rose Mary Ammiratti," Range said, starting the car. "But she's more like a cousin."

When they were parked out in front of her place in Southside he said, "You like Jay Jay, don't you?"

"Who wants to *know?*" she said, pouting, fluttering her lashes. She was the most breathtakingly beautiful creature he'd ever been near. Her presence was like the fulfillment of every desire of man. He thought he would faint with longing for her. Thought he would fall into those huge dark eyes and drown. Woulda ate a mile of her shit, he told himself, just to kiss her pretty brown ass. He had an excruciating case of the stone aches.

"Jay Jay," he said. "He wants to know."

"Jay Jay? Jay Jay?" she said breathlessly.

And Range, for all his will to resist (and though he knew the answer quite well), could not prevent himself from blurting, in a plaintive voice, "How come you like him more than me?"

"I like you, Delanito," she said, patting his cheek, "but you are a little shifty-eyed. Jay Jay's more the sincere type."

"You know what he said about you?"

"I don't want to hear it from you. You're going to say something nasty, I can tell."

"He said, 'I'd fuck her but I wouldn't be seen with her in public.'"

"Liar!"

"That's what he said."

"Liar! Liar!"

She slapped him twice, three times. He did nothing to defend himself. She jumped out of the car and ran into the house. He did nothing to stop her.

All the way home to the Vanducci ranch he kept telling himself, "Oh, shit, you done it now, boy. Done it now. Fucked things up on both angles. Fucked 'em up good."

And yet he was completely careless and cold. And he knew that if he wanted he could sleep like a dream.

Plink. Plink.

Bruno must have been out irrigating again.

Plink. Plink.

And tonight Range was tempted beyond all hope of resistance.

Plink. Plink.

He jumped out of bed with his prick in his hands. Held it hard out in front of him like a flashlight, as if it could see in the dark. Tiptoed through the silent cluttered house, tripping over mounds of clothes and rubbish on the floor. Up the stairs past Jay Jay's room: A little sliver of yellow light showed under the door.

The door to Angie's room was not locked. He went right in. The door squeaked, but she did not seem to hear. She was naked, wearing only her high-piled black wig that she put on for the Saturday night dances. She was leaning over the windowsill, dropping coins. Had them lined up before her on the sill in little piles. From up here you could barely hear them fall . . . *plink* . . . *plink*. He crept up behind her. Her white curving flanks were presented to him in the moonlight. Had she heard him come in? He stretched his prick out in his hands. She gave a start, but relaxed immediately. He thrust himself between her legs from the rear, exploring the damp pubic hair. Smoothed his belly up against her soft ass. Dropped his dizzy confused head upon her sharp-boned shoulder. With trembling hands he milked her small hard breasts. She stayed leaning out over the windowsill, kept dropping those pennies, as if Range were still below, and this person behind her now was not real. There was grave danger in this, Range knew. But he didn't care anymore. She helped him now, helped him to find the right hole. She moaned out the window; he could barely hear her. She spread her legs wider, leaned further out into space, wiggling her bottom against his thighs. He fucked her slowly, wonderingly. When he came his legs went weak. He was afraid he might fall to the floor. He came and came. With a mighty thirst, her body drank it down. He was half afraid she would suck him dry. Finally the milking was done. Now he wanted to take her to bed. Wanted to lie down with her because he was so tired. Wanted to suck her titties, suck them and suck them. Because he felt so dry. And now it was his turn. Urgently he spun her around, drew her toward the bed. She resisted. He pulled harder. She stopped, dug her heels into the rug. He jerked her arm. She yanked it out of his grip.

"Get out of here!"

He could see the whites of her eyes in the moonlight and her bared fangs.

"What?" he said, but he understood perfectly. He had even foreseen this possibility.

"Get out! Get out!" she cried. "Get out or I'll . . ."

She left her threat unfinished. But Range could guess its intent. And he slipped out of her room, cock in hand, with extremely mixed feelings.

He was euphoric. He was despondent. He was proud of his psychological perception this morning. Yet he was devastated that it had turned out to be so accurate. He was a man at last. But he had lost yet another mother. It was time to go.

He went down the stairs and crept through the silent untidy house, collecting his belongings from amongst piles of Vanducci things. The 'Duccis had been living here for thirty-seven years now, but the place looked like they'd just moved in and were only going to stay a brief spell. For years Angie had been after Bruno to get old Tony to fix the place up. And reluctantly Bruno had gone to his father, time and time again, only to be sternly lectured on "priorities in the agro-industry" and turned down flat. It seemed that the more they pressed the old man, the more stubborn he got and the more he let the house go. Till now it had become such a mess that it was something more than merely untidy. To Range its disorderliness seemed wrong on a cosmic level, at odds somehow with the harmony of the universe.

Some of the rooms in the house were bare, lampless, rugless, drapeless. Others were crowded with tattered couches that faced the walls, the windows and doorways. The house was full of half-unrolled rugs, broken TV sets, easy chairs with their springs poking out, lamps that didn't work, pictures off kilter on the wall. The interior was completely unfinished. The walls were still covered with white plasterboard. Electrical wiring hung down from the ceiling. The plumbing was exposed. Some of the rooms were separated merely by wood frames, and you could walk from one to the other without using the door. Others were roofless. Others were floorless. The Vanduccis, however, treated them as if they were quite finished, and referred to them as the "sewing room," the "service porch," or the "rumpus room." Yet, if you attempted to utilize the "rumpus room," for example, you'd suddenly find yourself in the swimming pool, thirty feet below. Range was certain the Vanducci house would never be finished. They'd never thought of building closets, for example. Everyone's clothes, clean and dirty, old and new, were spread out all over the house. They were lying on the floor, in the bathtub, on couches, chairs, all mixed up, one person's with another's.

For all its messy eccentricity, Range had not been unhappy in the Vanducci house. Or at least that's the way it seemed to him now. True, he had never been accepted as a member of the family. But, all in all, he didn't feel he should complain too much. To appreciate his own good fortune all he had to do was compare his situation with that of his sister Debbie, currently residing in the Ventura Home for Girls.

He began to wish now very hard that there was some way he could stay.

Once he'd got all his belongings together, he packed them in a large paper bag, took his King Kong poster down from the wall, rolled it up, stuck it under his arm, and was about to slip out the front door when it came to him suddenly that he wanted to murder her. He wanted to murder them all. He was powerfully tempted to reach up on the gun rack and get one of Bruno's pistols down, the Italian P-38, maybe, and sneak up the stairs and stick it in Jay Jay's fucking colorless ear and blow his colorless brains out all over the bed and then get his grandpa at the other end of the house and come back for his mother and rape her and kill her and fuck her again when she was dead and burn down the house to destroy the evidence. It would go up like kindling wood. It was a fucking firetrap, anyway.

He opened the door and looked all around, then turned an ear to the warm east wind. For a long time he stood there listening. But all he could hear was the cottonwood leaves rustling in Angie's garden, the tin pumphouse door banging, the whirr of the old windmill on the hill, and a small animal, a badger or a weasel, stirring the wild oats behind the house.

Bruno was still far out in the field, irrigating. No one was nearer. No one would hear.

The sky began to color over the Sierras. It seemed to be leading him on.

He left the Vanducci front door wide open and walked off east down the dirt driveway to Corral Hollow Road and then three miles northeast across the tomato fields in the pleasant early morning cool. The air was clear and clean, and he was almost sad he hadn't shot them all in the head. At the same time he was delighted that his practical, rational side had won out. Birds sang all around him. The fields smelled of rich watered San Joaquin clay and pungent tomato leaves and sweet dewy alfalfa. He walked into town and all the way across town, listening to the early morning trains hooting in the rail yard, the early morning traffic rumbling through on Highway 50. It took him an hour to walk to the World's Largest Truck Stop, and all the way he felt at once as old as the world and as new and breathless as the morning.

S ELENA WONDERED WHAT had happened to the little gringo. Day
after day she waited for him to show up at work. She hadn't meant to be
so harsh with him. In some way she felt responsible for his disappearance.

Rudy didn't help much. And neither did Connie. Every day they
kidded her unmercifully.

"Eh, what you do with that poor leetle *gabacho*, poison heem?"

"Ay, *primo*, that is no lie!"

"Last time he was seen alive was in her *compañia*."

"*Ay ay ay!*"

Summer turned to fall. Selena went back to high school and could
only work on weekends. The sun lost some of its ferocity. The rains
came. The Dootch died of a sudden heart attack and Bruno, trying to
hide his joy, assumed control of the Vanducci enterprises. Mama
gave birth to a plump dark baby girl that Aguilar named Rio. Tomato
season sped to a close. And still no Delano Range. Selena had to admit
that she did miss that little Anglo.

And for the first time in years she remembered the second grade,
when she would see him trudging over the railroad tracks on his way to
North School, swinging his lunch pail. It was a new yellow lunch pail
with a decal of Annette Funicello and the Mickey Mouse Club on it.
Inside she imagined neat Saran Wrapped meat sandwiches and giant
Hershey bars. And she envied him with her whole soul. For she and
Rudy only had greasy old paper sacks, and chile peppers wrapped in
newspaper, and refried beans rolled up in flour tortillas.

"How come he gets to go to North School?" she asked her mama.

"*Güero*," she said, shrugging her shoulders, as if that one word, that
one listless physical gesture, would explain everything. And Selenita, the
seven-year-old *morena*, envied him all the more.

And she remembered a few years later, when Del was living up the
hill with the 'Duccis. In the swiming pool after Angie's summer school
he would impress hell out of all the kids with his incredible performance
on the diving board. Front flips, back flips, double flips, half gainers,
full gainers, one-and-a-halfs, cutaway ones, cutaway twos, half twists, full
twists, and an unbelievable two-and-a-half with a double twist.

"Ape Man, Ape Man!" Jay Jay and the others would tease. But Range
wouldn't listen. Once he was airborne he left all worldly cares behind.

He'd get this faraway look on his face, and you knew he never wanted to come down. Selena got him to teach her a few dives, but she never got beyond the swan dive and jackknife stage.

And then later, in the seventh grade, when Selena went up to Anglo-land to attend Calmento Junior High, she thought Delano was the cutest boy in school, with his curly black hair and his pretty little sharp-pointed face, and she stuck his school picture in her bedroom mirror, right next to her own. But by then he had other interests, gringo interests, and a pale-faced girl friend named Cheryl Payne, and he couldn't be bothered with a little *morenita* from the wrong side of the tracks.

She didn't see much of Delano for the next few years. She stuck close to home, concentrating on her studies. At school the gringo boys only looked at her with lecherous eyes. And when the Mexican boys asked her out on dates she almost always refused. She cared for nothing but her future, and escape at any cost from Southside Calmento. She swore to herself that before she became a contented *mamacita* or a career agricultural worker, she would drown herself in the San Joaquin River or sell her ass on the streets of East Oakland.

Then last summer on the conveyor line, after so much time had passed, all of a sudden here was Delano Range, casting shy glances in her direction. But by then it was too late for Range. A relationship between him and Selena had nothing to recommend it. Neither of them had any prospects or resources. All they could do was drag each other down.

Yet, they did have a lot of fun together on that conveyor line. All summer long they made the hours just fly. And through Del, she told herself, she would have eventually met the boss's son. In this way Selena justified her very strong feelings of affection and compassion for the orphan boy. She often did this kind of thing, in her head. Even her most kindly and generous impulses she had to justify to herself on the grounds of self-interest. It was an instinct of survival.

Then one Saturday night ten weeks after Range's disappearance, a letter came from him, right out of the blue. She took it into her throne-room and read it over and over. And the more she read it, the more she thought it might be the answer to all her prayers.

Next day at work she flagged down Jay Jay the first time he came around on his forklift.

"Hey, I got a letter from your *amigo*," she said, smiling up at him, concentrating on him like she'd once concentrated on some little wet-backs at his grandfather's labor camp and nearly brought them to their knees.

"What *amigo?*"

"Range."

"Well, I'll be damned; we had the whole county looking for him. Where's he at?"

"Want to read it?"

"Naw. Why don't you read it to me?" he said, switching off his engine.

"Okay," she said, and she read it to him loudly and carefully, her voice carrying over the noisy machines . . . read it as if it had been an important philosophical treatise, rather than a note from a half-literate boy. Last night she had even practiced reading it in front of the mirror, on the off chance that he'd want her to read it aloud.

All the Chicanas on the conveyor line were jealously listening now, pulling their bandannas back from their ears to hear better.

Connie got so carried away with her eavesdropping that she upset a loaded box and had to scramble on her knees, chasing green tomatoes all over the floor.

> Dear Selena:
>
> How are you? I hope fine. I am locked up in here in Juvie Hall in French Camp and am writing you now to apologize for my conduct on our first and last date I do hope you will forgive me as its been praying on my mind. Since I last seen you so many things have gone down some of them not so good to make a long story short I "borrowed" a car in San Jose trying to get down to see my sister Debbie down in Ventura and made it all the way to Santa Barbara before they caught me after many adventures. It looks like I will have to do some time in Preston Reformatory as they got me on some pretty heavy charges including Breaking & Entering, Burglary, Grand Theft Auto, Unlawful Flight to Avoid Arrest, Resisting Arrest, etc. So I won't be seeing you for quite awhile unless . . .??? Visiting time here is on Sunday afternoon between one and five pm and it sure would be groovy to see someone from Calmento. Say hello to Jay Jay and Rudy for me, okay. And all the best of luck to you, Selena. Take care of yourself.
>
> > Your friend (I hope),
> > Delano Lee Range

"Well I'll be damned," Jay Jay said again. "Funny the cops never gave us a call on this. They were supposed to let us know if they heard anything. You sure he's really writing from there?"

"It's stamped right here on the letter: 'French Camp, California.' And anyway, why would he want to lie about a thing like that?"

"Range?" Jay Jay said, guffawing. "He doesn't have to have a reason to lie. He lies out of habit. He lies just for kicks. Lies for the practice, so he'll be able to tell better lies in the future. He'll lie very politely right to your face, even when he knows you'll catch him red-handed. Then when you do catch him, he'll confess and make up a bigger lie to explain why he lied in the first place."

"Aw, come on," Selena said. There was an odd equivocal note to his voice, part bitter, part whimsical, that made her doubt his sincerity.

"I'm not kidding," he said. "I'll never forget the time . . . Del's got this big old tom cat in his arms, see? And he's standing in the living room by the fire, stroking its fur, petting its head. And my dad, he comes in and he says, 'Del, you know we don't allow animals in the house.' And Del says, 'But I didn't bring nothing into the house.' 'Oh no?' my dad says. 'Then where'd you get that cat?' And Del, he gets this real panic-stricken look on his face, and he starts looking all around the room, see? And he says, 'What cat?' "

"Wow!" Selena said, laughing. "Now I can see why you don't trust him too much."

"Trust him?" Jay Jay said, smacking the metal hood of his forklift with the flat of his hand. "Hell, I'm not even sure the little bastard is real. For all I know, he made himself up."

"You know, I never would've guessed you felt that way, Jay Jay. I thought . . . Del living out there with you all this time, and . . ."

"Now don't get me wrong," Jay Jay said. "I get a kick out of Range. Always kind of had a little soft spot for him, I guess. But as far as my folks go, they've had it just about up to here."

"Gee," she said. "What'd he do that's so bad?"

"Hey!" Jay Jay said. "What hasn't he done? You know, the reason he ran away . . . My mother caught him prowling around her bedroom in the middle of the night."

"No!"

"I'm not lying."

"What happened?"

"Well, she woke up, and there he was standing over her bed. 'Get out of here!' she said. But he wouldn't move. 'Get out of here,' she said again, 'or I'll call my boy.' Well, that did it. He got out of the house as fast as he could. Left the front door wide open. And we haven't seen him since. In a way, it's a good thing he left. When my dad came in, he blew his stack. I think he would've killed Delano if he caught him then."

"Boy!"

"Yeah."

"Now it looks like Del's hinting for a visit."

"Looks that way."

"Guess you wouldn't want to go up and see him."

"Oh, I don't know."

"Really?"

"Yeah. I'll tell you the truth. My mother has a kind of vivid imagination. And every guy she meets, she thinks he's madly in love with her. For all I know, Delano just wanted to ask her a question. Or maybe he was half asleep. Or sleepwalking, even. Who knows?"

"Right."

"What about you?"

"Me?"

"You going up?"

"I don't have a car."

"Oh. Well, why don't we run up together? Be a nice surprise for Del."

"Why not?" Selena said, watching him closely above her on the fork-lift, forcing him to lower his sad creamy brown eyes, the eyes of a great myopic pussycat, behind thick tortoiseshell frames and heavy lenses.

Jay Jay was so pale and smooth and blond, such a big old baby. La Palomita felt that she could conquer him effortlessly, if she wanted, with her magic, an Aztec magic that blew hot and cold, that cooed like a dove and screamed like an eagle, that cooled and burned, soothed and wounded, that giveth and taketh away.

Selena's affection for Range had grown enormously since she heard Jay Jay tell his story. Range had befuddled those gringos up there on the hill, blown their fucking minds. He'd laid down such an incredible barrage of jive and mystification that they would never forget it, never forget *him*. An orphan, a half-breed Mex, the only surviving son of the Range family, which (as everyone in Calmento knew) had originally owned this land and lost it through its own degeneracy, little Delano had made himself *felt* on the Vanducci ranch. Selena understood him perfectly. She would make herself felt too. Yeah. Cut this big Wop right down to size!

At the same time she felt rather tender and protective toward Jay Jay, and thought him attractive in some odd way, and felt she could be an asset to his life. That smooth young face of his was deceptive. Under it was a complex tormented soul, she thought, like Rochester in *Jane Eyre*. Like Jane, she would uncover the secret tragedy in his house and bring out his real heroic character through love.

At home that night at the dinner table Selena shamelessly misrepresented the case and told her *familia* that Jay Jay Vanducci, the boss's only son, had invited her out on a date. It was like she'd dropped a bomb in the kitchen. Rudy was speechless with jealousy. Mama was so excited she wiped the baby's face with a tortilla. Aguilar got up from the table abruptly, said, "You're on your way now, ain't you, señorita?" and left the room without another word. Connie said, "It's all a lie. It's a lie!" But no one believed Connie. Not even Selena. In her own mind Jay Jay had asked her out on a date: He was madly in love with her. And she gathered all her considerable charms and powers to make it come true.

"Everything depends on men; they are the chess pieces of life," she told herself, appropriating the quotation as her own, forgetting even where she had read it, and left her mother and cousin and little sisters in the kitchen to follow Rudy and Aguilar where they had gone.

She found Rudy in the living room, sulking in front of the TV set, and made up with him quickly with a sisterly kiss and a false confession to the effect that her interest in Jay Jay was cynical and purely mercenary.

She found Aguilar lying face down on his bed, and she knew this would be a more difficult case. She glided into the bedroom, smooth and silent, and swoooooped down on him, landing lightly by his side on the bed.

"I want you to know what a wonderful papa you've been to me," she said, as if she'd already been proposed to and was on her way out of town on her honeymoon. And the funny thing was, as she said it, she believed it. "You've been such a beautiful *jefito* to me," she said.

There were tears in his eyes when he turned to her. In the months since Selena lost the queen contest Aguilar had grown stouter and stouter from his heavy beer-drinking, heavy bean-eating, till now his cheeks were puffed out like a great fat dark squirrel with a mouthful of acorns, and it was hard to take his tears seriously. Selena looked down at him on the bed and suddenly realized that he was no longer part of her picture. She had created him out of nothing when she was a little girl, out of nothing more than a summer morning. She had done it with her magic. But now he was no longer part of her picture. It was a cruel thought, but true. She told herself it was true. She would make it true. To survive, to get away, Selena must be hard, *dura, dura, dura.*

She regarded this poor weathered laboring man beneath her and she remembered him the first time she met him, conjured him, when he looked like an Aztec god, and won her heart. . . . And suddenly he was like the ephemeral promise of all things Mexican to her. Great gay-colored fiesta balloons, they float toward the heavens, only to pop at a low altitude and fizzle to earth.

She had been mistaken in her quotation about men. At least about this big man beneath her now. This was no chessman. Or if he was, he was only a pawn in the game.

So Selena the ex- and never *reina* said to herself on the bed.

Then, "*Bueno,*" she said loudly, insincerely, meaning her insincerity to be perceived, "*me perdonas entonces?*"

"*No hay nada a perdonar,*" he said with sorrow, and she could see that he understood what she had meant to convey and yet still wished her well.

"Look out," he said, rising suddenly from under her. "I'm gonna go downtown for a beer. See you later."

That night Selena found it very difficult to sleep. Not only was her hair set in big painful curlers, but she'd gotten her period and was suffering from terrible cramps and tender swollen breasts. She tossed and turned, sweating under the covers. Across the room she could hear Jovita's steady breathing. Suddenly she felt guilty for her *corazón duro* and her decision to abandon her *familia.* She felt tenderness for her little sister, sleeping so sweetly across the room. And her brother Rudy, snoring innocently out on the couch in the living room. And the little baby, Rio, and Mama, and poor great Aguilar who had not come in yet from the cantina. What would become of them all?

It was so hot and stuffy in the little room. And her breasts hurt so. What a sight she would be tomorrow with no sleep! She threw the covers off herself. Removed her nightgown and panties. Pulled out the curlers. The hell with them. Her beauty sleep was the most important thing. Why couldn't she just drift off into dreamland? No way. She felt herself to be at an absolute turning point in her life. A little voice in her head kept reminding her that nothing had happened to change her. She was accompanying a vague acquaintance, her employer's son, to visit a boy in Juvenile Hall. That was all. But the little voice kept getting drowned out by a roaring flood in her ears, a raging fantastic sea of ambition. Finally the roar became a buzz and put her to sleep.

During the night her cramps and discomfort disappeared. A tingling sensation spread across her body and eventually brought her awake. It was dawn. Through her window she could see the sun coming up from behind the Sierras. Never in her life had she been so stirred. She felt her breasts. They were no longer painful. She ran her hands down her belly, her tiny waist, her full hips. She watched her hands, long brown hands. She felt her thighs, her pubic hair, her vagina, her Tampax string. She was all wet. She rolled over on her side and grabbed the pillow like it was a man and whispered, "*Oh, mi marido, mi amor . . .*" Now that she had said it, she would make it come true. And when it came true her *familia* would benefit too . . . "*Sometimes you're too hard on yourself, Selena,*" she said to herself. "*They are really never far from your thoughts. . . .*"

All the way up the freeway from Calmento the next morning Jay Jay was nervous and ill at ease, fooling around with the radio, changing it from station to station. Selena had dressed just for him, but he was afraid to look. She tried desperately to cast her spell on him, but her magic didn't seem to be working. Finally she said, "Is there anything wrong, Jay Jay?"

"Oh," he said, "it's just Range. You know, after you showed me his letter, I went home and told my folks about it. Turns out they knew he was in Juvie all along. But they don't want to have anything to do with him. And now they want me to go over there and tell him that he's not welcome on the ranch anymore. I just don't know how to break the news. Seems like he's got enough troubles without laying that one on him."

"Why tell him at all?" Selena said. "I think that in his heart he probably already knows. You'll just rub salt in his wounds. I tell you what: If it was me I'd avoid the whole issue. Just talk about pleasant things. Figure it this way: By the time he gets out of Preston he prob-

ably won't be a juvenile anymore. He would be out on his own in any
case."

"Maybe you're right," Jay Jay said.

"You know I'm right," Selena said, and she waited for him to say
something else. But he went back to playing with the radio, fidgeting
in his seat; and she realized that she had lost him again. And for the
remainder of the journey the little conversation between them was
strained and perfunctory.

Kellerman Hall Juvenile Facility was located just off the freeway in
rural French Camp, between the county jail, the Honor Farm, and the
county hospital. All four units had been constructed in the brick mono-
lith style of public buildings in the teens. Time and weather had not
been kind to them. Earthquakes sent jagged cracks up their walls. Tule
fogs off the nearby San Joaquin River turned the brick a moldy black.
The sun burnt all the windows an opaque blue.

When Jay Jay and Selena arrived at the front gate a guard asked their
names and whom they wanted to visit. Then he phoned the main building and got permission for them to proceed to the official parking lot.
The driveway was lined with large old valley oak trees. On one side of
the road Honor Farm prisoners were pitching hay. On the other, young
Juvie Hall inmates were digging in a vegetable garden.

Jay Jay parked the pickup truck. Selena got her lunch basket, and they
walked toward the picnic tables in the visiting area. It was a brisk sunny
autumn day, and there were several families out there, having lunch with
young inmates. Range was sitting alone on the grass. He was wearing an
oversized blue denim uniform and looked extremely small and thin and
old. He saw them and came bouncing across the lawn, his short thin
legs racing, his long strong arms swinging.

Selena was extremely conscious of the picture that she and Jay Jay
made against the backdrop of barbed-wire fence: Jay Jay huge and
smooth and moon-faced, but kind of clean-cut looking in his horn-
rimmed glasses and flat-top haircut, his striped Ivy League shirt, his
polished cotton pants and gray tweed sport coat. Selena slim and de-
mure in her dark brown sweater, tan cotton skirt, brown pumps, brown
leather bag, suede jacket, her hair pulled back into a severe Spanish bun
with a tortoiseshell hairclasp at the nape of her neck. She had dreamed
of just this picture, this moment; she had saved all summer to buy these
clothes, had bought them weeks ago, knowing the moment would come.
She hadn't let her mother touch her this morning with her vulgar Pocho
hands. She wore neither lipstick nor rouge nor foundation . . . a smid-
gen of eyeliner was all.

"Hi, hi, how are you, how are you?" Range hollered, loping up to
them. "Boy, what a surprise! God, both of you together? Wow, I'm
really in luck. It's the first visit I had. My first visit!"

He shook Jay Jay's hand frantically, shook Selena's hand too. His grip was tight, moist, compulsive. To Selena it was very moving. She had hated him for days after their date, ten weeks ago. But now she felt only compassion. It must be horrible being locked up in this old blackened brick monstrosity. And he looked so tired, so wan, so lonely, with huge dark circles under his eyes. Impulsively she pulled him to her, kissed him tenderly on his flushed hot cheek. Tears of gratitude filled his eyes. Jay Jay looked acutely uncomfortable. Selena saw that he felt guilty too, responsible in some way for Range's tragedy. It eased her own burden somewhat.

She laughed for no reason: "Ho ho ho!" Clapped Delanito on the back like a good old *compañero*. Said, "Come on, *vato, vamos a comer;* how 'bout some good *comida* for a change?" And led him across the grounds to an empty picnic table near the vegetable garden. Jay Jay followed sheepishly behind them. He had yet to address a word to his friend.

Selena sat down with Delano, facing Jay Jay across the table. Behind him she could see the fence, the Honor Farm's alfalfa field, and the line of willow and bamboo that marked the course of the San Joaquin River. Closer by, she could see two picnic tables, at one of which a skinny black mama was crying, holding her large black son by the chops, crying and treating him rough, shaking him up. At the other table she could see a gray-haired Mexican father lecturing his son sternly. You could tell all the way from here that the *vato* was not listening.

"Boy," Del kept saying, "boy, it sure is great to see you guys. Boy!"

His joy was so intense that it was pathetic, almost embarrassing. He couldn't leave off touching them, grabbing them by their sleeves, hugging them.

At first Selena was rather alarmed. Then she glanced over at Jay Jay and saw him start to relax and smile for the first time. Delano's emotion appeared to have struck a chord in him. This development pleased her no end. Now when they were alone on the way home the ice would be broken.

"Damn," Jay Jay said. "I gotta admit, it sure is good to see you, you little fart."

Delano beamed with pleasure.

Selena brought out her sandwiches and potato salad and her thermos full of lemonade. She had taken as much care preparing that lunch as she'd taken in preparing herself. It was a classy lunch. Just like she was a classy girl, if she took the time with herself. The potato salad was spicy with paprika, and delicious. The sandwiches were sublime, made with Larraburu sourdough bread, stuffed with the finest cotto salami, the best smoked provolone and hot green peppers. Range tore into his food like he was dying of starvation. Jay Jay wasn't far behind.

"Mmmmmm, good!"

Selena hummed with pleasure and nodded toward the building behind them, across the lawn.

"Where's your room, Delano?"

"In the basement."

"What's it like?"

"Grim."

"You get to work in the garden?"

"Are you serious?"

"Why not?"

"I'm on restriction," he said, the smile having disappeared entirely from his face.

"How come they let us visit you then?" Jay Jay wanted to know.

"Figger it'll improve my morale, I guess."

"Are they mean to you, Delanito?" Selena sang, touching his sleeve lightly with the tips of her fingers.

"Naw," he said. "They only been whipping me a couple of times a day, here lately."

At first she didn't know whether to believe him or not. His face gave her no clue. Then he burst out laughing, and she felt like a fool for having been taken in so easily.

Delano was one of those people who laugh with their whole face. He would have done better if he had less mobile features. When he was serious and kept his mouth shut, he was very handsome. But when he laughed his eyes crinkled up into ugly little slits and his mouth was too big for his face and his teeth were crooked and stained.

Then Jay Jay laughed too, rather shyly. He was one of those people who laugh rarely, but whose looks are definitely improved by mirth. His mouth was not nearly so large as Range's, and his teeth were small and stainless and even.

"Come on, you little bastard," Jay Jay said. "What's it like inside?"

"It's too depressing to talk about."

"Look, Del," Jay Jay said, touching his arm. "You know I was just kidding, out in the pickup that time. Don't you?"

"I don't know anything of the kind," Range said.

"Come on, man."

"No, I'm not kidding," Delano said, his voice full of self-pity. "You people never wanted me out there in the first place."

"Okay, that's enough," Selena said. "I do not like the direction this conversation is taking."

"Jay Jay started it," Range said.

"Right," Jay Jay said. "Let's forget it."

"Good idea," Range said. "So what do we talk about now?"

"Let's talk about Selena."

"Yeah," Range said. "What's new with you, *chavala?*"

"Me?" she said. "Oh, there's never anything new with me. Same old grind at the shed."

"What's happening in Calmento?"

"Nothing ever happens in Calmento."

"I'll tell you something new, man," Jay Jay said. "Did you hear about my grandpa?"

"Naw. What happened?"

"He died."

"No shit. I thought he would live forever."

"So did everyone else, including my old man. You 'member how he never would spend a dime, don't you, Del? How he kept my dad on slave wages for thirty years, living in four rooms in the rear of his goddamn old broken-down unfinished rat-trap of a house? You know, Del, how he did. . . . And everybody in Calmento said, 'Just wait till the Dootch dies; Bruno's gonna have himself a ball then!' Well, for weeks after Grandpa Tony died, Dad crept around the property, afraid to make a move. Like the old fart might actually come back from the grave and tell him it wasn't his yet. Then last week I guess it finally sunk in. And Dad went on a rampage you wouldn't believe. First, he took all his section foremen aside and let it be known that he would look with extreme disfavor on anybody who ever dared call him 'Brunino' again. Let it be known that he would not be averse to being addressed as 'The Dootch' from now on. Then he went out and bought my mom two new fur coats, one mink and one sable. Ordered two big new Lincoln Continental hardtops. Had an architect start drawing up plans for a gigantic new mansion with a V-shaped swimming pool. Made reservations for a grand tour of Europe next winter, with a finale in Sangiorgio di Rocca, my grandpa's native village in Sicily. Now it looks like he's gonna be as big a spendthrift as my grandpa was a miser!"

"Oh, yeah?" Del said. "Well, how's he treating you, now that he's so rich and happy?"

"Me? Shit! Treats me just the same. Kicks my ass every time he gets a chance!"

"You mean he didn't give you anything?" Selena asked.

"Give me? Hell, I'm lucky the sonbitch didn't take something *away* from me."

They all laughed. But Selena laughed too loud. The idea of minks and sables and Lincoln Continentals and swimming pools was immensely exciting to her. Yet, it was distracting and worrisome too, in some way. As if she had a kind of moral debt or imperative one day to acquire all those glittering accoutrements of prosperity and respectability. She suspected that Range might feel the same way. Perhaps he was even her competitor for Jay Jay's favor. This possibility did not make her ill-disposed toward Range. For some reason it actually made her feel closer to him. She even read the wishful future and saw the three of them together in the new big house on the hill. In her mind's eye it looked exactly like the Sicilian palazzo in Giuseppe di Lampedusa's book, which she had recently read. . . . "*Il Gattopardo*," the lord of the manor was called, "The Leopard." She saw herself as the loyal and loving little Latina wife of another tamer species of Sicilian cat, Jay Jay

"Tiger" Vanducci, the Third Dootch of Calmento . . . and little Delanito as majordomo, foreman-in-chief of all the 'Ducci lands. . . .

"Well, Jay Jay," she said now. "Jay Jay," she said again, as if she loved
to pronounce his name and thought it funny at the same time, "looks
like you 'Duccis run to opposites from father to son. I bet when you get
that ranch you're gonna be just as big a skinflint as your grandpa."

"Oh no," he said, laughing. "No way. I tell you, they're both ex-
tremists. Me, I'm more . . . American, more of a moderate sort of
person. I'm gonna try to strike a happy medium."

"Moderate?" Range said, making a face. "Why, you're the craziest
sonbitch I ever met! Lucky you ain't locked up in here with me right
now. Look at the way he drives, Selena—like some kind of suicidal
maniac!"

But Selena believed Jay Jay. And there was no question in her mind
that he would one day with his reason and moderation build the Vanducci empire into something that his volatile Sicilian forefathers would
never have dreamed.

Range finished his sandwich and started bouncing around on the
bench beside her. She had detected in the past few moments a slightly
hysterical note in his voice and sought now to calm him down and make
him feel more secure. In some ways she felt years older than both these
gringo boys, and felt quite capable of mothering them any time the need
arose.

"Delano," she said, turning toward him, smiling at him, "when are
you going to get out of Preston?"

"I'd rather not talk about it, Selena, if you don't mind."

"Come on, Del, tell us," said Jay Jay.

"It looks like two years," he said wearily.

"Gee, I'm sorry," Selena said, patting his cold little hand. It was
weird, being with someone who was going to be locked up for two
years. It was like he was in a special magical state beyond ordinary human experience, like a condemned man. It was like he wasn't fully . . .
real.

"Say listen, man. Is there anything we can do for you?" Jay Jay asked.

"Yeah."

"What's that?"

"Promise me you'll come and visit me every so often. You're the only
visitors I got."

"Hey," Jay Jay said, "for sure."

"Me too," Selena said. "I promise."

"But is that all?" Jay Jay wanted to know. "I mean, isn't there something else we can do?"

"Just one more thing," Range said. "Stop talking about the Joint. It
depresses me."

They did their best to comply with Delano's wish. He appreciated
their efforts and tried to keep his spirits up. They sat there for an hour

eating and laughing and gossiping about Calmento and talking about old times in high school. The boys seemed to forget that Selena had never been part of their set. She did not remind them of the truth. Actually she'd been a member of no set. Yet now she felt extraordinarily fine and close to these boys, as if she'd always been their pal. They both seemed so decent and intelligent to her, so fragile and sensitive and lonely and bruised by life. She saw them as being very much like herself. It filled her with hope for the future. Unsuccessfully she tried to remind herself again of this hope when they had to take their leave and she was made to contemplate smilingly the fading image of unhappy little Delano as he waved to them from behind his screen of trees and barbed wire.

"Poor little fucker," Jay Jay said, wiping his nose with the back of his hand.

"I know how it is."

"No you don't. I always treated him like shit."

"But he forgives you now, doesn't he?"

"Nope," he said. And he said it with such utter conviction that it determined her to put an immediate end to such random and profitless emotions.

"You know why he apologized to me in that letter?" she said as they drove off the grounds. "On our date we had a fight. He said you'd insulted me. I called him a liar and slapped his face."

"Now what'd he want to go say a thing like that for?"

"I don't know," Selena said, fixing her mouth in an expression that was like a grimace, yet ambiguous and indecipherable, "but here's what he said. He said you'd fuck me but you wouldn't be seen with me in public."

"I . . . I swear, Selena . . . I never did say anything l-like that."

"I never believed you did, Jay Jay. But it's nice to hear it straight from your lips," she said, and settled in next to him behind the wheel of his pickup truck. As they pulled out onto the freeway she peeked at him in the rearview mirror. His image there inscribed itself upon her imagination and years later she would often recall it vividly to mind: on his round and bland yet strangely tormented young face she read a smooth high-speed road map to her own rosy future, and her *familia*'s happy prosperous new life.

Six

A WINDY AFTERNOON in early spring. Jay Jay Vanducci, wearing a baseball cap with DIFOLATIN COMPANY—WE KILL TO LIVE written around the crown, was farting along at three miles an hour on a John Deere tractor, hauling a motorized herbicide dispenser behind him. He was smack dab out in the middle of a flat black fifty-acre field that appeared to be quite empty. But appearances are deceptive. Every twelve inches a small level ridge ran down the field, survey straight, as far as the eye could see. Every six inches in the ridge a little tomato seedling was growing, under the manicured California soil. It was Jay Jay who planted it there. Today was April 19, 1964, his twentieth birthday.

Above him the sky was a dark dirty color, the same color as the earth beneath his tractor. The world appeared to be drowning in peat dust. The dust blew in a strong blustery wind off the San Joaquin River delta, ten miles away, blew up against the wall of the Diablo Range where it was halted, backed up, to fall like ashes upon the young tomato plants of Calmento.

His lips were cracked and caked with peat. It was down his neck and back, itching like the devil. It was up his nose, clustered into black boogers that smelled of herbicide. Behind his thick horn-rimmed glasses, his eyes were teary and inflamed, hurting in the corners where the dirt collected.

He cursed his father and his name.

"Fuck you, Bruno Vanducci!"

Five o'clock this morning and the bastard switched on the bright overhead light and came stomping into the room in his boxer shorts, trailing cigar smoke behind him, bellowing his son's name.

"Time to get up, Jay Jay!"

"Too windy for spraying today, Dad."

"Damnit, I give you that fifty acres. Now get your ass outa that bed."

So he did as he was told, crawled out of bed, pissing and moaning, growling to himself.

"Use your head, use your head," Bruno was always saying, and then the stupid shit forced his son out in the wind and peat dust at 5 AM on a Sunday morning that just happened to be his birthday. When any idiot could see the poison would blow right away and the whole operation would just have to be performed again.

But he was always doing things like that, giving out absurd orders just to see if Jay Jay would obey without question. His old man used to do the same thing with him. It was fucking diabolical. It was like some primitive kind of tribal initiation or loyalty test that they'd devised, and had absolutely nothing to do with any rational needs.

"Use your head, use your head," Bruno said, when he was always the one to lose his cool.

Like last year when one of the wetback dormitories burnt down. There was Bruno out there running around like a chicken with his head cut off, yelling "They'll sue us for everything we're worth if anyone dies!" while Jay Jay was up on the dangerous flaming roof, spraying water into the fire with a garden hose, directing the whole operation, saving the day. His picture in the Calmento *Courier*, even:

HEROIC GROWER'S SON
SAVES FARM LABORERS

. . . a large young man, heavily built, with an enormous head, head too large even for his body, outlined by the press photographer against the burning building. Everyone but Bruno had congratulated him. And what did Bruno do? Next day, bright and early, "Get back out there to that fifty acres of yours and finish that discing!"

"What fifty of mine?" he asked, smart-assed, since that fifty hadn't earned him a nickel yet. And Bruno got so pissed off he nearly slapped him one upside the head.

Jay Jay had been laboring over that fifty acres of his now ever since picking time was done in November. Working in the evening, after classes at College of the Pacific in Stockton, and on the weekends, he had plowed it, disced it, land-planed it, chiseled it, and then he had let it lie under the rains till March. Then he had disced again and seeded it. Now he was applying herbicide to hold down the weeds. Next he would cultivate, and thin out the plants so they were exactly nine inches apart. Apply lay-by herbicide. Do the open and close ditching. Irrigate, staying up every night all through the summer. Fertilize with nitrogen, a hundred and fifty pounds per acre. Apply pesticide, quick-ripening agent, fungicide to prevent mold on the vine. And then he'd be ready for the real work, harvesting. Twenty-five tons of tomatoes this field would produce. And tomatoes in the supermarket at forty-nine cents a pound. And what did Jay Jay get out of it? Nothing. He worked for less than a Mex. Worked for just pocket money and his keep. "Just like I did," his father always said, "just like your Grandpa Tony did with me." Oh, by God there would soon come a time when Jay Jay would no longer have to take that kind of crap from his old man. You'd think the fucker was still back in the old country, the way he acted. *"Le teste dure,"* the local *paisani* used to call him and old Tony: "the hard-headed ones." Products of the extreme southeastern corner of Sicily—a land so poor and stony and wind eroded that the peasants had to build a ten-foot loose rock wall to enclose and free the ground for a single olive tree, and the countryside looked more like a maze of undulating stone walls than farmland—the Vanduccis had always been renowned for their stubborn, vengeful, and clannish qualities. Nothing was valued higher than family loyalty. Once a 'Ducci had set his course, nothing could deflect him from it. He would never forget a slight. He would never break a vow. Only twice in Jay Jay's recollection had a Vanducci gone against his word. And these two instances had been so earthshakingly significant in the life of the family that they had resulted in a nearly endless series of repercussions.

The way Grandpa Tony used to tell the story, on the day that he left for America he buried a trunkful of ancient Vanducci keepsakes of great sentimental value (*"l'anima di nostra famiglia,"* as he had insisted on calling it, "the soul of our family," when in fact it was nothing more than a bunch of old dishes, silverware, blankets, letters, land titles, and photographs dating back to the time of the Kingdom of the Two Sicilies) in his ancestral garden in Sangiorgio di Roccas. He hid his treasure behind a stone wall, he said, under an olive tree. And he vowed to come back one day and dig it up. He spent five years as an iceman, gandy dancer, and farm laborer in San Joaquin County before he figured he'd saved enough money to return to the old country. But just then Mr. Hardy Range, Delano's grandfather, came along and offered him fifty acres of level, well-watered tomato-growing land at a rock-bottom price. Grandpa Tony broke his vow and bought the land and, driving his wife and two sons and three daughters like farm animals, he turned that original fifty acres into a hundred, a thousand, four thousand acres! And he never went back to Sicily. Never even looked back till he was a middle-aged man, in 1943, and one son was dead in the Pacific and the other was about to get shipped overseas to Italy. Looking back, there was only one thing that old Tony regretted: that old rotting trunk that he'd buried in the ground back in 1919, under the olive tree, behind the stone wall, on the far southeastern coast of Sicily.

It was then that he sent his only remaining son, Bruno, on a sacred mission, a quest for the relics of his family's Mediterranean past: He instructed him to go dig up the trunk.

Bruno got R & R leave in June of 1944 and journeyed to Sicily. He arrived in Sangiorgio di Roccas. He located the old Vanducci property. And then, for some reason that to Jay Jay had always remained obscure, he chickened out. Turned around and went straight back to his Division Headquarters in Naples. Didn't even trouble himself to visit the house or the garden, or speak to his father's relations in the town.

Grandpa Tony had never forgiven Bruno for breaking his word. Bruno had never apologized. And the two of them had remained at odds on the matter till the day the old man died.

This kind of romantic yet unbendingly obstinate quality in the Vanducci character was at once the source of the family's spectacular success in Calmento, and of certain morbid possibilities too. In Jay Jay's breast right now, in fact—Jay Jay clambering back up on his tractor, Jay Jay starting her up again—there existed one creeping little virulent symptom of possible trouble.

Her name was Selena Cruz.

After two years of going secretly steady (sneaking to Stockton for dinner and a movie, parking on the levee on the way back, creeping into Southside on secondary roads) and after nearly three months now of defying his father and dating right out in the open. Jay Jay thought of the Mexican girl as warm and familiar and yet wondrous, like the magic of one of his own ripe tomatoes in the palm of his hand. She was as sweet and fecund as the earth he plowed beneath his big John Deere: He would plow her, implant her, care for her tenderly as he did his own field. He adored her, dreamed of her every night, never looked at another girl. He felt weak with anticipation every time they had a date. The first time he went inside her he thought he would die of love. And when he came, the first time he'd ever come into a girl in his life, it was unbelievably painful. The sperm felt like it was torn right out of his guts, taking his heart along with it. Yet, now that he thought of it, at each step along the way to her sweet wiry pussy he'd felt the same way. It was a feeling that hit him right in the solar plexus, painful but good, that made his heart beat like wild, made his pecker rise. He remembered now with his dick getting stiffer and stiffer on the tractor seat all the firsts of their relationship: the first time they went out, after their visit with Range (their *only* visit: after that the thought of poor suffering Delano was like a burr in the side of their love, and they avoided the whole issue) . . . their first kiss that night . . . the first time she let him touch her titties a month later, parked in front of her house in Southside . . . the first time she let him suck them in the drive-in movie . . . the first time she let him fingerfuck her on the Old River levee, the smell of her quim on his hand that he wouldn't wash away for days . . . that fateful night parked in his father's tomato field in the driving December rain when she had lain naked for an hour under his more and more frantic probing fingers; Jay Jay trying to find a girl's snatch for the first time in his life (in pitch blackness), jabbing his cock in her asshole, her peehole, her bellybutton, in any hole he could find, too scared and shy to ask her to help . . . and then finally spurting it white in the darkness all over her round brown belly, her fecund waiting field.

Every time they fucked after that he worried about knocking her up. Tried using a rubber, but couldn't figure out how to get it on. Stood out in the pelting rain on the levee rolling it and unrolling it for half an hour, unable to get it over his huge, pulsing hard-on. Got so impatient he ripped a prickhole right through the reservoir tip. After that they tried to use the rhythm method but their lust often got the best of them. . . .

Jay Jay looked at his watch. Still three hours to quitting time. And that damn field stretching away in front of him bleak and black as destiny. And yet, just under that smooth San Joaquin soil, little things that he had planted were growing, growing, soon to burst into life.

Wipe your face, Jay Jay. Atta way. Whew! Blow your nose. Phew! The snot comes out black as tar. Tie that bandanna around your face. Okay now, boy. You can do it. Drop that spray. At least now the fumes will blow away. Now drive, man, drive it, into the valley, into your future, into the teeth of the howling wind!

Halfway down the field he spotted his old man creeping along the Delta-Mendota Canal levee in his Ford pickup, checking up on him. Ever since Jay Jay was a little kid his father had been pulling this kind of shit. Always sneaking around, spying on him. Asking silly questions . . . the most intimate things: "Hey, tell me something, Jay Jay. Can you come yet?" he asked him this one time, when he was just a little bitty boy and didn't even know what the word meant. And another time, just as he was reaching puberty: "You get laid yet, boy? Lemme know when you want it. I'll take you up to the Mustang Ranch and get you the best that money can buy."

Jay Jay understood that his father meant well, was genuinely concerned for him, wanted more than anything to "make a Vanducci out of him." But enough was enough. He was already a 'Ducci, for Christ's sake, a grown man, and his patience was wearing thin. *I am no fucking Wop. I will be my own man, goddamnit, or I will not be around.*

Into the sun again. Back upwind. Sunward. Windward. An eternity later and Jay Jay was done. He drove up the hill and into the barn and switched off his engine. Mother so hot she kept turning over for half a minute *plump plump plump,* getting fainter and fainter. Then it stopped, and he jumped down. Locked the barn and trudged across the dusty farmyard to the new Vanducci "mansion."

Early evening, and the last rainstorm of the year on its way down from Mount Shasta. Across the black dusty fields, across the freeways and waterways to the north, he could see the clouds coming marching down the valley like fat gray soldiers. They would drop only light rain on the San Joaquin. They would save the heavy stuff for the Sierra Nevada and drop it there in the form of deep snow. In June the snow would melt. The water in a milion tiny rivulets would run into the streams and creeks and down into the eighteen great mountain rivers, rivers with names of poetic beauty to Jay Jay's ears: Kern, Tule, Kaweah, Kings, San Joaquin, Fresno, Chowchilla, Merced, Tuolumne, Stanislaus, Calaveras, Mokelumne, American, Bear, Yuba, Feather, Sacramento, Pit. And, gathering momentum as it went, the water would squeeze through narrow mountain chasms and flood into the huge reservoirs in the foothills and roll over the spillways of gigantic dams and spin the dynamos of hydroelectric generators and flow in an orderly manner into the great irrigation canals of the valley, the San Luis, the Delta-Mendota, the Friant-Kern, and finally trickling again in small ditches and furrows, it would end up on his father's own rich land which he could see below him now. The thought afforded Jay Jay a degree of satisfaction that quite made up for his day in the field.

To tell the truth, the Vanducci house was no mansion at all. The "Big House" of the new Dootch's dreams had never been built. What had happened was, Grandpa Tony's old eclectic place had been rebuilt and enlarged and modernized into a long split-level ranch-style house with a patio and a new V-shaped swimming pool. The house was painted pink with white shutters. This year had been exceptionally wet, so now the pink was kind of mud-splattered. After the first summer no one but Jay Jay's mother used the pool anymore. And Angie only used it for her annual summer school. Now the pool was moss-grown and forlorn, the cement cracking, and the patio sprouting weeds. The Lincoln Continentals were scratched and rusting out, their paint fading in the relentless valley sun. Nor had the new Dootch toured Europe as he had planned. He lived with his wife and son in his father's old house, and the minks and sables gathered dust and were eaten by moths. But such had been the way of the 'Duccis from time immemorial, and it was by no means to be taken as a sign of decay. Their fields flourished, their crops grew tall, their fruits won prizes at the county fair, their bank accounts grew like never before.

"I'm home!" Jay Jay called from the back porch, hopping up and down on one foot, struggling to get his dirty boots off.

"Hello, darling, how did it go today?" his mother said, swirling out from her new yellow kitchen.

She wore a pale pink sun dress with a décolletage that was somewhat daring for daytime use. And she smelled of cumin from the salad she was helping the Mexican maid prepare. The dress was in character but the smell was not: Angie generally avoided cooking chores like the plague.

"I worry about you sometimes, dear," she said, kissing him softly on his peaty cheek, ruffling his dirty hair with her slender olive-skinned hand. "You work too hard."

"I couldn't agree with you more," he said, with heavy meaning.

Angie laughed and rolled her big eyes to let him know that Bruno was home and he'd better watch the wisecracks.

"Will you be dining *en famille* tonight, darling," she said drolly, "or . . . ?"

"Naw," he said, heading for the bathroom, "got a date."

"Oh-oh," Angie said. "Better not let your father hear about that. You know how he feels about that young lady."

"Come on, Mom!" he said. His voice sounded ridiculously adolescent to himself. Every time the subject of his father came up it sounded that way.

"Buh, buh, buh . . ." she said, in her playful melodious voice, prancing up behind him, putting her arms around his waist. And then in a more serious vein: "But do come home early, Jay, Jay, please. Otherwise I will be the one who bears the brunt of your father's ire. . . . Okay?"

"Okay, okay," he said, disengaging himself. And went into the bathroom, slamming the door behind him. He was annoyed with her now. He had been very open with her about Selena, and she had appeared to sympathize. And now here she was using it against him, in the interests of the Dootch.

"Goddamn," he said to himself. "That's what you get for being honest."

Yet he knew that the next time she was just as likely to use one of Bruno's secrets in the interests of her son.

Jay Jay found his mother mysterious and dangerous and delicious and unpredictable. And he was a little frightened of her, in a way he could never be frightened of his simple, tyrannical father. Jay Jay had always found his father rather boring, except perhaps on those rare occasions when he would sit over supper telling stories of his years as a combat infantryman in Italy during World War II. Yet Angie never bored her son. On the contrary, he sometimes found her disquietingly attractive. She was fully aware of this, and was not above using it to her own advantage. She did the same thing with Bruno. All the time. Had him twisted right around her little finger.

Bruno never made a business decision without Angie's explicit approval. Though, if you asked her a question about ranch affairs, she would protest, and say, "Oh, that's in my husband's province, I'm afraid. I'm just the housekeeper around here." At the same time, she would voice her protestation in such a way as to call into question its sincerity. In this way she often tried to hide her intelligence from new acquaintances, hoping they would underestimate her. Then she would boggle them with some acute perception (something she'd thought out beforehand), encouraging them to overestimate her. It was a form of extreme vanity. Yet the vanity encompassed her family and manifested itself in a fierce pride and loyalty to the Vanducci establishment. For this reason Jay Jay was convinced that she loved him and his father truly, despite her apparently overweening self-absorption. Which is not to say that she didn't tease them both unmercifully and continually, and provoke her husband nearly past endurance. It was how she kept them in line. Jay Jay couldn't say he blamed her. Otherwise, he figured, the two of them would have just taken her for granted, and run roughshod over her, like all the other growers did with their wives and mothers.

So in the bathroom Jay Jay was still angry at his mom, as he removed his filthy workclothes, dropping them among piles of other dirty things on the tile floor, but even the anger was just part of the after-work luxury he was feeling now.

He spent an hour under the hot shower, dazed with bliss, thinking about his date tonight with Selena Cruz.

When he had finished his shower and shaved, he threw on a fresh pair of brown Levi corduroys, a white button-down shirt, a tan car coat, and started out of the house. Toed it through the kitchen with his finger to his lips. His mother and the fat little Mexican maid laughed and nodded encouragement and motioned for him to hurry on out.

"Hey!" the Dootch yelled, from somewhere behind him. "Where you goin', boy?"

"Out," he said, without turning.

"Wait a minute, goddamnit! You were so worried about that wind, but it looks like you did okay to me," Bruno hollered, bounding up behind him, grabbing him roughly by the arm, whirling him around.

Bruno was a hard, weathered man with a bulbous crimson nose, a heavy jaw, thick lips, and big tobacco-stained teeth. His cheeks were deeply pitted from a youthful case of acne. He was very hairy everywhere except on his head. All his hair was bleached pure white by a lifetime in the valley sun. There were patches of overexposure all over his skin, and the rims of his pale gray eyes were perpetually irritated. He was rarely seen without a cigar stuck in the corner of his mouth. To Jay Jay he had always been a mindless but overwhelming presence, like some great dumb vicious beast of the jungle, a Cape buffalo or a rhino.

Bruno was very excited about something now. He was bouncing up and down on the balls of his feet, laughing nervously, puffing his cigar at a furious clip. His face was so florid, his hair so bleached, the smoke so thick around his head, it looked like he was on fire. It was Jay Jay who excited him. Whenever he was around his boy, he acted like the heavyweight champ with a dangerous new contender. But the kid had no desire to challenge him, as yet. All he wanted was to be left alone. That was the one wish, however, that Bruno could not fulfill. In this way too he was like old Tony. It was a form of savage possessive love, the manifestation of which was an insane desire to alternately fondle and torture the loved one. Like a tomcat with a plump captured rodent, Bruno could not keep his sweaty hands off his boy. Was always taking liberties, poking him, punching him, squeezing his arm, patting his cheek, slapping his back, kissing him, even though he'd hated it when old Tony did it to him . . . or precisely *because* he'd hated it when Tony did it to him.

"Dad, I'm sorry, but I'm in pretty much of a hurry," he said. Gingerly disengaged himself and eased out the back door. "See you later."

Did not feel like getting into it with the old fart tonight. Did not want to spoil his good mood, his sweet inspiration. Hurried across the ranch yard and got into his mama's big Continental and was just about to pull out when the Dootch appeared outside, banging on the metal roof with his fist.

"Open up!"

"Whaddaya waaaaaant, Dad?" Jay Jay whined, rolling his window down.

"I want you to understand one thing, bimbo," he said, in the low, reasonable, slightly Italian-accented voice that disguised his deepest ire: "Till the day you figure you can whip my ass, you treat me with respect. You ever slam a door in my face again, I'll break your balls. *Capice?*"

Jay Jay sat there under his father's gaze, seething with rebellion, trying to determine if that day had come yet. But somewhere inside him he knew that fate would have it another way: The day would never come. And he would remain, like his father, in thrall to his father till he was old and gray, and victory had lost its sweetness.

". . . And another thing. I told you before but I guess I'm gonna have to tell you again," Bruno said, grinning as if he were about to say something slightly off color, "don't go getting any bright ideas about that little chiquita. You do and you're gonna find yourself disinherited so fast it'll make your head swim. Understand?"

Jay Jay said nothing, just kept sitting there in the Lincoln, slumped in the plush red leather seat.

"Understand?"

At last, very slowly and sadly, Jay Jay nodded his great head.

"Well, that's more like it," Bruno said. "Now, you might laugh, but I just can't figure out what's wrong with a nice Italian girl. I really can't. I mean, is Rose Mary Ammiratti some kind of *cretina* or something?"

"Naaaaaaw, Dad," Jay Jay whined, hating his own voice. "It ain't that. . . ."

"All right then," said the Dootch, reaching into his pocket. "Here's twenty, bigshot. And don't do anything with the little señorita that I wouldn't do, eh?"

It was then that Jay Jay blew his top.

"Nothing you do or say," he said fiercely, startling even himself, "nothing you do or say will ever keep me away from Selena."

"Oh no? Oh no? We'll just see about that."

"I'm leaving this place."

"No you ain't."

"Just watch me."

"You ain't got the *coglioni,*" Bruno said and started for the house.

"Fuck you, Dad, eat shit!" Jay Jay screamed after him, and spun rubber out of the yard.

He could see his old man in the rearview mirror, eating his son's dirt. Then Bruno ran for the other Continental. He was so furious that all his movements were exaggerated, stylized, like a bogeyman in a high school Halloween skit. He looked so ludicrous, hopping across the yard, that Jay Jay started laughing out loud.

Bounced over the dirt driveway to Corral Hollow Road. Floored it and headed north along the black cultivated fields, checking his rearview mirror all the time, remembering another time, another year, when he'd done exactly the same thing. Defied his dad on a windy, peat-dusty day in spring. Ran his grandpa's new Dodge pickup off the ranch, peeking in the rearview mirror all the time to see if Bruno was following. Wailed into town and screeched up in front of Tracy's Drive-In on East Eleventh Street. Range was in there: it was Saturday afternoon and he'd finished the house chores early and hitched a ride into Calmento. The whole gang was in there with him: Big John Ammiratti, Dirty Harry Fulcher, Donnie "Prettyboy" Pombo, Sammy Dog. They were standing by the jukebox and the pinball machine, dancing around, acting up, laughing, mouthing the words to songs. They could see Jay Jay as he came springing out of the Dodge. He did a little *hi-yi-yi-yi-hi-yi-yi-yi-whoopie* Indian boogie for them on the concrete under the awning.

"Hey, babies, lez go drink some wiiiiiiine!" he hollered, scatting it up to the counter. Didn't even know he was gonna say that. All the customers in their booths turned around to watch. He'd just been rapping, making an entrance. But now all eyes were upon his ass. "Do Ya Wanna Dance," is on the jukebox. " 'Well do ya do ya do ya, wa-a-nna dance? Do ya do ya do ya wa-a-nna dance? Oh bay-bee, do ya wanna da-a-ance?' " And he's all of a sudden feeling so cool that he says it again.

"Oohie, lez go drink some wiiiiiiine!"

"Yeah, man," says Dirty Harry.

"Lez do it," Prettyboy says.

"Yeahyeahyeahyeahyeahyeah," says Sammy Dog, stroking the mange-eaten mongrel at his feet.

"I could go for a little booze," says Big John, running his huge red hand around his hard pot belly.

"Where you gonna get it?" little Range wants to know. His voice sounds doubtful and a bit sarcastic.

Jay Jay slugs him one on the arm.

"Ow! What's that for?"

"For bein' cute."

"One thing you won't ever have to worry about."

"Hearty har har," Jay Jay says, and goes behind the little prick and gets him in a hammerlock. Dirty Harry, Prettyboy, Big John, and Sammy Dog all laughing, real dumb, with their mouths hanging open. Jay Jay is laughing too. Just at that moment in fact he does recall a

place where he can get some wine. He had forgotten it. Range is trying
to laugh. But he can't. Jay Jay bends his arm a little farther.

"You gonna d-drink some wine with me?" he asks the little fucker,
breathing hard.

"Sure, man, sure, sure . . ."

Accelerating down Corral Hollow Road in present time, Jay Jay continued to check his rearview mirror for his old man. Pretty soon he saw
the sonbitch come barreling out of the driveway, fishtailing all over
the road.

"Goddamn, looks like a race. . . . Whoopie!"

Sixty, seventy, eighty miles an hour Jay Jay rode his wild metal steed
down to Valpico Road. The intersection was crowded with laughing,
singing, beer-drinking wetbacks who were lounging around in front of
the general store with no idea what was coming down upon them at
immoderate speed. He skidded around the corner at fifty miles an
hour, broadsiding it, scattering greasers every whichway.

"*Pinchi vato cabrón!*" they screamed after him, shaking their fists.

"Fuck you too, wetbacks," he said to himself, as he burnt rubber
down Valpico. Behind him the braceros settled down and began to
collect again in the middle of the road. *Watch out, muchachos . . .*
He could see them getting smaller and smaller in his rearview mirror.
Fifty, sixty, seventy, eighty, ninety, hurtling down along the high
embankment of the Western Pacific tracks.

In his grandpa's pickup, he had gone fast too. . . .

*"Where we goin'? Where we goin'?" Dirty Harry wants to know. A
big redheaded freckle-faced New Mexican with innocent blue eyes, he is
renowned as the most inquisitive guy at Calmento High. Never got over
that stage in early childhood where you're always asking questions.*

"Where we goin'? Where we goin'?"

*"You'll find out when we get there," Jay Jay says, but he still won't
shut up.*

"Come on, come on, where we headed, where we headed?"

*Jay Jay just finally has to ignore him. East out of town he drives them
old boys. Past the huge echoing hangars of the World's Largest Truck
Stop, past the H.J. Heinz 57 Brands tomato cannery, across the SP
overpass and past the Hi-Way Drive-In movie. Right on Chrisman
Road. And now a straight seven-mile beeline past the US Army's Calmento defense depot to the hills. He makes it in five minutes flat in
that Dodge. Over the Delta-Mendota Canal and into the yellow-green
springtime hills, into Hospital Canyon, Joaquin Murietta's old hideout,
on a blustery April day. Winding around a white gravelly ravine lined
with old oaks, cottonwoods, buckeye, laurel, canyon maple, and yucca
trees growing on the flanks of the hills. The creek is dry. All the trees*

*are white, leafless, dying. Up ahead is the city dump, where Indian Bill
makes his home. . . .*

Now by the Western Pacific embankment in the speeding Lincoln
Continental there were telegraph poles on one side of Valpico Road and
tall red and white oleanders on the other, whizzing faster and faster by,
black-white, red-white, in the periphery of Jay Jay's expanding vision.
And the black asphalt road before him like a high, narrow-based triangle,
with the apex getting never and never closer. In the mirror now he
could see the spicks as tiny specks in the road. Errrrrr! There came the
Dootch now in his Lincoln, around the corner lickety-split. "Aaaiiieee!"
Wetbacks screaming, jumping for dear life. The Dootch hit his brakes.
Stupid fuck! Hit 'em too hard. Lost control. Spun in the gravel. Spun
all . . . all . . . all the way around. Landed right side up in the ditch
all in a swirl of white dust and dark writhing braceros. "Har har har!
Lucky the sonbitch didn't kill himself, or one of the greasers. . . ."

*The city dump is nothing more than a chalky gray cut in the hills,
an old quarry. Last week Jay Jay hauled some trash up here for his
grandpa. Noticed that Indian Bill had acquired some big sparkling
water bottles and filled them with the purple rotgut he makes from
dumped Gallo grapes.*

*As they roll up the white dusty driveway, it looks like they're in luck.
Bill's car is gone. A full-blooded MiWuk Indian, he often travels in his
ancient flatbed Hudson to powwows up and down the MiWuk lands
from Sonora to Strawberry Lake. At one time there were the valley
MiWuks and the Sierra MiWuks. Indian Bill is the last of the valley
clan and takes pride in representing his now defucked people on tribal
business in the mountains. That's probably where he is now, Jay Jay
reasons. Either that or down in Southside at some cantina. Indian Bill
is a notorious drunk.*

*They pull up at the quarry. Dust swirls around the truck, then blows
away. There is not a sound in the canyon but the wind. There is even
no smell of garbage. It is all blown away south and lost in the wild hills
and arroyos of the Diablos. The sky is clear in this region, very blue, full
of circling buzzards. The peat dust has fallen behind. You can see it
now, low and yellow-black in the air, at the mouth of the canyon.*

*Sammy's dog jumps over the tailgate barking and runs off to chase
rats, rats as big as cats. Boys bail out and sidle up to Bill's abode. The
home of a true city dump eccentric, it is made of every conceivable jetti-
soned material: sheet metal, cardboard, discarded lumber, plastic, fiber-
board, styrofoam. The tin roof is held in place with large stones. It is
now banging in the wind, threatening to topple one of the rocks. The
rear of the house is virtually hanging over the precipice. Scattered
around the other three sides are old tires, washing machines, tin drums,
barrels, car parts, old furniture, broken glass, rusty wire, and a mountain*

of .22 long shells that Bill fires off to keep the rat population down. The ground is covered with engine oil and gunk that he spreads around to hold the dust.

Long-legged, hair blowing in the wind, the boys approach Indian Bill's lodge silently, almost reverently, as if it were on medicine ground. Bang at the door. No one home. Go around the side. Here's where he's got his big bottles. Filled to the brim with vino! Lined up on the east side of the house, out of the sun, out of the wind.

"That answer your question, Dirty?"

"Hey, wow!"

"Yeah," says little Range. And he bounces over and tries to pick one up. Can't lift it. "Har har har!" Gets down on his knees. Tries again. The bottle topples over the edge of the quarry and smashes a hundred feet below. BLOOMB! Purple wine and shattered glass spray out all over the garbage and the white rocks. Big black buzzards hop and scramble, flapping their wings.

Sammy Dog is tall, shambling, platinum-haired, the cluffiest guy at Calmento High. His dog, a foul-breathed mongrel shepherd named Dog, never leaves his side. They eat together, sleep together, they even smell alike. Like crusty bachelors of the same family, they are always biting and growling and cuffing one another. Sammy Dog does most of the biting and growling. Jay Jay and the boys only let him hang around for laughs. "Ooooooh!" he hollers now, and runs for another big bottle. But he can't lift it. Prettyboy Pombo helps him. With much strain they pick it up and throw it over the side just to see it splatter again. BLOOMB! It erupts spectacularly. Twenty redheaded buzzards take to the air.

Jay Jay is standing there with little Range, watching. Getting kind of excited himself. Muscles start to popping and jerking. Knees get to knocking. Jaw starts to grinding. Teeth get to chattering. He runs, bends swiftly, heaves up a giant bottle singlehandedly, raises it high above his head, his eyes bursting, smooth muscles bulging. Holds it there. . . . Holds it. Boys looking at him . . . strange. . . . Wondering what he's gonna do next, with such a savage expression on his broad young face. . . .

Jay Jay turned now at MacArthur Road, bumped over the high Western Pacific railroad embankment. Growled into town along the beet fields, vineyards, eucalyptus windbreak. Passed the Calmento Municipal Cemetery, where his stillborn baby brother lay, where his old pal Dirty Harry lay, where his Uncle Mike had been entombed since '43, where his Grandpa Tony and Grandma Letizia were interred, where his mother and father and even he himself and all his progeny would rest someday . . . in a crypt as big as a small house, quite visible from the road, made all of pure white marble, with VANDUCCI cut into the rock on all four sides in Roman capital letters.

Zoooooooooooooom went the big-ass Continental. Zoooooooooooooom!

*Jay Jay holds that enormous bottle up high in the air . . . longer
. . . longer . . . till the boys are almost afraid of him. No human
being can do such a thing, perform such a feat of power.*

*Then with a mighty roar, he throws it through the window of Indian
Bill's shack.VAVOOOOOOM! It explodes inside, flooding the house
with rotgut wine and broken shards of glass.*

*"Woo, woo, woo!" go the boys, dancing in the greasy city dump dust.
They never seen such a thing. Never been so impressed. Sammy Dog
runs around to the front and kicks in the window. CRASH! Hops
around on one foot, giggling hysterically, "Ohboyohboyohboyohboyoh-
boy!"*

Big John kicks in another. Blam! Cuts his leg slightly.

*The sight of blood, or the sound of glass breaking, galvanizes the
others into action. Dirty Harry, broad-shouldered, bull-necked, junior
varsity fullback, Dirty Harry puts his head down, pumps his legs, screams
"Yaaaaaagh!" and charges right through the wall . . . slips on the wine
and glass, and falls flat on his face inside. Comes up purple from head
to foot, bleeding from several small cuts.*

"Lucky you didn't cut your fucking head off!" Jay Jay hollers.

*Boys just standing around him in the black dirt, slit-eyed, open-
mouthed, keening with laughter.*

*Even Dirty laughs, his last laugh, lapping at the wine on his silly
young freckled face. "Yum yum!" he spouts. "This stuff's good drinkin'!"*

*Suddenly they are all in a frenzy . . . breaking things, kicking things,
picking them up and throwing them to the ground, stomping them,
smashing them, listening to the glass as it shatters and tinkles and skids
on the debris. In half a minute the house is demolished, and Indian
Bill's pathetic belongings flung in a mindless fury over the side. . . .*

"Oh-oh!" Here came the Southern Pacific embankment. DANGER—
UNDERGROUND CABLE said a sign by the side of the road. Jay Jay slowed
to fifty for it. Bounced once—*wump*—left the land behind, soared
through the air. *Wham!* Landed, bottomed on his mama's springs,
stepped on it again, bumping along the rough blacktop county road.
The valley flat and darkening all around him, his valley . . . the sun
going down red behind the Diablos, eddies of red dust in his path, red
tumbleweeds blowing across the red road. Left at Third Street now,
heading into Mexican Town. Even if his dad got his car going again,
he'd never follow him here. He'd never been in Southside in his life, as
far as Jay Jay knew. Had no business there. Very few gringos had. If
they wanted workers, they hired them through a labor contractor, or
shipped them up directly from Mexicali by bus. To the white people of
Calmento, the place didn't really exist. If you showed it to them on a
map, that third part of town on the wrong side of the tracks, they'd
look at it strangely, like they'd forgotten all about it. And yet it was

the oldest part of town, settled alongside the SP tracks by old James
Catlin Range in the year 1878. . . .

*Jittery with guilt, the boys stand on the ruins of Indian Bill's house,
trying to decide what to do with themselves. Very very spooky now,
jerking their heads around all the time. When a crow caws nearby they
nearly jump out of their skins.*

*Only Jay Jay serene. The violence has purged his demons, it seems.
Even his nervous desire to punch Range, to twist his arm and pull his
curly hair, even that is gone, and he regards the little fucker now even
with a certain measure of affection and laughs with him at Sammy Dog
who's chasing his dog who's chasing a cat who's chasing a great fat rat.
Sammy finally gets Dog and drags him back to the pickup. Prettyboy
and Big John load the last wine bottle that they have saved from destruction. Just about ready to crank up the Dodge and split when Dirty
Harry kicks one last shard of glass into the quarry, loses his footing, and
disappears over the edge. . . .*

"*Aaaaaagh!*"

*Happens so quick nobody can believe it. They look at each other half
grinning, suspecting a practical joke.*

"*Help! Help!*"

*Race to cliffside, peer over, and there is Dirty Harry, lying on an abut-
ment of rock forty feet below.*

"*You all right, Dirty?*" *Jay Jay yells, while out of the corner of his eye
he spies Indian Bill's Hudson flatbed winding up Hospital Canyon
Road, kicking up a trail of white dust.*

"*Oh, oh, oh! I . . . I think . . . think I broke m' leg!*" *Dirty Harry
screams. He can't stop moaning, shrieking in pain . . .* "*Aaaaaagh!
Aaaaaagh!*"

"*Okay, now listen to me!*" *Jay Jay hollers, nudging Range beside him.
Range looks over his shoulder and spots that Hudson, wailing up the
road.* "*You stay put, Dirty. We're gonna get you some help right away.*"

"*Don't . . . don't leave me!*"

"*Got to, Dirty. Got to get help.*"

"*He'll kill me!*"

"*Who?*"

"*Indian Bill!*"

"*You just stay quiet, man. He'll never even know you're down there!*"

*Boys run for the pickup, pile in. Dog leaps up in the back. Jay Jay
barrels that Dodge down the driveway, onto the road, down the canyon.
Indian Bill passes, spots the wine. Spins in the sand, gives chase. Jay Jay
careens down the dirt road, hits the Delta-Mendota embankment doing
sixty. Passengers commend their souls to Jesus. Heads carom off the roof.
Dog floats a full six feet above the truck bed, treading air. Wine cata-
pults to the sky, erupts a purple flower in the white road. WHOOMP!*

The Dodge lands. Boys come down in their seats with sore heads. Dog
makes a four-point landing in back. Pickup fishtails in the soft dirt,
skids, skids. . . . Floor that mother, Jay Jay! Straightens her ass out,
picks up speed. Hudson slows for the canal and the broken glass, and is
left far behind.

Jay Jay screams for the freeway, fast as the thing will go. Screeches
up at the first gas station, phones the county sheriff and the ambulance
service, giving a phony name.

But it's too late. By the time they get out there, Indian Bill has al-
ready picked off poor Dirty with his .22 pump gun.

Up Third Street Jay Jay drove, thinking about that tragedy when he
was only sixteen. Thinking about life, how unfair it all is. The Dirty
Man eats it at sixteen. Others at a hundred and sixteen. It's all just a
roll of the dice. If Indian Bill hadn't got sent up to Folsom, Vanducci
might've been next on his hit list. . . .

Now up along the dirty juniper trees of Southside he drove, the cactus
plants, rose trees, and oleanders in the dirt front yards. Goats, donkeys,
chickens in the road. Up South Central Avenue to the raucous sound of
ranchero music, blaring out of loudspeakers set in the cottonwood trees,
on this rapidly descending Sunday night.

His heart started firing like a pom-pom gun as soon as he turned into
Selena's driveway on South "C" Street. Pulled up in her front yard and
turned off his engine. Stayed put in the Lincoln for a moment. He had
that good smarting nervous twinge of love in the pit of his stomach
again. It made him weak. He was trying to make it go away. Concentrating, sweating with the effort, he finally got rid of it. Embarrassment
helped him get rid of it: He could see Selena's little sister Jovita in the
window, staring, giggling at him. . . .

For months after their first date Selena wouldn't let him come visit
her at home. Too ashamed of her rude family, her poverty, the torn
curtains in the windows, the faded linoleum on her floors, the ragged
furniture in her front room, the knickknacks and *chingaderas*—castoffs
of the white man—that they picked up at thrift shops in Stockton.

Then after they made love everything changed. Suddenly she was no
longer ashamed of her family. "You are my family," she said. "I have
nothing to hide." And thereafter he spent hours at home with the Cruz-
Aguilars, eating with them, playing cards with them, watching TV, lots
of TV. At first the smell of Selena's house, the smell of many people in
a small space, the smell of heavy perfume, oily skin, bean sweat, frijoles,
cornmeal, unrefined grease, tripe soup, chile peppers, hot sauce, cactus
apples, goat cheese, the smell made him sick to his stomach. But then
it kind of grew on him. And now when he was away from it he missed
it. To him it was Selena's smell, and he could think of nothing he'd
rather be than surrounded by it, inundated with it, for the rest of his life.

When Jay Jay first started visiting the Cruz-Aguilars, they had trouble relating to him. In order to cover up their embarrassment, they laughed frequently. But laughter was not something that came easily for them, in his presence. What happened was, it came out hollow. "Hee hee hee," they would all begin, as soon as he got in the door. Laughter was just another Vanducci job to them, like picking his daddy's fruit or driving his sulphur rig. Their minds were on other things, on food or drink or TV or the payday that was coming. They had no time for emotion with a stranger. At bottom they were not even convinced that this gringo in their house was made of flesh and bone. They trusted nothing, not even their own senses, in dealing with those outside their own family and *raza*.

But then slowly over the months he had started to win them over with his friendly unaffected attitude, and his interest in their food and their customs, and his refusal to play the young lord. That is to say, with much work Jay Jay established a rather uneasy friendship with the family that held within the walls of their home. However, if he saw Aguilar out on the job, working the Dootch's sulphur rig, or if he saw Connie and Rudy taking the drag in Northside, he ignored them as he had always ignored them, as they expected to be ignored. It never occurred to him to do otherwise. They were not like Selena, clean and good-looking and always dressed neatly like a gringa. They were greasy and unsavory and too Mexican-looking. Even they knew this. Selena certainly knew it; and she would never have permitted them to accompany Jay Jay and herself to the movies, for example, or to Tracy's Drive-In for a milk shake.

Jay Jay got out of the car. Jovita disappeared shyly from the window. He trotted heavily across the dirt yard, up the rickety wooden steps to the porch, *clump clump clump*; his big feet sounded loud, shaking the porch, setting the swing couch to squeaking. His heart was going like mad again. There was nothing he could do to prevent it.

Selena opened the door and closed it behind her. She was wearing a tight gray woolen skirt and a tight black cashmere sweater that he had bought her for Christmas. Brown-skinned, black-eyed, beaming at him, she was so outrageously fucking lovely that she was not real.

He swept her into his arms right there on her porch with the neighbors looking on. Squeezed her tighter, tighter, feeling her full titties under the soft cashmere, rubbing up against his tense pecs. Ran his hands down her ribs, waist, round the swell of her hips and her magnificent ass. Felt like he was holding the whole fucking world, all of existence. Felt like the Mediterranean conquistador who conquered the Americas only to be vanquished himself by the Aztec maiden Malinche. Loved his Selena with such rapture he was scared he would expire right on the spot. At the same time, he felt like her savior. In her Indian eyes he read the whole suffering history of her *raza*. As stout Cortés with his sword and salvation had won a savage queen for civilization, so Vanducci with his imagination had found his love like a rose on a burro-shit accumulation. As Hernán had decamped with the king's *carnala* and kept her as his personal chattel, so would Jay Jay win the Señorita Selena and keep her from the economic battle . . . yeah!

She led him now by the hand into her clapboard shack, into the vulgar glow of her black and white TV. The house was so tiny inside! First time he walked in, he bumped his head and they all laughed. Inside it was like a miniature house, a playhouse for dark-faced dolls that smelled strongly.

"Hi, Jay Jay," said Mama, sitting on the couch, cradling the baby.

"Hi, Jay Jay," said Rudy, barely looking up from the TV. A tag team wrestling match was on, and everyone was glued to it.

"Hi, Jay Jay," said La Trucha Connie, with her usual uncheerful unoriginality.

"Hi, Jay Jay," said little Jovita, insinuating herself shyly between the lovers, rubbing her little hip against Jay Jay's thick leg.

"Hi, everyone," he said, and sat down on the linoleum with Jovita on his lap. Jovita was warm and plump as a little piggie in his arms. He could feel her tiny heart beating furiously under his hand.

"Hey, where's Aguilar?"

"Where you think?" said Connie.

"Down at the cantina?"

"How you guess?"

Selena brought Jay Jay a plate of beans and sat down beside him. He wolfed it down, watching the television over Jovita's little head.

"Aw, these guys are faking," Rudy said. "He didn't really hit him that hard."

"Faking? Faking? What you mean, faking?" Mama said. "Look, you can see for yourself. They really do it. *Mira, mira!* Watch him knock that guy down. See?"

After a while Selena leaned over and whispered, "I got something to tell you. Can we go for a drive?"

Immediately his heart began to palpitate again.

"Jay Jay and I are going for a Coke," she announced, and rose to her feet.

But Jay Jay had such a hard-on by now that he was embarrassed to get up. He hesitated for a moment and then rose, still holding Jovita in his arms, but lowly, covering his privy parts. Carried her all the way out to the door that way. Gave her a big kiss and set her down in the doorway.

"See you later, folks," he said, and split to the car with Selena.

When he told her how it happened she cracked up. Scooted over beside him and snuggled up.

"You can let him go back up now, if you want," she whispered.

"He wants out."

"Go ahead and let him out. . . ."

And stroked him all the way to the Middle River levee.

Just as they hit the drawbridge he came in her hand. Quickly she got a Kleenex out of her purse and cleaned up the mess. By the time she was done he was already getting hard again.

"What is it you wanted to tell me?" he asked, when they were parked under the willow trees, sitting together in the Lincoln's luxurious back seat.

"Wait till we make love," she said.

He began tearing at her clothes.

"Stop it," she scolded. "Take them off carefully. Fold them up and lay them neatly on the front seat so I won't look a mess when I get home."

He did as she said, as he did every night they parked. Over the months it had become a ritual, and Jay Jay's frustration only added perversely to his delight.

Slowly he pulled her sweater over her head, folded it, placed it carefully in front, unbuckled her bra, placed it on top of the sweater. His fingers trembling, he unzipped her skirt, pulled it around her hips and ass, down her legs, over her feet, folded it, placed it beside her other things in front. Now she wore only her panties and stockings and shoes and garter belt. He took off her shoes, placed them on the floor in front, leaning all the way over the seat with his feet in the air to do it. Slid her panties over her hips, smelled her fragrance, slid them down her long legs, over her slender feet while she kicked, folded them, and placed them on top of her skirt in front. Now she wore only her garter belt and stockings. He was afraid he was going to have some kind of heart attack.

Moaned and fell face down on her pubic hair, babbling: "Oh, ah, oh, aaaaaah . . ."

"Stop it," she said. "Stop it. Take all your clothes off and lay them neatly on top of mine."

By the time poor Jay Jay had done all his cruel mistress demanded, he was foaming at the mouth.

"Aaaaaaaw!" he yelled, and thrust himself into her.

Selena was one of those ladies who speak in tongues when lost in the throes of passion.

"Basicka-balucka, goficka-gofucka," she chanted, driving him wild.

Lunged at her, drove her deep into the Lincoln's plush back seat. Nothing but instinct between them now as they tore and bit and heaved and sweat and strained till they came together in what he would remember as "six great blazing spasms."

As soon as he got his breath back, he jumped into the front seat, started the engine, and turned on the radio and heater. He was an expert at this parking stuff by now. They had made love in that back seat through the heat of summer, the rain and fog of winter, and the peat storms of spring. They'd been stuck in the mud three times. They'd been rousted out naked by a gang of vandalous Portagee irrigators with a pickup truck and a spotlight. They'd run out of gas and had to walk all the way back to town in the dark. . . .

He jumped back over the seat and lay down on top of her again.

"I love you," he said, gazing into her eyes. "More than anything."

"I love you too," she sighed, smiling up at him. "If only you knew . . ."

Theirs was a love as confined and self-contained as the inside of the automobile where it was born and continued.

"We are one," Jay Jay said, and at that instant he meant it literally.

"*Más que sabes tu,*" she said, pushing him off her, sitting up.

"What?"

"Nothing," she said, reaching into her purse.

"What is it you wanted to tell me?"

"It can wait," she said, dabbing at herself with a Kleenex, peering down between her spread legs in the darkness.

Selena's habit of evasiveness was one of the few things about her that annoyed Jay Jay. Her immodesty was another. He knew why ladies had to clean themselves after making love, and he knew the Cruz-Aguilars' casual attitude toward the body functions. But it repelled him anyway, in the same way that menstrual periods repelled him.

Across the seat Selena was still wiping between her legs with the Kleenex. But now she was flaunting it shamelessly and bringing it up to her nose, sniffing it.

Another of the things that annoyed him about her was this predilection for shocking his sensibilities all the time. Oddly enough, she was like his father in this way: It was her manner of putting his love and loyalty to the ultimate test.

"Come on," he said, "quit it."

"I wanted to find out what it smells like."

"It smells of Clorox."

"It smells of love."

"Love doesn't smell."

"That's where you're wrong, Buster," she said, laughing, waving the Kleenex in his face.

"Why do you talk like this? You take all the romance out of it."

"I don't want romance."

"What do you want?"

"I want you to see me for what I am and love me for it."

"That shouldn't be too difficult," he said flippantly, "if you'll clean up your act."

"We'll soon find out how difficult," she said.

"How's that?"

"*Soy embarazada.*"

"What?"

"*Encinta.*"

"Come again?" he said. He was afraid he understood her.

"*Llena, repleta, preñada . . .*" she intoned, driving a little wedge of apprehension into his already tenuous heart.

"What are you talking about?"

"I'm pregnant, Jay Jay," she said. And then: "What's so funny?" For suddenly he had begun to laugh.

"I'm thinking about my folks," he said. And the instant he said it, it became a fact. "Especially my old man," he said. "Can you imagine his face when I drop the bomb?"

"Are you going to tell him?"

"What do you think?"

"I don't know. I was kind of worried."

"Your worries are over now, kid," he said, still laughing. Why he was laughing he could not say.

Now Selena was laughing. There was nothing to laugh about. They were not laughing. They were desperate. Yet very soon they were rolling all over the car, laughing harder and harder. Laughed so fucking hard the Continental could not contain them. Rolled out the door, across the road, down the levee and out into the asparagus field, naked as jay-birds, throwing mudballs at each other.

By the time they got back to Selena's house they looked like they'd been in some kind of terrible accident. Raging with laughter, they bailed out of the Continental, ran up the front steps, and banged at the door.

Mama Aguilar opened it up. She took one look at them, exclaimed, "*Dios mío!*" and fell back into Rudy's arms.

Tracking mud and squished asparagus plant, they staggered into the house and collapsed in a fit of giggles on the linoleum floor.

"You're getting married," said Connie the Trout sadly.

On his way home to the 'Ducci spread, Jay Jay looked back over the course of his affair with Selena and tried to think of all its beautiful moments. But he found that he could consider the matter in general terms. True, the fucking had been outrageous. Yet, any one fuck was hard to remember in detail. It was only a teenage romance, after all, conducted solely in the back seat of an automobile. Who knew where it might have gone? But as it was, it was nothing more than it seemed.

He felt himself slipping, backsliding.

In order to firm up his resolve and encourage the growth of compassion within him, he tried to visualize the results of a hypothetical betrayal. What would it feel like to get dumped on by Jay Jay? What would Selena do if it happened to her? Would she cry? Rage? Plot revenge? Leave town? Languish away?

But it was no good. He hadn't a clue. And he felt his resolve and compassion seeping out of him now surreptitiously, like evil morning gas in Sunday High Mass.

"Stick to your guns, boy, stick to your guns!" he kept telling himself, striking the steering wheel with his fist for emphasis.

Then he tried another tack. Tried to figure out the best way to handle his parents when he broke the news of his betrothal. Whether to be very sincere and adult, or whether just to be deliriously happy and overwhelm them with his joy. Finally he decided on bliss as the best policy.

"Yippee, yippee!" he went, trying to stoke himself up for the coming confrontation. "Yippee!"

By the time he hit MacArthur Road he had worked himself up into a perfect frenzy of bliss.

But in his heart he knew he was damned. He broke down and cried. He prayed to God. He begged for mercy, for guidance. He cried out, "I want to be good, I want to do right, help me, help me. . . ."

He stepped on the gas.

It took him approximately forty seconds to make it the mile to the cemetery at Schulte Road. It took him only seventy seconds to make the two-mile run to Valpico Road. Ninety, a hundred, a hundred and ten, a hundred and twenty . . . Before him he could see trees, fields, houses, barns, packing sheds, orchards, mobile homes, gas storage tanks, pickup trucks with camper attachments . . . shrieking by in his headlights.

He knew the Western Pacific railroad embankment would be coming up soon. So it was vital to get his foot off that fucking pedal. But it was like he had some kind of muscle spasm. His foot was locked. He saw the embankment coming up. WARNING—UNDERGROUND CABLE. He shut off his engine. Started to hit the brakes with his left foot but decided it would throw him into a spin. The best policy, he figured, was just to ride it out.

All this went through his head in a split second. He coasted into the high hump straight and silent at seventy-five miles an hour. Big Lincoln rose slowly, majestically into the air. Went higher, higher. Looked like the beast never would come down. Below him he could see towns and cities and railroad tracks and irrigation canals and factories and fields and the great valley, the meandering rivers, the Sierras and the Diablos, the Delta, the Carquinez Straits, San Francisco Bay! Higher and higher went that big-ass Continental. Right into fucking orbit it went.

Then it descended from the most extreme heights, and he could see the roadway quite clearly below him. And the white line. The bumps and cracks in the asphalt. The soft shoulder.

There was a definite possibility that Jay Jay was going to wind up in the ditch.

On the other hand, maybe he would land safe and sound and continue on his way to his parents' home where, he knew, he would quickly and callowly capitulate to all of their demands.

At the moment he had no idea which way it would go.

But he was delighted that it was out of his hands.

Seven

FIVE MONTHS LATER, on a Saturday morning in September, Aguilar woke up with a hangover and he did not want to go to work. What he wanted to do was grab a few more zees and fuck his dear fat wife and stroll down to El Chico's cantina and have a few more hairs of the dog that bit him. But what could a man do? With his stepson Rudy drafted into the army, and his stepdaughter Selena disgraced and disappeared, who was there to help? Who would make the car payments, the TV payments? Aguilar, that's who!

Victorino envied his wife Delia today. All week long she came to the fields with the little ones and they helped him pick. But on Saturday they stayed home to do the week's shopping and washing and cooking, and Aguilar had to go out alone. Had to. There was no getting around it, for the rent was now far past due.

So, moaning and groaning, he rolled out of bed. Groped for his dirty smelly work clothes on the floor. Just one damn drunk after another all summer long . . . It was like Selena rolled up all the joy in his life and took it with her when she left town last spring. Without her nothing mattered, nothing counted, and the days and the nights they just came and went. Aguilar thought of his beautiful Selena now. He saw her radiant face on the night of her betrothal. Saw her wake up next morning looking the same way. Saw her wait for her fiancé's phone call all that day. And all the next day. And the next. Saw the soul go right out of her eyes. And the love. Saw the anger come marching in. Watched her call him at his place. Heard his mama say he'd gone away. "Well, you just better find him," he heard Selena say, "or there's gonna be hell to pay!" Three hours later the Dootch showed up outside the house. He didn't knock. He didn't come up the front steps. He didn't even leave his Continental. He honked, twice. And Selena came running. "Here's enough money for a trip to Tijuana and a four-year college education," the Dootch said. "Take it now, *bella*. Sign this paper and get out of town. Or the next time I see you it'll be in court." And she took it! Aguilar saw it with his own eyes. She signed the paper and snatched the greenbacks out of his hand and ran back into the house like she was scared he might change his mind. Then she counted out half and handed it over to Mama. "But what about that college education?" Aguilar said. "Don't worry about it, Papa," Selena said. The first time she'd ever called him that. With tears in her eyes, her lips starting to tremble, and all. And he damn near broke down himself. Then she packed her bags and collected her cousin Connie and the two of them left town that night on a Greyhound bus and no one had seen or heard from Selena since. Except for a card now and again. Well, in reality, she never forgot them. That was the truth. And always remembered to put a little something, a ten or a twenty or even a fifty once in a while, in the envelope. And it sure did come in handy. 'Cause his debts and drinking had eaten up his part of that blood money awful fast. And that was no lie. *Ay la vida, ay!*

And at that point Aguilar left off thinking about the matter. It was too focking depressing. Better not to dredge up the past, *cabrón!* Better not to curse the 'Ducci boy, who arrived back in town as soon as Selena departed, nor his father, who out of sheer spite fired Aguilar off his cushy job on the sulphur rig soon thereafter. Fired Rudy, too, just out of deviltry. Better not to lament over one's own irredeemably broken heart and the loss of all one held dearest in life, or remember that last little poignant look through the Greyhound window, that last little heartbreaking cry that escaped Selena's lips as the bus pulled out of the station. . . . *Qué no!* Better just to empty the head of such thoughts.

Ay, but Virgen María his head she was spleeting now, his eyes they was blind with pain!

Cursing loudly in Spanish and English—*hijo de la gran chingada cabronada maldita que fue la pendeja que te digo you bastard focking sonofabeech*—he struggled into his jeans that were stiff with tomato juice, his boots that were caked with clay. Got his sweat-stained straw sombrero down off the hat rack, clapped it low on his head, and staggered out to the kitchen. There on the table was the sack lunch that Delia had made him last night with careful hands: refried beans in a little jar, rolled corn tortillas, green peppers wrapped in aluminum foil, a thermos jug of iced coffee. He picked it up and stumbled across the green linoleum of the living room and outside into the black early morning and pitched down the dirt driveway to South "C" Street and thence to the Golden Taco Cafe.

The Taco was jammed with dark loud tomato pickers waiting for the Vanducci labor bus. Many of them were *amigos* and others were pretty *mamasotas*, but Aguilar had no desire to *charlar*. His black mood cleared a space of one seat on either side of him at the counter. Even Alma the waitress avoided speaking to him, him the possible *papá* of one of her six *muchachos*.

Coffee after black Mexican coffee he poured down his gullet, but nothing could diminish his gloom, his pain . . . *ay pinchi vato soy yo!*

The jukebox was turned up to top volume. "*Mira Bartola, ay peso sobre peso, paga la renta, el teléfono y la luz . . .*" Jorge Negrete lamented. And Aguilar was without defenses to deflect his terrible lamentation that shrieked now directly into his ringing ears, his molten brain, *aiiiiii!* Now his ears would burst. Now his eyes would pop out of his head. . . . He rose and hastened to the *escusado* and stuck his finger down his throat to vomit, but all he got for his effort was the dry heaves.

Somewhere in his echoing brain he could hear a horn honking. Reeling with nausea, he made his way through the empty cafe and out to the bus. Alma yelled, *"Adiós, Aguilar!"* But he did not answer, and left the door wide open behind him. It took all his strength of will just to put one foot in front of the other.

The bus lurched off down South "C" Street toward the fields of the Dootch. All of the pickers, they started laughing and joking and talking loud. Aguilar, he just ignored them. Leaned his head against the oily bumping glass of the window and closed his eyes to sleep. But he was too sick to sleep. So, what he did was, he pretended to sleep. More than anything he dreaded having to talk to some person, or smile. All he asked of his God was to release him from this diabolical torture of his *cruda*, his *ratón*, that was now eating his belly and brain from the inside. Pretending to sleep, Aguilar pretended to dream. . . . A clean cold morning in his native mountains. Waking up with a clean young *cabeza* at the first cockcrow. In the Sierra Madre, Aguilar remembered, you would always wake up with the cocks. All around you in the morning you would hear the *familia* snoring, all of them piled one on top of the other for warmth. The air of the *choza* hut was close and stale, Aguilar remembered, and it smelled of charcoal, cornmeal, refried beans, chile pepper, and urine. Of all the odors, urine was the strongest. Aguilar loved the smell of the *chozita*, and the feel of all his *familia*, his mama, papa, the baby, his little brothers and sisters, and each and all of their skins touching his own upon the straw pallet.

At first light he would rise and step over the sleeping bodies and go out into the morning. In the Sierra Madre the morning hits you in the face like cold water. Over the blue eastern ridges, ridges that rolled steeply one after the other like waves upon the sea, you could watch the sun come up out of Durango, red as hot iron. And down the shadowy western flanks of the cordillera you could see the wide Pacífico, purple as octopus ink. Closer, you could see your own poor mud and straw village spilling down the incline, and a thousand tiny terraced red-dirt corn and marijuana fields hacked into the green mountains. And smoke spiraling lazily up from a hundred morning woodfires to lie white and flat as a corpse upon the chill motionless air.

In the morning, Aguilar remembered, the first thing he would do was take a deep breath, holding it a long time in his spacious mountaineer's lungs, listening to his heart thumping strongly in his chest. Then he would offer up a brief prayer to Topo, the Gray Mountain.

Topo was made of solid granite and squatted on the horizon like a great fat mole. Topo was the father of Aguilar's people, and he had been from time immemorial, from the time of the Trogloditas, when men burrowed into the hills like moles. Topo had a son whose name was

Adán, and a daughter named Evita, and they were man and wife. They
had two sons. One was named Baltazar, and the other was Victorino.
Baltazar was called the *Malo*. And Victorino was called the *Bueno*.
Aguilar's mother had named him Victorino in hopes that he would be
a good boy. In that hope she would be often disappointed. The family
name meant "eagle handler," so his father had high hopes for his
cojones. In that his hope would be achieved perhaps too well.

Now the boy would run down the green grassy hillside barefoot to the
río. Sometimes he would tie a rope around the neck of the family pig,
a swift skinny animal like a clever little dog, and drag him down to
play. Once he rolled all the way down the hill and into the river with
the piglet, laughing all the way.

The *río* was clear and cold and fast, and flowed all the way to Mazatlán. In the reeds on the far side there lived a *brujo*, his father said. He
was a dwarf who dressed in the black robes of a priest. He had long red
hair and a red beard, and his name was Lázaro. If a woman went into
the *río* when she was bleeding, Lázaro would enter her from under the
water and nine months later she would give birth to a fish.

Every morning the boy would strip and squat down by the side of the
stream with his testicles dragging in the grass and the mud squeezing
up between his wide-spaced toes and he would look at his reflection in
the water: It was just a little copper-skinned Xixime boy, that was all
. . . an aboriginal American with a round face, thick black hair, and
narrow slanted eyes. Then he would plunge his hands into the water
and splash his head, blowing air like a mule. He loved the feel of his
heavy wet mane of coarse hair whipping across his face and neck. He
loved the water, the bubbling stream, the *brujo* in the reeds, the piglet,
the *chozita* on the hill, the village, the smoke curling up from the
morning fires, the mountains all around.

But most of all he loved his mama. Every morning he would watch
her when she brought the baby down to the water. She always wore the
same thing, winter and summer, day and night, year in and year out.
She wore a long striped black and red cotton skirt, a cheap white
blouse, a red and green rebozo for the baby, and a black shawl over her
head. Embroidered on the shawl in orange and blue were pictures of
fanciful birds, fish, monkeys, and jaguars.

Aguilar's mama, she had a funny way of walking. She would shuffle
along, taking tiny quick steps, rocking her body sideways from foot to
foot. But she moved very fast, and nothing could stop her. She went
over rocks, fallen trees, fences, and obstacles of every kind. And she could
keep it up for miles with a heavy load of firewood and a baby on her
back, never slackening her pace. He loved more than anything just to
watch her walk.

When she got down to the river in the morning, the first thing she
would do was wind the baby out of her rebozo and wash his little ass in
the water. The shit would flow away yellowish-green in the clear *río* and

disappear quickly. Fifty meters round the bend and Señora Benicta would be rinsing out her morning bowls. All the time Mama was wiping the baby, she would be talking to him. In Xixime, not in Spanish, she would be talking, in a humorous vein, trying to cheer him up. "Ho, ho, ho!" she would go. "What you bawling about, boy? We gonna have us a nice old time today. Look at your big brother there. See what a happy boy he is. Shush, now, shush! What is there to cry about on such a fine day?"

After a breakfast of chocolate, beans, and tortillas, the *familia* would walk three kilometers down the canyon to work in the rows of corn and marijuana, even Mama. She would work all day with the baby right on her back. Sometimes if it got too hot she would wrap him up in the rebozo and lay him on the ground. But mostly she just kept him right on her back. He didn't mind. No baby did. The motion put them right to sleep.

When the work was done, everyone but Victorino and his mama would straggle home and collapse on the floor of the *choza*. Mama would have to make supper. And Aguilar would have to go out and feed the animals. They had chickens, goats, a pig, and a donkey. When he was very young his papa warned him about the animals. He said if you were ever tempted to engage in sexual relations with a goat or a donkey, Topo would blow his top and the crops would go bad and the animals would sicken and die. But Eusebio the neighbor boy said Papa was full of shit. Eusebio taught Victorino to fuck the goat and the donkey, and the two of them did it for years and nothing bad ever happened.

Then one day Papa caught him at the nanny goat and a month later the crops failed and the goat died and Mama had a miscarriage and Papa chased his ass clean off the property. For months he lived like an animal in the mountains, all alone, eating roots and insects. Potato bugs were the best eating. They tasted of anise seed.

One time when the family was in the fields Victorino came down and sneaked into the larder and ate all the food. His papa came home and caught him and beat him with a plow trace. "Go on now, get out of here!" he hollered. "And don't you ever come back!"

Sadly, Aguilar left his family and village behind. Only his mother watched him go. Only his mother waved good-bye. He swore to himself that one day he would come back a rich man and build her a house on the hill. But he never went back. Did he really never go back? Nope, he never went back to his *pueblocito*, the name of which was Aztlanito.

The bus clattered and bounced to a halt in the middle of a great flat field of tomatoes. Its own dust caught up with it and descended on the passengers in a blinding cloud of white. Dizzy, choking with dust, Victorino awakened from his reverie and allowed himself to be impelled forward by the mob of farm workers. They shuffled and bumped down the stairs, out onto the white dirt road, and over to the Vanduccis' flat-bed truck. There they waited in line to receive their boxes. Two little *cholos* stood on top of the truck giving them out. They threw one box down. The first picker in line caught it and held it low against his thighs. Then the *cholos* threw one box on top of another till they were stacked up six high in the picker's trembling hands. Then he teetered off across the canal bridge to the field.

Standing in line, Aguilar dreaded his turn. The idea of any physical exertion at all made him sick to his stomach. He could barely fucking stand up, for Christ's sake. So how was he gonna carry them boxes? And yet when they began to throw them down at him he caught them handily and did not shame himself in front of the campesinos. The trouble came when he set out to carry his boxes to the field. They were stacked up so high in front of him that he couldn't see. If he tried to look around the side he lost his balance and the boxes started teetering precariously. He knew that the canal bridge was coming up, but he couldn't tell if he was on the right track or not. Yet he had too much pride to ask anyone the way. Slowly, one foot ahead of the other, he made his way toward the field. He found the bridge by approaching it from the side and regarding it out of the corner of his eye. He crossed it by following the edge. He did not make a laughingstock of himself by falling into the water, as many had done before.

Unsteadily but undisgraced, he walked into the tomatoes to stake his "claim." His claim was two rows of tomato plants that extended east from the Corral Hollow Canal to the end of the world, to the rising sun and beyond.

Then, like his dark fellows in sombrero and gay-colored kerchiefs, he dropped his boxes at strategic locations along the furrows, returned to his starting place at the canal, fell to his knees in the clay, and disappeared among the high green wall of plants.

It was a miracle, but he had made it. He pushed his sombrero back till the chin strap caught on his neck. Let his head fall forward and into the dirt. Pressed his brow into that cool hard soil that would soon be burning hot. Let it rest there unmoving for five full minutes. But it did nothing to soothe his hangover.

Then, since there was nothing further to be done, he began to pick. It was six o'clock in the morning. He would pick from now till noon, his head spinning, his stomach wanting to retch.

Now one was nothing more than oneself, Victorino, he of the little victories. Victorino who was sad and ill, perhaps, but still himself alone in a claim of his own making.

To the tomato picker, the furrow and the row of plants were like a whole little cosmos. On your knees in the black-eyed yellow clay you were at one with the dirt clods, the beetles and centipedes and scorpions. On your knees the tomato plants seemed as big as cottonwoods, their fruits like red globular tree houses, their flies and gnats like buzzing birds. On your knees for six straight hours with a hangover, in a field over which the air temperature would soar to ninety-seven by ten o'clock in the morning, the great world outside—the world of pickup trucks and tractors and grain elevators and railroad hoppers—disappeared completely. Now it was just you and the furrow. Now it was rhythm without ritual, discipline without purpose, meditation without philosophy, a quietude of spirit that Victorino would have preferred never to know.

Quick, deft, methodical, Aguilar worked. He worked the hangover right out of his system, sweated it right out of his pores. The perspiration beaded on his skin, soaked through his clothes and his shoes, sopped his hair and kerchief and the hat band of his sombrero, and dropped down his shiny brown forehead and fell off his curved Aztec nose and dropped to earth to fertilize the fields of the busy red ants.

After he had begun to work, after he had sweated for a few hours, work became its own raison d'être. Work had its own life, its own way, a way that was different from all else. By eleven o'clock in the morning, when the temperature was hovering at a hundred degrees in the shade and there was no shade, except for the ants, Victorino's very name was work: Trabajo Aguilar.

"*Trabajar, trabajar . . .*" he sang, a popular Mexican song, getting into his work, wasting no motion, his fingers flying through the leaves.

All was repetition. And yet each plant was different and presented different problems to be solved. Each plant was a war, with its own plan of attack. He assaulted it section by section, working his way around the plant till each ripe prize was captured and separated from its stem and placed neatly in his POW box.

Picking was a science, and Aguilar was an expert. There was a way for everything. A way to place your boxes in the row not too far apart. A way to crawl in the furrow so as to save wear and tear on your knees. A way to keep your hat down and your head swathed in a kerchief so as not to risk sunstroke. A way to pick each single tomato.

The way Aguilar did it was, he did not jerk the tomato from the vine, for that would injure the plant. He did not uncover its unripe mates, for that would expose them to sunburn. He did not pull it straight out, for that would break the branch. The way Aguilar picked his tomato was, he pulled at it steadily and gently, tipping it slightly, spinning it on its stem simultaneously. That was the way he did it. And he'd always had grand success. The checker said he was the best peeker she'd ever seen, from the Imperial to the San Joaquin.

The secret of Aguilar's success in the tomatoes was, number one, he was a beeg focker and had huge hands that could hold a lot of fruit. And, number two, he worked with both hands close together, moving them as one, filling them with fruit, and then moving them together toward the box. Never did he throw them. In that way he avoided getting marked down for bruising the fruit, and losing money. In that way he maintained his reputation, even when he had a hangover.

When he had filled all his boxes, he chalked his picking number —77—on each box and carried them one at a time to the end of his claim. There he stacked them up neatly with the numbers facing out. Then the checker, a pretty Filipina, came along and gave him credit as was his due. Then he had a drink of water from the common jug, picked up six new boxes, and went out to work again in the field.

In a one-acre field there are approximately two hundred and fifty thousand individual tomatoes. By seven o'clock that evening, Aguilar had picked one twentieth of an acre. Twelve thousand five hundred big beefsteak tomatoes had gone through his hands. Each tomato was worth about thirty cents at the supermarket. For his labor, which produced a gross profit of $3,750, the campesino Aguilar got a buck an hour and a dime a box. At the end of his twelve-hour day, a day that saw the temperature rise to a hundred and five degrees, the foreman paid him off with $15 and Victorino thought he'd done amazingly well.

He stopped off at El Chico's on the way home and had a few *cervezas* to cool off. He bought a round for his *compadres,* for it was only right, and it gave him pleasure. When he got home he had nine dollars in his pocket.

His wife yelled at him. The kids began to scream and jump up and down. He left the house in a huff, supperless, and went again to El Chico's for a few more rounds.

By the time Chico closed, Aguilar was very drunk and very broke.

But he looked at it this way: All he had to do was get himself up in the morning and he was good for another fifteen bucks.

PART **II**

Eight

A CAT IN THE SLAM is a thing of status. It is the hardest pet to come by and the most difficult to maintain in your space. But a cat is definitely the grooviest animal to have. It is warm. It is fuzzy-wuzzy. It purrs. For the kinky it scratches. A cat is a scene. A cat is a crib of your own, with a lace curtain over the bars and a terry-cloth cover on the open commode. A cat is love, a symbol of hearth and home. Nothing in the Joint shows more class. Such was Inmate Range's class. And his cat, a great big battle-scarred tiger-striped tom, was known as "Pussy" all over his section.

It had taken Inmate Range twenty months to scam himself a place in the Clinton F. Duffy Halfway House outside the San Quentin walls. It had taken him five months of faultless good behavior and a hundred-dollar bribe to get into the Honor Section with unlimited TV privileges, open-ended lights out, conjugal visit rights (unfortunately, however, he had no wife), and a pet of his choice.

Thinking of all these comfortable perks that he would have to relinquish on his approaching parole date, and of his exceedingly good chances of winding up in the slammer again, and of all the aggravation it would cost him to regain the same high level of penal-living standards, Inmate Range sometimes titillated himself with a momentary regret that they were letting him out.

The truth was, his last few months in the Joint were the happiest of his short and unhappy life. It was spring and early summer 1970. While Cambodia got invaded by ambitious armies of Americans and gory gangs of gooks and Viet Nam went up in smoke and universities all across the USA exploded in the last unpremeditated violence of the New Left and the Soledad Brothers went on hunger strike in the Quentin Adjustment Center and young Jonathan Jackson put the final touches on his foolproof breakout plans for his big bro, Range passed his time in the Outside Care & Treatment Center mimeographing copies of *The Warden's Weekly Report*, "improved his mind" by reading Dostoevski's *Crime and Punishment* during his lunch and coffee breaks and conducted an imaginary love affair with his immediate superior, a beautiful forty-five-year-old divorcee with the biggest tits in the Department of Corrections.

After two years in the South Block, the Mainline, after more than twenty-four months behind forty-foot piss-yellow walls, after seven hundred and some odd nights locked up in a bare four-by-ten concrete and metal cage with a three-hundred-pound child molester from Manhattan Beach who masturbated up to three times a night while simulating the love calls of both man and maid, life in the Halfway House was to Inmate Range a veritable paradiso, a Switzerland for his soul. Every morning he awakened on starched white sheets, with his kittycat curled up at his feet, in the basement of a quaint red brick building constructed in the era of sailing ships, when inmates wore balls and chains and black-and-white stripes, and their guards went around on horses. Every morning he sniffed sea fog and eucalyptus trees just out his window and thanked his sweet BeJesus he was out from behind those obscene blood-splattered yellow walls. Then he'd leap up, do eleven minutes of Canadian Air Force exercises, take a long hot gloriously private shower, slip into a fresh starched blue denim uniform, clap his billed denim cap on his head, and jog down Bull Nelson Terrace and Sonny Rolph Road to the Outside Mess Hall with nothing more important on his mind than what was for breakfast, or what to do with all his boundless excess energy, or whether he'd ever get into his boss's panties.

Incredibly enough, his chances at the moment did not look all that bad. In the office where he was employed, the betting was even money. And the odds got slimmer and slimmer every time she blushed bright crimson, or giggled like a virgin, or unconsciously tidied her coif when she saw him. It appeared, strange as it might seem, that Mrs. Desiree A. Bartlow, a mature chief counselor with an M.A. degree in psychology and twenty-two years of experience in care and treatment, had conceived a most ill-advised (and indeed quite illegal) schoolgirl crush on Inmate Range, the youngest of all her charges.

She bumped into him by the coffee machine one time, quite inadvertently, and blushed to the roots of her salt and pepper hair, though he apologized profusely for being in her way. Another time she became so fixated on his small tight un-American ass ("queer bait," they called it Inside; and it had cost him a tooth, a good deal of nose cartilage, and a six-inch knife wound under his right arm to maintain its charms unsullied) that she tagged along behind him on his mail run for fifteen minutes, like a little dog, before she came to her senses. A few days later she absentmindedly followed him halfway into the men's latrine.

Everyone kidded him about it on the job. The civilian employees called him "Loverboy." The convicts referred to him as "Sweetmeat." It was getting to be almost embarrassing.

Then one Friday afternoon a couple of months before his parole date she dropped all pretense. Called him into her office and locked the door behind him. He wasn't really too shocked. Women had always gone for him, older ones especially. Younger women said he was attractive because he had a "smooth way of talking." Older women didn't say why, but latched right onto him. Actually, his secret with them was his orphan routine, which he'd perfected over the years.

"Inmate Range?" she drawled. She was tall, dark, voluptuous, puffy-lipped, and kinky-haired. One of those southern belles with highly ambiguous antecedents. To explain her dark coloring she claimed to be "half-cajun," though she was born in Beaufort, South Carolina, a thousand miles from the bayous. There was a slight delectable down under her broad and pretty nose, and something rather Semitic about her looks. Since she was apparently neither Jewish nor A-rab, and attended the First Baptist Church in San Rafael, prison bigots (both con and bull) had arrived through the process of elimination at the conclusion that she was "passin'," and had a great big nigger in her woodpile somewhere down the line. Yet her ex-hubby was a blue-eyed Yankee from Connecticut, and her kids were "as white as you and me." In the image-starved environment of the Joint, Mrs. Bartlow had become a woman of mystery. Half the dudes in the Yard were in love with her. The other half wanted to see her prosecuted for miscegenation.

"Yes, ma'am," Range said, highly encouraged by the expression on her face, which could only be read as . . . playful.

"I see here," she said, pointing to a file on her desk, "that you been approved for early release."

"Yes, ma'am."

"Now, I also see here that you were in trouble a few times, early on, with fights and what not, but here lately looks like you been doin' right well."

"Doing my best, ma'am."

"Uh-huh," she said. "You got a job all lined up for when you get out?"

"Afraid not, ma'am."

"Well, you better get one quick."

"Pardon me?"

"I gather you not aware of the new rulin' on early release?"

"Don't believe I am, ma'am."

"Well," she said, nodding toward a mimeographed sheet tacked up on her bulletin board, "that jus' come down from Sacramento. It might behoove you to have a look at it. Paragraph nine."

Range did as he was told. The last line of paragraph nine had been underlined in red ink. It read: *"Parolee must obtain bonafide offer of employment prior to discharge or release; there will be no exceptions."* Range's heart stopped. He had been a professional dope smuggler far too long to have any "lawful" job connections. As a matter of fact, he had not been legally employed since that summer eight years ago when he was set-off man and Selena Cruz was glue girl at the Vanducci Packing Shed. Through an ex-cellmate he had lucked into a lucrative Mexican grass scam the minute he completed his first prison bit, and he hadn't done an honest day's labor since. Which is not to say that he hadn't developed certain latent talents: He could speak fluent colloquial Spanish; he was an excellent deep-water sailor and navigator; in a pinch he could copilot anything up to a Beechcraft Bonanza; he was an accomplished mountaineer; he had an expert's eye for the leaf quality of several high-cash crops; and he was an internationally recognized authority on clandestine shipping, packaging, and marketing techniques.

"Oh my God!" he gasped.

"I thought so," she said. "Now, the important thing is, do you have anyone you could write to, some friend or relative who would give you a job?"

"Unfortunately not."

"Well, who was your last legal employer?"

"We didn't part on the best of terms."

"Oh boy, you in trouble, ain't you?" she said. "Well, looky here. You think it would do any good if I sent that man a letter on your behalf?"

"It might," Range said guardedly. He had not particularly wanted to get involved with the Vanduccis again. It wasn't pride. He wasn't even sure he knew what that word meant anymore. Two times in his experience, once by the side of a dirt road in the high Colombian Andes, and once in a crowded bar in Culiacán, Sinaloa, he had found himself in a position where he had to get down on his knees and beg for his life. After that the notion "pride" had no more application to his life. And it certainly would not have kept him from making contact with his former foster family, if such a contact proved useful. Nor was it anger or hurt feelings or jealousy that held him back. He didn't believe the 'Duccis could move him that much emotionally anymore. It was just that Calmento was a chapter in his life that he had closed, and he didn't see any point in opening it up again. However, the way things were beginning to look now, he would probably have no choice in the matter. "I guess it might be worth a try," he said.

"All right," she said. "I'll do it for you . . ."

"Why, thank you, ma'am."

". . . if you'll do somethin' for me, in return."

"Anything you say, ma'am."

"Can you guess what it is?" she teased.

"Uh . . . I don't think so," he said, trying to keep a straight face.

Then she waved her hand and said, "Oh, don't go gettin' all hot and bothered. I'm just shuckin' you, boy. I'll tell you what it is. They given me this new house here on the grounds. A bigger place, on account of my seniority. And my boys, they all away at college. So, I'm goin' need someone to help with the movin'."

"Anything I can do . . ."

"Fine," she said briskly. "Then I'll look forward to seein' you tomorrow mornin' at seven. The address is Institution Residence #64, Max Rafferty Road. Okay? And don't worry about your supervisor at the Halfway House. You just tell him to give me a call and I'll fix everything up. . . ."

Next morning he got up early, had a quick cup of coffee and a piece of toast at the mess hall, and briskly hiked up the hill through a grove of eucalyptus trees to Mrs. Bartlow's house. The fog was very thick that morning and hung in a heavy impenetrable blanket just a few feet above the tips of the tallest trees. A fine misty drizzle was falling. It dripped from the curled white limbs, off the green umbrella of gum tree leaves overhead. It formed crystal globules on the ubiquitous bracken fern underfoot. The air was redolent of medicinal eucalyptus. Mist fell too in tiny droplets on Range's coarse black hair, kinking it. It clung to his long heavy eyelashes, the lashes that women loved, like clean tears, tears with no sweat or pain, unearned. He took a shortcut through the wildest part of the grove. He was all alone. Not a bull or a con or a trustee in sight. All he could hear was his heart beating strongly, swiftly, and the crunch of his free-world Frye boots on the fallen leaves, and the monotonous but altogether pleasant sound of automobiles racing over slick pavement on the freeway in the distance. Inside the walls, life had been hot, clamorous, sharp, deadly, bright fluorescent white, a detonation of sights and sounds: too real. Here in the foggy Pacific woods, Zen woods, all was cold and quiet and obscure: unreal, insubstantial. After the shank-tipped paranoid reality of the Big Yard, where an average of twenty-one men got murdered every year and fifty were wounded and you could buy a life with a pack of cigarettes, the true meaning of things was no longer important to Inmate Range. He was too fucking glad to just be capable of normal respiration and ambulation to give a shit about anything else.

"Hah, hah, hah," he breathed, trotting up Quarry Hill, recalling another trot, a long and dramatic cinematical one across the midnight rounds of Preston Reformatory, over the fence, across the plowed black-mud fields of winter to the silent Sacramento River, where he hoped for a dark towed beet barge bound for the Holly Sugar Mill in Calmento, bound (he fervently wished) for a happy reunion with his friends Selena and Jay Jay, whose long and inexplicable silence had driven him over the walls with anxiety . . . *a visit is a big thing in the Joint, people don't realize, it means everything* . . . and reached the river only to find it empty of barge traffic, its banks patrolled by loud-talking county sheriffs with high-powered flashlights and baying bloodhounds. . . .

"Hah, hah," he respired now, delightedly. Comparing his present prospects with those of that younger, sadder, lonelier boy, he thought he might faint from bliss.

Range had been locked up so long he had no sense of perspective.

Every half-pint state official seemed to him like a god or goddess. Now that he had Mrs. Bartlow eating out of his hand, he could envision absolutely no obstacle to his early release. He looked into the future and he could see his whole life of crime laid out before him like a long and empty book at the printer's shop with not a word on any page, only a THE END after many heavy numbers.

He reached her street and continued up the hill past a long line of little pastel-painted row houses with neat front lawns. At last he reached #64, an exact replica of all the others. A large red moving van was parked out in front. Lyon's Van & Storage men in brown uniforms pattered in and out, taking small quick steps, with couches and easy chairs resting on their bent backs. Next door an inmate gardener was mowing an officer's lawn. Down the street a team of inmate ditch-diggers on a sewer-laying job were leaning on their shovels.

"How you, boy?" Mrs. Bartlow called, beaming a smile at him across her neat flower-girdled yard. It was a positively radiant smile. She was a remarkably attractive woman, for her years. She had the kind of oily Latinate skin that does not wrinkle. It stretched tautly over her high elegant cheekbones and softly under her neck. Her age was betrayed only by the crowsfeet about her dark eyes and the two deep grooves that ran from her nostrils to the corners of her turned-down mouth.

"Morning, Mrs. Bartlow, I'm fine," he said, leaping a flower bed. He laughed, "Hup, hup!" distractedly, for he was truly smitten by her, for the moment.

Standing there above him on the wet bermuda grass, tall and ripe and desirable, in a black turtleneck sweater and bell-bottom blue jeans cinched tightly with a thick belt to accentuate her tiny waist, her vast and still fecund hips and breasts, Mrs. Bartlow was looking Range over. He had dressed as carefully as she, within the limitations of prison uniform regulations. He had worn his best street boots, his best set of starched and pressed "boneroo" denims, and a black turtleneck sweater much like her own. He had teased his shortish hair in such a way that it appeared to be semi-Afroed. And he had worn shell beads around his neck and a turquoise bracelet around each of his wrists.

As it happened, Mrs. Bartlow had worn a combination of similar beads and bracelets.

"Well I do declare," she said, "damn if we don't look like the Toni Twins!"

They were both happy for the excuse to laugh. She pressed his hand warmly. Range quivered with anticipation. This was decidedly not the way an institution official greeted an inmate of the opposite sex.

She took him inside and put him to work. While she packed the kitchen things, Range swept and mopped up after the moving men. He applied himself to the job with vigor, and by the time the truck was loaded, the cottage was spic and span and ready for immediate occupancy by its new correctional tenants.

Range and Mrs. Bartlow got into her Rambler station wagon and followed the Lyons truck down Max Rafferty Road to Perimeter Road, where they turned and went along the yellow prison wall past the Ad. Building, the Front Gate, and the Crafts Center. Then they turned left again and dawdled up Front Street, with the muddy bay on one side and the mansions of the warden and associate wardens and chief psychiatrists on the other. They turned left once again at the Employees' Service Station and climbed a steep hill. About halfway up they turned right and parked in front of Mrs. Bartlow's new and larger place in the Senior Employees' Housing Area, overlooking San Francisco Bay. A rambling old gray-shingled Cape Cod–style home with white shutters, it lay tucked into the hillside in such a way that the inner prison complex was completely invisible. The prospect from her front deck was of of forty or fifty old, individually designed wooden houses descending the steep incline in steps, and an expanse of gray, white-capped water. If it hadn't been for the high barbed-wire fence that ran along the shoreline it might have been a fishing village on the Oregon coast.

The Lyons men would not let Range help carry the furniture inside, so he allowed himself to be persuaded to sit on the terrace with Mrs. Bartlow, eating liverwurst sandwiches and drinking Lipton's tea. The sun came out from behind the clouds, banishing the gray from the bay, turning it an inky blue. A land breeze sprang up, blowing the scent of sage, scotch broom, manzanita, and wild oats in their direction. The two old cypress trees in her yard weaved against the scudding clouds, groaned with age, while blue jays and woodpeckers screeched at each other in their highest limbs. Far above the bare brown ridge behind her house, a red-tailed hawk rode the updraft, hanging stationary in the air, watching for rodents a half mile below. And higher than the hawk, four thousand feet above the Bay area, the air defense radar scanner at the top of yellow and green Mount Tamalpais went round and round, searching for incoming enemy rockets and bombers. The noon whistle went off at the jute mill. Air force reserve fighter planes took off from Hamilton Field, winged out over the bay and into the sun. Closer, Range could hear children playing somewhere down the hill, and a man chopping wood, and a fusillade of M-16 fire from the prison firing range.

"Whewie!" Mrs. Bartlow said. "Sure is grand to see the last of that fog."

"Nice, huh?"

"You know," she said, gesturing out over the bay, "this here is the purtiest damn state in the union."

'The weirdest," Range said, just to make talk. Actually, he couldn't conceive of living anywhere else.

It seemed to him as he sat there with Mrs. Bartlow on her pleasant deck-terrace that things were getting to the point where he was going to have to make his move. And yet he was afraid to make it, despite the encouragement her eyes appeared to be giving him. He hoped she would make some more overt sign, so there could be no mistaking her desires. Range remembered many times in his life when, bedazzled by a woman's beauty, deceived by his lust and his own egocentricity, he had been sure that she was beckoning and had made his move, only to be angrily admonished or even slapped in the face. He was aware of how men fool themselves about women, convince themselves that the most innocent glance is an invitation, and act upon their illusions. He was also aware that certain women provoke a man, just to prove their power, and then scream bloody murder when he makes his move— Angie Vanducci being a case in point. And he could not take the slightest chance of offending this woman who, after all, was his correctional superior and held his parole papers, his life, in her hands.

All through lunch they chatted of inconsequential things, squinting at each other in the sharp sunlight, squirming in their wicker chairs, each of them apparently hoping it would be the other who would get up the nerve to break the ice. Range even read the wishful future, saw them lying together naked in bed, laughing about how shy and silly they'd been before they made love.

It was nearly three years since he'd last had a piece of ass. And that was off a two-hundred-pound Cartagena prostitute and small-time cocaine dealer with a brood of kids who kept squealing and shooting off cap pistols around the bed.

After the Lyons men left, he helped Mrs. Bartlow do the little things they'd left undone. He set up the kitchen for her, cleaned the gas tubing and lit the pilots on her kitchen range, put up pegboard and hung all her pots and utensils. He hung pictures, drapery, curtains, and flowerpots with burlap slings in the windows. He went over the redwood walls from one end of the house to the other with Old English Scratch Remover.

"Can you come in here and help me for a second?" she yelled at him from the bedroom finally. "I can't get this open," she said, indicating a dresser drawer. But he pulled it out with no trouble. Then she insisted that he stay. "I'm gettin' bored in here. Got to have me some company."

So he helped her tack the straw rug to the floor. They worked side by side on their hands and knees, tap-tap-tapping with little hammers.

"Say, Range," she said. "Where you from, anyway? That's probably the one thing I neglected to look up in your file."

"Out in the Valley," he said.

"Is that right?"

"Yes, ma'am."

"Don't call me 'ma'am.' Call me Desiree."

"If you like . . ."

"And you don't have any family at all?"

"Nope."

"Really?"

"Well, I did have a sister. But she got snuffed out."

"What?"

"Murdered."

"You puttin' me on?"

"No lie. It was down in Berdoo. They found her floating in Lytle Creek with her old man, this Hell's Angel type. It was never solved."

"Boy, that kind of grim, ain't it?"

"I guess so. But I don't like to dwell on the past. I look to the future. Always have."

"Why, that sound purty healthy to me."

"Yeah."

"Guess I'm lucky. I come from a big happy family," she said quite unconvincingly, the belabored cheerfulness of her tone utterly impugning the validity of her affirmation. There was something in her tone that *wanted* to be impugned, Range believed. "My mama and daddy still alive and kickin'," she said, her accent thickening when she spoke of her native state, "and madly in love, after forty-eight years of marriage. They live in a beautiful old antebellum house on the Battery in Beaufort. We big on tradition down in our parts. Nigrahs, they still talkin' Geechee and Gullah. You wouldn't understand a word of that. My family been happily residin' there in Carolina since long before the War Between the States. Been livin' in the same house for over a hundred years. My daddy, he a lawyer, one of the finest in the South. Jus' like his daddy and grandpappy before him."

"Wow," Range said, "that really is something, isn't it?"

"Uh-huh," she said warily.

"I really am impressed."

"You makin' light of me, boy?"

"What makes you say that, Desiree?"

"I don't like your tone."

"That's too bad."

"Okay, what's this all about?"

"I don't believe a word you say," he said. And then he wanted to kick his ass for saying it. All through his life Range had made slips of this kind, with rather suspicious frequency. He'd lost out on more than one pretty lady through such cleverly self-laid traps, more than one parole date, more than one incredible dope deal. For years it seemed he'd been working furiously to further his own selfish cause and, quite concurrently, doing everything in his power to hinder it. He could not understand his own irrational counterpurposes.

"Why, what you mean by that?" Desiree said. She had turned and confronted him now on her knees, with the little hammer poised in her hand. The expression on her face was difficult to describe. To Range it seemed irate and at the same time rather . . . guilty, like she was just looking for him to catch her in a lie.

"Oh," he said, "you know."

"No, I don't. Why don't you tell me, smart ass."

She was breathing very hard, and her face had gone all red. He was half afraid she might hit him over the head with her hammer. Or worse, call the duty lieutenant and have him thrown in the hole.

"Tell me!"

Range backed away from her. "You are jive," he said.

"You callin' me a liar?"

"I'm calling you a nigger," he said, at once thrilled and appalled by his own audacity.

As soon as he had said it, he was sorry, and pitied her with his whole heart. But by then it was too late. His words had stung her like hybrid African bees, making her wince and whimper with pain.

They were sitting on their haunches at the foot of her bed, with their little hammers in their hands, staring at each other. He was sure she would hit him, right in the chops. He would do nothing to prevent her. He deserved everything she gave him, he felt.

Instead, she burst out crying.

"I didn't mean it," Range said bleakly, reaching out to touch her face. "Please don't cry, please," he said, finding himself suddenly in the jaws of a grief as virulent and ungovernable as her own.

And then for some unlikely and unplanned reason he was crying too, real tears, that ran down his cheek and splashed on the straw.

"Don't cry," he said again. And it was like he was saying it to himself.

"Aw, shucks, you right, boy," she wept. "You lookin' at a nigger, sho nuff."

"We're both niggers," he said.

"And I'm old enough to be your mama."

"I ain't got a mama."

And allowed his head to drop onto her soft, unutterably soft breast.

"Oooooooh!" she moaned, and fell over sideways onto the straw mat. They dropped their hammers at the same time; they hit the floor and struck each other and clattered against the wall. Range crawled onto her and got off instantaneously into his prison-issue boxer shorts. Tore then at her sweater, unquenchable, unstoppable, jerked it up around her neck while her head lolled back against the bed. "Oh! Oh! Oh!" Ripped her brassiere clean off her torso. Sucked brown, sucked nip and the minuscule zits around in a circle till she begged him to quit before she died of excess. She lapped softly at his ear, his eye, nose, and throat. Kissed his salty lips. Opened her legs to him, rolled slowly back and forth like a boat on the water, heaved like the sea. "Oooooooh!" she shrieked, thwarted, louder, straining to get her blue jeans and bikini panties down over her swelling buoy, her bell of hips and ass and thighs, while Range tupped at her instinctively, attempting simultaneously to get his pants and yolky shorts over his now cocked again pride . . . plunged then down into her wet and deep round.

"Aaaaaaagh!" she hollered, and bucked like a dolphin.

"I . . . I . . . I!" he shouted.

"Oh you . . . you . . . you!" she cried, in total delirium.

"I . . . I . . . am . . . am . . . home!" he cried, managing at last.

"Now I'm goin' turn you over my knee and spank you, boy," she whispered. "Then we goin' do it another way I know . . . hear?"

At four o'clock in the afternoon the fog crept back in through the cypress trees in her backyard and the First Count whistle blew in the Joint and it was time to go. She held his head between her perspiring breasts. She said, "Say, you know, soon's you leave, boy, I'm goin' get right to work on that letter to your last employer, just like I promised. How that sound to you?"

"Sounds great," said Range. "But this sounds better." And he blew "Pleeeeeew!" into her cleavage, a cleavage of color extraordinary, the highest yellow known to man.

"Oooooooh! That tickle!" she protested, and clamped down on the head of her inmate seducer and held it tighter in her motherly cleft till he begged for mercy.

Then, just before he suffocated, she let him come up for air.

Nine

LIKE MEDIEVAL ARMIES they faced each other across a county road in the heat of late afternoon, hurling invective.

"Come on over here and fight, pig!"

"Eat shit, chilibean!"

It was late in the month of May 1970, Year II in the reign of Richard M. Nixon.

One army stood in a long ragged line on the Santa Fe embankment, with the railroad tracks and somebody's apricot orchard behind them. The other army stood in a long straight line on the shoulder of Fresno County Road 189, with a drainage ditch, a row of oleander shrubs, a tomato field, and the smooth undulant yellow foothills of the Sierra Nevada behind them.

One army was small in stature, wearing dirty clothes, ragged straw hats, and bandannas. The other army was goliathan, wearing armored vests, riot shields, hard plastic helmets, loud little transistorized walkie-talkies, gas masks, and goggles, and carrying sawed-off shotguns, gas guns, pistols, billyclubs, and Mace.

One army was the attacking force. The other was the fortress. Inside the fortress was a two-hundred-acre Bugatti Brothers tomato field full of scab short-hoe weeders shipped up from Mexicali at great expense, and protected over the past three hot and bloody days through force of arms.

The leader of the defensive force was certain that he could fulfill his appointed task. Indeed, with his helicopter and his one hundred picked men from three counties, he had already done so three times this afternoon with merciless dispatch and devastating effects upon the attackers, half of whom were now POWs, handcuffed and guarded like captured Cong in neatly squatting rows behind his paddy wagons, while the rest were suffering from Mace burns, tear gas exposure, bruised bods, broken bones, and busted heads.

The leader of the offensive force had a much more difficult task to perform. She had to charge across the road, break through the enemy's line, reach the scabs in the field who had broken the back of her wild-cat strike, wrecking all her fondest hopes and plans, and convert them to her *causa* in the approximately thirty seconds she would have before the cops were on her back.

Any normal person, confronted by such odds, would have concluded that the task was imposisble. But the leader was Selena Cruz. And her task had not been assigned by any temporal authority, such as the Superior Court of the County of Fresno, California. Her task was self-imposed and preordained. She was therefore just as certain as her opponent that she could accomplish her objective. Indeed, she had already planned how she would do so, already outlined the plan to her *compañeros* in secret. She would provoke the opposing force into abandoning its defensive posture. She would send a diversionary unit toward the enemy's left flank. When he moved to stop this feint, she would take her main force, run down the railroad embankment, over the drainage ditch, across the road, around the enemy's right flank, across the ditch behind him, and up the incline to the line of oleanders. Then she would wriggle through the foliage and race for the spot one hundred yards into the field where the scabs were bent over with their *corte* hoes, weeding.

Like medieval champions, the leaders stepped out in front of their armies now, to taunt one another through portable loudspeakers.

"THIS IS MY LAST WARNING!" cried the little gray-haired county sheriff. "DISPERSE! DISPERSE IMMEDIATELY OR FACE THE CONSEQUENCES!"

"THIS IS MY LAST WORD, PIG!" Selena yelled, flipping the bird at him. "YOU GOT NO FUCKING AUTHORITY TO MOVE US OFF THIS PROPERTY! ONLY THE SANTA FE RAILROAD CAN DO THAT!"

"OH NO? OH NO?" he shouted. "WE'LL JUST SEE ABOUT THAT!"

Selena turned her back on him, disdainfully, to survey the ragged line of her valiant *compañeros*. After three days of relentless warfare their ranks had been decimated. Only twenty-four of them left now, standing there above her along the railroad tracks, squinting into the hot east wind, their sombreros and bandannas and loose clothes flapping . . . fat Chalie Romero, who'd been with her ever since she led her angry Young Turks out of the United Farm Workers . . . bad Sonny Vargas and his acne-scarred brother Tony, her personal bodyguards . . . hook-nosed, myopic Cookie Madrid, her most valued adviser . . . quick, clever, tiny Mary Quintana, "La Morenita" . . . Dusty Gomez, the ex-Madera High School track champ, now her most trusted courier . . . Timmy Jones, the ponytailed gringo college kid . . . Benjamin "Speedy" Gonzales, the slowest, laziest, most useless and yet indestructible man in her organization . . . pretty flaxen-haired Shelley Friedmann from Berkeley SDS . . . the long-haired half-Navajo Manny "El Loco" García . . . Tito Bejár, Esteban Patricio, Jorge Feliz, Raímondo Gallego, Estanislao Tomás, Martín Ramírez, Primo Morales, Melchior Sánchez, Pepe Hinojosa, Guillermo Pérez, Carlos Sainz, Raúl Baeza, Ernesto Castillo, thick-skinned little peasants from the mountains of Mexico, her finest troops . . . and last in the line was La

Trucha Connie, her little fish-faced cousin who over the years had developed into her most devoted disciple and her most effective organizer in the field. Which is not to say that, on occasion, she couldn't be just as bitchy and contentious as ever.

So this was Selena's little army. Dark army, dark Indian faces for the most part. She felt like Geronimo before his last charge on the Mexican border. Like Chief Joseph on his last stand in Montana. As she looked over her army, all her soldiers seemed like one great being, her own being, as much a part of her as her breasts or belly or gashed head or bruised arm or twisted knee. She ignored her people's little assorted entities now as she ignored her own little assorted aches and pains and personal problems. She thought of them not in the plural, but in the singular, as the *"pueblo,"* united.

"El pueblo unido, jamás será vencido, el pueblo unido, jamás será vencido," she chanted now, loudly but absentmindedly, scanning the line.

And the army took it up: *"El pueblo unido, jamás será vencido . . ."*

Selena was concentrating all her efforts now on just firing herself up for the coming battle. She had to employ her "tunnel vision" to do it. Had to abolish all the nonessential periphery of fear and doubt and worry from her sight. Had to puff herself up, distend herself, intensify and amplify her ass till she was hotter than fire, louder than thunder, larger than life. *Yeah.* It was not easy. After all, she was only human. To win she must achieve a victory over reality. It was impossible. But it must be done. It had been done in the past by certain remarkable individuals. She had watched Cesar Chavez do it with her own eyes. Selena could do it. She knew she could. But only with the aid of the mysterious, the spiritual, the intangible. She would have to climb down into her deepest self and tap the source at the heart of the species. *Right on!* She would then have to take this source and light her own torch, a powerful torch that would lead her past all the gates and boundaries, out of the land of the reasonable, the orderly, the ordinary. It was a hell of an order. But she could fill it. 'Cause she was Selena, La Palomita. She could feel the truth of it right down in her center, where the Dark Virgin dwelled, her bright fire, her molten core that was stronger than life, stronger than fate, stronger even than her own death. And it would last, would last, she was convinced, as long as her *raza.* For she was the rage of her *raza*, the *niña princesa chicana*, the carnal queen. . . . *Run it down, now.*

The part of Selena that was supreme, sublime, was like a stranger inside her, a kind of public-spirited parasite that fed off her private life. She called it her genie, when in reality she knew that it was nothing more than a servant of the Dark Virgin whom she revered. It had little to do with that everyday Selena Cruz who ate and slept and fucked and shit and bled like other people. It was a foreign body and had its own weird and wonderful ways, its own kind of smarts, its own imagination, its own plans. The genie's plans had always been a good deal less concerned with Selena's physical well-being than with the "historia," the myth she would leave behind. *Get it on, girl, get-it-on.* This myth was a living presence in Selena's mind, and had been ever since it came to her one day spontaneously when she was on her way to her freshman English teacher's office in Dwinelle Hall, Berkeley, in September of 1964. It had been months since her harrowing experience on the abortionist's table and she was still not over the shock, but she had just written a paper on Marcuse's *Hegel and the Rise of Social Theory* that had inspired this red-headed, rough-hewn, yet curiously effeminate young graduate assistant to write "Brilliant! Wonderfully Chaotic! Impassioned!" all over her paper. She arrived at the appointed hour in a dowdy skirt and sweater, feeling rather desperate. She flitted about his office like a trapped bird for several minutes, unable to calm herself, or even sit herself down. At first he stared at her like she might have lost her marbles. Then he saw that she was merely anxious, and assumed (as he would tell her later) that she was distressed about meeting him in private for the first time.

"How'd you know so much about Hegelian social theory?" he asked.

"I don't *know* how I knew," she said, stopping suddenly in the middle of the room. She was trying to look serious. She frowned, furrowed her brow, stroked her chin. She felt compelled to put on an act, to create a dramatic situation, even though she happened to be telling the truth. He saw through the act, but believed her anyway. Later he would write to her and say: "There was something frenzied, intuitive, something Rimbaudian about you. Like Rimbaud you appeared to have reached the 'unknown,' made yourself a 'seer,' through some sort of derangement of the senses. Like Rimbaud too, you had appeared out of nowhere, unannounced. Like life in the tidepools of eternity, electrically charged, under a benevolent sun, and all the proper conditions of chance, you had simply *created yourself*. I was convinced that you might spontaneously combust right there before my eyes. The room was ready to burst inward with your presence. You were, without question, the most magnetic human being I had ever encountered. . . ."

Selena remembered him praising her work, her exceptional gifts, her great future at the university. As for herself, she was barely listening. She was concentrating on some deeper aspect of his presence. He was a nice man, a queer little man, possibly a homosexual. . . .

All at once she exploded, interrupted him in mid-sentence, began tearfully pouring out her whole life story, her myth, the epic of her family in Calmento. Ranting, raving, crying, moaning, laughing, shouting, marching up and down his office, she spent two hours baring her soul. She told of her father's grisly death beneath the treads of the 'Ducci D-1, her mother's insanity of grief, the visitation of the Virgin, the stepfather she found by the road: Aguilar, the eagle and the cactus plant, the snake he killed with a rock. . . . She told of the queen contest, her shame and embarrassment at the gaucheries of her poor *familia*, her work in the packing shed, her fight with Delano, her love affair with Jay Jay, her broken promise to the imprisoned Range boy, her abandonment by the callow Vanducci boy, her payoff by the wicked father, the obscene abortion down in Tijuana with her cousin in attendance. . . . She mythologized her pathetic Calmento existence, made it a heroic battle of giants, with herself as the heroine.

Long before she was finished, she knew absolutely that she had won his sympathy. He was a kind man, a pleasant man, a generous man, a man of the liberal Left. He would show her the way, introduce her to art, ideas, aesthetics, social consciousness, intellectual friends and comrades, politics. He would help her in many ways, and Connie too. They would live together as communal friends, helpmates, soul mates. He would make only emotional demands.

And preposterous as it might seem, that is exactly the way it happened. His name was Lamoille Huffacker. He was not a homosexual. He was an ex-seminarian, impotent due to a traumatic childhood injury, something to do with having been molested and mutilated by an insane older cousin. He was utterly selfless and spent all his time thinking up nice things that he could do for his friends. He had private means, inherited from his mother. He owned a shingled ivy-covered Maybeck cottage in the Berkeley Hills and a beach house in Bolinas. Though his interest in liberal and radical causes never went much beyond the theoretical stage, he was tolerant of Selena's rapid radicalization on the Berkeley campus. He had long been acquainted with everyone in the local movement. He gave generously. He was on every mailing list from the Free Speech Movement to the *Viet Nam Day Committee*. He was like putty in Selena's Chicana hands. And in time he even developed a genuine affection for Connie. They lived together for four years as brother and sister and cousin. And he never asked anything of either of them beyond sympathy and companionship. This they were happy to give. They parted tearfully and affectionately in June of 1968. Lamoille was on his way to Princeton and a new teaching position. Selena and Connie were on their way down to the southern San Joaquin Valley to join Cesar Chavez and his United Farm Workers as volunteer organizers.

Lamoille's last words to Selena were "Take care, love. You don't have to write. I'll be hearing about you soon enough."

"Hey, you can count on it!" she exclaimed, with characteristic drama and self-confidence. "But I'll write anyway. It's the least I can do. I owe everything to you."

Now on the Santa Fe embankment above the fields of the Bugatti Brothers, two years after that final parting, Selena felt the same kind of self-confidence surging through her veins. Her pulse was jumping. Her heart was pumping adrenaline. She began to sweat, to go hot and cold, to breathe faster, harder, to hyperventilate. She read the signs of transcendance within her, read them with rapture in her boogying heart. Opened her mouth wide, took great gulps of oxygen. It was working. She was hot, she was popping. Her eyeballs were bulging out of her fucking gourd.

"*Ai ai ai aiiiiiii que viva la huelga en el fil!*" she screamed aloud and whirled to confront her porcine *enemigo*. "Aiiiiiiiiii!" she shrieked, like some kind of demented witch doctor, impervious to the white man's bullets. And, while her army looked on, shit-faced with wonder, she ran clomping and tripping down the embankment in her heavy Mexican riding boots, picked up a smoking gas canister mindless of her burning hand, clambered across the ditch and, holding the fizzing grenade over her head, charged the leveled shotguns on the law's left flank—a one-woman diversionary force.

It took a long mute lifetime to cross that road. She heard nothing but the meadowlarks singing in the tomato field. Saw nothing but the round black eyes of the shotgun barrels. At the center white line she stumbled over a spent gas projectile. In mid-flight, falling forward, she flung her grenade. Heard it blap against a plastic riot shield. Heard it thwunk hollowly in the dirt by the side of the road. . . . Then she came down on the asphalt, scraping her elbow and her knee. Rolled over and leapt to her feet, expecting to be blown instantly away.

Yet, for some unknown reason or command (or fear of witnesses from the press), the police took mercy on her. They ignored her, in fact. And she was left standing alone and foolish in the middle of the county road, crying tear-gas tears.

Silent, skittish as cavalry, her army stood above them on the railroad tracks, outlined against the milk-white sky.

"*Muerte al puerco!*" she cried out at the top of her lungs, bending half to the macadam with the effort.

And Connie took it as a sign. A tiny shapeless figure in wild Afro hair, a faded orange fisherman's smock, torn Levi's, and muddy huaraches, she whirled to the front of the line, screaming "*Al asalto! Al asalto!*" at the top of her lungs.

Howling like dervishes, throwing railbed stones and dirt clods, they charged down the embankment, over the ditch, across the road, and broke through the enemy's dismayed right flank.

Taking heart from her own success now, Selena spun around, dodged past a fat little Madera County sheriff's deputy, hurdled the ditch, climbed the bank, and slithered on her hands and knees past the leafy barrier of oleanders. She could hear him now right at her heels. He was breathing hard behind his mask. He wanted to hurt her. She could hear him clomping up the incline, fighting his way through the bushes, hampered by his heavy equipment.

Now she was on her feet and running again, full out, running due east down a muddy tomato furrow with a low blue-green wall of plants on either side of her and the yellow rolling foothills of the Sierras bouncing up and down in front of her.

"Halt! Halt or I'll shoot!"

She was running toward the stoop laborers whom she could now see in the middle of the field. All around her in the furrows were her *compañeros*, little Connie, slender Dusty, the stocky muscular Vargas brothers, shouting at the top of their lungs, kicking up little cleats of black mud behind them as they ran.

"*Viva la huelga!*"

Someone fired a shotgun over their heads. Selena could hear the little buckshot whizzing over them, peppering the ground in front of them, sounding rather harmless, like hail or hard rain.

They reached the scabs. *Esquiroles* they were called in Spanish. Surrounded them quickly where they cowered like squirrels among the plants.

Selena took a deep breath and started bellowing out her prepared speech in Spanish: "*No tiene miedo,*" she said, "have no fear, for we are of your own *raza* and we have known hunger too. But why should one poor campesino take bread from another? And why should a man labor like a burro with a short-handled hoe that will break his back by the age of forty?"

And that was all she got to say, for the law was upon her, and confusion reigned all around. She could hear the blows of lead-weighted truncheons to her left and right. She could hear the screams of pain and fright. She could see mud, green plant particles, blood, sweat, pieces of hair and bone, bits of chipped plastic flying through the air in the periphery of her vision. Yet, for her own part, she was elated still, even when she saw the Vargas brothers go down beside her. And the noise seemed far away. For this was not the private Selena, out here in the field. This was the public Selena, La Palomita, who looked at current subjective reality with the sketchy blurred objectivity of some future historian concerned with only "the long view."

Then like some gargantuan god of war in helmet, shield, armor, and black pig-snout mask, a Fresno County sheriff came tramping over the rows, squishing unripe fruit beneath his enormous black boots. There was haste and nervous anticipation and *desire* in his step. He had found the enemy leader, and he could already imagine the kudos in the locker room later, the citation in his permanent record, the laurel wreath round his fat head. Selena dropped in the furrow, bent her knees up to her chin, covered her head with her hands. He drew back his club, long black club, thick at the end. She could hear it rustling in the tomato plants behind him. . . . *Now I die. What does it feel like to die—*

"You got me, officer! I give up!" someone yelled behind him. It was

Connie La Trucha. The sheriff crouched, spun, split her head with several great whistling blows.

How many blows Selena could not tell. For the instant she heard that club break bone her consciousness went completely private on her, subjective as a menstrual cramp. And she took off running. Ran so fast her hair blew out behind her like a black flag and the plants flattened out in their rows. Beside her, running like jackrabbits in other furrows, were three of her *compañeros*, Carlos, Raúl, and Martín, small sweating Mexican males in workboots, tattered tan shirts, wind-bent sombreros, and dirty blue jeans . . . and the fear of God written indelibly upon their muddy frozen faces. Above them all, hovering in the air, kicking up a storm of dust, was a police helicopter broadcasting their position and direction over a loudspeaker mounted on its Plexiglas canopy: "GOT FOUR OVER HERE A HUNDRED YARDS EAST, OVER. LOOKS LIKE THEY'RE MAKING FOR THE WATER, OVER."

Halfway to the Friant-Kern Canal and Selena gave up hope. A cloud of white dust on the levee marked the presence of three squad cars. She made a sudden decision. Dropped out of the race without warning. Dove headfirst into the mud. Struck out diagonally across the field, flat on her belly, like a salamander or a snake, allowing her *compañeros* to lead her pursuers away. *For without the head the body will die.* Made for Charmichael Road and the eucalyptus trees that lined the Tulare Canal. Swiftly she slithered through the rows of tall green plants, across the black humped furrows. Every time she heard the helicopter clatter overhead she stopped and lay still, at one with the earth and vegetation. She felt like little Charley in his paddy, listening to those great huge Americanos behind her, clomping nearer and nearer through the vines, imagining what they would do when they caught her, and her beautiful pink and white brains splattered like fertilizer over the rich soil.

At last she reached the edge of the field. Crawled over the last hump, wriggled through the last row of plants, poked her head out. And found herself staring directly into the blue and yellow striped pantleg of a Tulare County sheriff's deputy.

Slipped back into her greenery again without a sound.

She could hear him now, smiting out at the mustard weed with his war club, moving off east down the drainage ditch. Behind him, fifty feet or so away, she could hear another one . . . and behind her in the field, beating up toward her through the rows, yet another. She took three deep breaths—*Do it!*—sprang to her feet, switched quickly through the last row of plants, ran down the rocky incline and across the muddy drainage ditch, keeping her eyes on the ground ahead. Clumsily, falteringly, she moved up the other side of the ditch over beer cans and broken glass, gained the gravel shoulder of the road, and started across the blacktop.

"Stop! Stop or I'll shoot!"

He fired his police special. She could hear it zing over her head, sounding much more potent than the shotgun pellets.

She had gained the trees now, by some miracle, and was crackling over a thick layer of medicinal-smelling gum tree leaves, leaves that fall summer, winter, autumn, and spring. Bullets ripped through the branches over her head.

Through the trees she could see a government gray metal fence, and a sign:

DANGER
STAY ALIVE BY
STAYING OUT

PELIGRO
NO ENTRE
ALARGUE SU VIDA

Tripping, falling, listening to her own rapid breathing, she ran for the fence, leapt up on the chain links, and climbed, hurting her arm, cutting her hand and hip on the jagged ends on top.

Dropped to the ground on the other side, barely able to stand. And flung herself down the steep concrete bank and into the silty swift-running waters of the Tulare Canal.

Breathless, she let her boots drag her down and heard what she thought was a bullet striking the water over her head, ricocheting, pinging off the bank.

A shadow passed over her head: the County Road 189 canal bridge. She fought her way to the surface, gasping for air. Her pursuer was invisible now beyond the high bank and the bridge.

And she allowed the current to carry her down into an impossibly ordinary afternoon on the other side. She dropped her boots in the water. She was alone and barefoot now, dog-paddling through an apricot orchard. Birds twittered in the trees. Dragonflies dove close to her long floating hair. Bees buzzed around the sweet grass and purple wild flowers at the canal's edge. A cloud of gnats swirled about her face. A muted reddish light and the round shadows of fruit trees dappled the tepid brown water.

She could barely believe she was alive.

She was not alive, yet.

She made for the canal bank. It was very high and steep, a forty-five-degree angle at least. And beneath the waterline it was slimy with green moss. When she was a girl in Calmento High, three of her classmates had drowned in a canal just like this one because they couldn't find a way out and panicked. *What I need is a long branch or a limb.* She swam and swam in the more kindly current on the other side of the bridge, looking for what she needed, listening carefully to everything around her.

The noise that she heard was mostly what she'd been hearing all along: copter rotors, sirens, loudspeakers, shouts and screams, but it was coming from a much greater distance now.

She was listening for one special sound, a striker's chant: *"Viva la huelga!"* or *"No nos moverán!"* or something. But nothing of that nature could be heard. All she could hear, all around her, was the sound of defeat.

Then, to kill time as she swam along the canal bank, she thought of her family whom she'd not seen in years; of her mama, who had cried so hard and long when she left town; of Aguilar, who had lost his job on the sulphur rig; of Rudy, who got drafted into the army and was now in military prison; of her sister Jovita, who was "growing up now," as she said in her letters, and still had to wear "torn and embarrassing little-girl dresses to school"; of the baby, Rio, who was too young for sorrows and worries, yet. . . . Selena wondered what they were all doing now, right at this moment. She tried to picture them all sleeping peacefully, having a nice late afternoon siesta, curled up on the beds in fetal positions. But their images kept flickering away from her, just out of reach.

She blamed herself for all of their troubles.

For years she'd been dreaming of doing something for them, something that would turn their lives around, give them hope, self-confidence, a second chance. But so far there had been little she could do beyond sending them a little money now and then. *"Happiness is a steady income,"* she said to herself. . . . And at that instant she thought of Jay Jay Vanducci. And the memory of his great moonface, his huge smooth-muscled body, his pale skin, owllike eyes, high tenor voice, tiny even teeth, and his oddly attractive smile caused her suddenly to fold in upon herself in the water. She retreated to her deepest, hardest core, treated herself again to her most shameful secret sore. Strangely enough, what smarted most was not Selena's memory of the monstrous lie that Jay Jay told, nor his phony fond parting on the night of their betrothal, nor the endless sinking days of waiting for his call, nor the humiliation of having to leave town, nor even the horror of her Tijuana abortion. The most painful wound, the one that lay open and festering still, was her memory of accepting money from his father's hand. She would never forget the day it happened, a windy, peat-dusty day in April of 1964. She would never forget the feel of that hand. It was a rough, hard hand. It could have crushed her little hand into pulp. "I thought so," the Dootch sneered when she took his wad of greenbacks. Softly he said it, so no one in the house would hear. "That's what you were after all the time, wasn't it, *bimba?*" And she wanted to throw it back in his leering red face. But she hesitated, fatally, her quandary being this: whether to keep the money, accept the truth of his allegation, and gain therewith the means (education, experience, political power perhaps) one day to work her revenge on him —or to return the money and leave vengeance to the Lord. What had finally tipped the scales was a purely personal consideration: She wanted to study, to learn, to *be somebody*. Still and all, Selena would never forgive herself for taking that money. And she would impose a harsh penalty on the Vanduccis for offering it, and on herself for keeping it, whatever good came of it in the end.

At last Selena found a piece of wood, a waterlogged young apricot limb. It was not what she would have liked, but it would have to do. She swam along till she found the metal wheel of an outlet duct. The wheel sat in a little rectangular groove in the cement, about nine feet above the surface of the water.

Very carefully she nudged the end of her limb up onto the incline, leaving the heavier, thicker end floating in the water. Then, pushing it little by little, relying on the natural adhesive qualities of cool, wet, slick wood against hot, dry, rough concrete, she worked the skinny tip of the limb slowly up the bank.

While she worked, she thought of Jay Jay again. She could not recall what had brought him so suddenly to her mind. Maybe it was the headline she had read the other day in the farm news section of the *Fresno Bee*: VANDUCCI & SON IN MILLION-DOLLAR LAND DEAL. Whatever the case, the sweet thought of future vengeance gave her the strength to do what she had to do. . . . She had finally reached a point in her struggle where almost half of the apricot limb was out of the water, lying up against the steep concrete bank. She rested for a moment, treading water with one hand. Then she took a deep breath and heaved the limb upward with all her might. The tip went in between the spokes of the metal valve wheel. She twisted sharply. It held!

Now firmly but gently she began to pull herself upward, and thirty minutes later she was out of the water.

She pressed the rough cement like a lover, with her head on his hard unbeating heart, letting his warmth run down her breasts, belly, mons veneris. Then, gripping the tiny bumps and furrows and gritty parts of the concrete with her fingernails, using the limb sparingly as a brace, she made her way slowly upward, hour by hour, watching the red ants run up and down with impunity, an inch from her eye.

By nightfall she had reached a place where she could smell the sweet grass and wild flowers that hung over the edge. Her body was one great howling ache from head to toe. She was tempted now to lunge upward and grab for the concrete groove and pull herself up. But it was risky. If she missed she would never have the strength to haul herself out of the water again.

Just then she heard voices, soft Spanish voices, whispering nearby.

". . . *oye, Manny, donde 'stán los . . . ?*"

". . . ahorita vienen . . ."

Yet for some reason unknown even to herself she kept her silence. And soon she could hear them moving away toward the lights of the town, north through the apricot trees.

Then a few minutes later she heard the sound of conflict on the road beyond the orchard, and the thwunk of truncheons on soft Mexican-American skulls. And grieved for her people, whom she had led to destruction. At the same time, she was consoled somewhat by this fresh evidence of her genie's premonitory powers, powers that seemed to work even in these moments of inglorious defeat.

And it occurred to her that there were many kinds of defeat and many kinds of victory. And if you couldn't win against the pigs, then you could just as well win against the bloody concrete bank. Cheered by this wild and amoral notion, Selena vowed again her devotion to the dark Virgin, took three great gulps of air, and risked everything in one last mighty grasp for the lip of the canal.

Ten

ROSE MARY'S GARDEN was a masterpiece of functional beauty. Delightful equally to her husband's eye, his belly, and his sense of order, it provided most of the Vanducci family's flowers and vegetables and not a little of its outdoor pleasure. Jay Jay knew it was much more than a hobby to his wife. It was her life's work.

Five years ago, on that desolate hill behind their little foreman's house, she had started blocking out the garden with stakes that she hammered into the brick-hard ground, twine that she ran through the rustling wild oats. Meticulously she set about drawing up her plans on blueprint paper, in white ink, with all dimensions exact. "Picture my garden like an upended flag," she told her young husband, "with three equal-sized bands of color. The first band is a patio of red tile. The second is green lawn. The third is black composted soil for my kitchen garden."

Next morning Jay Jay came around with his little Ford tractor with bulldozer attachment and, in a dirty half-day of blowing dust, made it flat as a drawing board for her. The rest of the day he spent trucking up a few tons of the finest Vanducci bottomland and rolling it flat. Then, with her own hands, Rose Mary built the fence. She made it out of redwood, high on the west and east sides, to break the prevailing winds, and low on the north, for the view out over the valley. When she was done, she planted oleander shrubs and fast-growing eucalyptus on the outside of the fence, and roses, grapes, ivy, and fruit and nut trees along the inside. After that she planted her lawn. When it came up, she tended it carefully, rolling it, watering it, fertilizing it, and clipping it by hand. Next she started her kitchen garden. She dug her furrows straight as a ruler, and between them planted peppers, pear tomatoes, eggplants, zucchini, carrots, garlic, red lettuce, English cucumbers, dandelion greens, artichokes, fava beans, peas, cauliflower, spinach, swiss chard, sweet basil, oregano, thyme, and rosemary, like her name. At the end of each furrow she drove a stake into the ground, and impaled the seed package on it. Then on the grass, which by now was thick and soft and smooth as a golf green, she constructed a circular fishpond and a birdbath of wagon-wheel dimensions, on opposite sides of the yard, equidistant from the fences. Next, she poured the concrete for the patio, and laid red tile on top. Then she stretched a large canvas awning over the patio, from the roof to the fence, and tied it down neatly with nylon twine. Last of all, she set out garden chairs and lounge chairs and a white metal coffee table.

Now at eight o'clock on this bright morning in early June, while university faculties went on strike across the nation and American embassies were besieged all over the world and casualties in South East Asia went over the million mark and the Cambodian Central Command Post of the Viet Cong remained as elusive as ever, Jay Jay sat with his wife under the awning sipping coffee, munching on a breakfast of toast and marmalade and browsing through a pamphlet entitled *Trends in Production and Marketing of California Fresh Market Tomatoes.*

Goldfish flashed in the pond. Grasshoppers jumped on the lawn. Bees buzzed among the flowers and vines along the fence. Sparrows splashed in the birdbath. Hummingbirds flitted in and out of the fruit trees, the sun catching their wings. Little Frankie, naked as the day he was born, fed breadcrumbs to the fish and birds. Vince was busily irrigating the vegetables with a garden hose. Ripe and green now, the plants grew almost as tall as the tan, shirtless boy. And beyond the boy, over the low back fence, the last yellow fold of the Diablos rolled down to the new Westside Freeway, where late-model cars and trucks were screaming by, heat waves rising off their metal roofs. And beyond that . . . the flats, the endless fields, the empire of the Dootch, over which Jay Jay would one day preside.

"No, Vinnie, let the water in slow, slow!" Rose Mary hollered, setting her coffee down on the little white table beside her. "All right now, that's much better."

Rose Mary was a tall hefty woman with a narrow pretty face that was a trifle too small in proportion to the rest of her. Seven months pregnant, she wore a gray and white striped smock with matching white shorts, and a pair of white leather sandals. She painted her toenails orange. Her frosted blond hair was cut short and curly now, in anticipation of the baby. Deeply tanned and freckled, she was the picture of maternal vitality. Her gray, good-humored eyes sparkled in the sunlight. To her husband, Rose Mary had always looked marvelously . . . ample. Even when they first started going together, back in the days when he was still on the rebound from Selena Cruz, he had found her so.

But Jay Jay and Rose Mary had gotten together originally through the offices of her mother, Tosca Ammiratti. Tosca called Angie one day and asked if Rose Mary couldn't ride with Jay Jay to college while her car was being repaired. They were both commuter students at College of the Pacific in Stockton at the time. Rose Mary was a sophomore majoring in home economics. And Jay Jay was a junior majoring in marketing. And Angie had said, "Why certainly, Tosca," without even bothering to consult her son. And he had been furious with her about it, he remembered. "It's a goddamn conspiracy!" he had ranted.

Yet, from the moment Rose Mary got into his pickup truck that morning he had been amazed and delighted by her . . . amplitude. And the fresh Lifebuoy Soap smell of her body. And her tan skin and good-humored eyes. And the pastel-colored sleeveless summer frock that she wore.

Two days later they went out on their first date.

A month later they were engaged.

And in June, to nobody's particular surprise, they were married at Saint Bernard's in Calmento. The ceremony, performed by white-haired old Father Murray, and the reception afterwards at the Calmento Golf & Country Club were long and elaborate affairs, attended by every major Catholic family in the northern San Joaquin Valley.

Rose Mary was a virgin till the second night of their honeymoon at Lake Tahoe.

Jay Jay spent their first night together confessing the whole long and complicated story of his relationship with Selena Cruz, and begging his wife's understanding (it was no little thing, in Calmento, to have sullied oneself publicly with a Mexican girl). Rose Mary spent all the next day reflecting on the matter, and that night she forgave him at last.

And on the following night baby Vincent Michael Vanducci was conceived.

Now, looking back on those first fruitful nights of their marriage, and on all the nights since, and recalling a scene that had taken place in bed this very morning before the kids got up (Rose Mary on top, like she always did it when she was this far along), Jay Jay leaned over and kissed his wife tenderly on the cheek. Her cheek was warm and fleshy and it smelled . . . clean. Smelled of Lifebuoy Soap, just like on their first date. It was a scent that Jay Jay had always loved, ever since he was a little kid.

"God, I'm so happy this morning," he said, "I oughta feel guilty."

"Guilty?" Rose Mary said, turning toward him, smiling, shaking her head. "What for?"

"Oh, I don't know. We got it so good here, honey, wonder there ain't some law against it."

"Get outa here, Jay Jay!" she said. Her voice was high, harsh, and very nasal, like his own. It was the accent of the San Joaquin. Though Jay Jay was aware of its cumbrous and inelegant qualities, he had always found it rather reassuring, like the homely monotonous *put-put-put* of his John Deere.

"No, really," he said. "Here's the thing: What have I done to deserve all of this? It's too good to be true." He gestured with his chin toward the garden, the boys, and the fields and canals and freeways beyond.

Rose Mary was a no-nonsense Calmento farm girl. Came from a line of Sicilian asparagus growers as hardheaded as the Vanduccis—without their fatal romantic streak. Her brother Big John Ammiratti, who had taken over the family ranch on the death of his father, had a rep as the most literal-minded guy in Calmento. One cold foggy winter day when they were in high school together, for example, Jay Jay had come up to the big Wop in auto shop, and said, "Goddamn, John, it's colder than shit out there today!" And Big John had turned to him and said, in his family's characteristically slow measured drawl, "Shit ain't cold." "Well, what I mean is," Jay Jay had said, just trying to make conversation, "it's freezing out there." "I don't see no ice," Big John had said.

His little sister Rose Mary was just like him. She had a way of dispelling the mists and cobwebs, fears and doubts that tended to form in Jay Jay's brain with a mere sniff and a wave of her hand.

"You think too much, boy," she said. "Now why don't you just run along to the cockfights with your dad, huh?"

She spoke to him in a gently scolding tone, laughing and shaking a finger at him. Her size and weight, her maternal condition, her suntanned, crinkly-eyed face that was aged beyond its years, her slow drawling laugh, all gave Rose Mary an air of wisdom and authority in Jay Jay's imagination. He decided to obey her without further question. The very act of obeying would, he was sure, relieve his vague anxieties.

"And take the boys along with you," Rose Mary said. "Your mom's starting up that summer school of hers again this week. And she said she wanted them over there at eight o'clock on the dot."

"Summer school?" Jay Jay said. "But it's Sunday today."

"I know that," Rose Mary said, "but I never argue with your mom, once she gets her mind set on something."

Jay Jay laughed and nodded agreement. Then he went into the house, dressed himself in Levi's, a tan western shirt, a pair of hand-tooled Tony Lama cowboy boots, a white straw Stetson hat, dark tear-drop sunglasses, and headed back out to collect his boys.

Rose Mary had them dressed in shorts and sandals now, and he took them each by the hand, and led them out the side gate and up toward the big house, raising dust with every step.

A warm morning in June. The sun still hovering low over the blue Sierras. The air still fresh and clear. In another two hours the valley would be hotter than Hades, socked in with smog the whole five hundred miles from Bakersfield to Red Bluff.

Cows were mooing in the yellow hills behind the ranch. Cocks were crowing. High tension wires were whining over his head. Traffic roared on the freeway below. A loud little Stearman trainer was dive-bombing the tomato fields beyond the freeway, pissing a stream of white poison out his rear end.

"What's that for, Daddy?" little Frankie wanted to know.

"Don't be stupid," Vince said.

"Come on, what's it for? What's it for?"

"Go ahead," Jay Jay said. "Tell him, Vince."

"To kill," Vince said. "To kill the bugs that eat the plants."

"Is that right, Daddy?"

"Uh-huh," Jay Jay said, laughing, pleased with his boys, and himself, and the morning, "just as right as rain."

Jay Jay's anxieties had at last receded, and he was beginning to enjoy himself. He firmly intended to enjoy himself. From mid-July till the rains of November no one on the Vanducci ranch would have a moment to himself. Five thousand acres of fruit to be picked, packed, and shipped.

Over at the big house the Dootch was sitting at the kitchen table finishing up a huge farm breakfast: linguisa sausage, eggs, toast, hash browns, coffee. Angie was working over the stove, where her old-fashioned upside-down Italian pot sang merrily. Beside her, at the sink, the Mexican maid was doing last night's dishes.

Jay Jay's parents were still in prime physical condition. It was a mystery how they did it. Ate like pigs and never seemed to gain a pound. Neither of them had aged a day since Jay Jay was Vince's size.

But Jay Jay and Rose Mary, on the other hand, they were very careful about what they ate, and went on a diet every few months, and seemed to get plumper and older-looking every year.

Jay Jay felt almost as if he were catching up with his parents somehow.

This morning when he got out of bed he had regarded himself in the mirror very closely. What he had seen was a face that was still smooth and round and colorless. But it was getting puffy around the eyes and jowls, and his hairline was receding dangerously. He was a contented family man, and it showed. Had a fat ass and a belly like a beer barrel and he looked ten years older than his age. A common American type, he looked like a great big aging baby boy. There was something indefinably sad in his countenance, something very vulnerable and sensitive, like he might bust out crying any minute.

"Mornin', fellas," Bruno said, waving his eggy fork, smiling fondly down at his little grandsons.

"Mornin', Granpa."

"How about some hotcakes, boys?" Angie said, motioning toward the blackened iron skillet on the stove in front of her.

"They already ate," Jay Jay said. "Anyway, I thought you were supposed to be starting your 'summer school' today."

"Today?" Angie said, puzzled.

"That's what Rose Mary said."

"Did I tell her that?" Angie said, smiling. "Now, whatever made me do a thing like that, Jay Jay?"

"I got a pretty good idea," he said.

"Oh, I guess I'll just have to admit the truth," Angie said happily.

"It was just an excuse to have the boys to myself for a little while. . . . How 'bout it, boys, how'd you like to go for a swim? Huh?"

"Oh boy, oh boy!"

"I thought you might like that," Angie said. "Actually, we'll be starting our summer school tomorrow, Jay Jay. We've got twenty kids this year, from six different ranches!"

Though Angie had finally earned her teaching credential from Merced State, she had never found the time to put it to use. So, her annual summer schools were still the only means she had of "keeping a hand in." And she was very proud of her work with the ranch children. And justly so, Jay Jay believed. When he reflected on the fact that his own boys would be attending the same summer school session by the swimming pool that he had attended with Rose Mary and Big John Ammiratti and Delano Range and Selena Cruz, it gave him a great feeling of continuity and permanence.

"Ready to go, son?" Bruno said, rising from the table, wiping his mouth with the back of his hairy hand.

"Sure, let's go," Jay Jay said.

"Whoopie!" Bruno said, doing a little jig out the kitchen door.

The Dootch truly appreciated his rare days off. And there was nothing he'd rather do than hit the cockfights.

"What time are you coming back?" Angie shouted, as they went out the door.

"Back around two," Bruno said.

"I knew I could count on you two fellows for Sunday dinner. *Non è vero, Brunino?*"

"*Si, si, Angelina, è la santa verità!*" said the Dootch, patting his hard belly, coughing up a laugh.

On the service porch the men picked up a couple of pairs of snippers and three covered wicker baskets.

"Say, I want to compliment you, son, on that job you did the other day," Bruno said as they traipsed over the yard to the cock pens.

"What's that?"

"Come on, you know what I mean. That quick-ripening agent. Laying it down on the whole South Section in one day like that. Couldn't've done it better myself."

"Just the way we always do it," he mumbled shyly. Now that all the rebellion was out of him, his dad tried to compliment him every time he got a chance. Jay Jay lived for those compliments.

"Now, you know I don't like to talk ranch on my days off, Jay Jay. But there's just this one other item. About that letter . . ."

"What letter?"

"From that woman at San Quentin," the Dootch said. "She beats around the bush so much with that bureaucratese bullshit that it's damn near impossible to figure out what she wants, exactly."

"It sure is," Jay Jay said, though he knew very well what she wanted. What *he* wanted was a little time to collect his thoughts. That letter from Quentin had come as a real shock to him. He had often wondered about Range, over the years, and it was sad and pathetic to hear that he'd ended up in the slammer. And he could imagine what it must've cost the poor little bastard in pride to get that woman to send a letter to the Vanduccis, after they'd written him off and abandoned his ass long ago. Jay Jay felt truly sorry for Del, and more than a little guilty too. . . . But this was the kind of emotional shit that he had to banish from his consideration now; and it was the reason he was playing for time.

The Dootch never asked a question without some definite purpose in mind: Maybe this was another test.

"She is Range's counselor in prison," Jay Jay said. "She wants you to send him an offer of employment so he can get an early release on his parole."

"So," Bruno said, shaking his hand limply at waist level, "I'm supposed to employ a jailbird, just 'cause he used to live on the ranch?"

"That's up to you, Dad."

"Let's say I don't send it. Then what?"

"He stays in Quentin."

"How much longer?"

"Six months to a year. It depends."

"Hell, that ain't much time. What do you think?"

"If it was me, Dad, I wouldn't do it."

"Why not?"

"Well, I'll tell you. I've given this a lot of thought. And I asked myself, where has Range been all this time? What's he been up to? Why is he thinking of us all of a sudden? What's he got up his sleeve? We don't know. And we don't have any way of finding out. All we know is that the whole thing smells kind of fishy. And also, I remember things that Range used to say, when we were kids, a kind of resentment that he had, that he couldn't hide, about us Vanduccis being the owners of this land that used to belong to his grandpa, and all of that. . . .

"Well, Dad, here is the way I thought it all out. . . . If there is ever any doubt in a situation, first thing on my mind is, 'What's good for the ranch? Is this gonna be a benefit?' And I'd have to say on this thing, 'No.' It's a charity case, at best. And we ain't in the charity business, or the sucker business either."

"Why, goddamn, son, that's just what I wanted to hear. Couldn't have expressed it better myself," the Dootch said proudly. Then he handed Jay Jay the other pair of snippers and his wicker basket, and let himself into the wire mesh cock pen.

There were three large birds in there, each in a separate cage, each one named for a color: Red, Negrito, and Blue. Red was the largest of all. "Big Red," they called him. A huge powerful old Hatch Shuffler with mean yellow eyes, he crouched now warily in a corner, watching the Dootch come toward him across the soggy chickenshit, the pecked corncobs and mud-covered feed. Bruno spread his muscular arms out wide and fixed Big Red with a stare. The little fucker didn't move a feather. Just stayed still and nice, hypnotized by that big man who was coming nearer and nearer. Bruno got ahold of him, picked him up with a quick deft movement, holding him by the wings and legs, and motioned to Jay Jay with his head. Cowering in their pens, the low sun shining on their feathers, the other birds clucked nervously, scratching the ground, throwing little mudballs up against the chickenwire fence. Jay Jay let himself into the pen, set the baskets on the ground. The Dootch got down in the mud and trapped Big Red between his knees. With both hands he held his little head very tight. Jay Jay took one of the snippers and cut back the bird's comb and wattles. That way the other birds couldn't get a grip on him in battle. When they were done with Big Red, they put him in a basket and performed the same operation on the others. Then they carried the three of them out to the Ford pickup in the wicker baskets and put them down in the truck bed. Walked around and got in the cab and headed out for the cockfights on Roberts Island. The Dootch drove. In the glove compartment was a small polished mahogany box. Jay Jay got it out and opened it. Inside, resting in fitted felt grooves, lay three tiny metal files and a selection of wicked-looking gaff and slasher cockfighting spurs. As they drove out under the freeway bridge, down Corral Hollow Road past fields full of ripening tomatoes and barley, up Calmento Boulevard past wetback camps and wrecking yards, across the sleepy asphalt and neon little town, out of town going north past the old brick Holly Sugar refinery, over the Middle River drawbridge, past asparagus fields and high yellow levees and groves of great valley oak trees, Jay Jay absentmindedly sharpened those evil little spurs.

He could tell that his old man had something ticklish he wanted to say but didn't quite know how to bring it up. The Dootch kept running his sweaty palms over the steering wheel, switching the radio from country music to farm news, and scratching his ass. Once he even called the foreman of the East Section on his radiotelephone and woke him out of bed, just to pass the time of day.

Whatever his dad had to say, Jay Jay was not particularly anxious to hear it. He had no great love of surprises. And he'd received enough in the last couple of days to last him quite a while. "I'm a farmer, not a romantic," he told himself, though it was not strictly true. What he knew was this: His current familial bliss was a very rare, very precious and fragile commodity in this fickle world. He saw it in his mind's eye as a kind of crystal palace, threatened all around by destructive forces. This was not mere idle speculation on his part or some kind of paranoia. It was a simple fact of existence. He'd known this ever since he took a course in physics at College of the Pacific: "The Second Law of Thermodynamics asserts a simple cosmic fact: that the universe is constantly, irreversibly, becoming less ordered than it was. It is this behavior of the universe that accounts for the one-way direction of events and the irreversible passage of time."

The signs of this decay of order were all around Jay Jay in the valley. Farm union organizers were stirring up trouble. Suburbs were gobbling up all the arable land. A cry was being raised in certain liberal quarters to abolish farm price supports, child labor, and subsidies for not growing crops. Ranch families were breaking up all around. Kids were leaving the farm, going to the city, joining communes and urban guerrilla bands. Divorce was almost as frequent as marriage. People were leaving the church in droves, joining kooky religious orders and cult groups. Women were getting abortions, popping the pill like candy, seeing psychiatrists, attending primal scream sessions and encounter groups. Respected elderly Catholic men were abandoning the Elks Club and the Knights of Columbus for weekends at Esalen and Tassajara Hot Springs. Growers were selling out their heritage to fast-talking eastern subdividers and retiring to Leisure World. Nobody knew what to do with themselves anymore. Everyone was nervous, touchy, uptight. Everyone drank too much. Most people were overweight and unhealthy. Cancer had invaded the valley with a vengeance: This area had the highest incidence of cancer in the entire contiguous United States. No one knew why. Stanford University was doing a study on it. Meanwhile everyone felt as if they were being eaten alive by disease. Friends and relatives were dropping like flies. Jay Jay's cousin Sal last year with cancer of the colon . . . Rose Mary's dad just five months ago with lung cancer . . . her little nephew with leukemia, the poor little guy, only a year to live, the doctors said. . . . Every time Jay Jay succeeded in abolishing the anxiety from his mind, the old grim reaper struck again. Seemed like he was getting closer every time.

So Jay Jay was not in the mood for any bad news at the moment, not from his old man or any other source.

"I don't know how to tell you this, son . . ."

"Then don't tell me."

"Har har. But you don't mean that, do you, Jay Jay?"

"You bet I do," Jay Jay said.

The Dootch had no appreciation of humor. And he was quick to take offense. When confronted with irony, he narrowed his eyes down to little blue slits and often reacted violently.

"The hell with you then," he said. "I'll let you find out for yourself." And all the way out to the cockfight there was nothing Jay Jay could do to change his mind.

The cockfight that Sunday was held out on the sandbar where Trapper Slough runs into Middle River. You could tell a fight was in progress by the number of cars and pickups parked up and down the dirt farm road. Bruno pulled up under a big cottonwood tree. He and Jay Jay got their baskets and walked down through the black peat of the asparagus field and over the yellow grassy levee and down through a bamboo thicket to the fight. Somebody had built a ring out of driftwood on the hard-packed sand. There were about two hundred men and a few women standing around the bar, sitting on the levee under the oak and willow trees, watching the action. Most of the spectators were Mexicans, Filipinos, and Okies. Only a few Wops, Portagees, and native Anglos. Nigger vendors came around from time to time, selling beer and pop from large iced buckets. There was a tremendous racket at the fight—cheers, hollers, songs, laughter, shouted bets.

Jay Jay and his dad went right to the ring with their baskets. The Dootch was hot to match up. He was one cockfighting man. Jay Jay remembered when he was a little boy he asked him one time how come he liked the cocks so much.

" 'Cause they got *tanates*," he said, using the Mexican term. "They'd rather fight than eat."

"How come they like to fight so much, Daddy?" he asked.

"Been bred for it," he said, "ever since Bible times. Every time a guy finds one who's a coward, he wastes him, wastes everything even remotely kin to him. So, what's come down is the baddest breed in the world. Make bulls look like mama's boys. Little buggers, they never quit fighting, even when they're dead."

"Even when they're dead?"

"That's right. And I want you to remember that."

Jay Jay remembered it, but he never understood it.

As soon as they put their wicker baskets on the ground a lot of Mexican guys started coming around, wanting to match up. The Dootch had a rep as a big gambler around Calmento, so they wanted a piece of his action. Also, they sniffed his green. Even though most of them were dirt poor and their birds were scraggly and mongrel, it would never occur to a Mex that he might drop his stake. You could count on them to go for broke against impossible odds and take them at your leisure. That is what Jay Jay's old man had taught him when he was just a little bitty boy, and it was true to this day.

One of the Mexicans who came around wanting to bill up was Aguilar. He still held a grudge against the 'Duccis, after all these years. So every few months he'd come around wanting to fight birds. Every time they fought, the Dootch's high-bred cock would take Aguilar's mongrel in a minute flat. Eat him right up. Aguilar wouldn't say a word. Just pay up, go home, and start raising another cock from the egg, saving his *dinero* for another big bet with his ex-*patroncito*. Then the next time they met up the whole thing would happen again. It was fucking pathetic. Seemed like ever since his stepdaughter Selena left town, he'd just gone completely to seed. Sure, he was the biggest Mex that anybody'd ever seen. But there was something weak and slobbery

about his face now. His eyes were always wet and red, like he was about
to bust out crying. He'd gone all soft and paunchy. And he had a kind
of unhealthy yellow color to him. His Pancho Villa mustache had
turned all gray. He looked like some wino that you might see down at
the freight yards.

Aguilar and Bruno bargained for a few minutes and then Bruno said,
"That new bird of yours is smaller than mine, Pancho. I'll spot you
twenty and bet you a hundred that Big Red'll snuff him out in three
minutes."

Aguilar raised his straw sombrero and squinted into the sun. He was
thinking it over. But the Dootch wouldn't leave him be.

"What's a matter? What's a matter? Eh? Thought you was a
gambling man."

"Focking right!" said the big Mex, taking the bait.

"All right then, gaffs or slashers?"

"Slashers," Aguilar said, spitting into the sand.

Now your Mex, he will usually go for the slasher-type spur. It is fast
and deadly. Your gringo, he will prefer the gaff. It is slower, and makes
for a better spectacle.

Once they had come to their agreement, Aguilar moved to the other
side of the ring to get his bird ready to fight. All the Mexican spectators moved with him. Bruno took out his mahogany box, selected his
cruelest slasher, and fitted it to Big Red's spur. All this time there was
an incredible racket going on all around them: referees calling, bettors
shouting, losers crying out, winners hooting with joy, cock auctioneers
yelling out prices over portable loudspeakers, all in a wild mixture of
languages and dialects from opposite ends of the earth. The sheriff's
deputy, heavily tipped, stayed miles away on Mandeville Island.

The only quiet thing about the cockfights were the cocks themselves,
who fought and died without a sound.

At the first lull in the noise, Bruno picked up Big Red, climbed over
the fence, and met Aguilar on the packed white sand in the center of
the ring. The ref talked to them for a moment. A great big pot-bellied Mex and a stocky red-faced Wop, they glared at each other as if it
were they, and not their birds, who would fight now to the death.

The cockfight was all a very serious game, all symbolic. Jay Jay figured
it was a pretty good way to work out human aggression. As far as he
was concerned, the world would be a long sight better off if we fought
all our battles with animal surrogates.

The ref gave his signal and they billed their birds up: let them peck
at each other from a distance till they were good and pissed off.

"A la prueba!" a Mexican woman yelled.

Then they let them go.

Immediately the spectators set up a loud clamor. All the Okies had
their money on Big Red. "Go git 'em, big feller!" they hollered. The

Mexicans were for Aguilar's bird, whose name was Moreno. "*Mátalo, mátalo, Morenito!*"

The Flips didn't say a word. They are sporting men, but not at all sentimental about animals. One of their great national delicacies is barbecued dogmeat, the higher bred the better. And they never wasted a tear on a chicken. When they placed a bet, they never said a word, never changed their sure calm expressions. They just raised one finger, two, three, signifying ten, twenty, thirty. . . .

Each of the races kept to its own side of the ring.

Moreno was a fast, mean little dun-feathered Pyle Roundhead who probably would have done better on the defensive. But he tore right into Red. And, for a moment, he scared the bigger bird. Red ran like a fuck-shy hen, and they had to bill them up again. The Dootch's face showed his embarrassment. Red had never done that to him before.

"*Cobarde, cobarde!*" all the *cholos* hollered. "Focking coward!"

"Bullshit!" the *gabachos* yelled. "Bullshit, he was just maneuvering!"

"That's right," a female voice piped up from the Mexican side, "maneuvering his little tail outa danger!"

Everyone broke up with laughter. "*Qué hembra!*" the spicks shouted. Even the dour leathery Flips cracked a grin or two among them.

To Jay Jay that small Mexican female voice presented a definite problem. When he recognized to whom it belonged, the "bad news" his father had attempted to convey was no longer a mystery. Before he could wonder how his father had found out she'd arrived, or what she was doing here, what monkey business she had planned for Calmento (her defeat in Fresno County was a matter of common knowledge, and for a time when she was with Cesar Chavez, Jay Jay had watched her exploits nightly on his TV set), he was afflicted with a severe pain in his left arm. Then it raced up his left shoulder, up the left side of his neck, and into his head. For an instant he was afraid he might fall to the ground. He scanned the other side of the ring and there she was, a small dark oval face in a sea of dark-skinned faces in the second row. She hadn't changed a bit. Stood out from among that drab assemblage as clearly as if she'd had a circle drawn round her head. She was wearing a white-sequined headband and a white Mexican dress or blouse with red and green piping on it. Regarding her across the ring, Jay Jay felt ugly and square and out-of-date, with his pot belly and flattop haircut and his trimmed long sideburns and his cowboy outfit. Watching her, he felt as if something were dreadfully wrong with him, as if he would soon die of cancer or something. He broke into a cold sweat. The pain in his arm went all the way down his left side and into his leg. His left testicle began to ache like mad.

Across the ring Selena seemed to be smiling at him. Was she smiling at him? Yes. A whole tide of memories engulfed him. Then all the memories coalesced into a single memory of perfect construction, clarity, and beauty. He saw her before him as she was then. For an instant he loved her again as he had loved her in his mother's Continental, in his future father-in-law's asparagus patch. Greedily he rifled the larder of their past, gorged himself on memories, vomited dreams. Whole scenes rose up before his eyes. He saw them in the most vivid detail: two teenage lovers, one light and one dark, on the night of betrothal, the night of betrayal. He regarded them with great fondness, for all their human frailties: the little Mexican girl who, out of the exigencies of poverty, had convinced herself that she loved the bossman's son . . . the deliriously happy boy whose delirium itself was induced by his subconscious knowledge of the future.

Even as they rolled with love in the mud he had known he would betray her.

Even as they kissed and announced their betrothal she had known her ass was for sale, that her love could be bought, and bought off.

For all that, their young affair did not stink in Jay Jay's memory. Indeed, it semed even more poignant for its delicate ephemeral qualities, and the heavy irony of its unplotted two-way double cross. He saw their romance as a kind of youthful tragedy, infused with pathos, even grandeur, a kind of *Romeo and Juliet* of the Far West. The idea was sufficiently glamorous to his hungry imagination to bring him nearly to the point of tears. He began to ache all over. His belly felt like an empty grave, a hollow in the earth, a deep cavern, wherein this cold fire burned. His emotion began to consume him from the inside. For a second he felt his life to be utterly base and without meaning. She stood before him at once as a dream of his former transcendant joy, a memory of lost youth, glorious rebellion . . . and a source of monstrous guilt.

Was she smiling? Yes. But it was a smile that could kill.

With a massive effort of will, Jay Jay shattered the memory like a blown wine jar in his mind and swept all the tinkling little shards over the edge of his consciousness.

Below him on the sand, Moreno tore into Big Red again. But this time Red did not run. They rose in the air again, wings flapping. They seemed to hang in suspended time, with the feathers flying off their wings in slow motion.

When finally they hit the ground, neither one seemed any worse for wear. Up they went again. Moreno was putting up a hell of a fight, for such a little thing. Up again, wings hitting, feathers falling. Suddenly a small streak of blood appeared on Big Red's wing. All the Mexicans cheered.

"A lo macho!"

Selena was screaming: "Mátalo! Mátalo!"

Up again went the cocks, pecking, clawing, slashing furiously. Now blood was showing on Moreno's breast. *Wham wham wham* went their wings, beating the air. When they landed the next time, Moreno looked a bit dazed. All the Chicanos hushed. Moreno weaved around for a long moment, like he couldn't find his way. There was just this thin line of red coming out from under one broken breast feather. His throat was cut.

"Eeeeeeh!" a woman screamed from across the ring. It was a primitive cry. It pierced through all the other sounds of the cockfight and chilled Jay Jay to his marrow.

"Eeeeeeh!" she shrieked again, like an Indian, like some kind of fucking stone age squaw.

"Die, die, die!" all the Okies hollered.

"Die, you little brown bastard!" the Dootch yelled.

"*Levántate, levántate, macho!*" the *cholos* cried.

"Eeeeeeh!" Selena shrilled, letting old Jay Jay know right where things were at. "Aiiiiii!" she cried. "*A la muerte, a la muerte!*"

He heard her loud and clear. From the very beginning he suffered from no illusions. Actually, clearing the air like this, it relieved him of a dangerous burden of guilt. If that was the way it was going to be, well, then . . . He wondered if she knew this about him. He thought she did. Her motives were beyond him.

Moreno got dizzier and dizzier. But he did not want to die. Big Red stalked him warily. Everyone hushed, waiting. White sun beating down on the white sand ring. A hot east wind sprang up, blowing black peat dust off the asparagus fields and into the spectators' faces, flecking their dark glasses.

Across the sand Jay Jay could see Selena begin to cry. Could *hear* her cry. Out of all the noise of the fight he was able to isolate that one small sound. It entered his brain and seared. His strength left him again. There was a moment when he was so weak and vulnerable that if she had asked he would have run to her side, would have cheerfully abandoned farm and family forever and run away with her, Lord knows where.

Moreno keeled over on the sand. "Eeeeeeeh!" He was dead. But his eyes were still darting, getting duller and duller. Big Red came prancing over to give him the coup de grace and got the surprise of his little chicken's life. He was pecking away at Moreno's eye, peck peck peck, when dead Moreno slashed out, caught him just below the breast, and cut his leg nearly clean through. He hopped away, hippedy-hop, on one foot, dragging the other like so much excess baggage.

"*Un gallo a toda madre!*" Selena yelled.

"Goddamnit!" the Dootch hollered. "That was my best bird."

"Crybaby! Crybaby!" all the greasers called.

"They never give up," Jay Jay said out loud, "even when they're dead."

"Who wins?" the oddsmakers wanted to know.

"Red wins," the ref said.

"Yippie!" went the Okies.

"Don' do heem moch good," said big Aguilar, grinning through tears.
The Flips just kept their mouths shut, and counted their loot.

"Sheeeeeeit!" the Dootch cried, and cut Red's cocky little crested
head off with one blinding swipe of his pocket knife.

More blood; it splattered all over the sand as Big Red kept dancing,
one foot, one foot, with no head.

Moreno's blood had splattered too, all over Jay Jay's face and shirt.
But he wouldn't know that till later, when he got home and looked in
the mirror.

Aguilar jumped into the ring and picked Moreno up by his scaly little
yellow legs. His head hung limp. Blood was running out of his open beak
and onto the white sand.

"*Bueno*," he said, "I owe you eighty bucks."

"Lemme give it to heem," Selena shouted, in an affected Mexican
accent, pressing her way through the crowd, climbing through the fence.

She wore leather sandals and a long white cotton dress with a silver
medallion round her neck. On the medallion were engraved a snake,
an eagle, and a cactus plant. She looked like some kind of vision from
another era, some savage time long before the white man's arrival out
here on this flat dry plain by the river.

"Naw," Aguilar said, "*lo debo yo*."

"I wanna do eet," she said . . . and Aguilar shut right up. No one
in the crowd said a word. There was something about Selena, some
energy that flowed from inside her, that demanded total attention.
Part of it was her eyes. They were not the same eyes that Jay Jay had
known and loved as a boy. There was something new there, a self-
awareness and brilliance and excitement that were truly ferocious. But
the thing that set them apart from all other eyes in the crowd was the
fact that they appeared to be illuminated from within, quite unnatu-
rally so, as if she had two little electric light bulbs wired up in her
head. The light was extremely powerful and shone all the way across
the ring. The quality of this light was impossible to describe. It was
. . . dark. The notion was hard for Jay Jay even to conceive of—dark
light. But that's what it was.

When Selena moved, every eyeball in the assemblage moved with
her. The air was absolutely static with her presence. Sand crackled
beneath her sandals like dry lightning. If poltergeists were to be sum-
moned, then she was the one to summon them.

"I don't give a shit who gives it to me," the Dootch said, attempting
a joke, "long as I get it."

But nobody laughed.

Jay Jay cowered among the crowd.

Selena had the money in her hand. He remembered that hand. It
was very long and narrow. On its back side the brown hairless skin was
transparent, and you could see her pale blue veins.

She stepped up to the Dootch, trembling with excitement. Involuntarily, he took a short step backward. She looked him in the face disdainfully. He could not confront her gaze.

She became more and more agitated. Her face contorted with loathing. She clasped the money in her fingers so tightly they went gray. She appeared to be holding her breath. Her eyes bulged out of her head.

"Here is your money, gringo!" she said.

But Bruno still wouldn't look at her.

"Go on and take it, gringo!" she said, holding out her hand.

It was an impossibly long and *dramático* moment. She had designed it that way.

Everyone knew about the Dootch's temper and wondered what he would do. At first it looked like he might haul off and hit her in the mouth. Then it appeared that he might actually take money from a woman.

"*Toma*, gringo!" she said venomously, shaking it in front of his nose.

At last the Dootch reached out, smiling but shifty-eyed, and accepted his winnings.

Selena laughed once, staccato, "Ha!" then turned on her heel and left him standing alone in the ring.

"*Viva la raza!*" someone yelled. And the Mexicans headed triumphantly for the cars, with their heroine at their head.

Jay Jay slumped down among the Okies and hid from her till she was gone.

Bruno was so pissed off he didn't say a word all the way home. Then, just as they pulled in the 'Ducci driveway, he stopped his pickup truck by the mailbox, turned to his son, and said, "Goddamnit, that's what I was trying to tell you on the way over."

"I'm sorry, Dad."

"She's here with that little cousin of hers. They been over there in Southside for quite some time, I hear, on the q.t. Say they want to register voters, get one of them elected to the City Council. But I know better."

"Yeah," Jay Jay said, almost sadly, "they definitely got other things on their minds."

"Now I tell you, Jay Jay, they stir up some shit in the field this year and I'm gonna lose my ass. Too much late rain. Small enough crop as it is. And I bought that fuckin' new section . . ."

"That's the way I see it, Dad."

"So what am I gonna do?"

"Damned if I know," Jay Jay said, stroking his jaw. And then, an instant later: "Range."

"Huh?"

"Range. Maybe you got a job for him after all."

"Hey!" Bruno said, smacking the wheel with the flat of his hand. "But your mother ain't gonna like it."

"I'll handle her."

"How?"

"I'll make her see there's no other way."

"She told me she never wanted to lay eyes on that kid again."

"She won't have to," Jay Jay said. "You'll just keep him on for this one job, Dad. Then you'll show him the road."

"Goddamnit, son," Bruno said, grinning broadly, slugging him softly on the shoulder, "I knew there was some reason I sent you to college!"

Eleven

A F RISCO MORNING in late July. Colder than a witch's tit. Drizzle over Bayshore yard. Gray wind. A whiff of burnt coffee from the Hills Bros. plant. And diesel oil. Salt sea. The look of gritty factories. Telephone poles. Electrical wires. Smokestacks. Drawbridges. Drydocks. The superstructures of container ships and naval destroyers.

Everything just as Range remembered it. Behind the Southern Pacific yard office, across the tracks, a view of that fateful SP employees parking lot that he knew so well.

Standing on the passenger platform at Third and Townsend, waiting for the San Joaquin *Daylight* to pull in, Range was so fucking excited that his stomach was going acidic on him, threatening to bring up last night's final carouse with Desiree Bartlow. He popped a Tums to settle things down. It was the first day of his new job. And his second day of freedom.

"Say, how come you don't take the Greyhound?" Desiree wanted to know in their motel room this morning. "Nobody takes the train no more."

"I dig the train," he said.

In his head much of Range's life was tied up with the railroad. All through his childhood he had dreamed of a career as a brakeman on the SP. And even though he hadn't laid an eye on his old man in sixteen years, didn't know where he was or even if he was alive, he could still sing from memory the words of his corny song, *"Life Is like a Railroad Train."*

The *Daylight* pulled in and screeched to a stop. The conductor cried out "All aboard!" and swung his lantern. Range climbed on with his duffel bag flopped over his shoulder and found himself a seat near the window. It was a scruffy seat, with cotton stuffing coming out and gum stuck to the arm rests, but he paid it no mind. The train eased out of the station and headed down the main line. Range was observing the caboose park across the rail yard. He checked all down a long line of SP cabooses for number 4337, his dad's old caboose, but he couldn't find it. Maybe it was laying over in Calmento today. Or maybe they had finally retired it from service.

One time when Delano was down out and in San Francisco, after a disastrous dope run to Mazatlán, he had snuck into this same Bayshore yard on a rainy night and cracked his dad's old caboose for shelter and

read the daily report on the desk and was absolutely shit-faced to discover that the conductor was Mike the Irishman, who used to be rear
brakeman with his dad. Feverishly Delano had searched through Mike's
things, his clothes, waybills, fusees. In a way, he was pretending they
were his father's things. In the pocket of an old rain slicker he found
a ten-dollar bill. He hated to take it, but slipped it into his wallet just
the same. In the morning, just before he caught a fast freight for
San Luis Obispo, he wrote Mike a note:

> Dear Mike:
> Sorry I had to do you like this but I am hungry. Soon as I get
> back on my feet I will reimburse.
>
>   Yours truly,
>   An Old Friend

Now, the first thing Range wanted to do when he got to Calmento
was make good on his word.

The train pissed along, stirring up swirls of seagulls from the tracks.
Over the salt flats of the Visitacion Valley to Brisbane and South City.
Down along the foggy forested suburbs of the peninsula to Menlo-
Atherton. Now east across the muddy south end of the Bay on a long
landfill and rickety trestle bridge. Just as they reached the end of the bay,
on the red iodized salt farms of Fremont, the train tunneled out of the
overcast into brilliant sunlight. Rays invaded the half-empty passenger
car, making everyone look peaked. Over his shoulder Range could see
the billowing ominous mass of fog: a great frothy tidal wave, sweeeeeep-
ing in off the Pacific, rolling over the Coast Range, tumbling down on
the tranquil bay.

His heart like a watchtower M-16, going like mad. Here he was now,
heading back to the only place in the world he could call home. And
the lonesome whistle of the train. The ties going by just a *clackety-clack*.

Now they were winding into the hills of the Diablo Range. Smooth,
round yellow hills, hills like the humps of camels . . . stands of oak
and buckeye in the arroyos. Now they were rattling up into steep rocky
Niles Canyon. Across the sere Livermore Valley. Over the treeless Altamont Pass. The sun getting hotter and hotter all the while, the sky
getting whiter and whiter.

From the top of the Altamont, where the air was so dry, the sun so
hot, that the grass was bleached silver-white and the Herefords never
strayed a mile from their trucked-in water, Range could look down
three thousand feet and survey his native valley all spread out before
him like a green and brown crisscross quilt on a gigantic well-made bed.
The sky was absolutely opaque now, a hot white dome, the roof of an
enormous geodesic greenhouse.

At the edge of this colossal fucking valley, four miles from where
the irrigated lands ran into the yellow hills, there was a large agglomera-
tion of buildings, houses, streets, water towers, grain elevators, a junc-

tion of roads and freeways, railway lines and hydroelectric power lines, rivers and canals. That was Calmento, the town that his great-great-grandpa had laid down:

CALMENTO
AGRICULTURAL CENTER
AND TRANSPORTATION HUB
OF THE GREAT CENTRAL VALLEY
POPULATION 10,000
"NOT JUST ANOTHER WIDE SPOT IN THE ROAD"
WATCH US GROW

It was a two-hour journey from chill, civilized San Francisco, but it might have existed in another world.

In Frisco the SP was discreet. It slipped into town at Bayshore and Mission yards and you barely noticed it amid the industrial gnarl. In Calmento, however, the railroad was the whole show, the be-all and end-all, the raison d'être. It sliced the town into two unequal pieces of cake: Northside and Southside, gringo and Mex. Nowhere were you ever out of the sound of the freight yard, the whistle, clatter, roar, and bang of the train.

Range's train stopped only a minute in Calmento and then it wailed off toward Fresno and Bakersfield, leaving him standing alone on the platform. As soon as he hit the asphalt he started to sweat. He sweat veritable rivulets down his neck and forehead, into his eyeballs. Peeked into the waiting room, but it seemed hotter than outside. Dragged over and set his duffel bag down in the shade. A thermometer on the station read 93 degrees Fahrenheit: a cool summer morn for the San Joaquin. Swabbed his face with a hanky, and it came up black as coal.

Plopped his ass down on a bench and endeavored to program his next move. No one on the platform to intrude upon his reflections. Out on the white hot yard a switch engine went by, hissing. A telegraph was bleeping somewhere inside. He raised his buttock carefully off the bench and let a slow evil poop. He was feeling distracted. Instructions on the telephone had been vague, to say the least: "I want you to come over on Sunday, 'cause that's when they're gonna be having their big celebration."

"What celebration?"

"A big fiesta, they're having. So, you just come on over, *bimbo*. Then, first chance you get, join up. Then play it by ear. Understand?"

"By ear?"

"Why sure."

"All right," he had said. But now that he was actually on the scene, sweltering in the heat, "playing it by ear" seemed a much tougher gig than it had in the city. The fiesta did not happen till tonight. That gave him a whole day to snuff.

Though he had left Desiree this morning without regret, without any intention of ever seeing her again, he was already starting to miss her. "Call me first chance you get," she had pleaded. "Sure, sure," he had said. And now he actually wanted to do it. What would he say to her? I'd rather suck your tits than fuck you? That was the truth. Her cunt had incisors, her womb a digestive tract. But her tits were magnificent. And when he flopped them over his dork and fucked her in the ribcage, he never failed to get off.

Slumped, wilted, Range sat for a long time on the shady side of the railroad platform. The acid of early morning had eaten all his excitement away. Now it was coming out as depression, a gassy bad-breathed nervous depression.

Not five blocks from this action lived the mother of his father, his own grandma. He even recalled her address: 143 Bervedor Street. The color of her crib: white with neat green trim. She would not like to hear his story.

In his memory Calmento had once loomed so large! Now it seemed such a tacky, dungy little place, sitting out here on this windswept plain, baking in the sun. When he was growing up, the town had been his very definition of reality. Now it was fucking with his mind: He was overcome with a strange feeling of unreality. It seemed suddenly like a toy town, a make-believe town. The station was merely a movie set for *High Noon,* or *The 3:10 to Yuma.* The narrow two-story Victorian buildings along the tracks were merely facades held up by braceboards, with nothing but weedy vacant lots behind. Up until Range left town eight years ago the realm of possibility had always seemed extremely limited and rigidly defined in Calmento. Now anything seemed possible, any weirdness.

But it was always like this when he hit the street. Always felt a little bit . . . frightened. It was spacy in the free world. So many fucking decisions to make, so many ways to go. And any one of them might prove fatal. In the Joint there was only one way to go, and everything was covered, everything was solid and real. There were no surprises, not in the physical routine, and not in human relations. If a cat was bad, he acted bad. If he was skippy, he acted it. In the Joint you got to know a dude. You knew him by his jacket, his rep, and his actions on the yard and in the block. You knew him overnight (his dossier was a matter of public record, and preceded him into the slam by mail and mouth). But on the outside, you never knew what a cat might do. Nothing was certain, nothing was clear. It was enough to give you the heebie-jeebies, when you first got out. So many fucking crazies running around. Inside there were crazies too. But they were identifiable. On the street you just never knew. Never. Not even about your own self.

The sun, glowing like a great motel heat lamp through thick safety glass, rode west along the rails till it lined up directly over the boxcars in the yard. A scorching wind sprang up, blowing white dust and the sound of Mexican ranchero music from the cantinas across the tracks.

Winos sluffed by, dropping their empty bottles, shattering them on the gray and white gravel between the ties. Switchmen rode by on the tops of boxcars, making up trains. Off-duty workers strolled by, headed for the yard office: tall Okie trainmen in bibbed overalls and black and white striped caps, Chicano hostlers, roundhouse helpers and gandy dancers in suntan pants and straw sombreros. Trains went by (men he remembered they were called, in railroad slang), hotshot cross-country freight men, deadhead special men filled with train crews, long yellow reefer men loaded with fruit and veggies for the city. A military man loaded with tanks, trucks, ammo, and chemicals for Viet Nam. Local men with gangs of hoboes and wetbacks riding on empty flatcars, taking the breeze. Every time one of them men went by, Range got a blast of hot dry air.

Then for an hour or so he closed up shop. It was not an unnatural state for him. All his life, ever since he was a little kid, he had gone through periods like this. The machinery of his brain would just shut down and go numb for a while. At school they had called it willful inattention and sent him to the principal. At the Vanducci place they had called it daydreaming and poked fun at him and snapped their fingers in his face. In the Joint nobody bothered him about it. They all did the same thing.

When Range came to again, he occupied his mind by trying to determine his next move. First he figured the best thing to do would be to check into a cheap railroad hotel, have a quick douche, change into some different threads, and get rid of the duffel bag. Then he decided the best plan would be just to show up at the door of the Calmento Community Action Committee all scruffy and sweaty, with his duffel bag over his shoulder. It would be a good psychological ploy that way. It would be self-evident that he'd just hit town. Selena would not be able to turn him down.

After he'd thought things out that way, Range hoisted his duffel bag up onto his shoulder and made his way over the railroad tracks. When he got to Southside, he followed a line of gaudily painted clapboard and cinderblock cantinas till he came to number 109 Fourth Street, which was the address he had for Selena. Potholed and treeless, Fourth Street fronted on the rail yard. At this time of the early afternoon it emitted nothing but the most forlorn of vibrations: amplified ranchero music.

The message got to Range. Stopped him for a moment cold in his tracks. Memories of Mexican Town bubbled up out of his blood and almost overwhelmed him. And for an instant he was tempted to walk down to Mount Diablo Avenue and visit the old Range place, his old house. Then he remembered that it had never been rebuilt. Last time he heard, it was still just a blackened hulk on the edge of the tomato fields.

CCAC headquarters was an old unpainted two-story wooden building with a steep green tarpaper roof and a rectangular false front. A vacant lot lay beside it, littered with beer cans and broken wine bottles. Across the side of the house someone had painted a huge mural in the popular Chicano street style. Yellow, green, and red were the predominant colors. The style was Rivera-like, monumental, elemental, with massive crude figures of dark sweating campesinos, fat white gringos with cigars stuck in their mouths, and the inevitable Aztec god in his loincloth and parrot feather headdress, with a swooning Mexican princess in his arms. And the eagle on the cactus plant on the rock in the lake, with the snake in its beak, under the two snowcapped mountains, Ixtaccihuatl and Popocatepetl. Above the mural, stretching the whole length of the building, was printed a slogan: EL PUEBLO UNIDO JAMAS SERÁ VENCIDO. Below the mural the same slogan was printed in English: THE PEOPLE UNITED WILL NEVER BE DEFEATED. A vandal had thrown white paint against the building, partially obscuring the mural.

The front of headquarters was plastered with Chicano propaganda: VIVA LA CAUSA! VIVA LA HUELGA EN EL FIL! ALMA CHICANA/CHICANO SOUL. VIVA LA RAZA UNIDA! BROWN POWER DE LA VALLEY. PODER PACHUCO!

Someone had tacked a card to the door:

CALMENTO COMMUNITY ACTION COMMITTEE
Selena Cruz, Chairperson
Victorino Aguilar, Secretary
Consuelo Pescadero, Treasurer

A few steps down the cracked grassy sidewalk was a large display window. A sign in brown letters ran across the top: SOMOS LA RAZA SANTA DE AZTLÁN, SOMOS LOS NIÑOS DEL QUINTO SOL. Across the bottom it was written in English: WE ARE THE SACRED RACE OF AZTLÁN, WE ARE THE CHILDREN OF THE FIFTH SUN.

A beat-out Pontiac was parked at the curb. Down the street, in front of a dilapidated building with BAÑOS 50¢ printed on the side, was a cream-colored Calmento Police Department squad car with a tall young policeman leaning on the fender.

Range peeked in the display window to see if anybody was home. The office inside consisted of a desk, several fold-up chairs, three telephones, an old mimeograph machine, a long table, and a wall full of posters of Che Guevara, Cesar Chavez, Fidel Castro, Reis Tijerina, Benito Juarez, and Pancho Villa. The office appeared to be empty. In the window some dusty paperbacks were displayed. Among them he noticed: Pocho, by José Antonio Villareal; Chicano, by Richard Vásquez, Huelga, by Eugene Nelson; Sal Si Puedes, by Peter Mathiessen; and The Labyrinth of Solitude, by Octavio Paz. Above the paperbacks hung a picture of a somber mustachioed Mexican in charro gear, pistolas, and crossed bandaleros, with the quotation:

The land belongs to everyone,
like the air, the water, the
light and the heat of the sun;
and all who work the land with
their own hands have a right
to it . . .

EMILIANO ZAPATA

Range stood there stupidly, staring at Zapata, too shy to knock at the door. The duffel bag was getting heavy. He was sweating profusely. The cop was staring at him from down the street. He didn't know what to do, whether to split or what. He wondered if the cop knew who he was.

Just then he heard a noise. Squinted through the display window and saw someone come out from the back room. She was a small, dark-skinned Chicana with an Afro that billowed out a foot above her face. She had a funny-looking bod. It was neither fat nor thin, round nor angular. It was . . . tubular, with a small head, short thick neck, small shoulders and breasts, short arms, large waist, small hips, wide thighs and calves, and tiny feet. There was something streamlined and almost . . . nautical about her. She was built like a submarine torpedo, all curveless geometry from shoulder to toes. Yet she was not at all slick or speedy in her movements. On the contrary, she seemed rather calm, slow, and precise, and appeared to reflect seriously before committing herself to any action.

She had not noticed Range in her window. She sat down at the desk, picked up one of the telephones, and dialed. Range set his bag down by the door and knocked. All at once he felt very confident. Who was this fucking broad, anyway? Just some chick from the barrio. He shoved the door but it wouldn't open. He knocked again.

"Just a moment, please!" she called. There was an impressive authority and self-possession in her tone.

Range leaned against the door, waiting in the sun. His own self-assurance had disappeared as suddenly as it had appeared. He felt weak, tired, and a little dizzy. It occurred to him that he hadn't eaten in hours.

Knocked again.

"Just a moment, I said!"

She had very careful diction, like someone who'd undergone a strenuous and long-term course in self-improvement. He was familiar with the type. The Joint was loaded with them. An "idealist" she probably called herself, when all she was really looking for was a piece of the pie.

To Range her jacket was nothing but cunt.

He considered just wheeling around, walking back across the tracks to Northside, and checking into a hotel. But the thought of the heat, the distance, and his heavy duffel bag finally dissuaded him.

Eventually she opened the door. She did it so suddenly that Range almost fell down.

"Yes?"

She was dressed in a pair of men's desert boots, baggy army fatigue pants, and a white sweatshirt with WE WILL NOT BE CO-OPTED; WE WANT IT ALL, printed across the front in fiery red letters.

Up close the Chicana's face seemed vaguely familiar to him. Her wide flat nose looked like it had been shaped by a difficult feet-first birth. It angled sharply upward from the bottom, pulling her tiny round mouth with it, permanently exposing her two front teeth, giving her a look of youthful athletic good humor.

It was Connie the Trout, eight years older, eight years reduced and dezitted and politicized.

They had recognized each other almost instantly, but pretended they didn't. It was an automatic reaction, the result of an instinctive mistrust.

"Hi there," he said. "Is Selena in?"

"I'm afraid not," she said. Her voice was deeper than he remembered, and resonant with self-confidence. Its flat ill-humor belied her looks.

"You know when she'll be back?"

"No."

"Hey, well dig it, I'm an old amigo. Just got out of the Joint. Just hit town. And I was wondering, could I leave the duffel bag here?"

She chewed her lip for a long moment and then reluctantly opened the door.

"Put it over there by the desk."

Range slipped past her and dropped his bag on the green linoleum. It was pleasantly cool inside. An old water-cooler rattled away in the corner.

La Trucha hung in the doorway, itching to send him on his way. But he was in no hurry to go back out into that heat. Along the eastern wall of the office there was a large table full of Chicano propaganda—magazines, pamphlets, newspapers: *El Grito del Norte, El Malcriado*. . . . He browsed through them for a moment, then looked up.

"Hey, you mind if I leaf through this stuff for a few minutes?"

"Why?"

"Well, it's interesting. I might wanna take some with me."

"Help yourself," she said. And slammed the door behind her. Walked over and plopped at her desk.

All the time that Range ran his scam, La Trucha just sat there eyeballing him—*I got your number, chum*, said her eyes—drumming her fingers on the desk, trying to make him uptight enough to split. But Range, he would have none of her shit. A great resistance was building inside him now, a sense of almost . . . moral outrage. Who did this fishy-looking cunt think she was, anyway? She was here at CCAC to organize people, wasn't she? That's what her propaganda said. Well, goddamnit, Range was people. Born and bred in Southside.

"Hey then listen, baby," he said, jiving extra heavy for the bitch, "you don't know where I could pick up on Selena, do you?"

"No."

"She gonna make the fiesta tonight?"

Reluctantly La Trucha had to cop to the fact that Selena would indeed be at the fiesta, that it would be held at the Southside Improvement Association's Community Hall, which was located in an abandoned Chinese grocery store on Mount Diablo Avenue.

"Gee, thanks for the poop, dear," Range said, keeping his voice very very sincere. "Say, you wouldn't mind if I hung out here till then, would you? See, I don't have no place to go."

La Trucha looked like he might have just shoved a pencil up her ass. With all her heart she wanted to say, "Negative." Her face pinched up with distaste. She ducked the issue for long moments, hoping Range would take a hint. Her animosity was as virulent as his own. Their pretense that they were strangers to each other, which had begun in distrust, embarrassment, and a kind of tacit understanding, was now impelling them into uncharted zones, and it would soon be too late for even a rapid and expedient "reacquaintance" to get them back on course.

"I got a lot of work to do."

"Won't be no trouble."

Finally she forced a smile and said, "Sure."

"Gee, thanks. I really appreciate this," Range said, walking toward the desk with his palm outstretched. "Delano Range is my name."

"A pleasure," she said, as if she'd never laid eyes on him before. "I'm Connie Pescadero."

"Real good to meet you, Connie," Range said, pumping her hand. A hard callused hand, used to men's work. "I think we used to work together at the 'Ducci shed, way back when."

"Maybe," she said. "And now if you'll excuse me, I have work to do."

"Hey baby, go 'head an' do yo thang," Range said, and collected a pile of propaganda from the table and sat down on the floor near Connie's desk to study it. *Too near.* She immediately started fidgeting, stamping her feet under the desk, going through drawers, searching nervously through stacks of papers, forgetting what she was about. While Range just hunkered down there happily on the linoleum, whistling through his teeth "Sergeant Pepper's Lonely Hearts Club Band," and other numbers, reveling in the havoc he was creating in this ill-tempered bitch's anal-retentive life.

The phone rang. La Trucha looked relieved to have something to do. The caller was from a local liquor store. Desired to know how many cases of beer would be needed for tonight. But the cunt couldn't make up her mind. Futzed about, telling the dude one thing and then another. Finally she must have pissed the cat off.

"I don't have to take that kind of talk from you!" she yelled into the phone and hung up.

But this bitch, she was fly. She was the kind who could never abide by her own decisions. Immediately jingled the jobber back again and apologized profusely and embarrassedly and told him to use his own judgment and bring as many cases of beer as he saw fit.

The phone rang every few minutes after that. Most of the calls had to do with arrangements for the fiesta. In the middle of one call, Range looked up and whispered conspiratorially, "Say, babe, you wouldn't happen to have a shower here, would you? My pits are ridiculous."

La Trucha clapped her stubby flipper over the phone and, trying valiantly to contain her temper, said, "Just a minute. I'll have to show you where it is."

After that, Range figured he had her number: On a gut level she hated people, hated doing things for them, hated being around them. On an abstract philosophical level she knew she was supposed to dig them, hang out with them, be good to them, help them out any way she could. Through sheer force of will La Trucha had been able to overcome her natural misanthropy. You could therefore trust her to put on a sour face, go against her nature, and be a nice broad.

Once Range had her down like that, he figured he'd be able to lead the cunt around like a pussy on a string.

After his shower, he went down and asked if he could raid the fridge. Even had the chops to ask if he couldn't use her bed for a nappy-poo. Made it a point to fall out wet and naked and get it all sweaty and mussed up, and drop cookie crumbs and pubic hairs all over the sheet.

All the time he was resting there, alone in the large air-cooled loft, he was thinking: *Goddamn, I'm the Man!*

Copped a gander out the front window. The cream-colored cop car was still parked on the street.

Later he checked the accommodations and dug that Selena slept alone.

. . . And went through La Trucha's things. All he found was a five-dollar bill and a partially completed letter to Cesar Chavez:

Dear Cesar:
I am worried about Selena. It was a mistake to let her talk me into coming here. Her motives are so obvious, so pathetic. They diminish her: she has her own private reasons for hating the local growers, especially one family. Such a tragedy, to waste someone of her unique talents in some blind goose chase in Calmento, California. . . .

Range snaffled the five out of pure reflex, but he left the letter in the pocket where he found it.

When it was time to leave for the fiesta, he went downstairs and said, "Say, Connie, do you mind if I tag along with you?"

Swallowing her bile, the bitch said, "Not at all, not at all."

They drove over in her Pontiac, the cop car trailing along behind.

"They always follow you, like this?"

"Usually they try to stick with Selena. But sometimes she can ditch them."

"They ever hassle you?"

"Are you serious?"

"What do they do?"

"Hit us with phony traffic tickets, make up excuses to search our head-quarters, slap us with fake building code and fire code violations, let high school kids and rednecks from the Posse Vigilantus harass us—"

"How?"

"Huh?"

"How exactly do they harass you?"

"*Caaaaaabrón,* how don't they? I mean, every day some *chingazo* tosses a rock through a window or defaces a mural or beats up on one of our organizers or runs one of us off the road or fires a twenty-two through a window— One time some bastard even sawed through the steering rod of one of our organizer's cars. Nearly got him killed."

"Gee, that is too bad," Range said sarcastically, wondering why he was driven, in opposition to his own interests, to such incredible lengths of antagonism. Cool it, man, he told himself. But he found it difficult. There is something phony and slimy about this bitch, he told himself. When he knew it to be quite untrue. And one would have to go miles, all the way to Berkeley or Salinas, to find another young woman as dedicated as she. The truth was this: In his heart he detested her for achieving such a remarkable self-improvement. If she had stayed her old fat, pimply, ignorant, unhappy, gum-chewing self he would have probably responded to her immediately, in his old friendly condescending way.

The doorway of the Community Hall was blocked by a crowd of wild-looking chooks, *vatos locos*, the kind who used to be his arch-*enemigos* in high school, used to pick fights with him at football games and dances, used to call him a fucking paddy gabacho and try to kick his ass if they caught him alone at Tracy's Drive-In. Even now the sight of their oily acne-scarred satchels, their mud-colored skin, their coarse billowing shoulder-length hair, their hard squat little bods, was enough to send a chill up his spine: He'd had run-ins with their elder brothers in the Joint. And those tight black pants they wore, their white tank tops, four-inch platform shoes. The beads, chains, swastikas, shark's teeth, Aztec eagles around their necks. Home-drawn tattoos all over their shoulders, arms, and hands.

Bad as they looked, soon as the chooks spotted La Trucha they were all giggles, bowed and scraped like peons, and ushered the two of them into the hall. In this way Range dug that she was some kind of sacred cow around here, and he'd better watch his mouth.

They entered a narrow crowded lobby and marched up to a small table. Selena's mama Delia was sitting there, hawking tickets, stamping wrists with a CCAC rubber stamp. She looked the same as ever, fubsy as ever, five by five, cross-eyed, raven-haired.

"Hi, Mrs. Aguilar, 'member me? Delano Range, a friend of Selena's. Maybe you remember my mom. Rita Robles?"

"Rita Robles? Why . . . why sure I remember," she said, flashing her gold teeth. "Where you been, *muchacho?*"

"Been in prison, ma'am," he said, apologetically. He had detected a note of pity in her tone. Mrs. Aguilar recalled his evil unhappy mama, and his sad fate as a little boy. It warmed the cockles of his *corazón*, it did. All his years coming up in Calmento the un-*moreno* Delano had loved and expected this kind of sympathy as his due.

"Well, you know, I am so glad to see you back safe and sound," said Mrs. Aguilar, and clasped his hand warmly, patted his arm, and gave him a free ticket.

The dance floor was crowded with hundreds of laughing, gesturing, loud-talking Chicanos of all sizes, shapes, and ages. Skinny railroad men in white shirts, clean gray workpants, and narrow-brimmed cowboy hats. Stout prosperous cantina owners in summer-weight slacks, sport shirts, and white shoes. High school honchos in T-shirts, Levi's, and huaraches. Farm laborers in denim shirts, pressed khaki pants, straw hats, and thick mustaches. Slim pretty girls in halterless summer frocks and long black hair. Tomato-packing women in red bandannas. Fat perspiring matrons in pastel dresses, nylon stockings, white pumps, and high-piled hairdos.

Everyone hanging out on the dance floor, drinking beer and orange soda pop, eating tacos and frijoles out of paper plates. Dozens of swarthy children ran and played and squealed underfoot.

The stage was all done up in green, white, and reddish-orange paper streamers. Posters and banners hung all over the walls and rafters. VIVA LA CCAC! BRONZE POWER! PODER DE LA PLEBE! ABAJO LA TIRANIA DE CITY HALL!

A group of ten young Chicano students from Berkeley was onstage, singing and playing guitars. *"El Flor del Pueblo,"* a banner proclaimed them. Loudly they sang:

> *"Yo no le tengo miedo de nada*
> *A nada le tengo miedo yo*
> *Unos pierden y otros ganan*
> *Pero a mi no me gusta perder . . ."*

The boys were small, dark, and handsome, all duded out in white pants, white embroidered guayabera shirts and red kerchiefs. The girls were short, plump, brown and pretty, wearing long red Mexican skirts and white tunics with burlap peasant belts.

Range ditched Connie in the crowd and headed across the floor for the bar. All of a sudden it was grand being out of the slam again. The scene put him in mind of the Palomar Ballroom in Stockton when he was a high school kid and used to go to the Tito Puente and Perez Prado and Celia Cruz dances. All the Mexican-Indian faces were familiar and congenial to him . . . and the Aztec noses, the slanted eyes, the short stocky stature of the men, the sweet plumpness of the women, their large bosoms . . .

Suddenly Range was getting off just hanging out here with his own half-*raza*. His mouth watered when he smelled the jalapeña sauce and melted cheese, hot tamales, tortillas. . . . Flor del Pueblo sang *"El Quelite"* from the Mexican Revolution and brought tears to everyone's eyes:

> *"Al pie de un encino roble*
> *Me dió sueño y me dormí*
> *Me despertó un gallito*
> *Cantando qui-qui-ri-qui . . ."*

The bartender was a paunchy pachuco who hadn't dug the scene had changed since '59. A true vet from the old days, he sported a black Sir Guy shirt with white buttons, ducktail haircut, a greasy pimp curl, a sparse black mustache and a tattooed cross on the web of his right hand; a yellow cigarette hung out of the corner of his turned-down mouth. He looked a little bit like Johnny Hotnuts, a comedian on the stage of the Club Suck in T.J.

"Hey," he said, "ain't you Del Range?"

"Yeah."

"Chale, ese! Don't you 'member me, *cabrón?"*

"Lemme see . . ."

"Rudy, man, Rudy!"

"La Rata, goddamn; you have changed, *cuñado."*

"No lie. Long time no see, huh?"

"I'm hip."

"Nel, mano, where you been keeping?"

"Just got out of the Joint, bro."

"Welcome home, motherfucker," Rudy said, grinning. "I just done a two-year bit at the Presidio Stockade."

"No shit? What was the beef?"

"AWOL."

"Hey, that ain't much of a beef."

"Oh no?" Rudy said. "What if you go AWOL with the company commander's private car?"

"I dig," Range said, though in fact he still considered it a cheap beef. "Yeah," he said, "well, that definitely puts another light on the subject, *mano."*

Snickering, the two ex-cons went for skin across the bar. Then Rudy bought Range a Mexican beer and wouldn't hear of being paid. Range got the feeling that things were looking up. And he waited impatiently for the moment when he would meet Selena again.

Flor del Pueblo terminated their set with *"Viva la Bandera Roja,"* and a rousing rendition of *"Solidaridad Pa' Siempre"* to the tune of "Battle Hymn of the Republic." Then the leader raised his hands for *silencio* and announced that "*Nuestra compañera muy querida, La Palomita,*" had a few words to say . . . and an unbelievably foxy Selena Cruz appeared in the wings with her mother and father.

For a moment Range almost lost his breath, nearly chumped his smitty, she was so fucking fine. And yet, Selena's presence was such a matter of total impression that he couldn't really see her in any detail. If she'd had a pimple on her face, for instance, a flaw of any kind, it would have passed unnoticed. Later he would wonder if this too wasn't part of her genius. Tall and dark, long-haired and voluptuous, with the carriage of a queen, she tramped across the stage in high Mexican charro boots, a pair of tan Spanish riding culottes, a white embroidered cotton blouse and, clasped at her long neck with a silver broach, an exquisitely wrought gray Nahuatl shawl and tassels that she let fall behind her like a train.

She stood there for a long moment, flanked by her pudgy parents—Delia in a shapeless green dress, Aguilar in worn khaki pants and a broken-brim sombrero—holding their hands in her own, smiling at the crowd below.

While they stood there at the front of the stage, acknowledging the applause of the people, Rudy and Connie came out from the wings and pushed a large blackboard out behind them and left it near the curtain, so it could be seen by the audience. On the blackboard, in neat large block letters, was printed:

THIS IS THE EPIC OF THE RAZA SANTA, THE SACRED RACE OF AZTLÁN. THIS IS THE EPIC OF THE FIVE SUNS . . .

PRIMERO SOL: THE SUN OF EARTH AND NIGHT. BIRTH, GROWTH. MAN'S FECUND NATURE. SYMBOL: THE TIGER.

SEGUNDO SOL: THE SUN OF AIR AND WIND. INVENTION, CHANGE. MAN'S PROTEAN NATURE. SYMBOL: THE MONKEY.

TERCERO SOL: THE SUN OF FIRE AND RAIN. LIFE/DEATH. MAN'S ROUND OF EXISTENCE. SYMBOL: THE BIRD.

CUARTO SOL: THE SUN OF WATER. SUSTENANCE, FERTILIZATION. MAN'S SELF-SACRIFICE (WITH EACH CORN SEEDLING A FISH WAS SACRIFICED, WITH EACH HARVEST A HUMAN BEING WAS SACRIFICED). SYMBOL: THE FISH.

QUINTO SOL: THE SUN OF SPIRIT, BLOOD, VIBRANT LIFE, THE COHESION AND

CULMINATION OF ALL PRECED-
ING SUNS. MAN'S UNITY AND
BEAUTY AND CONTINUANCE.
SYMBOL: THE PLUMED SERPENT.

Then Selena began speaking very quietly in Spanish. "This is my mother; this is my father; here behind me are my brother and my cousin," she said. "I wanted them to be up here with me tonight because I am so very proud of them and perhaps there was a time in the past when I was not proud enough. Now before all the world I want to say I am proud to be their daughter, sister, cousin, proud to be a Mexican, a Chicana *de sangre pura, una mujer de la raza santa* . . ."

Selena's voice was hushed, breathy, rhythmic. The crowd strained to hear. Not a sound but her voice in all the hall. She swayed when she spoke, in time to her words. Her words came out like a paean, a joyous chant. Soon her audience began to sway back and forth along with her.

"I'm not going to talk to you of politics tonight," she said. "We've had enough of that for now. I'm going to talk to you of dreams, of myths, spirit, blood, earth, flesh, *raza*. . . . In the beginning this *raza* of yours and mine came out of the clay where you now stand. Do not believe the tales of stepping stones across Siberias, Aleutians, Alaskas. Our story is a long one, but it took place, and is still taking place, endlessly repeating itself, here in the land of Aztlán. There are and were four great suns before us," Selena said, turning to point at the blackboard. "We are the children of the fifth and final sun. We are the culmination and cohesion of all that came before us. Therefore, we grew out of this earth beneath our feet whose color we bear today, and we abided upon her for a thousand generations, under our benevolent Quinto Sol. . . .

"For this is the land of Aztlán and we are the people of the Fifth Sun, who by the rights of birth belong to this earth as it belongs to us. Sixteen hundred years ago we set out from this land on a great migration. The reason is lost in the mists of antiquity. Perhaps it was drought that sent us on our way, war, famine, a vision, or perhaps it was simply the will of Quetzalcoatl. Whatever the reason, we journeyed south for several generations, till we came to the land of Anáhuac. In that land, cradled in a valley beneath two great snowcapped mountains, was a lake. In the middle of the lake was a rock. On the rock grew a cactus plant. Beneath the cactus plant there lived a snake. On the day that we arrived on the shore of the lake, the snake crawled up and entwined itself around the cactus. An eagle dove from the sky, landed on the cactus, and took the snake in its beak. To our people this was a sign from God. And there in the lake we built our city, which we called Tenochtlitlán, which means "cactus upon a stone." In two hundred years our city was the greatest in all the world, greater than London, Paris, or Rome. Then out of the west a stranger came, a white man. He killed our king through treachery, raped our queen, ruined our city, and robbed us of our land. And from that day to this we have been landless peasants, in service to the *gachupín* and the gringo. Over the years, driven by hunger, we migrated back northward to the land of our origin. We rejoined our brothers from whom we had been separated for many generations. But here in Aztlán, just as in Tenochtitlán, we were a subjugated race in service to foreigners. Only now, after five hundred years of servitude, can there be heard a cry for freedom in the *corazón del pueblo del Quinto Sol*. Only now do we declare ourselves a free and sovereign people. Aztlán belongs to those who plant the seeds, water the fields, and gather the crops. It does not belong to the foreign gringos who exploit our land and destroy our culture. With our heart in our hands and our hands in the sacred southwestern soil of Aztlán, we declare the independence of our blood, our soul, our nation. We are Aztlán! The very minerals of this sacred soil flow within our veins. *Somos la raza santa de Aztlán,*" Selena keened. "*Somos la alma chicana. Por la raza todo, fuera de la raza nada! Ay!*"

The crowd broke out into a tremendous cheer. "*Viva la raza!*" they screamed at the top of their lungs. "*Viva la raza!*" The sound was deafening. The cinder-block walls of the hall simply would not contain it. Range put his hands over his ears. Even that wouldn't shut it out.

It was an astonishing scene. In the city he'd been cynical. "Hey," he'd said to his new employer over the phone, "what is it out there, anyway? Just a bunch of Pochos, doing the cha-cha-cha." But now that he'd actually arrived on the scene he could appreciate that some rather major changes had definitely gone down out here. Eight years ago Southside was one of the most conservative communities of one of the most conservative ethnic groups in the country. All week long they were down on their knees in the gringo Wop fields and all day Sunday they were down on their knees in the gringo Mick Church. "*A Dios gracias, tenemos lo que necesitamos.* Thank God we got what we need," was one of the phrases Range heard most often when he was a kid. Now here were these same fucking Mexicans, listening to radical speeches, radical songs, without batting an eye, digging them, in fact, singing along with Selena and Flor del Pueblo now, clapping in time to the music:

> *Viva la Revolución*
> *Viva nuestra asociación*
> *Viva la huelga en general*
> *Viva la huelga en el fil*
> *Viva la causa en la historia*
> *La raza llena de gloria*
> *La victoria va cumplir . . .*

It was some powerful fucking medicine that had been laid upon these poor ignorant greasers, to put them through such incredible changes.

And, even though Selena was brilliant, impressive, even intimidating, it couldn't *all* be her. Obviously, even before she made the scene with her cousin, these *hijos de la chingada* were ready and waiting, already primed. Who primed them? Cesar? Tijerina? Corky Gonzalez? Fidel? Che? The influence of Black Power maybe? Whatever it was, it was beeeeeeg, *mano*, beeeeeg. No wonder the Dootch was getting suspicious. Eight years ago these motherfuckers were nothing but small-time, small-minded, jealous-hearted, suspicious of change, anxious to get ahead, hot to suck the *gabacho*'s ass, toady up to the *patroncito*. Now everything had gone flip-flop. There was a *solidaridad* and heavy anti-gringismo among these *chingazos* that The Man must find downright alarming. After all, this wasn't some foreign country, where they were spouting this mumbo jumbo. It was right here in the USA. The Man didn't watch out, he'd have a whole fucking *revolución* on his hands down here in the Southwest, and a whole *raza* of *subversivos*, and a strike in the fields he would not fucking *believe*.

For the first time since Range accepted his new job, he dug exactly what it entailed.

Now that he dug it, he wasn't sure he wanted it.

But he did know one thing: He was not about to break the terms of his parole. He would definitely stick around and play out his hand. All he was holding was the gig and five a month. And his cards were not of the best. He had no idea how long he could hang with the bluff. But it did not matter awfully, since he personally had nothing to lose.

Flor del Pueblo struck up "De Colores," which was the song of the United Farm Workers and one of the most popular songs and catchiest melodies in the entire Chicano rep.

Everyone in the hall joined in the singing. Selena stood onstage between her relatives, holding hands and swaying to the music. The words of the song were very simple, very sentimental, very moving, *de colores*, *de colores*, about colors, the colors one sees in the fields of *primavera*, and the birds that return from afar and the chickens one sees in the farmyard and all the sounds they make, the cock with his *kee kee ree kee* and the hen with her *ka ka ra ka* and the little chicks with their *pio pio pio pio pi*, and then the refrain:

> Y *por eso los grandes amores*
> De muchos colores me gustan a mi
> Ye por eso los grandes amores
> De muchos colores me gustan a mi . . .

When the number was done, everyone including Range was reduced to tears. It was a beautiful song, no one could resist it. It would have melted the heart of even the great grape-eating *gabacho* himself: Richard M. Nixon.

Selena and her group exited, and a new band, a young long-haired Chicano rock *conjunto*, took their place. They dimmed the lights, cranked up some hot *salsa,* and everyone dried their tears and boogied down.

Selena showed at the bar with Aguilar and her mama, sat down, and began greeting well-wishers. Dozens of Chicanos, young and old, lined up to shake her hand, give her an *abrazito,* and bend her ear.

It took Range nearly an hour, but finally he got up the chops to stand in the receiving line. As he waited his turn, he got more and more uptight. Felt almost like he was some kind of assassin. Went on that trip. He was in line to blow her away. . . . The light was so dim there was no way she could recognize him till he was right up on top of her. How easy it would be to waste her, if anyone was ever so inclined. By the time Range reached the bar he was feeling almost protective toward her.

"Hey, Selena," he said, "how you been doin'?" And she nearly fell off her chair with surprise. Looked at him for a moment like she could not believe her own eyeballs, like he was some kind of fucking zombie or something that had just rolled out of the grave.

"Range . . . Range . . ." she stammers, trying to get her breath back, "is this really you?"

"In the flesh," he says, cockily but nervously, beating his chest *thump thump* as if to prove his own words.

"Oh, Del . . . ," she says, grasping his hands, starting to cry (her emotion is real, he determines; it is something far too spontaneous for dissimulation), "Del, you don't know how . . . how sorry . . . how I . . . I wondered . . . all these years."

"Were you really sorry?" he asks, awestruck himself now suddenly (the moment is stopped in time; everyone in the hall is looking at them, but they are looking only at each other). "Did you wonder?"

"Always," she says, wiping the tears from her eyes, "*siempre, siempre.*"

And then, in spite of his own profound emotion, Range finds himself playing his first card in Calmento (he plays his ace): "Maybe you did wonder," he says. "But not enough to pay the kid a visit when he was locked up for two long years in Preston."

"It wasn't that I didn't think of you, Del. . . . It was . . . it . . ."

"I know," he says, gently, generously, now that he can afford it.

"Do you?"

"Sure.".

"Will you forgive me?"

"Hey," he says, tossing it off as if he had not spent half his lifetime dreaming of exactly this moment, "it's automatic."

Then she smiles her magical smile and looks at him through those great wet dark eyes and leans down in front of all of her people and bestows a precious kiss upon his stubbled cheek, and he says, in the inadvertently surreptitious tones of a convict on the yard at San Quentin, "Say, could you let me stay at your place tonight, Selena? See, I got no place to go. . . ."

Twelve

"I THOUGHT Aztlán was in New Mexico someplace," Connie said.

"Aztlán is a place of spirit," Selena said. "I carry it around with me in my heart."

". . . And I thought the tiger was supposed to be a sterile sign in Aztec mythology."

"Well, I do admit to a certain amount of . . . poetic license," Selena said wryly.

"What you mean is that Aztlán is an illusion."

"Aztlán is what I make of it."

"And all this crap the other night about tigers and monkeys and birds?"

"And fish . . ."

"Yes . . . and *fish!*" La Trucha scoffed.

"All in a good cause."

"You're incredibly cynical, you know that?"

"Not really. I believe everything I say . . . at the moment I say it."

Just then the phone rang. Selena reached for it on the desk in front of her.

"Hello? Hello? Hello?"

She cupped her hand over the receiver.

"It's 'The Breather' again."

"Hang up on him."

"We are armed and dangerous!" Selena screamed into the phone. "And we will not be intimidated!"

"You reap what you sow," Connie said after Selena hung up.

"Oh, Connie, everything you say is such a cliché. And you always lay it down with such a solemn look, like you were the one who invented it. I mean, really. What are we supposed to do? Just lie here and take it?"

"There are worse things."

"You ought to go back to the United Farm Workers."

"Not a bad idea. That's where everyone else went: Chalie, Mary, Manny, Timmy, Cookie," she said, rubbing it in. "Even the Vargas brothers."

"What're you waiting for, then?"

"You."

"My work is here."

"You got to go where you can do the most good. They aren't ready yet, up here."

"Look how far we've come already."

"Yeah, look."

"We got the Vanducci packing shed workers in the palm of our hand."

"The shed!" Connie sneered. "He's only got two hundred Chicanos working in that shed. And most of them are natives of Southside, people you've known all your life. I'm talking about the field. The place where ninety percent of his employees work. I'm talking about his field workers, his campesinos, the people who count. What have you done with them?"

"All we need is a little more time . . ." Selena said, vaguely. She was lost in thought. Her cousin had just given her an idea.

Connie had ridiculed her success with the packing shed workers. But it was really quite a respectable achievement. Granted, the Dootch's wages were niggardly, his working conditions abominable, his fringe benefits nonexistent, and any self-respecting packing shed worker would have walked out on the job years ago. But there were other growers in Calmento who were even less generous. And none of his employees had ever had the temerity to complain. And certainly not one of them had ever spoken the word "union" aloud before. Also, Selena's subversion of the packing shed workers had been concluded in a remarkably short period of time. Moreover, it had been accomplished (not without a certain amount of carefully applied intimidation, veiled threats in obscure Pocho dialect), in *total secrecy*. And most important, it had been *one hundred percent effective*.

Unfortunately, however, Connie was justified in her derision of Selena's efforts in the field. The Vanducci campesinos had so far resisted all her most resourceful and imaginative attempts to organize them. In fact, the only field workers she had been able to organize, in all her weeks in Calmento, were her own closest relatives.

There was only one plus that she could point to, in her record in the field: Aguilar had managed to persuade or intimidate the campesinos into keeping Selena's recruiting efforts, and the identity of her recruiters, strictly to themselves.

The main reason the campesinos had resisted organization, Selena believed, was the fact that they were strangers in Calmento, strangers even to one another. They came from all over northern Mexico and the southwestern United States. They happened to be collected together here in San Joaquin County simply because of tomato season. They had no unity, no fellowship, no feeling of *raza*. In the field it was every man for himself and his own family. When the season was over, they would all go their separate ways.

Unlike the packing shed workers who had homes in Calmento

(humble though they might be), the field workers could not go on welfare or receive food stamps when the going got rough. Their only home was the road, and the field where they happened to be working at the moment. Many of them were illegal aliens, constantly on the run from *la migra*, the Immigration Service. The only thing that stood between the campesino and destruction was his own quick wits. He concentrated all his efforts on earning as much money as possible while the brief harvest season lasted. Everyone in the family worked: grandma, grandpa, mama, papa, the kids, even the baby. Each farm worker worried and fretted and plotted against his fellow employees, trying to figure out how he was going to feed and clothe his wife and children through all the long San Joaquin winter. For in winter there were no picking jobs. And the whole great valley closed down tight from the Ridge Route in the south to Shasta Lake in the north, lying under the rains and tule fogs till weeding time in March and April. This was the dreaded time of the year when many an imprudent fruit picker found himself homeless, hungry, jailed for vagrancy, shipped back across the border. And whole big Mexican families sheltered in pup tents, one-room labor shacks, abandoned automobiles, boxcars, stacks of tomato lugs, hibernating through all the long cold months of the rainy season on two hundred and fifty pounds of red beans and ten kilos of moldy tortillas.

Selena's idea was this: If by some diabolically clever ruse she could fool the Dootch into believing that his field workers were the ones who were organized for a strike, and his packing shed workers were still loyal, then maybe (and of course this was a giant maybe), maybe by some stroke of luck he could be provoked into summarily firing his field workers and putting scabs to work in their places.

It would be a perfectly natural and reasonable decision, under the circumstances. The Dootch might well attempt to defuse the "strike" in just such a manner, Selena thought.

Her great hope was that the field workers would be so infuriated by the injustice of their spurious dismissal (at the height of summer, when their short-termed earning power was greatest) that they could be goaded into throwing up a picket line around the Vanducci Ranch and joining with the packing shed workers to close down the entire 'Ducci operation.

Even if Selena's plan was only partly successful, she believed that she still had at least a fighting chance of winning the strike. Most of the real money in the tomato industry was earned by speculators and middlemen, fruit and produce men who lived in San Francisco, Chicago, and New York. The grower's profit margin was exceedingly slender. A week or two of agitation, subversion, dissension, and obstruction in and around his ranch and packing shed, and the Dootch would be hurting badly. And once he was hurt, and his tomatoes were beginning to rot on the vine, then maybe (and this was another of those great maybes that she had to take into account), maybe he could be persuaded to come to the bargaining table.

It was a fine strategy. Selena had plotted it all out step by step, link by link. The plan so far contained only one flaw, one gap in its chain of cause and effect.

How was she going to provoke the Dootch into making his first (and fatal) mistake?

"Time!" Connie was saying, sneering at her cousin again. "Time, you say! Listen, we are gonna need a hell of a lot more than that, *querida,* believe me."

"You got no faith, *prima,*" Selena said.

"Don't be funny," Connie said. "*Fawny,*" she pronounced it still, quite unconsciously, despite her four years in Berkeley. Selena found it rather endearing. "This could get hairy, here. Especially with these growers."

"I tell you what, Connie. I look on those growers as our ace in the hole."

"Sure you do."

"I mean it," Selena said. "It's like guerrilla warfare. Their strength is their greatest weakness. Everything they throw at me, I'm just going to take and use against them."

"*Ay caray!*" Connie said, shrugging her round little shoulders. "What am I going to do with you? . . . And now this Range character."

"What about him?"

"It doesn't add up."

"Why not?"

"Just too much coincidence that he shows up right at this time."

"Come off it," Selena said. "I've known him all his life."

"You've never known him as an adult. What's he been doing all this time?"

"He's been in prison, for God's sake. Do you think he's a cop?"

"All you know about that guy is what he wants to tell you."

"I like Del," Selena said. "He was always like . . . an outlaw. Like Rudy. I left Calmento, I discovered I was better off with the outlaws than with the straights."

"Selena, I admire your courage. But I can't say much for your common sense," Connie said, pacing up and down the office, taking short little choppy steps, staring into Che's face, Cesar's face, without seeing them. "Wouldn't mind so much, but a lot of people could get burned."

"No one's going to get burned. Delano is cool. And we can use him," Selena said. And the instant she said it, she knew that it must be true.

"It's a fatal flaw in you," Connie said. "Letting your personal feelings make your political decisions for you."

"Maybe so. But there's a word for it. It's called heart."

"It's called vanity," Connie said, and picked up her bag and went out the door without saying good-bye. She was bound for Berkeley to drum up support for the strike. But Selena had another reason for sending her there. What was needed in Calmento at this point was not Connie's tight ass. What was needed was a little mystery and audacity and sleight-of-hand.

Now, however, as she watched her cousin's funny little tubular frame disappear out the wings of her display window, Selena felt an almost heartbreaking pity and affection for her. And raced out the door and chased her down and grabbed her, spun her around on the cracked gray sidewalk.

"Oh, damnit, Connie, listen," she said. "*Te quiero, sabes?* And I will always stick by you, no matter what."

"Always?" she said doubtfully.

"*Promesa, promesa,*" Selena said in Spanish, which always seemed to make the promise more truthful. "*Promesa,*" she said again, while the Calmento cop in his squad car pretended to look the other way, and the tin cans and broken bottles in the vacant lot glared, and the sun beat down on their heads, and switch engines hooted by on the railroad tracks across the street.

"But you've got to trust me now, *querida,*" she said, using her most beguiling voice. "If you don't trust my common sense, then trust whatever it is that makes me what I am. . . . Trust my genie. Now, *buen viaje,* and good luck."

"Save it," Connie said, getting into the Pontiac. "You're the one who's gonna need it."

When she was gone Selena breathed a sigh of relief. Simultaneously she felt a stab of guilt and a thrill of naughty anticipation. It had been months since she last made love. And that had been a hasty, frustrating, almost pagan prebattle rite with a sex-crazed young half-Navajo named Manny "El Loco" García in a midnight Bugatti Brothers tomato field. Now she would be left alone with Delano for two whole nights in the loft. . . .

Naturally, Selena had her own doubts about Range. But she had been able to lay them aside. Selena had a tendency to see people in terms of symbols. People were never what they appeared to be. And the thing they symbolized hadn't necessarily any connection with any real qualities they might possess. . . . Thereby, she saw her mama as a symbol of resilience, Aguilar as a symbol of strength, Rudy as a symbol of resistance to oppression, Jovita and her little sister Rio as symbols of purity, Connie as a symbol of enlightened moderation, and herself as a symbol of hope for her *raza.* In a less remarkable person this tendency would have proven fatal. But Selena had an amazing record in making her symbols come to life, Connie herself being a prime example. And, already since Selena's return to Calmento her family and friends seemed to be getting bigger and better. And as long as she could keep puffing them up, she knew they would keep right on growing. On the other hand, she had no illusions about what would happen if she ever lost her breath.

In Selena's mind now the half-Chicano, half-gringo Delano Range had come to symbolize the whole struggle in Calmento. If she could win him, if she could "do a Pygmalion on him," as Lamoille Huffacker had done on her, then she believed she could win the town.

She owed him the transformation. It was a debt for her thoughtlessness in the past. . . . *He may not know it, but whatever I do will be strictly for his own good.*

Actually, she was fairly certain he was a spy of the Vanduccis. And she had not so much laid her suspicions of him aside as deferred them until they were resolved. And now she had just determined on a method of resolving them, in such a way as to kill two or three birds with one stone.

Range was the stone.

If she was wrong in her suspicions about him, she had nothing to lose. If she was right, she had everything to gain.

Range was the missing link.

Connie had been wrong about her cousin. Selena no longer allowed herself a private life, private loves. Everything she did, no matter how pleasurable it might incidentally turn out to be, had an ineluctable aim. Revolution was her aim. "Land to the Tiller" was her slogan. She felt herself to be a work of cosmic political art, with all her parts dedicated to perfecting the whole. The work was beautiful and harmonious, she believed, composed of balanced portions of dark and light forces, positive and negative charges. Thus, she was impelled by love, a love for the *raza* she loved more than herself. Thus, she was impelled equally by hate, and felt herself to be little more than a ticking time bomb up the ass of the landowning class.

Her motives were irrelevant to her. What would the campesinos care about her motives, when they had won the land that was rightfully theirs?

The Anglo mailman came walking down the street while Selena was still outside. He left her a letter. Someone had printed it crudely in heavy dark pencil, in an attempt to disguise the handwriting:

From: Field HQ   8 July 1970
Posse Vigilantus
Kalmento, Kalifornia

To: Ms. Selena Kruz
Arch-Kunt, KKAK

Dear Bitchdog:

We do hearby ASPERM our DEEZIRES to aid in yor ORGANZ. cuz we belive in yor work and in SPICKLOVERS all over state of Kalif. We belive in you the ARCHWHORE and in all yor little GREASERS CHOLOS MEX'S and we belive in yor DEEZIRES to FOX the pore KAWKAZIANS and KRISTIANS of Kalmento and to take over our lawful MENSTRUATIONS of this hear place with BEANFART-ERS FLIPS and NEEGARS (rimes with CEEGARS, case you did not know). We belive you will be KILT (shot, rapped, drawn & quartered—in jest what order we aint sure yet), if you do not git yor purty brown ASS out of town inside of 48 hours flat and we are wishing to help and see you make it safe. We belive in you, we want like you want to see this great nation turned over to KOMMUNISTS JEWS NEEGARS BLED-ING HEARTS DRAFT KARD BURNERS RAPPISTS MURDERS THIEFS CIVIL WRONGS AKTIVISTS EARL WARREN THE JEWNITED NATIONS CHARMIN MAO and old UNKLE FIDO KASTRATE so you may count on us. You are in danger of losing yor cute TITTIES to the KNIFE of JUSTICE and gitting them stuffed up yor little brown PUSSY. Leave yor door open tonight so's we can come over and help you OUT.

Yors Untruly,

Posse (Pussy) Vigilantus

An hour later Delano came in from a meeting with his parole officer in Stockton.

And the first thing Selena did was show him the letter.

"What's this shit?" he said.

"Oh, just the kind of thing we get around here every day."

"What're you showing it to me for?"

"Connie thinks you are one of them. Says she can spot a pig, and you look like one," she said, watching him very carefully. In eight years Range had changed amazingly little. After many months of imprison-ment, and Lord knew what else, his face was still without a line or blemish, his step light and springy. Apparently, the only scars he bore were the ones he'd acquired as a child. Really, the only change in his physical appearance was the bushy mustache he now affected, and his frizzy growing hair and beard. As for his character, it hadn't changed either, as far as she could tell. His behavior was still a mixture of bravado and bashfulness, self-love and self-contempt, and it was still difficult to predict when one or the other would be ascendant. In his dealings with Selena, he was still trying to get the best of two worlds: simul-taneously he attempted to evoke her pity and her admiration, alternately he played the orphan boy and the macho.

"You think I am a pig?" he asked, allowing a plaintive quality to creep into his voice. He had begun to sweat now, under her even gaze.

"What were you in prison for, Del?"

"Dope," he said, playing with the ring on his middle finger, a large Burmese star ruby in a hippie-made setting: a purple petrified rat pellet in a gilded volcano. Slipping it on, slipping it off . . . "Actually," he said, "it was just a minor altercation over a kilo of hash that turned into a shoot-out almost by mistake. I mean, if we hadn't been armed to the teeth, we would have come out of it with bloody noses or something. As it was I got nailed on a manslaughter beef. And it would've been a hell of a lot worse if I hadn't copped a plea. . . ."

"What all that means," Selena said, "is that you killed a man. Right?"

"Right."

"Wow."

"Yeah," he said, sniffing in a self-deprecatory manner. "Reason I got into so much trouble, since I last saw you, I had a man to support."

"Who's that?"

"Coke Jones," he said very seriously, taking himself very seriously. "Wanna hear the rest?"

"Naw, forget it," she said, smiling at him all of a sudden. "Most of the time Connie is full of it, anyway."

"Hey," he said, smiling back, rather uncertainly. "Hey, come on out and have a look at my new car."

He led her outside and showed her a beat-out chocolate brown Dodge Dart.

"Next to the Model A," he said, "these are the best cars ever made in this country. Can't get 'em to use any oil. And they are virtually indestructible. I had this one old Dart one time," he said, laughing at the memory, patting his car on the fender, "on a dope run from Sonoíta, Sonora. Supposed to be met in the mountains by three hippie backpackers who were gonna hike the stuff over the border. But nobody showed up. So, I just hunkered down in the Dart and drove her for two days up a dry riverbed in one hundred and fifteen degree heat till I crossed the border in the middle of the Gran Desierto. That fucking Dodge, going through quicksand, over boulders, across beds of spiny cactus a half-mile wide, the sonofabitch wouldn't even slow down, let alone heat up. I owe everything to that old car," he said, as fondly as if it had been a human being. "She saved my life. And she gave me my first start in business."

"Oh, yeah?" Selena said, trying to keep herself from laughing out loud.

"Yeah," Range said, proudly, blissfully unaware of her irony. "Not a bad buy for four bills," he said, patting its fender again, "huh?"

"Not bad at all," she said, allowing him his ease for the moment. Selena's experience with men was that, like Churchill's Germans, they were either at your feet or at your throat. She used a combination of flattery, intimidation, and brilliantly orchestrated surprise to keep them

at her feet. Her motto was *Siempre de Improviso*—"Always the Unexpected."

"Take me for a ride?" she asked.

"Where to?"

"Take me someplace where it's quiet. Where you used to park with
your girl friends," she said. Then she ran back into the office and got
her purse, a bottle of wine from the back room, and a bumper sticker
off the propaganda table. She made sure to lock the door behind her.

When she got into the car she said, "I deserve a leetle rest, no?"

"Rilly," he said.

"See what I put on your bumper?"

"Naw. What is it?"

"A slogan."

"What?"

"*Viva La Raza!*" she said, and he laughed and seemed genuinely
pleased. It occurred to her now that he might not have believed in his
heart that she would accept him as one of the *raza*. She decided she'd
never call him a gringo, *gabacho*, paddy, *pinta*, Anglo, or *bolillo* again,
even in fun. And why should she? She could still remember him when
he was a little curly-headed Chicanito and lived over here in Southside with his mama *muy morena*. He always looked so small and
frightened and lonely, so very cute. As a little girl she had envied his
light-olive *güero* skin with her whole soul. As a big girl she rather pitied
him.

In late afternoon light, black and white, Delano drove her out of
Southside. East on Sierra Avenue they went, under the long shadows
of eucalyptus trees, past the Mi Ranchito Market & Tortilleria, past El
Chico's, The Golden Taco Cafe, Our Lady of Guadalupe Recreation
Center, the Southside Improvement Association. In recent years the
people of Southside had made great attempts to spiffy up their barrio.
Many of the old clapboard houses had been painted bright colors:
turquoise with red trim, canary yellow with green trim, kelly green
with blue trim, mustard gold with purple trim. . . . And the trees
had grown taller, fuller, shadier, the gardens lusher, greener, full of
high-growing corn, sunflowers, cactus, rose trees, carnations, and oleander shrubs bearing masses of beautiful pink, white, crimson, and
purple flowers. Planter pots and bird cages with plastic parrots were
suspended from the crossbeams of front porches. Year-round Christmas
lights decorated the windows. And flags of Mexico and UFW black
eagles hung on the walls. . . . Yet, under all this contemporary veneer,
little in the barrio had really changed. The loafers in their straw
sombreros still sat around shooting the breeze on the metal pipe hitch-
ing rail in front of the Mi Ranchito Market. The pachucos and *vatos
locos* still sat on the sagging old davenport on the sidewalk in front of
El Chico's, in their undershirts and heavy gold crosses, beating the conga
drums and sipping wine. Low-riding Cheebies and battered pickup

trucks were still parked in all the driveways. Public buildings were still covered with graffiti: "*C/S*," "*La Clover y la Freeway are still in love*," "*Chooko City*," "*El Carnal del Candi y el Ponchi*," "*Mota Powa*," "*Rifa is my Weed*." Chickens and goats still roamed the yards and unpaved alleyways, horses whinnied over backyard fences.

Down MacArthur Road he drove her, over the Southern Pacific embankment. The Calmento cop car fell off their tail, and a San Joaquin County sheriff's car picked them up. Selena could see the face of the driver in the rearview mirror. So could Del. It was Donnie "Prettyboy" Pombo, the Portagee undersheriff of the Calmento substation. They both knew him well. They had all gone to high school together. At noon hour, Selena remembered, she used to see Del and Donnie sitting up in the gym together with Jay Jay Vanducci, Harry Fulcher, John Ammiratti, and Sammy Dog, eating their sack lunches and snickering at the girls passing by.

"Hey, Del," she said, "there's your old pal behind us."

"No pig is a pal of mine," he said, and Selena chose to believe him.

It was the first time since the cockfight that she'd been out of the city limits of Calmento.

"Turn on the radio, will you?" she said. And Del got on some schmaltzy Muzak-type music from Stockton, with lots of weepy violins and sentimental saxophones. "Perfect," she said, and lay her head back on the seat and relaxed for the first time in weeks. Suddenly she knew that whoever Delano was, whatever he had become, he would not hurt her, not her personally. She knew this absolutely. She got the vibrations right off his skin. It was positive. She had known him far too long to mistake it. With this knowledge at her disposal, Selena felt quite ready for any eventuality.

South they went, toward the burnt yellow hills of the Diablo Range, past modern ranch-style farmhouses with pine trees in the front yard, past the cemetery which had grown twice as large in the last eight years, past Mr. Passalaqua's alfalfa and bean fields, past the Dootch's tomato fields. Though Selena and Delano were now in the deep country, on a narrow blacktop county road, they were not by any means alone. Traffic was heavy. Giant semi trucks hauling trailerloads of sugar beets, bales of hay, boxes of fruit and vegetables, honked to be let by. Late model Cadillacs with radiotelephone antennas and American flag decals hurtled by. Carloads of sombreroed braceros went by, in old Fords with Mexican flags on their aerials and rosaries suspended from their rearview mirrors. Everywhere around her on the road and off Selena saw machines and metal devices. Tractors in the fields, little Farmalls and Fords, big John Deeres and International Harvesters, enormous Olivers and Caterpillars, pulling complicated farm equipment, kicking up dust that came out red now in the fading sun. Mobile homes parked on barren plots of land, camper attachments set up on blocks, pickups sitting in the driveways. Six-wheeler trucks out in the beet fields, loading directly from the mechanical harvesters. Great long tanks of butane and ammonia sitting in the farmyards. Aluminum roofs shining in the light . . . Now they reached the Western Pacific tracks, bumped over the high embankment. Delano turned and drove into the hamlet of Carbona, past the Banta-Carbona Irrigation District Office, past the Vanducci packing shed that they both knew so well. CAFONE BRAND FRESH-PACKED CALIFORNIA TOMATOES the sign still said out front. Past a Mexican labor camp painted turquoise blue. Past a big old wooden water tower. Past the WP station (an air-conditioned aluminum house trailer, pulled up by the side of the mainline track). East on Valpico Road they drove, past walnut orchards, almond orchards, peach orchards, tomato fields, vineyards. Houses were scattered around in the orchards, low modern houses. Along the road grew the ubiquitous oleanders, ten and twelve feet high. Oleander was in full bloom now, and the air reeked of it, bitter-sweet. Down to Chrisman Road they went, past the US Army's Calmento Defense Depot (an enclosed rectangular puzzle of khaki-painted warehouses with gigantic black numerals painted down their sides), to Durham Ferry Road. Now eastward again through Mr. Gallo's and Mr. Franzia's wine vineyards they went, through an automobile graveyard a half-mile square, down into the San Joaquin River bottomland now, floodland, covered with waist-high grass, tules, willows, cottonwoods, poplars, cattle grazing by the muddy river, the lifeblood of the valley. Over the corrugated metal drawbridge now, *clonk clonk clonk*, off the road going on a little dirt levee track, white sand track, white sand blowing, the sun going down behind the trees on the opposite bank . . .

Somewhere along the line they had left their sheriff tail behind.

Delano parked his little Dart on the high levee.

"Where you taking me?" she asked, in mock alarm.

"Come on," he said, "show you something."

She got out and followed him down the river side of the levee and into a willow thicket.

"What you got in that sack?"

"Got some wine."

"What?"

"Wiiiiiine!"

"Oh boy," he said, "long time since I been down to the river like this."

Selena followed him on a narrow sandy path through the trees. What she felt as they went down the levee was . . . all of a sudden . . . such a *girl*. She felt her light cotton summer dress swishing between her bare thighs. She felt her breasts heavy and full and bouncy. She felt her ankles slim, her feet small and pretty, her shoes too fragile for the rough country. It was a delicious feeling that no ideology could ever destroy. They followed the path till it came out on a perfect little curved white sand beach. Cottonwoods lined the bank here, and big oak trees. The river was low and dirty, only about a hundred feet across. The other bank was like a dark jungle, with vines and brambles and poison oak growing to the water's edge.

They sat on the sand. Selena spread her short dress carefully beneath her. Then she got a corkscrew out of her purse and opened the wine. She took a long quaff and handed it to Delano. He drank deeply and then plunked it into the sand between them. She picked it up, put it on the other side of her, scooted over till she was touching him, and kissed him on the earlobe.

"Mmmmmm, salty!"

She kissed him again, ran her fingers along his chest. She could feel his heart jumping under his T-shirt, and she thought, *If you got to have a spy, better a spy whose heart goes pitter-patter.* And yet at the same time there was something . . . sleepy about him, as if he'd been asleep for years and was just waking up. She liked his dark heavy-lidded eyes, his thin hard lips, his nervous preoccupied way of laughing, his slow complicated smile. The smile was the key to his character, she thought. *The world is slippery*, it said. *Things are never what they seem to be. They happen by accident. They change before your eyes. Deception is the rule. Everything is dangerous. No one knows what he's gonna do next. Trust no one, not even yourself.* She liked that about him. She felt just about the same way. Except she never let anything happen to her by accident. And she did trust herself . . . and maybe Connie, in a pinch. No. Not even Connie. Only herself.

"Not afraid of me, are you, Delano?"

"Maybe a little."

"Great big man like you?"

"You hurt my feelings once."

"That was when we were kids."

"I got a long memory."

"Why don't we just start all over from the beginning?"

"That's gonna be hard to do."

"I'll make you forget."

"Maybe," he said.

They sipped their wine for a spell, watching the last grip of bloody fingers slip around the Diablos and fall into the San Francisco night.

"How we gonna get back to the car with no light?"

"I know the way blindfolded."

"Is that right?"

"Sure. Been coming out here since I was a kid."

"Nice out here," she said, leaning on her hands, feeling the cool fine sand squeeze up through her open fingers.

"Body temperature."

"Yeah. Guess the mosquitoes will appear soon."

"They don't bother me."

"No? Eat me alive!"

"That is because you are so sweet."

"Thought you weren't interested."

"Never said that."

"This the place you used to bring girls, Delano, when you were in high school?"

"Naw," he said bashfully. "Jay Jay and us, we used to come out here and drink."

"Oh?" she said. "Pombo, too?"

"Prettyboy? Sure, most of the time."

"He's probably out there somewhere then, isn't he? Watching us . . ."

"Probably," Del said. "Do you mind?"

"Oh, not really," Selena said. "I guess you always wondered what happened."

"About what?"

"Between Jay Jay and me."

"Sort of," he said. "But then I had other things on my mind."

"Happened," she said, "is basically a very old story. . . . Knocked me up and split on me without so much as a word of explanation. Sent his dad over with some money instead. And . . . and I *took* it. Took it and ran away with Connie over to Berserkly," she said. "Hit town at probably the optimum moment in history. September 1964, when it all began. Fell in with some people, people whose names you would probably recognize, who wanted to change the world. I was in the same kind of mood. Maybe even a little angrier than the rest of them. 'Off the Pig!' seemed to make a lot of sense to me. Every time I heard it, I translated it into 'Off the 'Duccis!' "

Selena paused and laughed at herself. "Honestly, Del, in my heart I was nothing more than a little seduced and abandoned Catholic girl. Believe me, the ranks of the radicals are loaded with them. . . . Anyway, it took a very close friend, a very kind and gentle and intelligent man named Lamoille Huffacker, to make me see a lot of these things about myself, and the Movement, and to help me gain a little objectivity. After that I concentrated on the issues: Civil Rights, Free Speech, reform of the Multiversity . . . and then the war in Viet Nam, the *Raza*, the Farm Workers. Tried to keep as nonaligned and nonviolent as possible. Then, after I went down and worked with Cesar Chavez for a couple of years and watched the *policía* blow off a few innocent *compañeros*, I modified the nonviolence somewhat. That's when Cesar and I parted ways. He is a beautiful man, Del, one of the few really selfless people I have ever met. And I owe him a lot. But at the time I was too pissed off to care. Someday I will go to Cesar and I will tell him what I neglected to tell him when I left his union . . . that I love him. Anyhow," Selena said, chuckling to herself, "after that I got involved in a couple of Kamikaze attacks down in Fresno County—"

"Yeah," Range said. "I seen that on TV in the Joint."

"—and here I am," she said, and added, ". . . if it's ever that simple."

"Often wondered," he said. "How it all went down."

"Well, I made it, anyway."

"It was never in doubt."

"That's what you think."

"What I know."

"You don't know shit," she said. "But let's skip it. How 'bout you?"

"Me?" he said, sniffing again. "I don't know. With me it was touch and go for a while . . . in the Joint. And a couple of other times."

"What happened?"

"Well, in the Joint this big black blood with a taste for white meat got a yen for my ass. Caught me in the shower and pulled a shank and said, 'Fuck or die.' I knew I would rather die. Which I almost did. He got me under the arm, punctured my lung, missed my heart by a quarter inch. I blacked out and woke up in the infirmary. They asked me who did it but I couldn't tell. Would've gone worse for me on the yard. After that the blood left me alone. Said I'd paid my dues. Found another little honkey who looked just like me. . . . And then," Del said, "there was this other time, before I got locked up. In the Andes mountains, in Colombia. A coke run. Someone turned."

"That can be a problem."

"Yeah," he said, playing at understatement.

Men are so utterly transparent, Selena thought. And waited patiently for him to develop his little drama.

"Yeah," he said again. "Especially if you are holding thirty thou in cash. And it ain't the *policía* who is waiting in the mountains. . . . I'll tell you about it sometime."

"You do that," she said, smothering a grin. And then she sighed and said, "Well, at least here you are back in Calmento, Delano, safe and sound."

"That is exactly what your mother said."

"She did?" Selena said, laughing. "God, am I already beginning to sound like her?"

"Naw," he said, "but I wouldn't mind if you did. She's a nice lady."

"That's all you're looking for—a mother, isn't it?" she said, sarcastically, but he refused to hear her.

"Ain't it nice out here?" he said. "Listen to the river."

They listened to the San Joaquin for a long time. You could barely hear it over the sound of the crickets and electric irrigation pumps. It was a very low sucking sound, like water going out of an enormous tub. The mosquitoes had begun to bite. But Selena just let them feed on her. It was too nice out here to go home just yet. She had the distinct impression that a female ancestor of hers had sat out here in just this place, on just this kind of night, with just such a recalcitrant duplicitous lover, long before the white man came. She could feel the truth of it right down in her blood. It was Delano's blood too, part of it.

It was very dark now. All she could see of him was his white T-shirt and his face. She wondered if he could see her at all.

She smiled widely and said, "*Now* you can see me!"

"Ha ha," he said, insincerely, and then: "You seen him yet?"

"Just once," she said.

"Thought of calling him."

"Wouldn't do that, if I were you."

"That the way it is?"

"Yep."

"Wow," he said. "Yeah, well how's old Jay Jay doing these days?"

"Better than ever."

"Oh, yeah?"

"Richer than Croesus."

"No lie? How's he looking?"

"Predictable. Like what he is: the enemy. And . . . are you ready for this?" she said, gleefully. "He still wears that old flat-top hair-cut of his, just like in high school."

"Hey, that's kind of sad."

"I don't waste any tears."

"Cat really ran a number on you."

"To me he is just a symbol," she said, "a symbol of oppression."

"With me it's more personal," Delano said.

"What do you mean by that?"

"Oh, I don't know. Guess I'm kind of jealous. On account of the Dootch owning all this—this land," he said, gesturing across the river in the darkness, "that would have been mine."

"Fuck the land," she said. "It's only dust. And fuck the landowners too. They are merely parasites. What counts is the people who live on the land and work it with their hands."

"But you gotta understand how I feel."

"I don't care how you feel. I have no sympathy for that kind of nostalgia. The way I see it . . . another roll of the dice back in 1920 or '22 and I'd be fighting Ranges now instead of Vanduccis. So," she said, laughing, "just count yourself lucky you got screwed out of this land, boy."

Selena's last few words had escaped Range's attention. Her humor had evaded him.

"Never forget the times we used to come down here," he said. "Come down and drink wine and wrestle and play touch football. I was the kind of kid who always wanted attention. So a lot of times I'd pretend to pass out, just to make a spectacle. And Jay Jay, he'd always pick me up and throw me in the river. 'That'll bring the little fucker around!' he'd yell. And I actually used to bask in it, used to feel a thrill of pleasure flying through the air, getting dunked in the water, with Jay Jay and all the kids watching me, laughing at me."

"*Pobrecito*," Selena crooned, ruffling his wiry hair. And then, still in Spanish, she whispered, "You are a symbol, too. . . ."

"Huh?" he said, incredulously.

"Let me tell you something frankly," she said. "In my own mind, Delano, you have become a kind of symbol. A symbol of my whole effort here in San Joaquin County. Don't ask me why. Maybe it's because of your blood, which is mixed more or less like the population of the area. Maybe it's because of your name, which happens to be the same as the little town down in Kern County where I first joined the struggle in the fields. Anyway, the way I feel now, if I can win *you* over to our *causa*, then there is a chance that I can win Calmento."

"I don't believe in symbols," Range said. "I deal in facts."

"What else do you deal in, Delano?"

"Huh?"

"Oh, never mind," she said, rubbing her arms up and down frantically. "Let's go. These mosquitoes are eating me alive."

"They haven't touched me."

"Funny how they choose, huh?"

"Guess I'm just a bitter pill."

"Deadly poison, I wouldn't doubt."

"Oh yeah?" he said. "Then how come you let me hang around?"

"Dunno. Must have suicidal tendencies."

"Don't do me no favors."

"What is this shit?" she said. "Can't you take a joke?"

"Only if it's on someone else."

"You mean that, don't you, Del? I think you really do. You know what? You are hysterical. You ought to go on stage."

He laughed and rose to his feet and guided her up through the trees to his car. They got in and drove back to Southside. On the way he stopped at a liquor store for a couple of bottles of wine. He got Gallo.

"Now you go right back in there and trade those for some other brand!"

"What for?"

"They exploit their workers."

"Okay," he said meekly, and went in and traded it for some Almadén.

"That's more like it," she said. "They have a contract with the UFW."

"I will make it a point to remember that."

"You do that."

"You are one hell of an ideological lady, you know that?" he said, and tentatively put his arm around her.

"I will never make love with you till you join us," she said.

"Where do I sign?"

"Here," she said, and took his hand off the wheel and pressed it to her breast.

Thirteen

IN THE DREAM Range was a secret agent, contracted to eliminate a beautiful Communist spy. His attitude toward the target was like an architect's drawing of his tripartite heart. He could see it very clearly, laid out on a large operations table in a place that looked suspiciously like CCAC headquarters. It was a great red cherry pie with three equal slices. Each slice had a toothpick stuck in it. Attached to each toothpick was a little flaglike label. One label said AFFECTION, another said RESENTMENT, and another, COLD INDIFFERENCE.

"What is her true ident-kit?" he asked.

"Nobody knows who she really is," said Control, who looked very much like Jay Jay Vanducci, except that he smoked a pipe. "She is a woman of many devices, many disguises, many names. One must be careful."

Then Control sent Delano out on her trail. He searched for her all over the world, followed her for years; but he was always just a jump or two behind her. It became an obsession with him. He had to find her. At the same time, he did not want the search to end. It was like a game that was more fun to play than to win.

At last one day he found her in an obscure little town in the Central Valley of California. He knocked at the door of her hideout. She came to him bearing union-picked grapes with a UFW eagle stamp on the side of the box. He ate of the grapes and they turned into nipples. He sucked them and sucked them. The longer he sucked, the bigger they got. It was like she was made out of rubber, instead of skin. It was like he was blowing instead of sucking. Soon she was huge as an elephant. She began to pet his head with her enormous trunk. She petted him harder and harder till the petting became cuffing and hard strong blows. The blows smarted. Yet at the same time they felt delicious. His government contract was completely forgotten. She beat him unconscious. Then she lit the house on fire and vanished. He regained consciousness in a smoke-filled room and tried to find his way out. But the door was locked and the window wouldn't break. Outside he could see his target. She was standing on the grass with a white man who looked remarkably like Control. They were laughing.

When Range awakened his face was caught under the covers, Selena's arm was flung over his neck, and his nose was stuck in a hotspot between her full left breast and the sheet. Her bosom rose and fell slow, steady, snuffing his wind with each deep toke. He was dank with perspiration. His pits were ridick: they were oozing.

After he got his head back together, the first thing that came to mind was business: Last night Selena swore his ass to *chicano amorta* and revealed her plans in detail. The Dootch had been right: She was not here just to register voters. Already she had subverted his field workers, she said. Only his shed workers were yet to crack. . . .

Range's problem was this: He owed the bossman a tinkle this morning and he couldn't decide whether to lay the goods on him or not. If he copped, the scam would be offed before it even began.

It would indubitably be a feather in his cap if he blew the whistle. The Dootch would be amazed at the speed with which he'd penetrated her organization, at the highest echelons. Probably offer him a job as foreman, when all was said and done. On the other hand, it would put an end to his current gig, which was getting interesting, his five a month, which was a bird in hand, and his scene with Selena, which was outa-fucking-sight.

It was a tough decision. Range rolled over on his tight muscular ass to reflect upon it. The sweet aphrodisiac of last night wafted up from the bedcovers to tempt his senses. Selena's hand dragged across his tense pecs, limply fell by his flexed bicep. She stirred between her zees, dreamy, creamy. Stirring his memory and affection. He could not resist her slender brown hand. Squeezed it against his thigh, ran his nails over her knucks, his digits in that warm soft spot between her knucks.

"What is your true attitude, man?" he asked himself, and he had no answer right at the tip of his tongue.

Toward himself his attitude seemed rather neutral, at the moment.

Toward Desiree he apparently had no attitude at all: He hadn't thought of her in days.

In Selena's case an attitude did exist, but it was not readily definable. Now that they'd balled, Range was looking at things through different glasses: He no longer resented her teenage betrayal, for she'd paid him back with a mature surrender. He no longer felt that weak lovey-dovey thing in the pit of his stomach that he'd felt for her since he was a kid, for she was now removed from her pedestal. The idea of touching her, being near her, no longer brought tears to his eyes, for he had conquered her ass. On the other hand, there was now this acrophobic thing that he felt. He was afraid he might be embarking upon some kind of love trip. Having never traveled that way before, he was acquainted with neither its perils nor its specific route. But there was one thing he knew for sure: It was a detour from his own independent itinerary. And Range was not the kind of dude to take a journey like that very lightly.

Downstairs someone was monkeying with the front door. Opened it up with a pass key. Closed it quietly behind. Climbed the stairs. Tiptoed across the softwood floor of the loft. Pulled back the Mexican blanket that hid Selena's mattress.

He cracked his lids and stole a glance. It was La Trucha Connie, in Monday morning light, a ring of bright gray motes round her wild Afro hair. She looked tired and slumped and drawn. Looked like she hadn't slept a wink since she left town three days ago. She had a corduroy jacket slung over her shoulder and a heavy briefcase in her hand.

Range smiled at her sardonically, held her bleary wavering gaze for half a minute. Smiled her down.

She let the curtain fall and creaked in defeat across the room to her bed.

There had been just this one instant of doubt, when Range had wondered if it might not be better to worm his way into her creaky heart. But he drummed that notion loudly from his gourd: *The way to handle an enemy who is also an uptight asshole is merely to increase her aggravation. Then, when all her frontal defenses are up, take her from the rear with kindness.*

With that he turned his attention again to Selena.

It was not in his character to allow an advantage, no matter how small or seemingly insignificant, to slip by.

Selena lay in a pool of her own lush locks, dark against the white bedclothes. She lay on her side, curvaceous, pouting into her pillow.

Range woke her up and slipped it to her sideways, compressing up inside her like a cold greased thermometer to a fevered mouth.

Across the loft Connie stayed still as a trout.

The CCAC building had once been a cantina. Downstairs, behind the office, there was a former short-order kitchen where they took their meager chow. A tiny, narrow, high-ceilinged, unpainted wooden room, it was barren of any decoration save for an ancient gas range, a battered fridge, a rusty metal sink, a shaky card table, three rickety wicker chairs, and some worn green linoleum. For some reason it had been favored with four large windows, more than any other room in the house. And it was very bright and cheerful in the morning. At night they hung old sheets in the windows as a precaution against vandals and snipers and peeping toms.

When Range and Selena came down for breakfast, Connie already had the coffee perking, and was doing last night's dishes in the sink. As usual, her threads were nothing but the tackiest: short-sleeved white blouse with pics of boats on it, a pair of old polished-cotton slacks, and white imitation leather sandals.

Selena, in a gay-colored Guatamalteco smock, faded denim bellbottoms, and a pair of huaraches, trucked up and gave her a great big *abrazo* from the rear.

"So, Connie, how'd it go?" Selena asked, releasing her, bouncing energetically over to the stove to pour herself a cup of Colombian.

But Connie was playing it tight-pussy. Just kept sponging a big plastic salad bowl that she held in her soapy little fat fingers. Swabbing it over and over. Not even checking it while she worked. Squinting out through the window at the overgrown and abandoned backyard, slump-shoul-dered, sulky as a kid.

"What's wrong, dear?" Selena asked, slurping at her hot coffee, blow-ing on it, lighting a Pall Mall, slouching long-legged against the oven door.

She was genuinely perplexed.

Connie quit scrubbing the bowl. Let it plop back into the suds. Turned, purple-fingered, drippy-handed. And pointedly fixed her gaze upon Range . . . Range, who was now parked on his hunkers at the card table, devouring two biscuits of Nabisco Shredded Wheat simul-taneously, playing the monkey, stuffing his maw, attempting to stir with light farce any heavy shit that might be brewing.

"Oh, *him!*" Selena said, tittering, slapping her shapely thigh, while Range let Shredded Wheat dribble out of his mouth, down his stubbly beard, and back into the bowl.

And then, gesturing with her coffee cup as if to wave aside any ob-jections, she said, "Listen, Connie, Delano is one of us, now. Whatever you've got to say, you can say it in front of him."

Yet still the dikey bitch would not spill her jive.

"I feel like clearing the air," Range said finally. "Look, baby, I know what you think about me . . ."

"I wonder if you really do," Connie said at last, pucker-faced, turn-ing, drying her steamy hands on a dirty dish towel.

"Selena told me."

"Oh, and what exactly did she tell you?"

"Everything."

"Everything?" Connie said archly, plunking her shanks at the oppo-site end of the table, coffeeless. "Are you sure about that?"

"Sure I'm sure," said Range, glancing at Selena by the stove.

"But Selena doesn't know everything. And certainly not everything about me."

"Oh, yeah? Well then maybe you are the one with something to hide."

"Hide? Who said anything about hiding? Whatever brought that to your mind? Your own case, perhaps?"

"We all have things that we hide."

"Some of us more than others."

"Look, bitch, if you got something against me, why don't you just fucking spill it out?"

"You already know what it is, asshole."

"Oh, yeah?"

"Yeah."

"I do?"

"You are trying to sow dissension between us."

"Between who?"

"Between Selena and me."

"I'd say it was the other way around."

"You saw me come in this morning, didn't you? Then you deliberately took Selena and you started playing around with her on the bed and then you—"

"Did you, Del? Did you see her?"

"I was sound asleep."

"That's a lie!"

Range found himself to be quite as irate now as if he were actually being unjustly accused. All it took was a minimal effort to stoke his ire into real fury. "Get up outa my face, cunt!" he said, spitting milk over the table.

"Okay, that's enough, you two!" Selena hollered, holding her left hand up like a traffic cop, with her cigarette between her fingers. And yet there was a hint of amusement in her eyes, a hint of even . . . encouragement. It appeared to Range that on some level she wanted to allow their emotions free sway: Selena's kitchen cultural revolution.

"All right, look," he said, making a real attempt to be reasonable, "why don't we work things this way. I'll split the room right now. You two have your talk, discuss your business, and all that. Don't let me in on nothing. Then, when things start to pop, you can judge me by my actions in the field."

"Things won't ever 'pop,' " said Connie, "if you have your way."

"Jesus," Selena said, pointing at her cousin, "look who's talking now."

"My only concern is you, Selena."

"My only concern is the organization."

"My only concern is my ass," Range said. Nobody laughed. "It's a joke!" he said. "I'm just kidding, see?"

Connie pretended she had a sour taste in her mouth.

Selena merely repeated herself. "My only concern is the CCAC," she said, pouring herself another cup of coffee, lighting herself another cigarette off the one in her mouth.

"Right on!" said Range.

"So, as I was trying to say, Connie," Selena said, "how, for Christ's sake, how did it go in Berkeley?"

"It was a total bust," she said. "I'm sorry, but it's true. No one will help. No one will offer any money. No one will volunteer, even for legal aid. Their resources are stretched to the breaking point with the lettuce strike down in Salinas. And besides, they don't think you have a chance here, Selena. These people up here in the North San Joaquin, they have not been exposed enough to the movement, they say. They are very primitive as far as the issues go, they say, and it will take years to—"

"Uh-huh," Selena said. "And I bet you didn't break your ass trying to bring them around to our point of view, did you? Because in your heart you agree with them."

"You know I did my best."

"I don't know anything of the kind."

"Come on."

"No, Connie. You are capable of anything, if you think my personal well-being might be involved."

"Anything but lying to you," Connie said. "Anything but breaking a promise."

"I'm not so sure of that."

"You can rest assured."

"If you say so," Selena said, sighing. "Well then, I guess we're just gonna have to go it alone."

"Selena, if I might say . . ."

"Just a second, Connie. Look, Del, I'm going to take you at your word. You said you'd prefer not to be in on our discussion. Well, so be it. Now, here's what I want you to do this morning. I want you to go in and run off twelve hundred copies of the *Plan de Calmento* on the mimeograph machine. Okay?"

"Sure," Range said, with the appropriate show of enthusiasm. "And then I gotta drive over and see my parole officer in Stockton. All right?"

"Far be it from me, Delano," Selena said, winking at her somber little slant-eyed cousin, "to keep you from your lawful obligations. . . ."

The *Plan de Calmento* was Selena's blueprint for mobilizing Chicano political power in San Joaquin County. Range ran off the twelve hundred copies she asked for, and cleaned up the mimeograph machine. It took him a couple of hours, but the cousins were still in deep conversation (an extremely low-voiced conversation) when he was done.

He went outside, got into his car, and drove across the tracks to Northside.

The cop car did not follow him. He'd noticed what they usually did: Usually they stuck to Selena like glue.

Wheeled out to the freeway and brodied up at a Chevron station that catered to nonlocal traffic. Hopped to the phone booth and jangled the Dootch at his office.

Till the instant he got on the line, he had not the funkiest notion what he would say. As it happened, he told the truth.

"Hey," the Dootch said, "this is quite a little piece of intelligence. I'm gonna have to sit back and digest it for a while. Then I want you to call me back. Call me tonight. And . . . keep up the good work, *bimbo.*"

"Will do," Range said.

Then he got back in his car and drove over to the Southern Pacific yard office at North Central Avenue and West 6th Street, thinking all the time, "Boy, was he impressed! Damn if you ain't got it wired this time, man! On both angles! Wow!"

Parked and went into the office and looked for Mike McCabe's mail slot. Asked the dispatcher for a piece of paper and an envelope. Stuck a ten-dollar bill inside with a note:

Dear Mike:

It has been five years now since I borrowed this $10 from your caboose in Frisco yard. Better late than never, no? I am a man of my word. Seriously, I am very happy that I am finally in a position where I can pay it back to you. Sorry for any inconvenience I might have caused you.

Thank you,

An Old Friend

He was about to seal it and stick it into Mike's slot when he was overcome with a feeling of terrible inexplicable guilt. He took the note out and signed it, "Delano Lee Range (Son of Eddie Range . . . P.S. You haven't heard anything about my dad in recent years, have you?)"

He even went so far as to stick an additional five-dollar bill in as "interest," and give his local address: "C/O Calmento Community Action Committee, 109 4th Street, Calmento, CA."

Then he jumped in his car again and drove to the meeting with his parole officer.

"How come you're so late, Delano?" she asked him, soon as he got in the door.

She was stout and gray-haired and matronly. And her bark was worse than her bite. Range had responded to her instantly, in the same way that he had responded to Desiree in the Joint. He had a suspicion the feeling was mutual. Her name was Mrs. Jones. His life had been full of ladies of her kind. And they had come in all sizes, shapes, and colors.

"Mr. Vanducci had me out on a special assignment," he said, smiling sheepishly.

"Come on, Del. What kind of fool do you take me for, anyway?"

"I'm not lying. If you don't believe me, just pick up your phone and get him on the line."

"Ooooooh," she drawled, smiling back at him, "I don't think that is going to be necessary, Delano."

"Oh, Mrs. Jones, Mrs. Jones, Mrs. Jones," Range said, just under his breath as he went out the door, "I think we got somethin' goin' here. . . ."

Fourteen

R o s e M a r y had done wonders with their little four-room fore-man's shack. She'd repainted the outside: barn red with white trim. And she'd done it up all Bay Area rustic inside: a kitchen with hanging ferns and coleus plants, copper pots, red tile linoleum, a yellow antique stove, an oak-lined living room full of old farmhouse furniture she'd picked up in garage sales around the county. Now that she'd fixed it up, and the softwood floors were refinished, and the old braided throwrugs were down, the little place was really quite comfortable. Every night after they put the kids to bed they sat together in the living room: Jay Jay in his favorite rocking chair and Rose Mary on her brass daybed and patchwork quilt. They only watched TV for the news. Didn't have much time for the evening sitcoms and shoot-'em-ups. By the time the dishes were done and the kids were tucked in, it was already eight o'clock and only two more hours to bedtime. These were happy hours for the young Vanduccis, a time when they could relax and be alone, or read, or talk about the day's events, or discuss the kids, or their plans for the future, or whatever.

In the past few weeks, however, it had become a painful time for them both. It was all Jay Jay's fault. His mind wandered all the time. Rose Mary complained that he wasn't paying enough attention to her. And she was right. For long periods of time he was completely unaware of her existence. Then, when he was made aware of her, it was with a measure of unavoidable distaste. In bed her great pink and white body filled him with a violent disgust. He had not made love to her since the day of the cockfight seven weeks ago. Nor since that day had he properly shit, slept, eaten, or bathed. Nor had he taken any pleasure in his work, his children, or his home.

Selena Cruz was a devil in his flesh.

Rose Mary knew that the Mexican woman was back in town. The origin of his malaise was therefore no secret to her. Till now she'd had the good grace not to mention it. But he could tell by her attitude, as she sat squinting and swearing to herself, unwinding a major mistake in her knitting, that if he didn't pull himself together soon she'd have to say something. In a way he wished she would say something.

Barefoot, shirtless, on this hot Monday night in the last week of July, Jay Jay sat in his rocking chair now unrocking, pretending to be absorbed in a book on farm labor relations. Fiercely he glared downward into the white page, past the page, through the lines of dancing print, into a space beyond.

The Chicana girl lay before his eyes as she had lain on that iniquitous night long ago. He could smell her, feel her beneath his rough hands. She was soft and brown and beautiful. She smelled of love.

Rose Mary gave him a quizzical look now, a hurt harried look, but kept her own counsel, kept at her work: a white woolen Aran Islands pullover for Vince.

While Jay Jay, floating out there in the void, was overcome with a blind fear, a blind fury. He saw Selena as she really was: his enemy, dedicated to the destruction of all he held dearest in the world.

He dreamed of becoming her mortal conquistador.

The pressure on him was building day by day. Soon he would have a nervous breakdown, maybe, start seeing things.

Out in the field, here lately, out on the job, he tried to imagine what it was like to see reality coming apart at the seams. He looked out over the great valley and all the 'Ducci lands and imagined the pillars of the sky falling down, a great flood rolling in off the Pacific, a whole blue sea where the fields and freeways now lay . . . sailboats tacking across a sunken Calmento, only the water towers and grain elevators showing above the waves.

Then he thought: *It was once a sea; it will be again, someday.*

"Honey, you haven't turned a page in a half hour!"

By reflex he turned the page and sought a way between these new lines that confronted him. He ground his teeth with the effort, scratched the wooden arm of the rocker with his nails.

"Quit that damn fidgeting!" Rose Mary said, setting her knitting aside. "You are driving me insane, Jay Jay. Look at the errors I'm making."

"I'm sorry, honey," he said. "I—I'm worried about those irrigators out there, I guess."

"I know what you're worried about."

"Listen, Rose," he began, and he was just about to confess the truth to her when the phone rang.

It was his father.

"Jay Jay," he said, "I want you to do me a favor. That Range kid called me up this morning and gave me some info that is kind of suspicious. Now, he squealed like hell when I suggested a meeting. But I want you to run over to Manteca and have a talk with him."

"Where at?"

"Crash City."

"What time?"

"Ten o'clock."

"Then what?"

"Lean on him a bit, if you have to."

"Uh-huh."

"Find out what his game is. I just can't go for the story this *bimbo*'s handing out."

"What's he say?"

"You know what he says? They got us unionized in the field."

"Bullshit."

"That's what I think. Now, if he said the shed, I might swallow it. You get people from the same area, working together under the same roof, at steady wages, year in and year out, you are open to agitation. But the field? Shit, they don't even know each other, out there. And the poor bastards are so happy just to have a job . . ."

"That's the way I see it, Dad."

"But listen. If I could be sure this story was straight, it'd be a fantastic piece of luck. I could just fire the whole shootin' match and have another field crew out there next day. Cut the rug right out from under 'em. But before I go doing anything that drastic, Jay Jay, I want to be sure. They been working good out there for almost two weeks now. No use disrupting the whole operation for nothing."

Jay Jay got up out of his chair as soon as his father rang off. "Sorry, honey, but I have to go out and do something for my dad. Gotta check up on those irrigators," he said, wondering why he took the trouble to lie. "Mexican fell asleep last night and run seventy thousand gallons out on my ripe tomatoes. Damn near drowned 'em out."

"All right, go on," she said, standing to face him. "Might as well. Hell, you're no company to me."

He leaned over to give her a kiss, and sniffed baby powder. She already smelled of the child she would bear.

"Let me tell you one thing, boy," she said, drawing away from him. "Pretty soon you're gonna have to either shape up or ship out. And I'm not kiddin'."

"I will, honey."

"Is that a promise?"

"Cross my heart," he said, summoning a smile from somewhere. Then he padded into their bedroom for his boots and shirt, and hurried out the back door to his pickup truck.

A big half moon. The yellow lights of the big house across the yard. The twinkling lights of Calmento in the distance, and the other towns beyond: Banta, Carbona, Byron, Manteca, and Modesto and Stockton on the horizon. The rushing lights on the freeway below. The stars above.

Bumped down the dirt driveway along the barbed-wire fence and out onto Corral Hollow Road. Goosed her under the freeway bridge and out onto the flats, listening to her dual pipes rap off behind him. Turned into the dark tomato fields of the South Section. It was nine o'clock by the luminous hands on his wristwatch.

He would use this hour to find a few things out on his own.

He could picture Rose Mary in the window above him, watching her husband's lights below. Lights that bounced now over yellow-black dirt clods and dark water and struck the cat eyes of young Enrique Mendoza, his wide-awake irrigator.

Tiny and brown, wearing hipboots, Levi's, and a narrow-brimmed sombrero, Enrique stood leaning on his shovel in the middle of the canal, up to his thighs in muddy water.

Jay Jay pulled over and switched off his engine. Enrique waded out. Clomped up the embankment and across the dirt road to lean on the truck.

Jay Jay reached in the glove compartment for the tequila he always kept there for his men.

"Here, have a shot of this, *hombre*," he said, and handed it through the window.

Enrique raised the bottle. "*Salud!*" Took a big gulp, blinked, took another, capped the bottle, and handed it back with a broad, big-toothed grin, wiping his lips with the back of his hand. His face gleamed in the overhead light.

"So how's she goin', Pancho?"

"*Muy tranquilo.*"

"Just the way I like it."

"*Yo también.*"

For fifty minutes Jay Jay sat there in his pickup truck sipping tequila and shooting the breeze with his lonesome irrigator, speaking English and getting Spanish back.

He could smell Mendoza, his bean scent, the maguey scent of the liquor on his breath. He liked the smell. He could smell the tomato plants in the field, their ripening fruit, the damp fertile soil that embraced them. He liked that too. He could hear water running in the furrows, owls hooting, the roar of the freeway across the field, a train whistling on the Altamont Pass, the reassuring sound of Mendoza's soft humble Mexican voice: "*Sí sí* Meester Banducci . . ."

"Tell me, Enrique, is there a strike brewing?"

"*Donde?*"

"In the shed."

"*En el shed no hay nada.*"

"Positive?"

"*Absolutamente positivo. No es posible.*"

"And in the field?"

"*En el fil no sé. Quién saaaaaabe?*" said Enrique, grinning, shrugging his little shoulders till his head almost disappeared, raising his palms and eyes to the night.

"Right," said Jay Jay, and started up his truck. You could never trust a Mex, no matter how well you thought you were acquainted with him. Jay Jay knew no more than when he started. But with that tequila sloshing hotly around his belly, he sure felt a damn sight better!

It is twelve miles to Manteca. The freeway goes straight and fast as a bullet. At night it is two solid streams of light, one coming and one going, like airplanes shooting tracers at each other and missing narrowly.

Vanducci made it in ten minutes flat.

Fish-tailed onto the gravel in front of Crash City. Skidded into a parking slot in the shadows, just beyond the orange floodlights.

Crash City was a topless go-go joint just outside the city limits of 'Teca Town. Got its name from the gutted air force training plane, a T-6 Texan, that was "crashed" into the roof as an eye-catcher.

A loudspeaker in the spot-lit cockpit was now blaring out Otis Redding's "Sittin' on a Dock of the Bay."

" 'Sittin' on a dock of the bay,' " Otis sang, " 'watching the tide roll away. Yeah, sittin' on a dock of the bay, wastin' time . . .' "

Jay Jay climbed down out of his pickup truck and went inside. Stood for a time in the vestibule doorway letting his eyes get used to the darkness. For a moment all he could see was the little round stage in the middle of the room, and the two frugging go-go girls. One was short and fat and white, wearing only a black bikini bottom. The other was tall and black and slender, wearing only a white bikini bottom. Fatso had little bitty tits with big nips and Slim had great big tits with teeny nips.

Gradually Jay Jay was able to make out the bartender and the cocktail waitress at the bar, under a glimmering "Land of Sky-Blue Waters" beer display. Then he began to make out some of the customers, who were clustered at tables around the gyrating dancers. Most of them were dressed in either cowboy gear or trucker gear, Stetson hats or baseball caps, western shirts or greasy T-shirts. The men tended to thick necks and pot bellies. The women looked like fast-food waitresses on their night off. Jay Jay felt right at home. At the same time, he sensed the vulgarity of the place, and wished it wasn't quite so congenial to his tastes.

Every time he came into Crash City he had a good time. Every time he walked out he felt bad. . . . He did not want to be like these people. He was meant for better things. But only here could he get off. He came here often. Twice he'd even got head in the parking lot. "My wife is pregnant," he told the girl, a teenage bride from Escalon who only worked Saturday nights. "I know how it is," she said, with a mouthful of jizz.

They appeared unreal to him now, these people, outlandish, under the black light that filtered down from the plastic fishnet on the ceiling. When they laughed, their fluorescent teeth shone bright, their day-glo tongues stuck out, and their eyes went round and white as winter moons.

He was fatally attracted. If they hadn't existed he might have invented them now, as a personification of the squalid, uncertain, yet dangerous present state of his own fucked-up head.

Range was sitting alone at a little table on the far side of the stage. Slim and wiry, wearing a black kinky full beard and an Afro Latino, a white tank top with chains and gold crosses dangling down his hairy chest, he looked too hip, too urban, for a place like Crash City.

Looking over at him from across the room Jay Jay had mixed emotions. In a way, it was great to see old Delano again. And it would be fun to compare notes, and find out where he'd been, what he'd done. At the same time he was jealous of Range's style. Made him feel kind of straight, and old, and fat. Affected him like Selena had at the cockfight. Got him sort of scared and weird and unhealthily excited. Left him with an almost overwhelming desire to walk over and hurt Range, slug him on the arm, pinch his cheek too hard, give him an Indian burn.

"Lean on him," his father had said. Jay Jay was moved to interpret the phrase in its ugliest signification: *Maybe Range is taking his job a little too seriously. He's looking more like a greaser all the time,* he thought, though he hadn't seen him in years, and had no basis for comparison.

Range appeared to have affected the other customers at Crash City in much the same way. If Jay Jay hadn't shown up, the trendy little fucker would have probably had to fight his way out.

He had always affected valley people that way. He didn't even have to say anything. They just didn't like him on sight. There was something smart-ass about his Latin good looks, a cocky gleam in his eye, the way he bounced when he walked.

Jay Jay remembered the first day he showed up at the ranch, after Angie took him in from the county. Dusk on a winter evening. Cold and still and gray. Bruno and Del climbed out of the cab of the pickup truck and got his stuff out of the back. Two cardboard boxes tied with twine. Jay Jay standing with his mom, watching from the backporch window . . . At first he'd been delighted when he heard he was gonna have a foster brother, someone his own age who was already a pal at school. But soon he began to have second thoughts. He was standing there at the window, watching them come forward across the ranch yard, watching his mama smile and wave. *Crunch, crunch, crunch* went their feet on the gravel, the mist swirling round their legs. Range had such an adultlike expression on his cute little dark face. So smooth and worldly for his age. Jay Jay had a big yellow pussy-cat cradled in his arms. He was petting it absentmindedly on the head. Just an old tom they had on the ranch. Nobody even knew who it belonged to. After Range moved in, though, it became a bone of contention between them. One of them or the other was always petting it, combing it, stroking its fur. They grew to love it so much they had pitched battles over it. One time they nearly tore the poor thing in two, pulling it in opposite directions. They got so possessive they couldn't even agree on a name for it. In secret Jay Jay called it Miranda. Range called it Dolores. But in public they called it Pussy, which was neutral. . . .

Jay Jay went over and downed a double Tequila Sunrise at the bar. Bought two more and made his way to Range's table.

Till the instant he got there he had no idea what he would do.

Otis was singing "Try a Little Tenderness" now, ironically, starting slow, singing slow and smooth with a fast bossa nova beat behind him to ac-centuate the dramatic tension and heart-quickening an-ti-ci-pation in his voice. . . .

"Hey, you little prick."

Range turned around with an exasperated expression on his face. And the dye was cast.

"This is fucking ridiculous," he said. "Someone from the barrio walks in that door, man, and my cover's blown."

"You let us worry about that, Delano. Anyway, who said they let Mexicans in here?"

"All right," Range said, raising his hands in the air. "So what's your problem?"

"Hey, is that all you got to say to your old pal?" Jay Jay said. The booze was starting to get to him. It felt good. He had intended to give Range the other Tequila Sunrise. But now he decided to save it for himself.

"Let's put it this way—" Range began.

"Don't tell me," Jay Jay said. "Lemme guess."

"That's how it is, man. The way I look at it, a promise is a promise."

"You hold a *grudge!*"

"A visit is a big thing," Range said, "when you're a kid in the Joint."

"Hey, if your feelings were so hurt, Delano, what the fuck you write us for? You know, we didn't have to give you a job."

"That's business," he said.

"So?"

"So, I always keep that apart from the other."

"You got a lotta fuckin' nerve."

"I thought we came here to talk," Range said. "I don't get back soon, I'm gonna be missed at the CCAC."

"By who?" Jay Jay wanted to know.

"It's in the mutual interest," Range said, avoiding the question, taking a quick swig at his Heineken's mug, his slanty dark eyes shifting rapidly around the room. Jay Jay checked his pecs under the tank top, his muscular shoulders and arms: *Been working out on the rings and the high bar; they do that to kill time in the slammer.*

"Come on, Jay Jay, they really are going to get suspicious over there."

"I tell you what. Me and my dad, we are getting a little bit suspicious ourselves."

"Of what?"

"Of you, maybe."

"I just report what I hear."

"We just can't swallow it, Del."

"That's your privilege," Range said, shrugging his shoulders.

"Who told you this story about our fields being infiltrated?"

"Who do you think?"

"How'd you get in with her so fast?"

"Figure it out, man."

"Why don't you just go ahead and tell me, Del?" Jay Jay said, downing his second Tequila Sunrise. Or was it his third? He didn't know. Soon if he didn't watch out he was gonna lose his cool.

"She's one of the fringe benefits," Range said, grinning lasciviously.

"We sure got you well placed," Jay Jay said, trying a joke, trying to keep the bile from swelling up inside him, thinking: *He is telling the truth.*

And at that moment Jay Jay determined to go home to the ranch and tell his father that he believed the story. He detected Selena's guiding hand in all of this. It was a game they were playing together, maybe. Just the two of them. Over the heads of everyone else. Jay Jay wanted her to lead off. So, he would sacrifice his first pawn. Just to see where she was taking him. Just to see what he would do when she got him there.

It was then also that he warmed at last to his old pal and decided to set them back on a more pleasant track. But it was hard to switch like that, in mid-course. So, to disguise his extreme anxiety and his flaming envy and his insecurity, anticipation, feelings of inferiority, he turned his attention to the go-go dancers onstage. And soon he found himself completely absorbed in their act, which included a complicated routine in which they twirled their breasts in a clockwise direction while revolving their pelvises in a counterclockwise motion.

He was especially fascinated by the nigger dancer. There was something almost . . . savage in her demeanor, he thought. Coal black, woolly-haired, broad-nosed, fat-lipped, flat-footed, she looked like something just off the auction block, made to dance the bump and grind for her lewd new masters.

Watching her sweat and glisten in the black light and wiggle and roll her whites and swing her long loose arms, Jay Jay began to tremble violently. He was startled by the excessiveness of his reaction and quickly tried to control it. *Take it easy now, boy,* he kept telling himself. *It's just all this pressure you been under, here lately.*

Then, when he discovered that he could not control it, he tried to conceal it in a display of rowdy good humor. "Whoopie! Whoopie!" he bellowed, banging his glass on the table top. "Goddamn can you dance, goddamn!"

And soon he was gratified to hear other members of the audience taking up his cry.

"Yeah! Whoopie!" they hollered. "Do your thing, gal!"

Though at first the rowdiness was all in fun, and Jay Jay was sure that no one meant any offense by it, the black girl did not seem to care for it. There was something in their tone, perhaps (something that they themselves couldn't hear), that she didn't like.

Whatever the case, Jay Jay's trembling had ceased as suddenly as it had begun. Now that it had disappeared, he felt he had to keep on making a racket or it might come back again. "Yippee! Yippee!" he yelled. "Keep on truckin', gal, keep on truckin'!"

And then he did something so unexpected, so utterly without precedent in his life (which till now he had considered an exemplar of reason and moderation), so completely uncalled-for and shocking and . . . despicable, that next morning he would find it difficult to believe he'd ever done such a thing and would even (very briefly) consider the possibility that his brain had been invaded by an alien intelligence.

He would end up blaming the whole thing on the devil in his flesh. Under the bar table, he would remember, he had sprouted an enormous and unaccountable erection. . . .

What Jay Jay did, he started baiting the black go-go dancer. Crudely, rudely, unmercifully he baited her, like a red-neck Texan he saw one time at a topless show on Broadway in San Francisco.

"Hey, come on over here, Liza Lou!" he hollered, looking around for approval from the rest of the audience. "Lemme put a dollar bill in them there bikini panties!"

Nigger gal just frugging away, trying to ignore the peckerwood.

"Come on over here, honey pie, and lemme get a look at that kinky thing up close!"

"Yeah, go ahead, baby! Yeah, yeah, yeah!" cried certain members of the overweight audience, while their beefy red-faced fellows giggled encouragement. "Let him have a peek, just one little peek!"

"'Goin' to Kansas City,'" Otis sang now, "'Kansas City here I come. They got some crazy little women there and I'm gonna get me one . . .'"

Jay Jay stood up at his table excitedly, cupped his hands around his mouth, and was just about to bellow out something new when Range grabbed him by the arm and said, very calmly, "What are you doing, man?" And it was like a question Jay Jay might have been asking himself at that moment. And his response was like the response of somebody else, some Texan in a Frisco topless joint: "Jest havin' a little fuuuuuun," he drawled, in a voice that was not his own.

And broke away from Del and whacked the stage with all his might and boomed out at the top of his lungs: "Get your black ass over here, Liza Lou, 'cuz I'm gonna eat your pussy and howl at the moon!"

Yet, with Range's exception, none of the customers seemed to think he'd gone too far. On the contrary, his antics seemed to amuse them greatly. And several of them continued to shout out encouragement: "Go to it, 'Ducci! Sock it to her, boy!"

Someone even let go with a loud beer belch that made everybody laugh all the harder.

Nigger gal rolled her eyes again, looking to the bartender for help. But he was not too cooperative. He knew a thing or two. No one fucked with a Vanducci in this county.

Next time the black girl came shimmying around, Jay Jay made a lunge for her across the stage. Effortlessly she boogied out of his reach. He landed face down on the stage, laughing, banging the boards with his fists, his cowboy hat over his eyes. The whole crowd guffawing now, stomping the floor with their high-heeled boots.

Nigger bopped around Jay Jay and leaned over his table where she did something quickly, furtively, that he couldn't see, something that made the crowd laugh all the more. He pulled his hat back on his head and jumped into his seat. But he wasn't fast enough to catch what she'd done back there. Whatever it was, it had provoked an uproar of hilarity in the audience. They were slapping each other on the back, "Har har har!" banging the tables with their beer bottles.

"What'd she do?" Jay Jay asked, bewildered.

Range shook his head, rocking in his chair with merriment.

Nervously Jay Jay downed his drink. For some mysterious reason that put the crowd into an absolute shit-fit. They doubled over with laughter, clapped their hands, threw their hats on the floor. Black girl was laughing so hard she could barely dance. Only the white girl still keeping the beat, while Otis sang: " 'Well, I might take a train, I might take a bus . . . Kansas City, Kansas City here I come . . .' "

Jay Jay whirled and got Range by the throat.

"What'd she do, motherfucker?"

"Take it easy, man. All she did was sprinkle some pubes in your drink."

"*What?*" 'Ducci saw red. Leapt to his feet, plucking a nappy pubic hair from between his teeth. Grabbed Range's beer mug. Held it shaking in the air with his right hand, pointing at the black girl with his left. "*You!*" he said. The crowd hushed. Nigger gal slunk to the far side of the stage. Jay Jay wound up and was just about to let fly with the contents of the beer mug when Range caught him by the wrist.

"Cool it," he said.

Jay Jay strained against him, but Range forced his arm slowly to the table top. The beer spilled on the floor.

"Let's get out of here," Del said.

All of a sudden Jay Jay felt very juiced. And allowed his old friend to lead him staggering for the door. Around them the music was still playing. The girls were dancing again. The customers had quieted down, and now they were whispering and pointing.

Range stopped at the bar on the way out.

"Gimme a ten," he said.

Jay Jay fished drunkenly in his pocket. Range took the money and left it for the girl.

"Sorry," he said to the bartender.

The bartender nodded without looking up.

Later, out in his pickup truck under the lights, with the radio playing sad country songs, Jay Jay got the blues.

"Now, why'd I go and do that? Why in the world did I do that?" he kept asking, striking the steering wheel with his fist.

"You're always sorry, man."

"What do you mean, Del?"

"Look at that time when we was kids," Range said, sipping at Jay Jay's tequila. "Rousted them bums out from under the SP bridge. Shot 'em up with BB guns and slingshots from the bed of your grandpa's pickup. Got 'em madder than hornets. Then you run off and left me."

"I know, Del, I know . . ."

"And then, for Christ's sake, look at the fuckin' deal you pulled on Selena. First you knock her up and then you split on her without a word. Why the hell couldn't you have just come over and faced her and told her the truth? I mean, you only got yourself to blame, man, for all this shit you're bringing down on your family."

"Del, listen. Believe me. I know I was a bastard. But I haven't been that way in years, I swear. . . . Ask Rose Mary. Ask anybody. I just don't know why now I start in. . . ."

"I know why."

"Tell me," Jay Jay said. "Be frank."

"Like I say, let's keep this strictly on a business level," Range said, and started out of the cab.

"When this is all over, Del, you know you always got a job if you need one," Jay Jay said, forgetting the previous arrangements he had made on this matter.

"Says who?"

"Me."

"You don't say shit till your daddy's dead."

"He ain't gonna live forever."

"Don't count on it," Range said, and headed for his car.

Jay Jay waved to him as he drove out of the lot.

It was Saturday night. He unzipped his Levi's and, hating himself, played with himself for an hour, waiting for the teenage bride to arrive from Escalon.

Fifteen

AGUILAR GRABBED HIS SOMBRERO, slammed it down low on his head, and made his way to his pickup truck in the darkness before dawn.

It was Wednesday morning, July 29, 1970, the fifteenth day of tomato season.

"Kee kee ree kee! Kee kee ree kee!" went the rooster of Mrs. Alvaraz next door. *"Kee kee ree kee!"* Used to be old Morenito was the first one to sound off in the barrio. Now Moreno was fucked, *jodido*. But *jodido* for a good *causa*, no? What better way to go?

Never as long as he lived would Victorino forget the surprised look on Beeg Red's little beak when Moreno came back from hell to kill him dead. Never would he forget the look upon his Wop master's face, either. Ay, he would give a hundred lugs of tomatoes to see it again, just one more time. Already in his mind the *batalla heroica* of the little cock Moreno had assumed the qualities of myth.

Now he got into his old beauty and cranked her over. She never failed him, his Cheeby peekup, never. Bought her used in 1960, put a hundred and seventy-five thousand miles on her, and she'd never been a moment's trouble yet. Ay, she was his Chevycita Bonita and he would never let her down. He'd even written her name on her homemade wooden front bumper, in white paint and ornate Mexican script. He cared for her like he cared for his wife. Gave her everything she needed, in moderation: an oil change every twenty thousand miles, a lube job and filter every forty, retreads every fifty. Few women had been so good to him in his life. Few had he been so good to in return. *Bruuuuuum!* she wound out. A good old low-compression Cheeby Seex with overhead valves. Then he let her idle quietly for a few minutes, for that is what she liked.

Delia and the girls would linger over their coffee now, sitting around the kitchen table till he honked the horn. That gave Victorino five precious nonworking minutes when he could be alone. During these moments he thought of the past. He often thought of the past, lately. Why this was so, he could not say. Just seemed like . . . the older you got, the more there was to reminisce about. The road of life stretched out farther behind you than in front of you. He recalled the day he left his native village. He saw his mother on the hill, waving good-bye. He saw himself as a sixteen-year-old Xixime Indian boy, waving back, with tears in his eyes. He saw the boy go down to the *río* to wash. Then he saw him get up and walk up the path that went along the *río*. For a long time he walked up the *río*, without looking back. He followed it till it became a creek, till it became a stream that squeezed through a deep narrow chasm in the mountains, till it became a tiny spring spurting out of an alpine rock. He crossed over the summit to the plateau on the eastern side. There he found another spring and followed it till it became a rivulet, a stream, a river. He followed it through a great pine forest, and Salto, a town made all of rough-hewn logs. He followed it down into a deep canyon, and over a range of low dry hills of scrub oak and saguaro cactus and across a boiling desert of white sand. He followed it all the way to Durango. Someone had said there was work.

There was no work, and there was nothing to eat, and it was cold in the winter. But you could find newspapers and sleep under them in the bus stops. You could steal Coke bottles from behind the restaurants and sell them for a peso each. Still, it was a hard life. One day he went down to the Ayuntamiento and joined the Mexican Army. He was only seventeen but he looked twenty, and he was big and strong for his age. "The biggest fucking *cholo* I ever seen!" the sergeant said.

Aguilar remembered when he got out of the army nine years later. By then he was a lance corporal and a man of experience. He had lived in Tabasco, Chiapas, and La Capital. And he could read and write. Actually, he didn't want to leave the army at all. But his regiment was being disbanded for "budgetary considerations" and he had no choice. So one day he found himself on the streets again, just like when he was a kid. Except times were even harder now. In La Capital the restaurateurs tied vicious dogs behind their places to keep the Coke bottle thieves way. And all the newspapers were quickly collected by scavengers. Nowhere could he find a job. Finally he went down to the shoeshine boys union and applied for a permit. The shoeshine boys, it turned out, weren't exactly "boys." They were middle-aged men with big families of their own, and they hadn't let anyone into that union since it was charted in 1933. "*Lustre Número Uno—1933*," it said, right on the side of their shoeshine boxes. He kept trying every day, but never would they let him into that union. One day he stole the hubcaps off a big gringo car and sold them and took the money and bought some shoe polish and some rags and made himself a box and went down to the Reforma and started shining shoes on his own. When the union men found out, they caught him in an alley and ganged up on him, beat him and stole all his money and his shoeshine box.

The next day he had nothing to eat. He decided it would be easier to find food in the country than in the city. So he started walking. He walked up the Reforma to La Marqueza and out of the Valley of Mexico and into the mountains. He walked all the way to Caputitlán before he found anything to eat. He broke into an Indian *jacal* while the family was at work in the fields. He gorged himself on leftover beans and set out again on his way. It seemed he was heading north. That night he slept in a cold pine forest at a high elevation and he had a dream. He dreamed that he would find fortune in the north. "How far north?" he asked, in his dream. "As north as you can go," a voice said. In the morning he decided he was destined to be a farm worker in the USA. When his *fortuna* was made, he would return to his native pueblo and build a fine house on the hill for his mother.

He started walking. He walked for three months, across the states of Querétaro, Guanajuato, San Luis Potosí, and Nuevo León. He walked all the way to Texas. He swam the Rio Grande and got a job in Hidalgo. His job was digging potatoes. He dug potatoes for three years and at the end he had enough to buy a car. It was a 1937 Cheeby sedan, two-tone gray and green, with fender skirts, and it cost four hundred dollars. Already he was a man of property.

He set out for California with high hopes. He had youth, ambition, and a strong back. Surely he would be a grand success.

Victorino would work twenty years in the San Joaquin but never would he make the *fortuna* of his dreams, never would he return to his pueblo in the Sierra Madre, never would he see his mother again. Only in his memory, on times like this, when he was alone and awake for a minute or two, would he visit the old *chozita*, again and again and again. And often he would wonder how they were all doing now, his *familia* in the mountains. How had life treated them? Which of them had survived? What did they all look like now that so many years had gone by, now that the youngest of them, the baby, was a grown man? But try as he might, he just could not imagine. So, what he would do was, he would guard them in his graying *cabeza* exactly as they were on the day he left, when he went for the last time to the *río* to wash. And he would keep them that way and treasure them, and take them with him intact and unchanged on the day of his death, which he had already imagined too well: In summer he would die, on a day as cloudless as this. He would fall in the dust and fix his fading memory on his pueblo in the mountains one final time, and it would comfort him mysteriously, as it comforted him now, as proof of the sweetness of life.

Aguilar honked his horn. The sound was amazingly loud and abrupt in the morning silence, and it blew his daydream to smithereens.

Delia came out of the house with the girls and herded them out to the truck in the darkness. They fell asleep as soon as they got in the cab, Rio lying on her mama's lap and Jovita on her shoulder.

Clucking her tongue, Delia patted Rio's dark little head. Then she turned and smiled at her *marido* and sighed. He could barely see her across the cab. The sigh said: *Ay, here we are, a little* familia, *in our car.* Aguilar did not smile back at her, but made a pretense of a comparable contentment: Gently he clucked too, and stroked Jovita's long black hair.

Then he dropped his beauty into gear and bounced over the sandy driveway, his headlights going up into the clean silver-green of the cottonwood trees, down into the dirty yellow wild oats. Up and down, up and down to the smooth white gravel of South "C" Street. Then he turned left and headed out of town toward the Dootch's South Section.

Three young campesinos were walking up the road in the opposite direction, headed for the labor bus at the Golden Taco Cafe. They looked like a trio of *bandidos* in the darkness, Apache marauders, in their high leather boots, white pants, and Levi jackets, and the red and blue bandannas they tied around their shoulder-length hair.

"*Dónde van?*"

"*A los Banducci.*"

"*Vamos,*" said Aguilar. And they scrambled up into the truck bed.

And then it was only the night. The cab. The motor running. The little green lights on the dashboard. The smell of four warm human bodies in a small place, three of them female. Everything closed and cozy and self-contained: a *chozita* of metal. And the headlights bouncing on the road ahead. The murmur of the campesinos in back. The black canals and tomato fields all around.

Now they were rolling over a smooth dirt road, their headlights striking a line of thirty ancient jalopies parked by the side of the road. And bonfires in the drainage ditch. Sparks of cigarettes. White eyes, white teeth, and white straw hats. Six small circles of men, women, and kids in ragged work clothes and bandannas. Little people with shiny brown Indian faces, warming their hands, smacking their hands nervously, and stomping their feet, though it wasn't cold at all.

And then the brakes squealing. The braceros clattering over the tailgate, laughing about something. Their boots smacking the hard-packed sand. And Rio waking in the cab, whining. Delia scolding: "Watch that *boca*, señorita, or you gonna get a slap!" And the slam of the doors. The clean morning air. Mist rising off the irrigation ditch on the other side of the road. The crunch of boot heels on the gravel shoulder of the road. And kicked pebbles. Running water. Night birds. Early birds. Low-voiced conversation in northern Mexican dialects. The smell of burning brush, and damp clay, manure, dewy sweet grass, oleander, the piquant leaves of the mature tomato plant, and nitrate, fungicide, pesticide, chemical defoliant, artificial growth stimulant, sulphur. The flicker of the bonfire up close. The crunch of an old fence post going into the ashes. The fire crackling, popping, rearing up, sending embers to the unfathomable sky. And now the white lights and yellow lights, the barn lights and big-house lights, the spot-lit date palm twins of the Dootch's complex on the hill . . . And a sudden awareness of the *inmensidad* of his invisible empire all around, and the almost insurmountable difficulty of organizing any effective resistance. "What we wanna organize for?" the campesinos would always say, when Aguilar tried a little morning recruiting in the field. "Organize?" they would say. "That means *huelga. Huelga* means no work. No work means no pay. No pay means no eat." And then they would laugh foolishly and make the pantomime gesture for hunger: hands on the belly, head thrown back, eyes rolled up to God, in mock accusation.

Up till now Aguilar's morning had been as slow and familiar as a favored old fuck. Then all of a sudden it was like strange pussy. Things got weird and started coming at him faster and faster and he couldn't tell what would go down next.

A gray light appeared from behind the Sierra Nevada, revealing a large wooden gate with a large black sign:

VANDUCCI RANCH

SOUTH SECTION

NO TRESPASSING

SURVIVORS WILL BE PROSECUTED

. . . Revealing also a new blue Ford pickup truck with dual spotlights, radiotelephone antenna, and gun rack parked in the field behind the gate, fifty yards out, and a burly blond man in long sideburns, horn-rimmed glasses, and a white cowboy hat. He was sitting on the right front fender, with his boots propped up on the bumper. It was Jay Jay Vanducci, with a 16-gauge shotgun and a portable loudspeaker lying across his lap. On his left front fender a tiny stiff plastic American flag flew from the AM-FM aerial.

"*Qué pasó?*" went the murmur on its way around the fires.

"*Qué pasó?*" said Delia and the little girls. "*Qué pasó?*"

But neither Aguilar nor anyone else had the answer.

Finally one of the campesinos, a paunchy little guy named Corky DeJesus, got up the nerve to holler out: "*Qué pasó, patrón?*"

"NO WORK TODAY," Jay Jay said. His voice through the little speaker sounded loud, and at the same time very small and far away, like the Beatles, in a popular song that they sang on the gringo radio station.

"*Porqué?*" Corky said, shaking his pudgy fingers in disbelief.

"NO TRABAJO. BETTER GO ON HOME."

"*No comprendo,*" said Corky unhappily. Corky was the one who always took the lead in opposing Aguilar, when he initiated his recruiting drives. He was a fat-faced little chocolate-colored busybody with a huge ass and a waddling gait. Aguilar was delighted to see him get his comeuppance.

"WE JUST DON'T LIKE THE WAY YOU BOYS BEEN WORKING, HERE LATELY."

"*No es justo, patrón,*" said Corky, shaking his jowly head.

"DON'T TALK TO ME ABOUT JUSTICE," Jay Jay said, in an aggrieved tone of voice, striking the hood of his pickup truck for emphasis. "WE KNOW WHAT YOU BEEN UP TO, BEHIND OUR BACKS—AGITATING, ORGANIZING."

"*Pero no es verdad!*" Corky pleaded, casting an angry glance in Aguilar's direction. "Not true, *patroncito*. He try. Two, three times. But we say no. Always!"

"TELL IT TO THE MARINES," Jay Jay said, but Corky didn't understand.

"What's he mean, what's he mean?" he kept asking. But no one seemed to know.

Just then Selena appeared on the scene. Came speeding up the road in Range's old Dodge, raising a cloud of white dust.

"Hey, what's going on?" she asked through the car window, asked the whole crowd in general. From the way that she asked it, in such a loud stagy voice, Aguilar figured she already knew the answer. Other things were suspicious too. Rudy was with her, at the wheel. Where was Range? Connie was sitting in back, with a pile of CCAC propaganda on her lap. What were they doing out here, so early in the morning?

Aguilar knew his stepdaughter as well as he knew anyone. And something about her—her slightly flushed face, the contained excitement in her voice—told him that she was about to deliver a speech. And Selena never did anything, least of all give a speech, without a great deal of forethought.

"What exactly is going on here?" she asked again, making a dramatic sweeping motion through the window with the flat of her hand, a gesture that encompassed the field, the campesinos, the stout *patroncito* on his pickup truck.

"We just been fired off the job," Aguilar said, walking up to the door, with Delia and the girls trailing along behind him.

He looked in the window and discovered that Rudy and Connie were just as surprised as he. In Connie's case it was something even more than surprise. She was flat-ass astounded. Her eyes were popping right out of her *cabezón*.

Aguilar was no patsy. He picked up quick. Whatever mystification Selena planned, she would not find her step-dad out of step.

"Yeah," he said, in a more forceful tone, "they fired us for no reason. Us they fired. Can you believe it? The best they got!"

"Can this really be true?" Selena asked, as if she were shocked by the disclosure.

"*Sí, señorita!*" everyone cried at once.

Selena got out of the car and made her way through the crowd. She climbed onto the bumper of Range's car, the fender, the hood, and up onto the roof. She was wearing a sequined Yaqui headband, a sackcloth Mexican tunic, and a pair of white cotton pants that she tucked into her high-heeled vaquero boots. And the girl was really something to see.

The campesinos crowded around the car, pushing and shoving for a better view.

"Listen to me, *compañeros*," she said in Spanish, in a low breathy voice that made them strain to hear. "Who is this gringo to tell us we can't work? What have we ever done to him but slave in his fields at low wages? His lies do not deceive us. He's got himself some squirrels who will work for nuts. If we wait here we'll see them come up the road this morning. What do you say, *compañeros*, shall we wait and see?"

"*Que sí, señorita, que sí!*" they all shouted. How else were they to respond to that bewitching *sotto voce*, the sway of her body, the tossing and swinging of her long black hair, the easy self-confident tone in her voice as she spoke of the boss's son?

"*Bueno, amigos*," she said, smiling down on them, lighting them up with her eyes, "who's got a car?"

"*Yo!*" cried several men at once. "*Yo!*" they called again, standing to the front of the crowd, raising their hands up high.

"You," she said.

"Me?" asked a thin little middle-aged man with a Charlie Chaplin mustache, as if he could not believe his *fortuna*.

"Yes, you," she said. "*Cómo te llamas?*"

"Fulgencio."

"*Muy bien*, Fulgencio," she said, speaking to him in an extraordinarily intimate and confidential tone, as if he were part of her family, "I want you to drive down to the corner and blink your lights when you see a bus coming. *Te acuerdas?*"

"*No tengo licencia*," he said, as if there were nothing, not the smallest detail of his life, that he should hold back from her.

"*No importa*," she said, laughing at him like a mother laughs at an amusing child.

"*A sus órdenes*," said the grave and licenseless Fulgencio. Then clumsily, tripping over his big workboots, nearly falling, he ran to his antique Studebaker Land Cruiser and drove off into the dawn, leaving a billowing screen of acrid black oil smoke behind him.

"You see heem?"

"Yeah, he was weavin' all over the *camino*."

"No wonner they won' give heem a *licencia!*"

"Ho ho ho!"

Selena got back into Range's car and started writing something down on the back of a leaflet. Aguilar and the rest of them stood out in the road and down in the drainage ditch, eyeing the *patroncito* with suspicion, waiting for something to happen.

After a while Aguilar started them singing to kill the time. They sang "*De Colores*," "*El Quelite*," and "*Las Mañanitas*."

Then Selena said from the car, "Sing 'Adelita.'"

For some time they had all been casting sidelong glances in her direction, waiting for her to say something. They had been disappointed that she had ignored them for so long. So now they responded with gusto to her command. And they sang it over and over, that sad-happy song of the Mexican revolution, their raw peasant voices booming out and then losing themselves all too quickly, on that great misty morning plain, under the yellowing Diablos:

> *Si Adelita se fuera con otro*
> *La seguiría por tierra y por mar*
> *Si por mar en un buque de guerra*
> *Si por tierra en un tren militar*

> If Adelita runs off with another
> I'll follow her by land and by sea
> If by sea in a ship of war
> If by land in an armored train

Two miles away across the flats, Fulgencio blinked his lights. A vehicle turned the Valpico corner and started crawling up Corral Hollow Road. The campesinos strained their eyes to see.

Soon a large yellow schoolbus appeared out of the mist, filled with a bunch of worried-looking winos from Stockton's Skid Row. Actually, only about half of them were true alcoholics. What they were in fact was the dregs of the valley, the bottom of the heap—Negritos, Chicanos, Filipinos, Okies. They were just a stop-gap crew, Aguilar knew, something to make do with till the professional *esquiroles* showed up from Mexicali.

The driver honked his horn and gunned his engine, trying to make a way through the campesinos who blocked his path. But they would not budge an inch. He gunned his engine louder, leaned on his horn. The more noise he made, the less inclined they were to give way.

Several of them ran around to the side of the bus and started banging on the fenders and panels with their fists.

"*Fuera, fuera!*" they shouted. "Come outa there! Don' take our jobs away!"

The driver, a tiny harried black man of advanced age, got out and tried to negotiate his way creakingly through the mob on foot.

"Ah jes' woik heah, bros, ah jes' woik heah," he kept groaning, making his way toward the gate.

Jay Jay was at the gate, waiting just on the other side, his shotgun in one hand and his loudspeaker in the other.

"LET THAT OLD MAN THROUGH," he hollered. And the campesinos, reacting instinctively to the order of their ex-boss, let the little negrito go. He ran stiff-legged up to the gate, and there engaged in a long whispered conversation with the *patroncito*.

Meanwhile, Fulgencio blinked his lights again, and another bus load of winos appeared out of the mist.

The campesinos were furious now. "Give us back our jobs!" they yelled, and ran up to the second bus with Corky DeJesus at their lead, kicking at the fenders with their boots, banging on the windows with their fists. One of the Apaches even broke a window with a rock, cutting the wino inside.

"Gimme back my job, *cabrón!*"

Jay Jay left the old negrito at the gate and ran back to his pickup truck where he commenced calling frantically for help on his radio-telephone.

Now Corky had got some of the campesinos together, men and women, and they had begun rocking the second bus on its springs, threatening to roll it over into the ditch. *Boom, boom, boom,* went the rubber tires, every time they hit the ground. Inside, the winos were like . . . petrified. Some of them were even clawing at the windows, trying to get out.

Other campesinos had invaded the first bus and were intimidating its bleary-eyed passengers, grabbing them by their soiled collars, shouting "You gonna take my job, *chingado,* you gonna take my job?"

Aguilar looked for Selena. She was sitting in the Dodge Dart, bent over writing something. *Muy tranquila,* like nothing was happening around her.

Aguilar ran over to her and said, "Hey, Selena, why don' you do somethin'?"

She looked up at him very calmly and said, "What would you suggest?"

"Stop these people before they do somethin' loco."

"I don't mind a little *locura,*" she said, "as long as it's well-directed."

"Well I tell you, this ain't directed at nothin' but suicide," he said. "The Dootch show up with his goons and you find that out fas'."

Almost reluctantly, Selena got out of the car and climbed up on top of the roof.

She stood there for a while surveying the action, real cool, with her hands on her hips, like she was looking at scenery.

That's all she had to do.

Within seconds the campesinos were turning around, looking up at her, as if someone had tapped them each on the shoulder and said, "*Oye,* bro, look at that!"

"*Mira mira,*" said the Apaches in the first bus.

"*Watchala,*" said Corky and his boys, around the teetering second bus.

A minute later and she was surrounded by a milling crowd of *braceros,* waiting impatiently for her word.

Jay Jay quickly took note of the situation and signaled his drivers. They revved up their diesels and swung off the road. Barreled through the gate and out into the field, churning up a great storm of white dust.

The moment the winos were safely behind the fence, they all started cheering and shouting and cursing.

"Whoopie!"

"We made it, pardners!"

"Fuckin' Communists!"

"Eat shit, honey!"

Selena ignored their jeers and stood waiting on top of the car till there was not a sound to be heard but the meadowlarks singing in the fields.

All eyes were upon her, even the winos' eyes, even the *patroncito's* eyes.

At last she spoke. In that same soft intimate voice she had used before (it was almost a whisper), she said in Spanish, "See what happens? He tosses you out like garbage. And what do you do? You get mad. And you strike out blindly with no plan, no hope of success. Come with me now, *compañeros*," she said, her voice rising. "Come with me now before the enemy arrives in force and destroys you before you have even begun. Come with me into Calmento where we have friends of our own *raza*. Come with me now and I will give you organization, solidarity, and power. Come with me now, *amigos*, and I swear to you on my life that one day the 'Duccis will lie trembling at your feet. . . ."

Her voice was like honey and the campesinos were like ants. Her words were like milk and Aguilar was like a hungry calf. The day was like strange pussy, and things came at you faster and faster, and you never knew what would happen next. Nobody knew where he was going. Nobody seemed to care. Selena blew her pipes and everyone followed like rats. They abandoned the fields to the winos without a thought. They followed her down the road in their beat-out cars and all the way into town. They followed her through the barrio, honking their horns and waving their hats and calling the people outside to hear of the unparalleled *injusticia* of the Vanducci, who fired a man for no reason, at mid-season, and put a no-good gringo *borracho* in his place. They followed her to McDonald Park in the center of Southside, and instantly renamed it Parque Emiliano Zapata, in honor of her hero. They followed her all in a great hollering crowd out onto the yellow grass in the middle of the park and hoisted her up on their shoulders, chanting "Selena Cruz, Selena Cruz, Selena Cruz," and set her upon the bandstand above them, with all the people laughing and shouting and singing and the little kids running around in circles and the dogs barking and almost no one knew why.

Maybe Aguilar knew why: They were the limbs and she was the brain; they were the flesh and she was the spirit; they were the horse and she was the rider; they were the arrows and she was the bow.

The day was truly the strangest. In a long and promiscuous life, Aguilar never seen anything like it before. And the strangest thing of all was this: Never, not once through all of the speeches and all of the cheering all through the morning and afternoon and night, not one single time did Selena allow the word *huelga* to be pronounced aloud.

Sixteen

U P I N H E R L O F T bathroom on the following night, under a forest of flesh-colored underwear hanging to dry, Selena was girding herself for her coming task. All around her in the tiny steamy room were a gaggle of dark perspiring females. Mama, Jovita, Rio, Connie, Connie's obese elder sister Lita, Rudy's thin little pot-bellied wife, Gloria, they sat on the bathtub, the sink, the toilet, all of them laughing, talking at once, watching La Palomita as she stood at the mirror in her royal-blue terry-cloth bathrobe.

"*Ay que linda es!*"

"*Así chulita no hay ninguna.*"

"*En el mundo entero no hay.*"

"*No hay.*"

"*A la santa verdad!*"

She was plucking her eyebrows. Pluck, pluck, pluck, each little tweek of her metal tweezers a twinge of pain. She could smell them behind her, beside her, her plump *carnalas* in their farm workers' clothes, their blue jeans, khaki shirts, straw hats, and bandannas. There had been a time when she found that smell unendurable. Yet it swirled around her now, unsuccessfully drowned in perfume, and she barely noticed it.

Then she finished plucking. She reached down, picked up her eye-lining pencil, wet it at the tip of her tongue, and began carefully doing her eyes, leaning over the sink to observe her handiwork up close.

"That's all she uses, just eyeliner," said Lita, in tones of wonder, as if she were speaking of a movie star down in Hollywood and not her own cousin, whose full round ass was now almost directly in her face.

"No makeup?" Gloria asked.

"*Qué no!*" said slender long-legged Jovita, seated on the sink, gazing on her sister with passionate love.

"A natural beauty," said Mama. "Always was."

Selena finished her eyes and threw off her robe. Connie caught it, folded it, and put it away.

"Ooooooh, Selena, what happened to your back?" Gloria exclaimed, pointing to the chafed spot just above her bikini-clad buttocks.

"That?" Selena said, turning around, smiling, blushing. "That is none of your beezness."

"Woo!" they all crooned, teasing. "Woo!" chorusing, stamping their feet on the green linoleum. "Woo!"

La Palomita busied herself with her hair now. She combed it out straight and long and parted it in the middle. She coiled it up into a heavy blue-black bun and caught it with a tooled-leather hairclasp at the nape of her neck, like a Flamenco dancer.

"Now you can dress me, Mama," she said, when she was done. They all leapt to do her will. They dressed her in rags. They dressed her in soiled white cotton pants, a torn khaki workshirt, a sweat-stained neckerchief. They dressed her in the dirty clothes of a poor campesino. They put rough tire-sole sandals on her tiny brown feet. They clapped a battered Indian sombrero on her exquisite head. They disguised her as a man.

All the women sighed.

"Ah, qué maravilla esa!"

"Qué belleza, ay!"

She gave herself a last once-over in the mirror: her black slanted eyes under the low-brimmed straw hat, her curved Mayan nose, her lips full and red as wine, her little chin that threatened to point but didn't, her two front teeth that overlapped in the cutest way, her skin the color of soil ripe for planting, and her greatest elegance, her neck like Nefertiti's.

She was ready now for the ritual drama, the human sacrifice. She was playwright and actress, priestess and victim. Downstairs in the CCAC office her audience was waiting: her blood, her breath, her body, her extended soul.

The image that La Palomita had worked to create tonight, that she could see before her in the mirror now, had nothing to do with vanity, she told herself. It was important only as a symbol to her *causa*, to the *raza* she loved more than herself. She saw herself as only an organ, the most necessary and important organ of the body of *la raza* in San Joaquin County.

Selena had transformed political reality in Calmento overnight. The "*injusticia*" of the 'Duccis had mobilized the recalcitrant farm workers in a matter of hours. The entire Chicano community had rallied to their side.

Now even Doubting Connie had to admit that things were looking "fairly good."

Things were in fact almost perfect.

There was only this one last string untied.

"Mama, will you call Delano for me? We'll only be a minute. Please, all of you, wait for us outside the door."

Range materialized in a moment, looking rather peaked. He had looked that way for nearly forty hours now, ever since he heard what went down in the Dootch's tomato patch. That's the way she wanted him to look. She had left him to dangle like that. She wanted him to wonder when the ax would fall. And she'd watched his anxiety level rise compliantly to the point where soon he'd either have to make a run for it or bust wide open. Selena knew somehow that he would not run away. Why that was she couldn't say. Maybe it had something to do with what they had done together in bed. What they had done was very good: those long brown hands around that thick white penis, guiding it into her body. . . And then giving herself up to the tongues: "Basicka-balucka, goficka-gofucka . . ." There was also an emotional thing that went beyond the physical and mutually ulterior end.

Selena closed the door behind him.

"Sit down there, on the tub," she said, and swung herself up on the sink, with her legs dangling over the side.

"Now before you say anything else," he said, with an audaciously assumed expression of sincerity on his handsome bearded face, "please let me explain."

"Tell it to me, man," she said.

"They got me out on parole on the condition that I work for them."

"So?"

"So, any time they want, all they have to do is phone my parole officer and have me 'violated' back into the Joint."

"Hey, Del, that would be cold."

"Selena, believe me."

"What for?" she said. Her tone was ironical rather than angry, and not quite unfriendly; she was swinging her feet over the sink, hitting her sandals against each other. Her hands were folded in her lap.

"I felt so guilty the whole time."

"Sure you did."

"I even left you clues," he said, sniffing at himself in his habitual way.

"Now, why would you want to do a thing like that?"

"I don't know," he said. "To salve my conscience?"

"I doubt it."

"Look," he said, half-rising to his feet. "As soon as I heard what happened out in the field I knew I'd been had," he said, talking very fast. "Figgered I was bait and the Dootch was the bear and you had him by the claw. I coulda phoned him, Selena, any time I wanted. Coulda told him everything I knew. Coulda said it wasn't the field but the shed they had to watch. Coulda fucked up all your bad plans. Ain't that the truth?"

"Possibly."

"So, what do you want from me now?"

"I don't want any clues, and I don't want any phony admissions or confessions or expressions of regret. You know what I want from you?"

"No," he sighed. He was terrified. And yet what had he to be terrified of? He could get up and walk out the door right now and no one would stop him.

"What I want is this: I want you to work for me," she said, *siempre de improviso.*

His mouth fell open. But Selena wondered if he was really as surprised as all that. There was something in Range, some little kernel hidden very deep, that nothing could surprise.

"Really," she said, "I kind of feel like I owe you something."

"You're joking."

"Naw. You landed them right in my net, Del. It would've taken years without you."

"Who says I didn't do it on purpose?" he attempted, half-heartedly.

"Save it," she said.

"What about my parole then?" he asked quite unembarrassed, and with an energy and volume that told her he was already transmitting at his normal frequency again. That is exactly where she wanted him at.

"Don't worry about it."

"Why not?"

"We won't tell them you quit."

"You mean you're not mad at me?"

"Mad? Why should I be?"

"I just don't understand how you can forgive me so easy."

"Delano, the truth is . . . you are just another victim."

"A victim of *what?*" he demanded, with a characteristic exhalation through pursed lips. It was a pugnacious gesture, the opposite side of the coin from his self-deprecatory sniff.

"A victim of Vanducci exploitation," she said in deadly earnest, and dismissed him peremptorily from her presence.

Then she called for her female relatives. They took her by the hand and led her out of the bathroom and across the loft as if she were made of precious stuff.

Actually, the stuff she was made of was not particularly precious. But it was highly combustible: quick to flare up and quick to burn out. She let them adulate her a bit. It helped. In her conversation with Range she had allowed her carefully nurtured fires to die down. Now she had to concentrate all her efforts to rekindle them.

Below her on the floor of the CCAC office were her closest people: Rudy, Aguilar, Range, Lita's dark dour little husband Nacho, Fulgencio, Enrique Mendoza, Corky DeJesus, the three Apaches, and thirty other new organizers and picket captains whom she had selected and assembled after her speech in Emiliano Zapata Park. They all stopped talking as soon as she appeared above them.

Selena loved the thick atmosphere, the heat and smell her people generated in that small space, the electrical impulses discharged by their brains. She fed off the strength of the crowd. Soon she would be consuming herself again in her own great sunburst of energy. *Yeah.*

She was almost ready.

Like an incognito queen with her ladies-in-waiting she descended the stairs.

By the time she reached the floor she had her audience in an absolute trance, and herself with it. She halted three steps up from the foot of the stairs. Permitted her ladies to pass her by. And at last she stood alone above the crowd. *Tell it, now.*

When Selena looked at the crowd she was not concerned with individuals. If she looked for any single person among the masses she would lose her feel of the whole.

Yet, it was not pride or vanity that made her set herself above the others, she believed. It was transcendence!

What she saw before her tonight was one great picture, one great portrait, the face of the *pueblo unido*. It was this *pueblo* that she must ignite, must direct and move to victory against still tremendous odds. *Now get down, girl, get down.*

Selena took a long deep breath and started to speak. Till that very moment she'd no idea what she must say, what role she must play. She didn't even know in what language she would speak. She left all of that up to her genie.

It was the genie who began to talk now.

It chose to speak in *inglés.*

"Let me tell you all a story," Selena said, in the flat normal twang of the San Joaquin, with just the faintest trace of Mexican accent. "Just before I came back to Calmento I went to Cesar Chavez and I said, 'Cesar, I want your support. I'm going up to my hometown to organize my own people to strike for higher wages and better working conditions in the tomato fields. The tomato industry, Cesar, as you know, is the largest cash crop agro-industry in California, yet its workers are among the lowest paid in the state. They live in camps unfit for animals. They work in poisonous insecticides. They are bilked by unscrupulous labor contractors in collusion with the growers. Children labor like adults in the fields. There aren't even any field toilets for the workers; they got to squat like dogs in the furrows.'

"And Cesar said to me, *compañeros*, he said, 'Selena, I know that what you say is true. But I'm gonna have to turn your request down. And I'll tell you why. At the moment we got more than we can handle fighting the Teamsters and mobsters and lettuce growers down here in Salinas. It would cost us approximately fifty thousand dollars a week to finance a major strike up in Calmento, and the chances of winning are just about nil. The tomato growers' association is the richest, most powerful, most militantly antiunion farmers' organization in the whole state. They got enormous pull in the town, the county, and up in Sacramento: Reagan is their right-hand man. And they got the local police, the sheriff, the DA, and all the judges in their back pockets. They are gonna fight you tooth and nail and use every dirty trick in the book to preserve what they got. I'm sorry. Selena,' he said, 'but that's just the way it's gonna have to be.'

"Well, I thanked him for his frank appraisal of the situation, *compañeros*. And then in rebuttal I quoted the precedent of the workers of

Firebaugh. Firebaugh is a little town down in Fresno County with a large Chicano population. And one of the *carnales* down there, he got fired off a job for organizing. His fellow workers walked off the job spontaneously as a protest. The injustice of his firing galvanized all their energies. They drew up a list of demands, including wage increases. The whole barrio supported them, as our barrio here in Calmento has done for us in the last couple of days. They set up tents next to the orchards. They brought in stoves for cooking. The workers came day and night to eat there. The spirit of the people was strong. They helped each other, lived with each other, slept out on the ground. They didn't need no fifty thousand dollars a week. All they had to do was hold out for ten days. After ten days Cesar was so impressed with their *huelga* that he came up to have a look. He saw there were terrible grievances, injustices on the part of the growers. He saw that the workers were strong, there was community support, spirit, good humor, and an enormous desire for *victoria en el fil*. He endorsed their strike, went to the landowners, and got them to negotiate. In the end, twenty-three thousand acres and four thousand workers were won for *la causa*. All because the little people of Firebaugh took it into their own hands.

"When I was done, Cesar laughed and said, 'You got a powerful argument there, Selena, but I still have to say no.' Well, *compañeros*, I don't believe that 'no.' Just like I didn't believe him when he said it couldn't be done in Calmento. Cesar is a great man, but we have already proven him wrong. We are united, filled with hope, and a tremendous will to win. The time is ripe. We are primed and ready. The barrio is ready. The labor camps are ready. The packing shed is ready. The field workers are ready. I am ready. You are ready. The only people who are not ready are the growers, who will receive tomorrow morning the rudest surprise of their lives, who will be hit at the height of summer when their crops are most vulnerable to rot on the vine. And the unreadiest of all will be Vanducci & Son, the beegest, who will be distressed to find that our main efforts have been concentrated on him. It'll take another two days at least for him to get his professional scabs up here from Mexicali. By then we're gonna have his ranch sealed up so tight that, anyone tries to get in or out, the air is gonna go 'pop' like a vacuum-packed coffee jar. The Dootch can only last ten days without losing his whole year's· profit. If we can hold out till then he will fall into our hands like ripe fruit. Cesar will come up here then, I bet, and help us sign our contract. I believe this with all my heart," Selena said. And the funny thing was, the moment she said it, she did believe it. "The victory is ours," she said. "*Ya hemos vencido!* That will be our slogan. . . ."

After the speech she paused on the stairs to survey her audience. They seemed to have swallowed it, hook, line, and sinker. Only Doubting Connie seemed dubious; yet even she seemed to reflect upon it for a moment, asking herself if it couldn't possibly be true. And Selena wondered whether it had been her outrageous fictional story that had won them, or her false but necessary invocation of the name of Cesar Chavez. Whatever the case, they were an utterly captive audience now: No one had the courage to come near her, no one had the nerve to say a word, not even her own mother.

Selena was hot, she was popping. She felt that steam must actually be escaping from her ears and nostrils, flames shooting out of her eyes. She was half-convinced that she would glow in the dark.

"Follow me," she said to her family, and they trailed out the door behind her like baby ducks. "Say good-bye to me now," she said, when she got to Aguilar's pickup truck. "Then wave and drive away. I'll ditch the *policía* and meet you at the corner of Third and East Street in five minutes."

They obeyed without question, and rattled off into the darkness. She went back into the office and dismissed her picket captains and organizers. They filed out the door like soldiers, two abreast, still speechless with wonder.

That left her alone with Range.

"What about me?" he asked.

"Do what you want."

"I want to be with you."

"I'm leaving."

"Where are you going?"

"Come along and find out."

"I don't get it," he said, shaking his head in bewilderment.

"It's simple," she said. "I'm gonna let you prove yourself, just like you said you wanted to."

'But . . . how come you trust me?"

"I don't."

"Then . . . ?"

"Delano," she said, "the progress of certain historical forces is inexorable. And there is nothing you, the Vanduccis, or anyone else can do to impede it."

Then she turned around and marched through the house and out of the house and across the dark overgrown backyard looking neither right nor left, with Del trailing along behind her.

In the alley she ran into a prowler. Bumped right into him where he crouched like a scavenging animal in the darkness by the back gate, between the garbage cans. He grunted in fright, leapt to his feet, and ran off down the bumpy dirt alley, banging into fences, stumbling over tin cans and old tires.

Range nearly shit his pants.

But Selena barely noticed him. One foot ahead of the other, she trod purposefully down the alleyway past chicken coops and pigpens and horse corrals and garbage cans and courting cats and scratching rats, hearing nothing, seeing nothing but the path in front of her. She reached the rendezvous point and climbed over the tailgate and into the truckbed without a word, stiff and silent as a zombie.

Range clambered up behind her.

Aguilar dropped the Chevycita Bonita into gear and took off, heading for the country.

Selena let no one get near her.

She was like dynamite with the fuse burning. People were like water; words were like spit; they might put her out.

To deepest Carbona they rode in the hot valley night, the only sounds the drone of the engine, the clang of the tailgate chain, the squeak of the unlubricated springs.

Selena folded in upon herself again, treated herself for the last time to her deepest secret shame. Saw herself sprawled out naked in the back seat of a Lincoln Continental parked in a muddy asparagus patch. Watched herself confess her age-old predicament. Saw her moon-faced lover above her. Heard him start to laugh, cynically, as it seemed to her now. Heard herself laughing back, hysterically, perhaps. For six years the sound of those two young laughing voices had been ringing in her ears. Soon one of them or the other would be silenced for good.

The labor camp was all in darkness. Aguilar's headlights flashed on a sign at the gate:

CAFONE BRAND LABOR CAMP

PROPERTY OF VANDUCCI & SON, INC.

NO TRESPASSING

SURVIVORS WILL BE PROSECUTED

They parked in a peach orchard on Valpico Road and went in on foot. Selena led the way infallibly, as if she had radar built into her head. If there had been a fence, a wall, she would have walked right through it.

Near the entrance, between a row of labor buses, they were met by a delegation of campesinos. In darkness and silence they were ushered into the barracks, into the camp kitchen where the workers were assembled. They opened for Selena as if she had been the point of a dagger. Her *familia* the blade. Range the butt . . . She had no more worries about Delanito. Whatever his past, his ass now belonged to the *campesinita*. It was clear that no one could resist her. The night was like a secret religious ceremony. The campesinos were like Christian initiates in the catacombs of pagan Rome. Range and her family the acolytes. All was still save for an occasional cough or sniffle or the cry of a baby.

At long last Selena was in the heart of her enemy. Soon she would avenge all the suffering of her *familia,* her *raza,* herself. Soon with her Aztec knife she would begin to carve him up. From the inside. Ay!

She scrambled onto the table. She stood above the throng and let them see her in the light of an electric torch.

"Selena, Selena," they murmured, "Selena Cruz . . ."

She ripped the sombrero off her head and flung it to the kitchen floor. She unfastened her hairclasp and shook her long black hair out, let it fall all down her back and breast.

"*Ai ai ai!*" went the campesinos. Never had they seen anyone so fine, so dark and noble and tall. One of their own.

"This is the way I want you," she said in Spanish, in a compellingly gentle voice that she had learned as just a little girl. "I want you strong. I want you standing-up-on-your-own-two-feet. You see how I have freed my hair? So will I free you from the gringo's bondage. If there is any-one here who doubts in the ultimate victory of our *causa*, let him speak now. . . ."

Selena had to put her hair up and let it down several times in the course of the night, but never did anyone speak.

PART **III**

Seventeen

SWEATY, FRETFUL, SLEEPLESS, abed with his blissfully snoring wife at four o'clock in the morning, Jay Jay was startled to hear the telephone ring in the other room. An odd hour for a call. Yet after his initial surprise, he decided he welcomed the intrusion. And leapt out of bed and ran into the kitchen to answer it, hoping it would jar him out of the weird half-waking nightmare state he'd been in all through the night.

"Vanducci?"

"Yeah."

"Selena Cruz," she whispered.

"Wha-what do you want?" Jay Jay asked, shaking his head, trying to rattle some sense back into his brain.

"I want your assssss," she said, exaggerating the sibilant to the point of absurdity.

"Huh?"

"You got a strike on your hands," she hissed. "Your fields are surrounded by pickets."

The moment Selena mentioned the word "strike," a strange and wonderful thing happened. All the pressure that had been building up inside Jay Jay was suddenly released. *Sssss*, it went. And all the cobwebs and vapors blew out of his mind, leaving it clean as a whistle for the first time in weeks.

It was the suspense that had been killing him. Now that war had actually been declared, he could not wait for the battle to begin. If he had not received Selena's call at this time, he might have invented it. Maybe he had invented it. . . .

"Just a second," he said breathlessly. Dropped the receiver and ran out the kitchen door. Stood on the back steps naked, an ear to the warm east wind. For almost a minute he stood there in the darkness, hearing nothing but the pump-house door banging, the squeaking of the old windmill on the hill, the rustle of the wild oats behind the house. Then from over the property line on Corral Hollow Road came the sound of soft Spanish conversation, rising, falling, blowing in the wind.

He ran back into the house, picked up the phone, and said, "So what?"

"If you don't know now," she said, "you'll soon find out."

"You can picket us till doomsday for all we care, Selena, 'long as we're moving tomatoes."

"You're not going to be moving any more tomatoes," she said. "Not until you've signed a contract with us. Your labor camps have been liberated by their residents, and your packing shed employees have walked off the job."

"Whew," he said. "I don't get it."

Actually, he understood perfectly. Several days ago he had decided to play her game. Trouble is, she'd not only nabbed his pawn, she'd damn near cleaned him out with her first move.

"Sure you do," she said.

"All right, Selena," he said. "But listen, don't make the mistake of underestimating me."

"That would be an easy mistake to make."

"And don't underestimate the love I have for my family," he said, ignoring her sarcasm, "and the land that we hold in common."

"That kind of crap just does not enter into my calculations."

"The way I see things," he said, still refusing to hear her, "I'm just holding this ranch in trust for my boys."

"You had another boy once. You want to hear what happened to him?"

At last she had got through to him.

"Let me serve you warning," he said.

"You don't serve me shit," she said. "I take."

". . . I will not be swayed by emotion, or anything that might have been between us in the past."

"I've never accused you of being softhearted, Jay Jay."

"I just wanted to let you know how it is."

"I'm not interested," she said. "Now let's get down to business. If you want to talk, get your old man and meet us at your packing shed office in an hour."

Then she hung up.

When Bruno and Angie heard the news, they took it just about as well as could be expected under the circumstances.

"Tsk, tsk," Angie said, sitting up in bed, shaking her head. "That woman certainly set you fellows up, didn't she?"

"'Fraid so, Mom."

"If you'll remember," Angie said, "I advised you very strongly against trusting Delano Range. Didn't I?"

"Yep," Jay Jay said, "but . . ."

"Do you think she turned him, Jay Jay?" Bruno said, butting in, rolling out of bed in his boxer shorts.

"What do you mean?"

"I mean, do you think she won Del over some way to the other side?"

"Naw, Dad. Remember, we got his parole papers in the palm of our hand. A word from us and he's back in the slammer. I think what happened . . . I think she found out somehow that he was working for us. And she lied to him. Told him the field was organized and the shed was loyal. When in fact the opposite was true. And Del, he believed her, and passed it on to us. I guess she had it figured that we would fire the whole crew out there, if we suspected any hanky-panky. And she knew they'd hit the ceiling, if they got laid off for no reason, like that."

"Had us completely psyched out, huh?"

"Yes, you might say that, Bruno," Angie said.

"But what I want to know is this," Bruno said, ignoring his wife's ironic tone. "How in God's name did she figure out that Range was our man?"

"Good question," Jay Jay said.

"Maybe he just ain't a very good spy."

"Maybe she's just a little bit smarter than you fellows," Angie said.

"All right," Bruno said. "How would you do things, honey?"

"You're running scared, Brunino. You act as though we've no power base in this county."

"Maybe you're right."

"You know I am," she said, yawning, falling back on the pillow, pulling the blue bedcovers up to her soft unwrinkled neck. "Now go on and get out of here, both of you. And let me get my beauty rest."

Bruno turned off the lamp and marched out of the room, across the pink and white den, through the modernistic yellow kitchen and outside into the darkness, with Jay Jay right behind him.

"Okay, okay," he said, prancing up and down on the sharp gravel in his bare feet. "Let's see the strike. Where is it?"

Jay Jay ran over to his Ford pickup and switched on the spotlight, illuminating a circle of five little dark bow-legged Mexicans in straw sombreros, huddled in the road around the Vanducci mailbox. Each of them carried a sign—*HUELGA!*—on a tall stick. Jay Jay's spotlight had caught them by surprise. But instantly they recovered and struck up a chant: "*Hueeeeeelga, hueeeeeelga, hueeeeeelga*," shaking their sticks in rhythm to their words.

They did not look particularly angry. On the contrary, they appeared to be having a rather good time. One of them was little Enrique Mendoza, Jay Jay's good-humored irrigator. You could see his big teeth flashing from a hundred yards away.

"Okay," Bruno said, almost regretfully, "if that's the way they want it. . . ."

Then he turned and crept gingerly but purposefully over the gravel in his bare feet and dialed in quick succession (and despite the hour) his labor contractor, his county supervisor, his congressman, the sheriff, the chief of police, the mayor, the chairman of the Calmento Farm Bureau, the president and treasurer of the California Tomato Growers Association, and Judge Benetti of the Superior Court. Then, almost as an afterthought, he called his lawyers in San Francisco. And finally, winking lewdly at Jay Jay—"This is strictly off the record, son"—he phoned Mr. Smokey Dee Leevining of the Posse Vigilantus.

Jay Jay was mightily impressed. In the workaday world of the ranch you tended to forget. Angie was right. The Vanduccis were a force to be reckoned with in this fucking valley.

An hour later and they took off down the bumpy driveway in twin blue pickups, Jay Jay out front, his father behind. Ran the picketers off into the drainage ditch. Goosed their machines on Corral Hollow Road, and dove for the dark green tomato fields below. Dawn was just breaking over the distant Sierra. A pinkish light crept across the sky. A bluish light invaded the sleeping San Joaquin. Through Jay Jay's window the air came fast, fresh, and dry. He felt like an Italian ace of the Dawn Patrol, *La Pattuglia Aurora*, bound for a bombing run over Addis Ababa. The words of a song his grandpa used to sing kept running through his brain:

> *La nostra gente*
> *or non emigra più*
> *per sofrir!*
> *il fecondo lavor*
> *dei coloni*
> *tutta l'Etiopia farà*
> *fiorir . . .*

Jay Jay hurtled under the freeway bridge with his daddy right on his tail. Leveled out on the valley floor and roared for the Valpico corner. At every farm road there was a little bonfire, a line of battered old cars, and a dark circle of ragged Chicanos carrying picket signs. "*Hay huelga aquí, aquí hay huelga, hueeeeeelga, hueeeeeelga, hueeeeeelga!*" they chanted, shaking their picket signs in unison, shuffling in the dirt by the side of the road. What they looked like to Jay Jay was . . . barbarous, uncivilized.

Bruno swooped up behind him and blinked his lights. Jay Jay banked to the side without diminishing his velocity. Bruno drew abreast, his sparse bleached hair blowing in the wind. He grinned, gave him the high sign, yelled, "Let's go get 'em, son!" And neck and neck they yodeled off to Carbona, scattering spicks and picket signs every which way.

On Valpico Road they caught a line of them unaware and forced sixteen wetbacks into the cold irrigation canal. Quickly Jay Jay spun around on his own, caught them just as they were coming out of the water, and dunked them all again. Came so close to the soft shoulder that he almost followed them in with his pickup truck at eighty-five miles an hour.

When they reached Carbona the entire hamlet was overflowing with Mexicans. Old and young, men and women and little kids, townspeople and country folk, farm workers and railroad workers. Must have been two or three hundred of them out there, laughing and shouting and chanting and dancing and running in and out among their beat-out cars that they'd parked alongside the road. Probably less than half of them were Vanducci employees. But all of them carried picket signs. Beside the Vanducci packing shed gate they were holding up placards that said *HUELGA!* Next door at the labor camp they were waving red and black banners that read NO NOS MOVERAN—WE SHALL NOT BE MOVED!

And yet, through all of this, things in Carbona went right along more or less as they always had. Cement trucks from the open-pit concrete plant behind the shed kept roaring by on Valpico Road, heading for the freeway overpass project in Crow's Landing. A Western Pacific rail-testing crew was working its way calmly down the tracks on the embankment above the strung-out picketers, whistling and joking with each other and chatting about baseball scores. A white dog was trotting down the center line of the blacktop as if he were alone in the world.

Jay Jay blared his horn, revved his engine, sent the white dog yelping and scurrying into the drainage ditch, and turned in at the packing shed gateway. "Outa my way!" he hollered. "Outa my way!" And carried through the crowd of pissed-off Chicanos at a steady three miles an hour with his dad right behind him. The crowd gave, but not without some resistance: They snakedanced around his truck, chanting their slogans— *"Buscamos justicia en el fil!"*—shouting their grievances—*"Trabajamos como perros por nada!"*—shrieking their demands—*"Aumento de cincuenta centavos la hora!"*—kicking at his fender in anger, jerking at his radio antennas, making them whip through the air. A smart-ass kid with an Apache headband flipped him the bird through his open wind wing. Somebody threw a big rock that shattered his rear window and splattered his gun rack with glass.

There was a moment when Jay Jay was completely surrounded by the crowd that he experienced a tremor of paranoid fear: these dark little sweaty foreigners with their oily pockmarked skin, their slanted eyes and sharp pointed teeth . . . They would eat him alive if they could, take his land, destroy his family, cannibalize his soul.

And then very quickly he bumped and nudged his way through the crowd and made it through the gate. Burnt rubber across his daddy's immense dirt parking lot. Around his quarter-mile-long stack of empty tomato lugs. Around his long line of empty six-wheeler tomato trucks, some of them being warmed up by their early-bird drivers, big beefy white men, Teamsters in baseball caps with farm equipment company ads printed across the front. Skidded up in front of the aluminum packing shed in a swirl of white dust. His dad pulled up beside him. They got out and walked over and opened up the sliding main door. Turned on the lights and gave the shed a once-over. It pleased them both greatly to see that everything was in order. Outside chaos might reign, but here in the 'Ducci shed all was clean and cool and dry and everything worked. At the flip of a switch the machinery would spring to life.

Though it cost a fortune to light the shed during nonworking hours, Bruno kept it lit now a bright fluorescent white. Jay Jay understood the gesture perfectly: Darkness was barbarity, civilization was light. In a Vanducci home the lamps stayed on all night. And nothing was too good for the *plant;* no expense, no investment, no sacrifice was too great.

Penny poor and pound wise, the Wops and Portagees and Yugoslavs had come late to the valley, and were ridiculed and abused for their profligate Mediterranean ways with agriculture, their feverish acquisition of more and more irrigable land, their overplanting and underselling. And then within twenty years they had turned the cautious WASP husbandmen straight under, buried them in their own hot fecund soil that they'd not had the macho to truly stir. . . . Or, at least, that's the way that Jay Jay Vanducci saw things.

The 'Ducci & Son office was bright and roomy and modern. Here Bruno conducted not only his packing business, but all his other agro-interests as well. It was furnished with three large desks, one for himself and one for each of his clerks, several gray plastic conference chairs with seats contoured to fit the human buttocks, two big Selectric electric typewriters, a long standup workbench cluttered with waybills and receipts, a photocopy machine, and a small IBM billing computer. On the Dootch's desk at the rear of the room there was a neat stack of papers and folders, a small plaque with I FIGHT POVERTY—I WORK! written on it, a round wooden stand with two little flags stuck in it, one American and one Italian, and a twenty-year-old picture of Bruno and Angie and Jay Jay standing out in front of the ranch, with Grandpa Tony and Grandma Letizia beside them. The wall was covered with snapshots of Tony as a young farmer, yellowing photos of antique spike-wheel tractors and mule-drawn wagons, technical shots of different aspects of a modern tomato growing and packing operation, and a colorful display of various Cafone Brand tomato box labels over the years. The room had a white perforated soundproof ceiling, plastic fake-wood wall paneling, and a dark green astroturf rug on the floor. A wide bay window above the workbench looked out on the floor of the packing shed.

This was the place where Bruno spent much of his life, and it was arranged to suit his taste. Jay Jay spent a good deal of his time here too. Someday he would sit at his father's desk, under the picture of A. P. Giannini shaking hands with Grandpa Tony. Here he would spend the rest of his years.

It was a bit stuffy in the office, so Bruno turned on the air conditioner. Then he took a deep breath and went over to sit at his desk. Put his workboots up on the ink blotter, leaned back, clasped his hands behind his head, and sighed loudly.

"Put the coffee on, will you, son?"

Jay Jay did as he was told. Soon the delicious aroma of Medaglia d'Oro filled the room. He served Bruno his coffee as he liked it: black, thick with anise-flavored sugar. And himself: artificial sweetener and Pream.

"Now," Bruno said, slurping at his cup loudly, "before they get here, son, there's a few things I'd like to say. When they come in, we're gonna be all business, see? We listen to what they got to say. Find out exactly what they're up to. Then we show them the door. Right?"

"Right," Jay Jay said.

". . . I have no intention of negotiating with these people, under any circumstances. You can tell by the tactics they're pulling out there, Jay Jay, that we're dealing with Communists. Communists do not give a damn about the little guy, the fellow who will lose his harvesttime job. All they want to do is get the boss. Right?"

"Right."

". . . Now, here's the way I got it figured. They think they got us by the *coglioni* now, right at the beginning of harvest, in high summer, with the fruit out there getting sunburnt and mildewing on the vine. But look at it this way, Jay Jay. It's only gonna be twenty-four hours before our green-card braceros start showing up from Mexicali. Our winos from the Casual Labor Center in Stockton can hold the fort till then. And Buddy Baldocchi of the TGA has promised me three hundred top fruit packers from the Imperial Valley by tomorrow night. Then we crank up the shed and start moving tomatoes again. . . . But let's say we run into some kind of snag. No problem. I already got Jerry DeSylva of the Farm Bureau on the case. Any trouble and he'll get the governor to declare a crop emergency and give us a permit to import as many more Mexicans as we want. And not only that, in three or four days, Judge Benetti and my lawyers tell me I'm gonna have a court order in my pocket. And that court order is gonna prevent all picketing and agitation on or near Vanducci property. And it's gonna provide for a large force of county sheriffs to back it up. . . . So what do we stand to lose, Jay Jay? You tell me. Almost nothing, right?"

"Right."

After the pep talk and another cup of coffee, Bruno seemed much refreshed. He lit another cigar, picked up the phone, and dialed the county sheriff again.

"Hey, Jimmy, you got your boys in position yet? Yeah? Great! Now lookit. You just tell 'em to stay right where they are till I give the word. All right? Atta way to go, old buddy!"

Then, just because he was feeling his oats, he called the Calmento chief of police again and chewed his ass out good.

". . . Goddamnit, Myron, what kind of surveillance were you conducting on that woman, anyway? Hell, we should've been warned about this strike days ago. Jesus H. Christ, it's a disgrace, a waste of the taxpayers' money. And I don't have to tell you, do I, that I hold you directly responsible?"

Like denim-clad ghosts, specters of the 1960s, Selena and her cousin appeared out of nowhere on the packing plant floor. They spotted Jay Jay through the soundproof window, wavered, halted, whirled around as one, and floated smoothly together toward the door.

Watching them, Jay Jay could imagine very well the heavy shit they'd been into all through the late sixties, over in Berkeley and Salinas, down in Kern and Fresno counties. They were seasoned veterans now, little Mexican war-horses, each trained to compensate for the other's quirks. Watching them, it occurred to him that the outcome of this confrontation was not as clear-cut as his father might imagine.

His father had seen them too, and he was on the phone with the sheriff again.

"Go get 'em, Jimmy," he said.

Then one of the Chicanas knocked at the door. Bruno replaced the receiver quietly and leapt to his feet and ran across the room to get it. He was suddenly in an extremely agitated and excited state, which he attempted to control by imposing a slight stiff smile upon his very tense and serious face. It was not altogether successful. It was the smile he used to put there just before he gave Jay Jay a severe beating as a kid. Grandpa Tony used to do the same thing. Only he'd *kiss* you before he hit you.

Bruno opened the door, his mouth still frozen in a grin.

"Come in," he said, in what he intended as a not unfriendly voice.

"Hi, I'm Connie Pescadero."

Selena came in right behind her cousin. But she did not feel it necessary to introduce herself. Nor did she feel obliged to acknowledge the presence of her former lover in the room.

"Come on over and have a seat," Bruno said affably, leading them toward his desk. "Say, Jay Jay, you got that coffee going?"

"Sure do, Dad!" he said heartily, taking the cue from his old man.

"Well, bring these ladies some. . . . How do you like it?" he said, leaving no opportunity for refusal.

"Black," they said, almost in unison.

Bruno sat down. The women remained standing.

"Sit down, sit down!" he said, motioning them to the conference chairs in front of them.

Jay Jay brought the coffee, placing the cups and saucers on the edge of the desk.

"Maybe you'd like something a little stronger in it?" Bruno said, winking, reaching into his desk drawer.

Brought out a big white and blue bottle of Sambuca Romana, hoisted it into the air, and raised his sun-bleached eyebrows quizzically, comically.

Selena and Connie shook their heads simultaneously.

"You sure?" he said, appearing to be genuinely disappointed.

"No thanks," they said.

Then he offered the bottle to his son.

"Don't mind if I do, Dad," he said, and seated himself at his father's right hand.

Bruno poured a capful in Jay Jay's coffee, and a good deal more in his own.

"*Salute!*" he said in Italian, raising his cup.

Neither Selena nor her cousin seemed to know how to respond. Connie tried smiling but it didn't work. Came out more like a grimace of pain.

The Dootch sipped at his drink loudly, grandiloquently. He had achieved his aim. The women were obviously surprised, disconcerted, and neatly put off balance by his display of cordiality. Connie drummed her fingers noisily on her black leather briefcase. Selena wet her lips inadvertently.

"Now," he said, grinning naughtily, leaning back in his chair, flicking invisible ashes from his cigar, clicking his tongue and shaking his head to signify that the liquor was good, especially good when one dared to partake of its pleasure at this sober hour of the morning, "you wanted to talk?"

"Yes," Selena said, wetting her lips again, clearing her throat, speaking in an official tone of voice, "we have here, Mr. Vanducci, a list of our demands. . . ."

"Oh, is that right?" he said, leaning forward, feigning great interest, meaning his feint to be perceived. "Mind if I have a look?"

Selena took Connie's briefcase off her knee, unzipped it, and brought out two typed sheets of paper, one a carbon copy of the other. She handed the original to Bruno and set the copy on the table before her.

Her hands were trembling with excitement.

Bruno took the page from her, put his glasses on, and read the list of demands out loud:

1. Moratorium on poisonous or cancer-causing pesticides and herbicides.
2. Abolition of child labor in the fields.
3. Improvement of substandard labor camp housing.
4. Restriction of capricious hiring and firing practices.
5. Installation of adequate field toilet facilities.
6. Field Wages—From $1.50 per hour to $2.00 per hour. From 15¢ a box to 20¢ a box.
7. Packing Shed Wages—From $2.00 per hour to $2.50 per hour.

"Well, I tell you, this is quite a list you got here," he said, when he had finished. Then he looked up at his visitors and smiled. He appeared to be enjoying himself immensely. And yet, just beneath his show of geniality was a crude and venomous irony that he did nothing to hide.

Across the desk the union people tensed up visibly. Connie started grinding her jaw. A smear of perspiration appeared on Selena's upper lip.

". . . Now, I would like to try and sincerely reply to your demands one by one," Bruno said. "But unfortunately I'm not gonna be able to do that. And I'll tell you why. In all honesty, ladies, collective bargaining is just not a viable possibility for the tomato industry. We got a highly perishable product here. While we were sitting around the bargaining table our crop would be out there rotting in the field, and none of us would make any money. And besides that, I'll tell you very frankly, I just don't have the authority to negotiate with you on my own. Any inquiries you might have in regard to wages or working conditions should be addressed to the Tomato Growers Association."

The women appeared to be taken aback. Looked as if they expected him to go on.

"Is that your last word on the subject?" Selena asked.

The Dootch pretended to reflect on it for a moment, and then he said, "Gee, I'm afraid so. Sorry about that."

"But can't we at least discuss—" Connie began.

"No," Bruno said, rising to his feet, signaling that the interview was at an end.

"Now just a moment!" Connie said, leaping to her feet, grabbing the list of demands, waving it in Bruno's face. "Surely, you can't—"

"Can't?" Bruno said, still smiling. "I don't know the meaning of that word."

Connie started to say something else, but Selena caught her by the elbow and started leading her toward the door.

"Come on," she said. "What else is there to say?"

Bruno seemed undecided about what course of action to take. At first he sat back down in his swivel chair, attempting to maintain an appearance of dignity. But then he couldn't contain his excitement, and he jumped up and followed them across the room.

"You people," he said, circling them on his springy athletic legs, chopping the air with his stubby red hands, "see, you people don't understand—"

"We understand perfectly," Selena said, halting in the middle of the room, turning to face him haughtily, with her nose in the air.

It became apparent to Jay Jay then that she relished this confrontation, and the prospect of the coming battle, quite as much as Bruno, quite as much as himself.

"No, really," Bruno said. "Look, I don't work in a vacuum here. The growers of this county operate in concert. Now," he said, reaching out to tap Selena carefully on the shoulder. "Let's say I negotiated with you. None of the growers of this county would ever speak to me again.

I'd be ostracized from the Farm Bureau, the Elks Club, even the Knights of Columbus. . . ."

"You're breaking my heart," Selena said.

"No, listen, I'm serious. See, your people are migratory by nature. Me, I'm rooted to the same spot. That's why a lot of the time it's so hard for us to understand each other. Look, I'm part of the community here; I have roots here."

"Roots?" Selena said, disbelievingly. "Roots?"

Now it was Connie who urged Selena toward the door.

"Come on, let's go."

"Wait a second," Selena said, flinging Connie's hand away. "Here's a guy whose old man came over here in 1920. And he's talking to me, *una chicana de sangre pura,* about 'roots.' Now that is a laugh. . . ."

"Hold on now," Bruno said. But Connie pulled her out the door and closed it behind her.

"That fucking bitch," he said when they were gone.

He was standing there in front of the shut door, fuming, trying to make up his mind whether or not to pursue the matter. His common sense told him to stay where he was. But his anger got the better of him. He burst out of the door and ran after them.

Jay Jay also hesitated for a moment and then decided to follow his dad. When he caught up he was surprised to find him standing quietly beside Selena and Connie in the packing shed doorway. They were all staring fixedly at something that was taking place across the parking lot.

Over at the labor camp, under an angry cloud of boiling white dust, a strange and violent scene was just drawing to a conclusion. Sirens wailed through the hamlet, echoing off the peach and eucalyptus trees. Two-way police radios and portable loudspeakers blared. Mexicans cried out in pain. Burly deputies in tan uniforms grunted and cussed and barked out orders. Strikers jeered and chanted and shouted out furiously from across the county road. The white dust billowed up higher in the hot white sky, flattening the sun, paling it.

The San Joaquin County Sheriff's Department was evicting the labor camp squatters by force. The last few holdouts were getting bashed on the heads with billy clubs now, and stomped on the barbed-wire fence that ran around the camp. Others were being handcuffed and thrown into paddywagons.

When the last of the squatters had been locked into the police vans and hauled away, Selena turned to Bruno and said, very flatly, "Pig."

"What?"

"Pig," she said again.

"Hey, you can't call me that."

"Now, Selena," Connie said, soothingly.

"Pig!" Selena hollered, stamping her foot on the concrete, shaking her fist at him. "Pig! Pig! Pig!" she shrieked, working herself up into a frenzy.

And drew back her tiny brown fist and . . . swung on the Dootch with all her might.

He deflected the blow quite easily, laughing and dancing out of her way.

Connie grabbed her by the arm and started pulling her outside.

"No, just a moment, please," Bruno said, going after them, his hands raised high. "Wait, I got a proposition for you," he said, in the cunning reasonable slightly Sicilian-accented voice that disguised his deepest anger. "Come 'ere," he said, motioning Selena back into the shed. "Look, I tell you what, dear. Why don't we call it a day? What do you say I just hand you three thousand smackers in cash, on a personal basis, right here and now? No one'll be the wiser. And you can take it and leave town with your cousin and just forget the strike. How's that? Isn't that fair? No? Why not? You did it once before, didn't you? All right, I'll go as high as four thousand. But that is positively my last—"

Selena went for his eyes.

He slapped her hand down hard and shuffled back like an aging boxer, giggling. "Hey, why not? Why not, eh?"

Connie got her around the waist and tried to hold her back.

Bruno took out a thick wad of bills and dangled them gleefully in front of her: "Go on, take it. Don't be coy. A Mexican always has his price. Ain't that right?"

Selena broke loose and knocked the money out of his hands. It fluttered down on the gray steam-cleaned cement floor.

Bruno slapped her face then. It was not a hard slap. It was meant to offend, not to harm. But it sounded awfully loud in the packing shed, echoing off the high tin roof.

Selena kicked him in the shin with all her might.

"Ow, goddamn you!" Bruno hollered, and limped after her and was just about to whack her a good one when Jay Jay, figuring that things had gone just about far enough, ran up behind him, pinned his arms back, and hauled him off toward the office.

Selena ran after them and kicked him in the other shin while he was helpless.

"You fuckin' little bitch!"

"Please, please, Selena . . ." Connie moaned.

"Get her out of here!" Jay Jay yelled, struggling to hold his father back.

At last Connie got her out the door.

"Take it easy, Dad, take it easy now!"

"Lemme go, lemmo go, I'll kill her, I'll kill her. . . ."

Bruno broke free and trotted out the door, with Jay Jay panting heavily after him.

Bruno caught them just as they were getting into an old Dodge that was parked around on the shady side of the shed. Range was sitting behind the wheel. He was wearing a brown beret and an expression of mild surprise.

Connie dropped to the ground by the open right door and assumed the fetal nonviolent position as soon as she caught the look in Bruno's eye.

He kicked her in the teeth, stepped on her head, yanked Selena out of the front seat by the hair, and started dragging her across the yard toward the shed door. What he proposed to do with her there, Jay Jay had no way of knowing. He ran up and tried to make eye contact and convince him to let her go. "Come on, Dad, come on . . ." But the Dootch was blind to reason.

Range got out of the car. "Let her go!" he yelled, and ran around behind Bruno. "Let her go!" he said again. But Bruno refused to hear. Range dropped him with a loud cracking judo chop to the back of the neck.

Selena fell down at Jay Jay's feet. He picked her up off the ground, holding her tightly around the waist. Never had he felt anything so soft and delicious. "Now," he said, "now," holding her tighter, tighter. He was afraid he might accidentally break something. Tighter, tighter . . . He was trembling with desire.

"Now *what*, scumbag?" she snarled, and spat at him. Bloody red from the drubbing his father had given her, the spit flashed through space, struck him high on the nose, and started oozing down into his eye socket. He was so startled he relaxed his grip on her.

"Lemme tell you something," she said, stepping back from him, her breasts heaving. "Lemme tell you. You want to hear it?" she ranted. "Range fucked your mother one time. How do you like that? Huh? He told me himself. How do you like that?"

"What—what are you talking about?" he said stupidly. Though he knew quite well what she was talking about, had known, or at least suspected, it for a long time: ever since that night when in a place between sleeping and waking he heard what he thought he might have heard from his mama's room.

"This!" Selena hissed and, quick as a snake, coiled and sprang for his face. Raked his cheek to the bone. Then whirled, leapt in the car, slammed the door, locked it, and rolled up the window.

Confronted by an enmity such as this, Jay Jay was unable to react. He just stood there looking down at her, dumbly, numbly. *Nobody should hate anyone as much as that,* he thought. His glasses and his cowboy hat had fallen off and were lying at his feet. He made no move to retrieve them.

Meanwhile Bruno had recovered and was slugging it out with Range on the other side of the automobile. And Connie was just rising groggily to her feet and stumbling for the car door. Inside, Selena had scooted over into the driver's seat and fired up the engine.

"Jay Jay!" the Dootch called. "Jay Jay!"

Range had gotten the upper hand now, and he was beating Bruno's head against the front fender.

Jay Jay ran around and got the little fucker by the neck in a full nelson and dragged him off. "What'd you say about my mother?" he asked him, snapping his neck down farther and farther in rhythm to his words. "What-did-you-say-about-my-mother?" But Range stomped him then so hard on the foot that he had to let go, then spun around and swung for Jay Jay's face, hard. Jay Jay blocked it and hit him with a solid right cross to the jaw that felled him instantly.

There was Delano Range the unfaithful agent, lying stretched out full length on the ground. His brown beret was knocked off his head. His eyes were closed tight. Blood was bubbling out of his nose, out of the corner of his mouth, staining his curly Guevara beard. There was Delano Range the Latin lover, cold-cocked at last.

Eighteen

"Go on, son, kick him in the face!" Range heard Bruno say.

"What?" he heard Jay Jay say from closer by, right above him, it seemed. "You all right, Dad?"

"Yeah," Bruno said, coming up behind him, breathing hard. "Stomp him one time for me, will you, son?"

And Range blinked his eyes open just in time to see the sharp heel of Jay Jay's cowboy boot raised over his face. Instinctively he grabbed it by the heel and toe, twisted it sharply, and brought him down hard on his back, knocking the wind clean out of him.

Then he jumped up, straight-armed Bruno out of the way, and streaked for the Dodge Dart. Selena and Connie were sitting in the front seat, bent over forward, turned anxiously in his direction, big-eyed. Selena had the back door open and she was winding the engine out loud, creeping forward across the sand, riding the clutch, ready to pop it out when he was safely inside.

Range dove for the back seat. Even before he was fully inside the car, she had popped the clutch and was burning rubber. *Wham!* the door slammed behind him. *Bam!* he hit his head on the doorhandle. And then he started to black out again. From a million miles away he could hear someone, Bruno Vanducci perhaps, hollering, "Don't let 'em out! Don't let 'em out!" And then he went under.

In the space where he found himself for the next few moments he could neither see nor hear. But he could feel everything. He could feel the pain where he had struck himself on the head. He could feel himself impelled backward against the seat as the car accelerated. He could feel himself rolling forward, falling off the seat and onto the floor when the car braked suddenly. He could feel himself skidding on his face across the rubber floormat when the car swerved violently, and skidding back when it swerved the other way, sweeping up old gum wrappers and bottle caps with his nose. He could feel himself slam against the drive-shaft hump when the car struck deep potholes, and floating in the air with a sickening hollowness in the pit of his stomach when it went over ramps and embankments.

A thick cloud of fine dust came sifting up through the floorboard. He could feel it sticking to his lips, his eyelashes, to the short hairs on his arms. He could feel himself breathing it in, choking on it, coughing. It got thicker and thicker and thicker. And finally, like the fine dust of time, of distance and removal, it blotted him out, snuffed the present entirely. . . .

He was lying on the floorboard of a pickup truck. His mama was driving. She was going fast, skidding around corners, weaving crazily through the streets of San Francisco. He could see her bare brown legs and her green shoes as they frantically worked the control pedals. He could see the many-colored wires all twisted and gnarled beneath the dashboard. He could see the heater, the air vents, the dull gray under-belly of the radio, the dusty floormat with old bubblegum stuck to it, turning black. But this time he wasn't frightened. He was perfectly content, euphoric even, it seemed, as he rolled violently from one side of the cab to the other. He even started to laugh, he thought. It was like the times when she used to take him out on the back lawn and play with him, roll him over and over inside an old cardboard box while she laughed and the dog barked and little Delano giggled with hysteri-cal pleasure.

This time his mama was not gonna light the house on fire.

She would not want to hurt him, this time. This time he would remember to tell her he loved her. He would tell her even before they got home to Calmento. On the freeway, riding down from the Altamont Pass, he would give her a great big kiss and hug her tight and say, in Spanish, which she liked best, *"Te quiero, mamá, para siempre, siempre, siempre,"* and promise never to leave her. . . .

Then he woke up. Groggy, still being buffeted roughly about on the floor, he shook his head, blew the fine thick dust out of his nostrils. "Whew!" Then he hauled himself up by the arms and leaned over the front seat between Selena and Connie.

The car was still going very fast, bouncing over potholes, skidding in the dust, barreling around piles of boxes, lines of tomato trucks, junked machinery, and other obstacles. Selena was driving hard. She was bent over the steering wheel, shifting gears quickly, popping the clutch, burning rubber, turning her wheels frantically this way and that.

Connie was shrieking out nonstop directions at the top of her lungs: "Turn here! Now back around to the left! Step on it! He's right behind you!" Though she sounded anxious and scared, there was also this little tremor of elation in her voice.

Yet Selena was obviously not listening to a word she said. She was too busy driving the car, too busy delivering her own unbroken rap which, though just as feverish and high-pitched as her cousin's, betrayed none of its inner confusion: "Goddamn, did you see that fucking Bruno go down? Wow! Did Delano cop a sunday on him! Caaaaaaray! And did you see me spit in Jay Jay's eye? Right in his eye! Ay!"

All this to the high trilling pickaninny sound of the early Supremes on the FM radio, behind a relentless MoTown beat.

The entire inside of the automobile was filled with dark skirling female voices, light swirling clouds of powdery dust.

Range was holding on tightly to the seat in front of him, trying to retain his balance as the car swerved right and left, trying to make some sense of the scene that confronted him. He peered through the screen of flying dust, past the ghostly faded-denim backs and shoulders of his *compañeras*, past their voluminous bonnets of lightly dirt-frosted Afro and indigenous hair.

And finally dug what in the fuck was going down.

They had never gotten off the grounds of the Vanducci packing shed. The sheriff's deputies had shut the front gate on them, trapping them inside the high chain-link fence. And now they were careening wildly around the perimeter, desperately seeking a way out, with two Vanducci & Son pickup trucks in hot pursuit.

"Hey, champ!" Selena hollered, grinning back at him in the rearview mirror while simultaneously throwing the Dodge sideways into a power glide six inches from the rim of a forty-foot pit full of rotting tomatoes. "How you doin', boy?"

"Better," he said, as she straightened out her ass-end and roared across the bumpy dirt parking lot toward the front gate.

"Ay, *cabrón*, Delanito," she said, wailing by the front gate, past a sheriff's deputy in a straw cowboy hat who had drawn his revolver and was waving it around madly in the air, "did you show those 'Duccis! Boy! They never knew what hit 'em!"

"Yeah," he said, smiling back, as they flashed by a long line of cheering Chicanos who were leaning against the outside of the Vanducci front fence. "I guess I did."

"Hey, Del, can you tell us something?" Connie shouted, while her cousin wheeled down to the end of the fence, broadsided to within a foot of the edge of the Carbona Canal, and burnt rubber toward a long row of six-wheeler tomato trucks that crossed their path. "How the hell do we get outa here?"

"Without breaking the law," Selena added, calmly guiding the Dart through the row of trucks with only centimeters to spare, past their pissed-off drivers who were waiting in ambush behind, past a cloud of flung missiles, rocks and clods and rotten tomatoes that banged and shattered and splattered on the windows and body of the car. "I can think of better reasons to go to jail."

"Me too," Connie said, "about a thousand of them," as Selena brodied around the aluminum corner of the packing shed, neatly maneuvered past Bruno Vanducci's roadblocking pickup truck, and broke into the open rear yard. "But I can't think of too many of them here in Calmento."

"There's only one way out," Range said.

"How's that?" Selena wanted to know.

"Gimme the wheel," he said. And without hesitation, without moving her foot from the gas, Selena scooted to the side. And Range jumped over into the driver's seat.

Now with the automobile in his control, he felt some of the Chicanas' excitement coming across. Framed in the crosshair of his rearview mirror he could see the pickup truck that pursued him, the huge angry face of Jay Jay Vanducci behind the wheel.

"Yeah," Range said. "Yeah," he repeated. "Yeah, did you see me bring that fucker down? Yeah! And his old man too! Yeah!"

"Flat on their asses," Selena said, laughing, slapping the dusty knee of her Levi's.

Connie was laughing too. First time he'd ever seen her crack more than a smart-ass grin.

Connie had a black eye, Range noticed. Selena had a bloody nose. He figured he probably looked about the same. Or worse. But it didn't faze him. Didn't faze them either. They would wear their wounds like battle ribbons, he thought, like symbols of their first engagement with the enemy.

"Whoopie!" he hollered, and played with the big Wop for a while. Took the fucker on a tour of his grounds at sixty and seventy miles an hour. Round his stinking tomato pit one more time. Over the ties of the Western Pacific spur that ran down the east side of his shed, chattering his teeth, shaking his guts up. Down the dangerous embankment and across his enormous dirt parking lot again. Past his gate, his cop, his fence, the strikers, who were whooping it up on the other side of the fence, waving *huelga* signs. Through his tomato trucks and his tomato drivers another time. Around his daddy, sideswiping his daddy's pickup adroitly, sending him crashing into the aluminum siding of his own fucking packing shed.

And then three times around his pile of tomato lugs, his stupendous stack of wooden tomato boxes (each with the rustic smiling face of his departed Grandma Letizia glued to its ends) that was four pallets of seven twelve-inch boxes high and a quarter mile long. . . . Once clockwise, twice counterclockwise, and finally right through the heavy ropes that held down his tarp on the western end . . . and *boom!* The end pallets fell over. Hit the next set of pallets. And the next and the next, going eastward down the line. Till both Del and Jay Jay were left circling in awe, idling down to almost a crawl. On and on and on the boxes went, like gigantic dominoes that disintegrated when they struck each other. The racket could be heard for miles, Range was sure. It was like . . . this long slowly rising rumbling noise and then this wild (and to Range, highly symbolic) earth-shaking roar when the whole stack came tumbling down at the end, raising an enormous mushroom cloud of white dust.

"*Viva la huelga!*" shouted Delano, Delanito the spick, the Mex, the wetback, the chilebean-eating Chicano whose lifetime identity problem was resolved at last. Suddenly he was free of the past. Free of the chickenshit little half-breed within him, the part cringing, part arrogant little weenie who'd chaffed and worried him and fucked him over and set cunning self-sprung traps for him all of his goddamn life. Free of that fat fucking gringo inside him who had smothered his Latin soul . . . Free!

Free, that is, till the 'Duccis decided to revoke his parole.

Ah, but then they would have to catch him!

I will become a master of a thousand disguises, the Robin Hood of the West.

"*Ai ai ai aiiiiiiii que viva la huelga en el fil!*" he hollered out the window, and took his shell-shocked old ex-bro on another goose chase round his domain. Led him down through his family's private junkyard behind the shed. Twisting and turning through a maze of discarded trash barrels, old tires, wheels, tables, chairs, workbenches, aluminum siding, chains, belts, ropes, wires, ladders, pipes, tools, stacks of lumber and plastic irrigation chutes, boilers, conveyors, electric engines, ball bearings, abandoned toilets and beds and water basins and camper attachments, horse trailers, house trailers, boat trailers, tractor trailers, semi-trailers, flatbed trailers, tractors both tracked and wheeled, hay balers, plows, discs, graders, rakes, seeders, sprayers, sulphur rigs, and bicycles, tricycles, pushcarts, trucks, pickups, dumpsters full of twenty-year-old trash, Jay Jay's ancient red Fergy Forklift, and a rusted-out 1958 Ford convertible with a sawdust-filled crankcase that Angie once bought from a shyster car salesman in Stockton ("Top Deal, $895." was still chalked to the windshield) . . . Led old Jay Jay right out the ass-end of his packing shed lot. Blasted through his old wooden gate in its remotest corner, flinging splinters and woodchips and broken boards all over. Bounced across his railroad spur in hot white morning sunlight. Into the lower section of his labor camp property. Up through his apricot orchard, his torn-down walnut orchard full of rotting hulks of enormous uprooted trees. Around a forest of blooming cactus plants and red, white, and pink oleanders. Into the dusty main yard of his labor camp. Past rolling tumbleweeds, abandoned washing machines, stinking piles of plastic-bagged garbage. Past his tenants' sagging laundry stretched between his barracks, long low unpainted wooden barracks with hot tin roofs and windowless black apertures for air. Past his forlorn blacktop basketball court, its hoopless backboard baking in the sun. And the chickens of his peons, their ducks and goats jumping out of the way, their abandoned horse corral, their rabbit hutches along the side. Past his roofless stucco bathhouse with its rows of blackened porcelain basins and its mud-splattered Mediterranean blue paint job. Past his camp dining hall with the following sign swinging above the door:

ATENCIÓN
Favor de quitarse
el sombrero
antes de entrar

ATTENTION
Please remove
your hat
before entering

Range was just making for the gate on Valpico Road when in his rearview mirror he caught a glimpse of Jay Jay placing a call on the radiotelephone. Determined then and there that an immediate change in plans and direction was in order. Hit his brakes without warning. Ass-ended around in the dirt till the two ex-bros were eyeball to eyeball on the narrow driveway. Then, just as Jay Jay was about to ram him head on, he feinted to his left and, while Connie and Selena laughed and hooted and bounced in their seats, hitting their heads on the roof, made a long end run to the right, into the dry irrigation ditch that ran alongside the road, through a line of cactus plants, over a neat pile of old crossties and rusty iron rails, down along the furrows of somebody's field of tall corn. Weaved his way through the labor camp again, lickety-split, scattering domesticated fowl every which way. Back through the felled walnut orchard again, leaving a trail of billowing white dust behind him. Up onto the railroad spur again. Lined his wheels up with the rails, and rode the bucking crossties a hundred yards down the embankment to the open-pit cement plant that lay to the south of the 'Ducci property. Off the tracks at a cement truck crossing. Up the dirt pathway to MacArthur Road. Then north on MacArthur as fast as the Dart would go, along the tall eucalyptus trees that lined the Carbona Canal. Ran the Valpico Road stop sign doing eighty miles an hour. Hit the WP mainline embankment doing sixty, flew four feet into the air, hit, bottomed, skidded, straightened out, started to spin again, and attempted a swift foxy little saving right turn into a narrow dirt road that ran through somebody's plum-plum trees ("plum-plums" as opposed to "prune-plums," which were grown solely for canning purposes). Missed his objective. Skidded off the road and into the orchard sideways. His left wheels hit the black plowed ground and suddenly stopped skidding. His right wheels rose up, up, up. Car rolled right on over, narrowly missing a tree. Landed right side up and then damn near half-rolled again. Hung there teetering for an instant and then the wheels came safely back down to earth. And ended up stalled but unharmed, bouncing up and down on the Dart's squeaky springs in a blinding cloud of black dust.

Jay Jay was nowhere in evidence.

"We lost him," Range said. "Like I say: Can't beat these Dodge Darts. Best cars ever made. . . ."

Selena and Connie, who for the last two minutes had been holding their breaths, exhaled at last. And promptly broke into fits of coughing laughter.

"Oh, holy Jesus!" Connie said, fanning the dust away from her swarthy acne-scarred face.

"Goddamnit, Del, you are too much, too much!" Selena said, wiping her sweaty blackened forehead with the back of her hand. "Too much, too much!" she kept saying, while they all roared with laughter, whacking the dusty dashboard and steering wheel with the flats of their hands, stirring up new little eddies and swirls of dust, and the Supremes, undismayed, continued their long-playing album of their greatest hits.

Then Selena turned to Connie and said, "*Ese, prima, qué te parece?* What do you think?"

"Let's go back to the CCAC," Connie said.

"How come?" Range asked.

"To find out what's happening in the other sections, Del," she said, politer than usual. "I mean, we got people out all over the Calmento area. As leader, Selena is supposed to stick close to headquarters. You lose communications with your picket captains, you're gonna lose control of your strike."

"I don't know," Range said. "I think we ought to stick around awhile. Hide the car in the orchard, up near the railroad embankment. Sneak across the tracks, and join up with our picketers on Valpico Road."

"What for?"

"I got a feeling that we could reoccupy that labor camp."

"You're kidding."

"No, I'm not kidding. I noticed when we drove through there. There's only two cops guarding the whole place. And they're out at the front gate. I know a way we could infiltrate maybe twenty or thirty people back in there."

"Oh, yeah," Connie said. "And then what?"

"Then we would hold it," Range said. "At all costs."

"I tell you what, Range. It would cost a whole lot. They'd just come wading back in there again with tear gas and billy clubs and haul us all off to jail. We just don't have that many people to spare."

"It would make a lot of noise," he persisted. "It might be worth it. We'd get a lot of publicity on TV."

"Shit," Connie said, her patience at an end. "They'd have us all out of there and loaded into paddywagons before the cameras even arrived on the scene."

"She's right, Del," Selena said, laughing at Range affectionately, patting him on the shoulder. "But, I tell you what. I like your spirit. I really do."

Then she turned to Connie and, winking broadly, said, "What do you say, Consuelita? Should we let him back in the club?"

"He's gonna have to do a lot more than race-drive," Connie said, "to get back in my club."

"Your club was always a little more exclusive than mine," Selena said, and turned to Range and ran her brown fingers over his battered white face and kissed him on his puffy bruised mouth.

Then she said softly, but insistently, "Let's do like Connie said, Del."

And he obeyed her without further question: Cranked up the wrecked but amazingly still running Dart and headed for town.

The instant that Range felled the Dootch his fate had been determined.

Now that there was no going back, he had decided that he had no wish to go back. He was impressed by his own decision, surprised by the quickness of his reflexes, proud of his display of courage, astonished by the depth of his feeling for the Mexican girl who sat beside him in the car.

Now that there was nothing left but hope, Range hoped for the stars. He was astounded by their brilliance, number and variety. He wanted to live. He wanted to love. He wanted to fight. He wanted to win. He wanted a piece of his native place. He wanted to be one with his dark half-*raza*, to march arm in arm in their front rank, into the sunset of class solidarity with Selena at his side, singing a union song. He wanted everything, and he would not be co-opted. He wanted his life to mean something, in and for itself. He wanted to be remembered when he was gone. He didn't know what all he wanted. But all of a sudden he wanted it achingly bad. And he only had a little time to get it. For, whichever way the dice rolled now, to cell block or cemetery, prison yard or graveyard, too soon was old Delano gonna be back on ice.

Nineteen

EARLIER THAT MORNING, Victorino had slept right through his *alarma*. Why that was, he could not say. It was not like he didn't know where his duty lay. *Seguro qué no!* His motto was *Victoria o Muerte*. It was like—he had this funny feeling about getting up—like it might be better just to sleep this one out, right around the clock, and try again tomorrow. His whole little *familia* must have felt the same way. Because Aguilar, he was the first one up, at six o'clock in the morning, an hour late for his assignment. Quickly he awakened Delia and the girls. "*Rápido, rápido*," he kept urging them, as they dressed and washed and packed their lunches and wolfed down their breakfast cereal. For the first time in memory he dispensed with the five minute warm-up of his beloved Chevycita Bonita. Herded Delia and the girls directly out and started her up and drove down to Fourth Street in Southside. Pulled up in front of the CCAC office, "La Kack," as he called it, pronouncing the "a" softly, in the Spanish manner. Dozens of old farm workers' jalopies were parked outside, all over the place, up on the railroad embankment, in the glass-strewn vacant lot next door, on both sides of the street, up on the sidewalk, in every driveway in the neighborhood, and even up in the dirt frontyard of the house that said BAÑOS 50¢ on its wall. A young Calmento cop was busy ticketing anyone who was not parked strictly in accordance with the law.

Aguilar defied the law, double-parked in the middle of the street, and ran inside to apologize for his tardiness and to find his picket crew, if they were not already out on the line.

Yet, the first *compañeros* he spotted when he walked in the door were Corky DeJesus and the three Apaches. They were picket captains too, but here they were, standing around the front of the office, twiddling their thumbs.

Aguilar relaxed at once and moved past them into the office. Obviously, the strike was running late—*as what does not run late in the Mexican mind?*—and no one would notice his own dereliction of duty.

The place was packed with dozens of milling, shouting, violently gesturing picket captains, organizers, Chicano volunteers, union officers, and campesinos. The noise was deafening. All appeared to be chaos, under the bright office lights. But if you looked closely, you could see some evidence of organization. The walls of the office were plastered with maps, schedules, rosters, lists of growers and ranches, car pools, telephone numbers, picket instructions, union posters, and cartoons depicting growers in planters' hats and teardrop sunglasses, smoking fat cigars and carrying bullwhips. Some people were standing in line waiting for their assignments, others were drawing posters, running off propaganda leaflets on the mimeograph machine, answering phones, and giving out picket instructions. Everyone was laughing and talking at once. Everyone seemed flushed with excitement.

Aguilar could see Selena on the stairway. She was talking very rapidly to Del and Connie, gesturing with her hands. "I already told you, Connie," she said, as her stepfather approached her through the crowd, "I'm with you on this nonviolence thing. Just as long as . . ."

Victorino was glad to hear what he heard. He was *no-violencia* too. And not for the reasons of *filosofía*. It was a matter of common sense: The growers had the guns, the cops, the courts, and the judges.

Before Aguilar could make it to the stairs another group of people, poor campesinos and fruit packers, crowded around their leader, asking her innumerable questions, each one trying to shout louder than the others to gain her attention.

"Fock it!" Aguilar said out loud, and turned to find the picketers who would be under his command. It kind of pissed him off, all this attention she'd been getting. Seemed like, here lately, he'd not been able to get a word in edgewise, with her. *Caaaaaabrón,* all he wanted to do was wish her luck. Ah, well . . .

He rounded up his picketers, nine little peons from Mexico, and helped them to collect all their *HUELGA!* signs, posters, banners, and herded them out to his Chevycita Bonita, which, by some miracle, had not been ticketed yet for "blocking traffic." He directed his charges up into the truck bed and got into the cab beside his sleeping daughter Jovita and was just about to drive off when Selena ran out of the office and stopped him.

"*Eh, jefito!* Wait!" she hollered, jumping on the running board. She was all flushed and out of breath and in the highest of spirits, and it did Aguilar's heart a huge amount of good to see her there so big-eyed and beautiful, framed larger than life in the open pickup window. And he wasn't the only one. In the truck bed, nine sombreros turned as one, eighteen Indio eyeballs flashed on her *belleza increíble.*

"*Oye, como va, papacito?*"

"*Todo va bien,*" Aguilar said, avoiding her eyes.

"How you doin', mama?"

"Hi, sweetheart," said Delia, in her clucking voice, picking an invisible piece of lint out of Rio's dark hair. "I'm doin' fine, I guess, for this ungodly hour of the mornin'. You get any sleep las' night?"

"*No te preocupas, mamá.* I'm doin' just great. How you doin', girls?"

"Fine," said Jovita, squirming beside her father.

"Fine," said little Rio sleepily.

"Say, listen, just one more thing, *papacito,*" Selena said, talking to him confidentially now, breathing on him, stirring him. "Since I didn't get a chance to talk to you inside, I want to fill you in just briefly on where we're at. . . . So far everything's gone like clockwork. I sent Rudy and Gloria over to Stockton with five other people. They're standing out in front of the Casual Labor Center on Skid Row, offering a free fifth of Dago red to any wino who refuses work. And—Rudy just called —it's working like a charm."

"Hey," said Aguilar.

"Yeah," Selena said, not listening, her mind racing ahead. "Now, here's what Rudy says, *jefito*. He figures he can pull about half of them with wine. Then he's gonna put infiltrators on board the labor buses, so they can subvert the rest of them on the way down here. He figures he can pull another, say, twenty-five percent that way. If he does, that means the Vanduccis are only gonna have about two hundred and fifty very inexperienced and hung-over winos out in the field today, doing the work of a thousand. And in the packing shed they're gonna have zero. So, they are hurting, no?"

"*Sí, en verdad*," Aguilar said, regarding her very closely now. There was something odd about her expression, something he couldn't quite put his finger on, something . . . scary in her eyes when she spoke of the 'Duccis.

He knew she would never rest till they were buried, every last one of them. And, though he had little love for the Wops, it did make him kind of . . . nervous, contemplating their destruction: The Vanduccis were beeg, *mano*, beeg as they come. And when they went down, they were gonna take a lot of other folks with them.

"Alright now look, *jefe*," Selena said, running ahead, heedless of the look he gave her, the pat on her arm that said, *Easy down, girl, easy down*. . . . "I'm sending you out to that South Section main gate today 'cause you are my best man and I have a feeling that's where the action's gonna be later on. So, I just want to say, keep on your toes, okay?"

"Eh!" he said, angrily. "You ever seen me any other way?"

"Naw," she said, softly now. "You're right, Papa. I guess I just wanted an excuse to come out here and tell you people that I love you and I'm so happy you are my *familia* and it is for you that I do everything I do. Everything! You know what I mean?"

"Everything?" he said, revving his engine, preparing to go, pretending still to be angry.

"Well," she said, very seriously, "almost."

Aguilar noticed that there were tears in her eyes when she said it. And he'd always been a sucker for *sentimiento*.

"Aw, don' worry, *queridita*," he said. "Whatever thing you do is *perfecto con nosotros*. 'Cause we love you."

Then he dropped his Chevycita Bonita into gear and Selenita jumped off and waved at him and he roared off down Fourth Street past the parked cop car, thinking: *She is more than I can bear*.

There were tears in Aguilar's eyes too. He glanced in the rearview mirror but all he could see was the door to her office, closing.

He would never see her again.

"I jus' got this terrible premonition," he said.

"Get it outa your mind, honey," Delia said, in her clucking voice. "Just remember to stop at Señora Placensia's place so we can leave Rio off."

I will never see Rio again neither.

Nevertheless, by eight o'clock that same morning Aguilar had succeeded in abolishing the premonition from his mind. The way he did it was, he just kept repeating to himself, "*No es posible, no es posible,*" till it went away. It was like a great marble slab, a mountain of earth, a ton of tomato lugs being removed from over his head. *Ay, finalmente!* He took a deep breath and began issuing orders to his strikers in a strong clear voice. Now in place of the weak feeling of premonition there was a good tight nervous excitement growing in his belly moment by moment. It was like dawn on the day of the general's greatest *batalla*. The campesinos were like soldiers of the Mexican revolution, fearless and fatalistic and true. He was proud of them. And proud of Delia and slim Jovita with her tiny budding breasts. They were like women of the revolution, Adelitas, who caught the tails of their men's great horses and ran behind them from town to town.

"Jovita! Delia! Bring out them thermos jugs and give us some coffee. And Fulgencio!"

"*Sí, señor!*"

"I wan' you to take the *troca* and go down to Valpico Road, jus' like you did the other day, and blink your lights if you see anything comin'."

"*A sus órdenes!*" Fulgencio shouted, nearly clicking his heels with a desire to please. And Aguilar had to laugh. It was only an excuse. But it bubbled up free and clear. *Whatever they throw at me now, I am ready. . . .*

"Okay, let's get down to beezness," he said. "Lalo! I wan' you to take Paco, Flaco, and José. Go up there beyond the freeway underpass and cover Corral Hollow. And yell '*Abajo la tiranía Vanducci!*' if you see anyone sneakin' up the back way. And you, Hector! And Ernesto. You go down and cover that little gate down there halfway to Valpico. The rest of you stay with me. And keep your eyes open. No tellin' what they gonna pull."

Aguilar stood there a long time in the road with his little troop, waiting for something to happen. To kill time they walked up and down, shivering and smacking their hands and warming themselves by the fire, though it was not cold at all.

Then they started singing. First they sang all the union songs they knew. Then they sang all the revolutionary songs, the patriotic songs, and finally they ended up singing ranchero songs from their native northern Mexico. They sang, "*Concha Perdida,*" "*Justicia Ranchera,*" "*Vivo Tomando,*" "*Alma En Pena,*" "*Me Alegran Tus Ojos,*" "*No To-*

mare," "*El Tropezón,*" "*Mi Cobijo,*" "*Los Laureles,*" and "*Hace Un Año.*"

Just as they were finishing up with "*En Las Cantinas,*" Fulgencio blinked the Chevycita's lights. A vehicle turned the Valpico corner and headed up Corral Hollow Road. But it was too small for a labor bus. It was a pickup truck full of Mexicans! All of them dressed for work in sombreros and bandannas and Levi jackets.

"Go get 'em!" Aguilar hollered. And his little troop surrounded the pickup truck and brought it to a stop in the road.

Aguilar ran over, thrust a bunch of leaflets at them, and started yelling: "Ain't you guys heard of *la huelga?* Eh? What's a matter with you, anyway? Everyone's going out! *Todos van a salir!* In three days we gonna win and you gonna make up for the work you lost. Go on now and drive back into CCAC headquarters in Southside and sign up. You even get free food and a place to sleep. *Sí, sí, somos muy organizados.*"

The truck turned around and headed back into town. Everyone cheered on the picket line: "*Qué viva la huelga en el fil!*"

Then a few minutes later Lalo and his boys started screaming from the freeway underpass. "*Abajo la tiranía Vanducci!*"

And the 'Duccis father and son came hurtling over the hill in big new twin blue Ford pickup trucks. And if a truck could show anger, those Fords were two pissed-off machines. They were going so fucking fast that their wheels left the road at the crest of the hill. *Whooom,* they came down hard, skidded dangerously on the gravel, straightened out, and came roaring down on the strikers at ninety miles an hour.

"Outa the way!" Aguilar yelled. But his people, they just stood there gaping. "Outa the way!" he hollered again. But still those crazy Chicanos would not move. "*OUTA THE GODDAMN WAY!*" he shouted, and ran along the picket line shoving them roughly into the drainage ditch.

Just as he threw himself down in the dirt he felt the wind of the Wops' near miss, flapping at his pantlegs.

The fuckers had come so close that no one dared move a muscle for a minute after they were gone. You could hear those two big V8s winding out all the way to Valpico Road.

Then all was silent again. Except for the traffic on the freeway, the buzzing of the electrical wires overhead, a train coming over the Altamont, the jets in the sky, and a red-winged blackbird in the tomato field across the road.

The strikers got up off the ground, dusting their clothes, replacing their sombreros, adjusting their bandannas.

"*Asesinos! Asesinos!*" some of them cried, shaking their fists toward the north. But they did it softly. As if those terrible Italian *pilotas* might somehow hear them and come shrieking down upon them again out of nowhere: Jay Jay's tracks passed not a foot from the spot where Jovita's precious little head had lain. . . .

"Jovita, *mi corazón*, next time I say 'jump,' you jump, no?"

"*Sí, papá*," she said, giggling, and skipped lightly across the road to "warm" herself beside her mother at the dying fire.

How strange are the young, who do not value their own lives, thought Aguilar, who valued his own life greatly, but was not afraid to lose it if he could make it count.

Down the road Fulgencio blinked his lights again. The campesinos strained their eyes to see what was coming.

A big gray streamliner bus appeared out of the ground smog. It was filled with scabs. Another few seconds and they would be here.

"Get your signs ready!" Aguilar yelled. His adrenaline had started to pump. "And stop 'em if you can. But be careful, eh?"

The bus pulled over to the side of the road and stopped near the South Section gateway.

"*Hueeeeeelga! Hueeeeeelga! Hueeeeeelga!*" the strikers chanted. "*Vénganse a fuera, compañeros! Fuera! Fuera!* Come outa there!"

The driver was the same small harried old black man as three days ago. He stepped out of the bus, jostled his way through the picket line to the gate, stuck a key in the padlock, opened it, and swung it inward toward the tomato field.

Meanwhile Aguilar was running up and down beside the bus, searching frantically for the union infiltrator who was supposed to be inside. Finally he saw him through the green-tinted rear window. It was Rudy.

"*Ahora todos van a salir, Rudycito!*" he cried. "*El momento está llegado, mijito!*"

And Rudy smiled his slippery smile through the tinted glass, winked, and led seven Mexicans out of the bus: four men and three women, very poor, very frightened, obviously illegal aliens.

"*Qué viva nuestra santa lucha en el fil!*" everyone shouted, embracing Rudy, embracing their shyly smiling new *compañeros*.

The bus driver got in and drove into the field.

Aguilar ran over and gave his little stepson a great big *abrazo*. Rudy just about split a seam of his britches, he was so proud of himself.

"Pretty good, huh, Papa, pretty good, huh?" he kept saying.

"No lie, kid, no lie. Real good, real good!"

Now Victorino had sixteen *huelgistas* in his little *tropa* by the side of the road. He thought a moment, considering whether it was worth a criminal trespassing charge to slam and lock the gate again, and decided in favor. *Blam.*

When the next bus showed up, about five minutes later, the driver was forced to stop, get down, walk over, and open the gate again.

"*Todos van a salir!*" the strikers yelled.

And Lita's skinny little husband Nacho, who was the infiltrator, brought out every Pocho on board, ten of them, all men. Now they were twenty-six on the road.

"*Qué viva la raza unida!*"

The bus drove into the field. Aguilar slammed the gate again, locked it, and scrambled quickly back over the property line, stumbling over dirt clods and mustard weed: He had no illusions about what the 'Duccis would do if they caught him trespassing. He would never survive to be prosecuted.

Four buses showed up in the next half hour, carrying a total of ninety-seven tomato pickers, by Delia's count. Of that total, forty-six bailed out with the infiltrators at the gate.

Now Aguilar's little *tropa* was enormous, strung out all the way along the road on both sides, waving and singing and shouting at the winos in the field.

"Come on outa there, you scabs! *Vénganse, esquiroles!* Ain't you got no shame? *No tiene vergüenza?* Everybody's comin' out! *Todos van a salir!*"

The winos were having a very difficult time. Aside from the harassment from the sidelines, they had to unload their own boxes from off the trucks. And there was no straw boss or checker to direct them to their claims.

Aguilar couldn't understand why the Vanduccis and their foremen and grower friends had stayed away so long. The only thing he could figure out was that they were having such a rough go of it on the other sections that they'd not had time to deal with the South Section as yet. It was nothing to kick about, of course. It was actually very good luck. But it worried Aguilar. Made him feel kind of . . . creepy.

He sent Rudy running down to Fulgencio with instructions to drive into headquarters for news of the strike. While he was there he was to pick up a portable loudspeaker, if one was available, and more *huelga* signs and banners. Maybe even a few cases of cheap wine, if possible.

The sun rode up over the Sierra Nevada. The temperature soared. Heat waves rose over the field, the canal, and the long white road. Soon Aguilar was sweating under his arms, under his sombrero. Rank and salty, it burnt his eyes, soaked through his clothes, dripped off the tip of his nose. But goddamnit he was sure as hell not sweating like them poor hung-over winos out in the field. They were hurting now, hurting bad. Ay! Aguilar recalled very well what they were going through. The memory was engraved on the burnt brown ridges of his brow, in his bloodshot eyes, on his knobby knees and callused hands.

Poor fuckers, though. You could see them out there staggering under the weight of the boxes, falling down in the furrows, vomiting on the plants.

"Come on outa there you miserable sonsofbitches! *Vénganse, desgraciados!* What does it get you, eh? What does it get you? Heat stroke for a buck fifty an hour minus tax!"

One o'clock in the afternoon. The temperature way up there near a hundred. All over the wide fields an unnatural calm prevailed as Chicanos and winos sought shade where there was no shade, cool where there was no cool: under their hats, under buses and trucks, under to-mato plants and mustard weeds.

Then from the north came a cloud of white dust. The Chevycita Bonita, loaded up with cases of wine!

Aguilar ran over and jumped on the running board on the passenger side even before it had stopped.

"Rudy, *mijito, qué pasó?*"

"Beeeeeeg fight over at the labor camp, *jefito*."

"*Pues?*"

"*Pues*, they hauled at leas' thirty *huelgistas al juzgado*."

"And what's happenin' on the East Section?"

"*Problemas*," Rudy said, shaking his little narrow head. "*Los 'Duccis*, they got *este grupo enorme* de beeg bad-ass motherfuckers: Teamsters, Posse Vigilantus, off-duty *policía*, Wops *y Portugueses gigantescos*. And they are heeting us, *jefito, con* everything *que los tienen*."

"And the sheriff?"

"The sheriff? Sheeeeeet! Selena call heem ten times if she call heem once. 'Ah'm sooooo sorry,'" Rudy said, imitating the sheriff's Oklahoma twang, "'but ah jes' cain't do nothin' less somebody gits hurt out theah.'"

"How they holdin' out *en la línea?*"

"Where?"

"On the East Section."

"*En la línea del* East Section they are takin' everything they deesh out."

"*No-violencia?*"

"Us? *Sí*. Them? No."

"*Bueno*. And how many peekers they got in the field over there?"

"None."

"*Cómo?*"

"None, they say. Gloria bringin' them out in droves with vino."

"Ay! You hear that, Delia, Nacho, Jovita? You hear that?" Aguilar hollered, grabbing the portable loudspeaker out of Rudy's hand, turning to face the large crowd of strikers which had gathered around him. "YOU HEAR THAT, *COMPAÑEROS*? ON THE EAST SECTION NOBODY, *REPETO*, NOBODY IS WORKIN' IN THE FIELD. NOW, ARE WE GONNA LET THEM BEAT US, OVER THERE, OR ARE WE GONNA GET UP OFF OF OUR FAT *CULOS* AND PULL EVERY SINGLE *CHINGAZO* OUTA THAT FIELD?"

"*Que vamos a sacarlos en seguida!*" the strikers shouted. "*Vino gratis! Vino gratis!*" they shouted, grabbing bottles out of the bed of the pickup truck and brandishing them in the air. "Free wine for everyone who comes out. Free wine!"

And those fucking winos, out there slaving in the sun, hot and sweaty and dry and dying for a *trago de vino,* how could they resist? Every nonwhite picker in the field came running: Mexicans in straw sombreros, tiny Filipinos in baseball caps, big Changos with rags tied around their nappy black heads.

"*Vénganse, compañeros!*" the strikers yelled, beckoning them across the field. "Come on, don't be afraid!"

Aguilar got up on top of the pickup and started yelling "ALLEG-RIIIII, ALEGRIIIII, ALEGRIIIIIIA!" through the loudspeaker at the top of his lungs.

Just as the pickers reached the property line and were about to crawl through the fence, the Vanduccis came screaming over the hill to the south in their twin blue pickups. Roared down upon the winos at top speed, stood on their brakes, and screeched to a halt in front of them, barring their way, blinding them with dust, sending them scampering like rodents back into their furrows.

Then two more truckloads of big mean-looking motherfuckers came skidding up right behind them. Huge, hairy, pot-bellied, cigar-smoking, shotgun-toting bastards in teardrop sunglasses, Levi's, cowboy boots, Stetson hats, and ball caps with farm equipment ads printed across the front. They vaulted over the tailgates of their trucks, landing heavily in the dirt, stirring up more dust, and then came swaggering slowly over toward the picket line with the Dootch at their lead. *Crunch, crunch, crunch,* went their cowboy boots as they crossed the road: Smokey Dee Leevining, a great lumbering Okie-Indian with mean little red eyes. Big John Ammiratti, the brother of Jay Jay's wife Rose Mary, who weighed something close to three hundred pounds. The pop-eyed degenerate Sammy Dog, his puckered lips quivering with a desire to hurt. And fat-faced, four-eyed Jay Jay Vanducci came next, big as a fucking mountain, pointing his shotgun at the sky, firing off both barrels *boom boom* trying to scare people. And then the beefy self-righteous Wop and Portagee growers behind him, breathing fire and brimstone (their fields might be next, after all!).

Aguilar jumped down off the truck and started dancing up and down in front of the picket line. "Okay now, cool it, cool it. Remember, non-violence, *no-violencia!*" he hollered, as much to the 'Duccis as to his own.

Neither the Dootch nor his son gave any orders. Nor did they or any of the other gorillas make any attempt to talk or reason or parley or bargain with the strikers. They just came tramping right straight down the picket line in single file, elbowing people in the ribs, stomping toes with their cowboy boots, snarling; "Outa the way, greaser, outa the fuckin' way!"

It was almost more than Aguilar could bear, watching them grin spitefully (especially Jay Jay, who had been a guest in his home, broken bread with him) and stomp the pretty little brown toes of Jovita, who was wearing only sandals, the tender work-worn toes of poor fat Delia. Ay! You could see the farm workers' faces contort one by one. You could hear their cries, "Ow! Ow! Ow!" getting louder and louder, closer and closer. It was like . . . *absurdo*, the way it happened. Like a comedy you might see in the movies. Except it wasn't funny. 'Cause, *Thwunk!* next thing you knew it was your toes that was getting stomped and squished by sharp-heeled cowboy boots, and you were the one hollering "Ow!" and hopping up and down on one foot while the next gorilla tried to stamp on your other. . . . And then it was the turn of your next *compañero* down the line. And the comedy started all over again.

The 'Duccis and their allies made many runs in the minutes that followed, stomping, elbowing, cussing, spitting, hurling racial and sexual insults, firing their shotguns in the air. But the pickers refused to be provoked. In the end it got boring for the gorillas, so they retired to their pickup trucks and drove a couple of hundred yards down the road to discuss strategy.

Right away the picketers started up with "*Ya hemos vencido! Ya hemos vencido!* We already won! We already won!" which was Selena's slogan for the strike.

"Hey, wait a minute!" Aguilar hollered back at them. "We only won the first round. And look out in that field. They still got fifty or some-odd winos out there!"

But deep down in his *corazón* he was proud. For he had come to love his picket line. To Aguilar it was a living entity, of which his own life was an integral part. As leader of the picket line he felt unique and important only insofar as he was a symbol of the whole, an expression of its will. In this way he valued his people more than himself. For he was only a little of himself. And they were more. They were all.

"Ay!"

And still the sun was not at two o'clock in the sky.

Aguilar got hold of Jovita, handed her the loudspeaker, and lifted her onto the roof of the Chevycita. Figured she'd be out of harm's way, up there, and she might even turn out to be useful.

"What am I s'posed to do up here?" she whined. "What am I s'posed to do up here?"

"Why don' you call a few *esquiroles* outa that *fil* for us, *queridita?*"

She looked so cute up there, in bare feet and sandals, long brown legs and long black hair, and that short little summer dress that she wore.

"*Viva Jovita!*" all the strikers yelled.

At first she was kind of shy: "Now, come on, people, please come out of the field," she squeaked. But then after only a little coaching she got the hang of it, and shouted into the loudspeaker, over and over again: "*VENGANSE, AMIGOS, VENGANSE PARA VINO GRATIS,* FREE WINE, FREE WINE, COME ON, COME ON!" And finally she convinced a group of five multiracial winos to leave the field.

They ran for the fence while the 'Duccis were down the road. They reached the gate, climbed over, jumped down on the other side, and ran clumsily up the embankment for the road.

"VENGANSE, COMPAÑEROS, VENGANSE!"

The gorillas spotted them, but it was too late. By the time they'd clambered back into their pickup trucks and turned them around on the narrow road between the canal and the drainage ditch, the winos were getting kissed and hugged and congratulated with free swigs of *vino* on the picket line.

Now the Wops were really pissed off. They started driving up and down the picket line at sixty and seventy miles an hour, raising a choking blinding cloud of dust, trying to see how close to the strikers' toes they could get, trying to see if they could make them jump.

But nobody jumped. And the proceedings rapidly degenerated into a contest to determine who owned the shoulder of Corral Hollow Road.

To Aguilar the whole thing was ridiculous, and served no earthly purpose other than to make the 'Duccis madder than ever.

"Eh, *compañeros*, why tease them?" he said. "Jump outa the way if they come near." But nobody would listen.

The gorillas made another pass, even faster this time, missing them by mere inches, cutting them with flying bits of sand and gravel.

Still nobody moved, though some flinched and blinked, and others puckered their cheeks.

"*Viva la huelga*," they started chanting now, inspired by Jovita on top of the pickup truck. "*Y no nos moverán!* We shall not be moved!"

"Hey!" Aguilar yelled. "Don' be stupid. A peekup truck will move you, believe me."

Now the Wops came at them out of the south, father and son, two abreast, trying to force them onto private property where they could pick them off with their shotguns for trespassing.

"*No nos moverán*," the strikers kept chanting, swaying to the words. "We shall not be moved!"

"Wait a minute, if they gonna hit you, then move, okay?" Aguilar hollered. But they would not see reason. They would not be moved.

Aguilar saw tragedy in the offing. Either his people would move or they would be ground into dust. Desperately he looked around for help. And just then he saw Range's beat-out Dodge Dart turn the Valpico corner. Unfortunately, it was still too far away to have any bearing on the events about to take place.

"*No nos moverán*. We shall not be moved. . . ."

It was at that moment when Aguilar made his final decision, and bowed to the will of his *raza*: "*No es posible*," he said to himself, when he was reminded of this morning's premonition. "*No es posible, no es posible*," he kept repeating.

Then he stepped out into the middle of Corral Hollow Road, stuck his right hand out, palm open, and awaited the coming of his destiny.

Twenty

MEANWHILE, neck and neck with his father in his flying pickup truck, bearing down on the crazy defiant spick Aguilar, who appeared as a mere speck in the road before him, Jay Jay was overcome with a strange feeling of déjà vu. The scene bore an uncanny semblance to a story that Bruno had told many times over the years, always out of earshot of old Tony (for Tony had his own version of the story). And it flashed now across the screen of Jay Jay's consciousness not swiftly, but quite leisurely and digressive, as a man's entire life is supposed to pass slowly in front of his eyes in the accelerated instant before he dies.

In November 1943, the story began, Bruno shipped out of Oakland Army Base on a troopship bound for the Mediterranean Theater of Operations by way of the Panama Canal. His sisters, his bride Angie, Grandpa Tony and Grandma Letizia saw him off at the dock. Tony did all of the talking. Aside from the usual parental admonitions, he asked only one thing: what Jay Jay's father knew he would ask, what he had been afraid the old man would ask, what he had been anticipating with very mixed feelings.

He asked him to go to Sicily and recover the trunk that was buried there.

He gave him a detailed map of the Sangiorgio di Rocca area, and the old Vanducci property, with the place of the cache marked in red pencil.

Bruno was to ask permission to dig from his cousin Gennaro, who was the present owner of the land. He was to offer a handsome consideration for Gennaro's acquiescence. If Gennaro did not acquiesce, which was regarded as highly likely, then Jay Jay's father was to take it by stealth, or even by force if necessary. He was to empty the trunk and repack its contents and send them to America at his earliest opportunity.

In one way, Bruno said later, he actually looked forward to the quest. From his earliest years there had always been a kind of bond between him and Grandpa Tony, a love of the land they farmed, the crops they grew, the great fertile valley they lived in, and their heritage as tomato farmers that went back to the remotest antiquity in Sicily, back to the days when the fruit was as small as a cherry and wasn't even red, wasn't even called a tomato or even pomodoro but *pomme d'or*, "apple of gold," and graced only the tables of dukes and kings.

By the age of eleven, Jay Jay's father said, he could name every step in the production of tomatoes, from winter plowing and discing to spring irrigation and insect control to summer harvest and packing. And, through Grandpa Tony's endless stories and descriptions, he knew Sicily almost as well as he knew his own hometown of Calmento. He knew about the mountains rising from the sea and the towns built on the tops of hills for defense against invaders and the stony spent soil and the rock walls of Sicily and old Tony's trunk buried there. All his young life Jay Jay's father had been aware of that trunk, moldering in the ground, under the olive tree, by the stone wall.

But in another very definite way he resented it, Bruno said, the whole weight of this charge, this mission Grandpa Tony had set up for him. Why didn't the old fart just go back and dig it up himself? The war would be over soon. And he certainly had the money. Why hadn't he gone back years before, when his hero Mussolini was in power? It probably wasn't even there anymore, for Christ's sake. It had probably been dug up years ago. And what the hell was it, anyway? Nothing but a bunch of old worthless family keepsakes from the time of the Kingdom of the Two Sicilies.

And yet he *had* inherited it somehow, Bruno said, this silly debt, this pipe dream of his old man's.

Jay Jay's father reached Italy in time for the Anzio invasion, and landed with General Truscott's Third Division. He was wounded on February 19, 1944, on the Mussolini Canal, and spent the next four months in a pleasant hospital in the hills of Naples.

In June he found himself with a week's leave and decided he would at last honor Grandpa Tony's wish, much as he disliked the idea. He packed a rucksack with an army collapsible shovel, bought a ticket on the *Rapido* for Palermo, and two days later found himself riding along the south coast of old Tony's native island. The sun was out and the train puffed around the hills above the sea, a clear turquoise sea, and there was a large mountain above, bright with the temporary springtime green of semiarid country. And below there were flowers, poppies—not the golden California poppies he'd picked as a kid, but red ones, deep red, the color of arterial blood, running all the way down the steep slope and into the sea.

At Gela he got out of the train and bought a couple of bottles of wine, some bread and cheese for his lunch. It cost him an arm and a leg at blackmarket prices, he said, but it was tasty and worth every nickel. Just as he finished eating, the train came into the rock country, Vanducci country. And the landscape appeared exactly as Grandpa Tony had described it to him: steep and hilly, crisscrossed with thousands of gray rock walls.

Then he saw the station sign of Sangiorgio di Rocca coming up on the right. He raised his bottle, sucked the last few drops out, and put it on the floor. He got up and pulled his rucksack down from the rack. It landed with a heavy thud on the seat. He put his US Army raincoat on, for it had begun to rain. Then he swung his gear up on his back. All the passengers stared, as if they'd never seen such a queer-looking individual. The train stopped abruptly and Jay Jay's father was impelled forward, lurching down the aisle past the raised faces toward the exit, not knowing why he was even getting off, really. He would have much preferred just traveling on, right on around the island and back to the mainland. He had a superstitious fear of digging up the box. It was like some kind of Pandora's box, perhaps, in which all of the ills of the world were buried. Why look for trouble?

And yet suddenly there he was standing in the rain on the station platform. The passenger car snapped forward behind him. The train began to move. He was tempted to jump back on board. Instead, he walked into the station house. The rain beat loudly on the tin roof. He checked his rucksack at the *consigna*. An attendant in railway blue and a thick mustache eyed his American uniform warily.

Jay Jay's father buttoned up his raincoat, walked out of the station house, across an arched stone bridge spanning a brown seasonal stream, and up a muddy lane in the gray early afternoon. No one stirred. There were high walls on both sides of him.

In the town the streets were narrow and deserted. The houses were the color of the ubiquitous rocks. On one street something bright red ran down the gutter in the rain water, spilling over onto the cobbles, staining them in the dry places under the eaves of houses, the color and texture indicating that it had been staining them for centuries. Only later, as he climbed the hill, did he discover that it was blood and ran down from the public slaughterhouse. Near the top of the hill there was a square with no trees. On the square he found a bar. He raised the wet blanket that served for a door and entered. Inside he found he was in a tiny courtyard, a garden, with potted plants, a stone floor, and rose trees planted along the rectangular walls. Above, dipping heavy drops of rain on him, was an arbor of wet roses, red and white ones, blooming.

He went through an open doorway and found himself in the bar proper. It was dark inside. There were no windows. The collected whitewash of many generations had rounded the corners of the place, giving it the appearance of a cave. There were several tiny wizened peasants inside, dressed in ragged corduroy, drinking wine at small tables along the wall. It occurred to Jay Jay's dad that he might be related to some of them. He was not tempted to ask. All activity ceased the moment he walked in the door. He sat alone. A boy of about fourteen with a shaved head served. When he came over he smiled a toothless smile and stretched out his soiled little hand and said, in the tiny inhuman voice of a mynah bird, "*Hi, Joe, you gotta chewing gum?*" Bruno hit him with a pack of Spearmint and said, "*Vino.*" When the wine came he drank a glass of it down neat, refilled it, and took out the map that Grandpa Tony had drawn for him. He could see immediately that the ancestral home of the Vanduccis was on the other side of the station, that he'd come the wrong way. It didn't matter. He thought he'd wait till the rain let up anyway. Sitting down, he felt a little drunk. His head began to buzz. There was an ache at the bottom of his abdomen, dull, constant.

Though he had just eaten and was not in the least bit hungry, he ordered the meal he saw the other men order: bread, garlic, green olives, vinegar, and olive oil, lots of olive oil. He dipped his bread into it as he saw them do. It was good. They all watched.

Suddenly, for the first time, he liked Sicily, liked being there. He saw himself like in a movie, he said. There he was, Private Bruno V. Vanducci, US Army, twenty-one years old, sitting in a musty little bar, an undeniably quaint and wonderful little bar, with mustachioed Siciliano rock farmers orbing him, in a little stone village on the far coast of Sicily, Grandpa Tony's native village, six thousand miles from home!

Then, just as suddenly, his head was buzzing again, an insect let loose inside. The men at the tables stared at him. He stared back. That seemed to put them off, as if it weren't fair. Since he was the stranger, it was their right, not his, to stare.

Jay Jay's father paid his bill and left. Stepping out on the wet stones of the street that went down the hill, he could see the packed overcast thinning out over the mountains to the north, and patches of blue sky. The wind blew, the rain let up, and the clouds broke and ran down the valley like infantrymen.

He thought: *It was Montgomery and the Limeys that came through here. They came across the valley there. The Krauts regrouped in the mountains up there and came sneaking through that pass over there in the middle of the night and cut them off from the rest of the Corps for three days with their 88s.* . . . And then he refused to think about it anymore. It all seemed so long ago, he said. The war seemed so far away. And it had looked so different then, in the newsreels and magazines. It had been September, the month his brother got hit in the Pacific. The valley had been all dusty and yellow, full of maneuvering tanks. And Bruno had been at home on leave in Calmento, California, conceiving his first child: John Joseph Vanducci they had decided to call him, he said, "Jay Jay" for short. . . .

Jay Jay's father could see the river and the Roman arched bridge below him. And the white gravel highway, the slick wet railroad tracks, the station, the scattered farmhouses. And the rock walls growing everywhere out of the land, running together everywhere. The whole valley like a long narrow rat warren in his head, unclear now, even with the rain blowing in his face. And he also saw, had seen from the moment he stepped out of the bar, the great olive tree, the tallest in the valley, and near it the ancient graystone tile-roofed Vanducci farmhouse, with its neatly terraced fields of pomodoro tomatoes climbing the green hill in back.

By now, Jay Jay's father said, he thought he'd probably drunk enough to do it.

He clapped his overseas cap on his head and walked down the cobblestone street with the blood and along the high rock walls. The rain let up. People appeared. A peasant with a shiny bald pate, driving a donkey loaded with firewood, moved up the lane. He was a dead ringer for Grandpa Tony. "*Buona sera*," he said. Bruno nodded and walked quickly on. He went back into the station, waited at the *consigna* for the attendant to come out from the back room, and paid the charge for his rucksack. He would need the shovel he had packed.

He walked across the tracks, into another narrow lane, and out across the valley toward the farmhouse. He could see the olive tree clearly now. It was very thick and gnarled and tall. Its leaves flickered and glistened in the wind, silver on the bottom and green on top. It was planted at the base of a little hump in the earth, or what might have been a mound from olden times, and it leaned a bit, toward the house, away from the hump, as if it were getting slowly pushed over through the years. The rain stopped altogether now. The sun came out. The mud went plop under his combat boots, the sound hollow and echoing back, even that little sound, from the high walls on every side. There was no one on the road. It appeared so deserted that Jay Jay's father wondered if anyone lived out this way anymore.

It had become quite warm. He began to sweat. His whole head an insect now, buzzing, no place to land. And the heavy redness of the black-market vino inside him.

His pace seemed to be slackening. He felt he should hurry. He wouldn't have to worry about his cousin Gennaro, the present owner of the house. He wouldn't have to pay him anything since he was most likely dead in the war, or at least gone off somewhere beyond recall. He crossed a small ditch filled with muddy rainwater. His head hurt. He reeled from the wine. The way was much farther than it looked from the town, and the slope of the valley much steeper. His rucksack weighed heavily on his shoulders. His leg wound began to ache. The sun beat down on his bare head. He still wore his raincoat. It permitted no air to circulate underneath. His skin was trapped inside, clammy and wet. He felt hot, choked, as if he would stop breathing. His head a whole beehive now, buzzing. He took a wrong turn and walked several hundred feet before he realized his mistake. He rested a moment with his rucksack propped up on the wall. It was hot now. The wind hushed. The sun heated the walls. The place between the walls became an oven.

With great difficulty Jay Jay's father raised himself up. He staggered down to the crossing and turned up the lane for the farmhouse again. His leg hurt so bad he was afraid he'd opened it up again. He could've sworn he smelled his own blood. And the peculiar bittery smell of the wet tomato plant.

He hadn't gone far, he said, when way far off from the other end of the valley and over the hill, coming up the main coastal highway from Gela, he heard something he had thought he detested. But now its familiar rattle and groan seemed sweet to his ears. It was the sound of a high compression internal combustion engine, the six-cylinder flathead Dodge motor of a US Army two-ton truck.

Jay Jay's father spun, he ran toward the sound, he rushed down the valley between the walls, setting the rocks to rolling.

Grandpa Tony would never forgive him, he knew, for abandoning his task. Yet he suffered an unnameable horror of this place. And he could not face the past.

"Those goddamn old things, buried in the ground, they gave me the willies," he said. "Who knows what I might have found? Who knows?" he kept saying, again and again.

He thought of it as a kind of initiation, he said, "a weening away from my dad. . . ."

He was a man at last.

All of a sudden the whole world had changed. All its colors were sharper and clearer. The sky was bluer and the mountains greener. The air of old Tony's native island was sweeter, the sun brighter. Everything was tinged with the color of afternoon stainless steel.

He climbed up the rocky embankment to the white gravel roadbed. He saw an olive drab truck coming a mile away, fast, kicking up a storm of white dust. He walked out to the center of the road, under the hot sun, and raised his right hand, palm outward. The truck kept coming. Soon it was almost upon him and showed no sign of slowing down. The white American five-pointed star on the front bumper got bigger and bigger.

It came to Jay Jay's father suddenly that the truck would not stop, would roll right over him, squishing him like tomato in the road. Yet he was in no mood to run or jump out of the way. This too he figured was part of the test, he said.

And so it was now twenty-six years later upon a white dirt road in Calmento, California. Only it was Bruno and Bruno's son who were doing the driving now. It was they who were looking down at that little speck in the road that got bigger and bigger in the twin windshields of their blue Ford pickup trucks and became a man, a great big dark stubborn Latin man.

Father and son bore down on the fucker with their feet to the gas.

None of them knew what was gonna happen.

None of them was about to give in.

In Sicily, however, at the very last instant the truck had slid to a halt, the dust boiling up all around it, sifting into Jay Jay's father's hair, his eyes, ears, mouth. The white US Army star was not ten feet from the toes of his combat boots.

The driver was a tech sergeant in the occupation forces, and he was laughing.

"Oh, hot damn!" he hollered, in a Texas accent. "I'm sorry, soldier. Thought you might of been one of them A-rabs. Country's loaded with 'em. Moroccan de-serters. Nothin' they ruther do than hold up a lone driver. . . ."

Bruno got in and they geared off toward Ragusa, the canvas top of the truck flapping in the wind, the bright white road stretching out before them between the high granite mountains and the gray rock walls of Sicily.

"Where you headed, son?"

"Like to get a train in Ragusa."

"Oh, yeah? What you doin' in these parts?"

"Visiting relatives."

"Relatives? Well, I'll be damned. You don't look like no kind of Eyetalian to me."

"Yep. Vanducci's the name."

"Mine's Holmes. Holmes Watkins. Mighty proud to know you. Say, looky here. If you headed for Messina, I can take you all the way. 'Cause that is where I am bound."

"Gee, thanks a lot, sarge. I sure would appreciate that," Jay Jay's father said, and settled back for the long ride.

They bought wine at several small towns along the way. Jay Jay's dad did the treating. He felt like celebrating. Sangiorgio di Rocca was a million miles away. By the time they hit Catania the sarge was drunk as a lord, and Bruno had to take the wheel.

High on the black seaward flank of Mount Etna, in the middle of the night, an A-rab Moor in combat fatigues and khaki forage cap leapt out in the front of him on the highway and motioned for him to stop.

"Run the nigger down!" the sarge yelled.

And Private Vanducci did just as he was ordered.

Two hours later they were on the ferry for Reggio Calabria, drinking Scotch at the bar with a covey of plump ANZAC nurses, and the whole grisly episode was forgotten.

Later though, after they'd crossed the Straits of Messina, and the whirlpool of Charybdis, Jay Jay's father thought of it often. And later still, fighting up all the long valley of the Arno. And even after VE day, he thought of it. Even back home in Calmento, California, after the war. Sometimes, he said, he even dreamed about it. It was not a guilt thing that he felt. What he felt was just like something he had felt when he killed a big field rat as a kid. He had nightmares for months afterward, dreaming that the entire race of icky dirty rats, every last rodent on earth, was after his ass, seeking vengeance for the death of their own flesh and blood, he said.

Now with big brown Aguilar getting bigger and bigger and browner and browner in the white dirt roadway before him, Jay Jay knew his father must be thinking of those rats again.

And Jay Jay slammed on his brakes and skidded to a halt in the middle of the road.

But his father ran the poor fucker down in cold blood.

And then the two of them floored their twin Ford pickups and moved their tails for town at a hundred and ten miles an hour to evade and outrun the hordes of squirming squealing rodents that pursued them.

Screeched up in front of the Calmento Police Station at West Eighth Street and North Central Avenue and ran into Chief Downs's office to report an accident.

"Jeeeeeesus H. Fucking Christ, Mr. Vanducci! Don't you know better than to leave the scene of a fatal accident? That's a felony, you know. And it's already been reported. We just got a call on it. I was gonna have to swear out a warrant for your arrest."

"Look, Chief, that guy jumped right out in front of me. Ain't that right, Jay Jay? He's my witness."

"That's right, Dad."

"There's just absolutely no way I could've avoided hitting that guy. And those Mexicans out there, they were in no mood to discuss the matter politely, believe you me. Would've pulled my ass out of that pickup truck and lynched me on the spot. Right, Jay Jay?"

"Right."

"Okay, okay," said the little chief, licking his fat lips. "Then we better go in and see Judge Benetti and get him to help us with the deposition. Otherwise, goddamn, Mr. Vanducci, you are going to find yourself in a whole shitload of trouble. Hell, what you done, it's got a name, you know. It's called 'hit and run.' "

"Thanks, Chief. You don't know how I appreciate this."

"Well, Mr. Vanducci, I'm gonna be real frank with you. There will shortly come a time when you will be called upon to show your appreciation in a very concrete way."

"Anything I can do . . ." Bruno said.

And the three of them walked over to the judge's chambers next door and made out their deposition and shook hands all around and Jay Jay and Bruno left the building and they were just crossing West Eighth Street when an old white Chevy pickup came flashing at them out of nowhere. Someone had written *"La Chevycita Bonita"* across its homemade wooden front bumper with white paint, in a florid Mexican style longhand. Jay Jay could see the Chicano driver, a young dark man with a familiar weak-chinned rodent's face. And even before the name "Rudy la Rata" took shape in his mind, he knew his life was not worth yesterday's pasta.

Yet, by some miracle, he managed to twist out of the way. His father unfortunately was not so nimble. An instant later and BRUNO VITALE VANDUCCI, 1923–1970, FARMER, VETERAN & FATHER, was nothing but more tomato for the road.

Twenty-one

S E L E N A S A T in the Tsujimoto Mortuary surrounded by her bereaved female relatives and the *compañeros* of the deceased. Redheaded young Father O'Malley from Saint Bernard's sat beside her, his head bowed in prayer. Old Father Murray had begged off, refusing to attend Aguilar's wake on the grounds of illness, when everyone in Calmento knew he was thick as thieves with the Wops and Portagees, and made the poor wetbacks kneel in the back of the church, and was Angie Vanducci's private confessor.

Mama, Jovita, Gloria, Lita, all wept loudly, unconstrainedly, though it was eleven o'clock at night and they'd been sitting here on these hard metal fold-up chairs since nine o'clock this morning. Only Selena kept her emotions in check. Only Selena was calm and competent enough to accept condolences and receive flowers and Mass cards from the huge throng of *braceros* who had come from all over southern San Joaquin County to pay their last respects.

In the five days since his death Aguilar had become a martyr to his *raza* in Calmento, and his mourners' line went halfway around the block. Tsujimoto had to open every room in the place to accommodate the flowers: red and white carnations, white lilies, roses of every color, enormous flower displays shaped like bleeding hearts, like Christian crosses, like flags of Mexico. . . . One of them had the hero's marriage picture as a centerpiece. Another told the story of his life from the Sierra Madre to the San Joaquin.

The building positively reeked of flowers. To Selena the odor was overwhelmingly oppressive: too piquant, too pervasive, too . . . *dulce*, like the old clothes of the itinerate young Aguilar that she had burnt up in her mama's incinerator when she was a little girl.

In addition to the flower displays, special racks had been set up in the chapel to show off the dozens of Mass cards that had been mailed into the parish church. Aguilar's soul would be sung into paradise with a hundred Catholic Masses, each one bought and paid for by the sweat of the poor farm worker's brow.

Selena sat amid her weeping *familia*, looking at the ornate coffin before her on the altar platform. It was the best that Tsujimoto had to offer. Paid for by a special collection from the CCAC membership. Made of heavy pine, black lacquered, with gold-sprayed curlicues. Behind it, arranged on a display rack that resembled an artist's easel, stood a giant floral piece in the shape of an Aztec eagle. In the center, on gold cloth, was printed:

TO OUR BRAVE EAGLE
NUESTRO COMPAÑERO MUY QUERIDO
VICTORINO AGUILAR

In this his last resting place the hero Aguilar was dressed in the finest black charro suit that money could buy, resplendent with silver studs and buckles and antique coin buttons that ran down his tight black pants, up the sleeves of his short fitted bolero jacket. His black Mexican vaquero boots gleamed in the dim light. His white frilled blouse was starched and spotless and stiff as the corpse himself. His cufflinks were of pure Navajo turquoise, his neckerchief and sash of the dearest crimson silk. Yet his face was sallow and saggy and embalmed, with a rigidly imposed smile and rouged cheeks, and it bore only a mocking resemblance to the robust living man of days gone by.

Tasteless and vexatious as she found these proceedings (and expensive to the *causa*, and enriching to the capitalist Jap Tsujimoto), Selena was convinced they were absolutely indispensable to her aims. Indeed, even before the poor man hit the ground she had begun planning his martyrdom.

The important thing, therefore, was not taste, or any other bourgeois aesthetic considerations. The important thing was the ritual, the show. And in this she had achieved her wildest dreams. Aguilar's wake was a work of the highest and most artful vulgarity, a spectacle both colorful and grand. For its vulgarity, and the unseemly haste of its planning, he would surely have forgiven her. And its purpose he would have indisputably condoned: If Selena could attract national media attention to her strike, and the liberal support that inevitably accompanied it, then perhaps there was the slimmest chance it might succeed.

But in this hope Selena had been seriously disappointed. True, for two or three days after the double tragedy Calmento had been full of media people. And Selena's face had become familiar again on the evening news. But almost immediately the story faded off the TV screens. And, except for an enterprising young woman from the Berkeley *Barb*, no one attempted the deep background story that Selena felt was necessary and merited by the facts.

Liberal support stayed away in droves.

Selena suspected that certain powerful local agro and business interests with media connections had initiated a "conspiracy of silence." But there was little she felt she could do about it, short of going out and getting someone else killed.

And this was not the least of her problems in Calmento. For five whole days since Aguilar's death she had been obliged to relinquish operational control of the strike. And under Connie's cautious stewardship the strike did not advance. It atrophied. Luckily, the Vanducci forces were in a state of temporary disarray over the death of their leader, and Connie had so far managed to do only minimal harm. The professional scabs had arrived from Mexicali, but not in sufficient numbers to be of much use. Growers all over California had been hit with a spate of little wildcat strikes this summer. And the Vanduccis' labor contractor had found it impossible to import more than half the number of workers required for full production. What it all boiled down to was this: Half the 'Duccis' ripe tomatoes were still out there hanging under the hot August sun. The longer they hung there, the sooner they would begin to rot on the vine. When they began to rot, Jay Jay would have to negotiate or lose his year's profits. So Selena figured that she'd probably gained a little more than she'd lost in the past few days. But at what a cost!

Sitting here in this macabre mortuary all day yesterday and all day today (and still two more days to go!) she had been so prodigiously bored and uncomfortable she might well have gone bananas, she believed, if she hadn't let her mind wander. She had hoped that in its wanderings it would lead her into the realm of strategy, a useful and concrete place. But in this she had been disappointed.

Her mother was to blame, her poor suffering mama beside her who twice now in her forty-two years had been made to kneel in the dirt with the bloody head of a mortally wounded mate in her lap.

Watching Delia now, Delia who wept too loud, who was too tireless, too woebegone at her side, Selena foresaw the same perils as the first time around: the same orgy of endless grief, the same incipient Mama Loca. She tried to comfort herself with the thought that if she'd saved her mother once, as just a little girl, then surely she could do it again. But there was this one little doubt that kept gnawing at her. There had been just this one moment on Corral Hollow Road when she had gone weak in the knees, and fallen into despair.

Aguilar was down on the ground, his bashed-in sombrero ringing one of his upturned toes. Mama had his broken head in her bloody lap. She was bending over his ashen face, his dusty mustache, crying, "*No te vas, no te vas, me está volviendo loca!* Don't go, I'm going crazy, don't go!"

Aguilar was trying to say something: "Gotta . . . gotta . . ." But his legs were twitching so violently he couldn't get it out. Involuntarily he kicked the sombrero off his toe and it went rolling down the embankment and into the canal. Rudy ran down and fished it out. Climbed back up the embankment, tears streaking his smooth dirty cheek.

Jovita was standing on the roof of the Chevycita Bonita, speechless, pointing northward toward the rapidly departing Ford pickup trucks.

Selena got out of Delano's car, ran over to Rudy, and without thinking, grabbed him by his shirt collar and started screaming, "Go get 'em, Rudy, go get 'em!"

Rudy looked at her stupidly at first, as if she were speaking some kind of foreign language.

"Go get 'em, Rudy, go get 'em!" she cried out again, in anguish and frustration.

At last he appeared to understand. He clapped Aguilar's big wet sombrero on his small head, ran over and hauled his little half-sister off the roof of the Chevycita, jumped in the cab, and tore off after the assassins.

It was then that Selena felt the edifice of her will begin to quake and suffered her first temptation: She was enticed by the luxury of impotence and irresolution.

As Aguilar's lips went cold and blue, as the death rattle in his great lungs fainted out, as he died like a dog in the white road with his brains and blood puddling out around him like tomato paste, Selena attempted halfheartedly to comfort her hysterical mother, her little sister Jovita, who now lay in the dirt beside the body, dry-eyed, catatonic.

But it was no good even trying. For Selena was stricken with a grief of her own, an awesome soul-scorching guilt for the death of the heroic Aguilar, and for the coming events which she could already see too well: the extinction of Bruno Vanducci, the incarceration of Rudy Cruz, the resurrection of Mama Loca. And she felt this evil insidious numbness come stealing up through her limbs like sleep. And it was only through a concentration of the most powerful positive thinking, and the blithest rationalization of her life, that she was able to turn it back at last. . . .

Late on the last morning of the wake Selena gave her mother and sisters over to the care of her obese cousin Lita and left with Gloria to visit Rudy in the San Joaquin County Jail. They rode in the Chevycita Bonita, the weapon of revenge, which Selena had now inherited by default: Delia couldn't drive, Jovita was too young, and Gloria now had Rudy's car. Prettyboy Pombo trailed along behind them in his green and white Sheriff's Department sedan.

As they drove up the freeway toward French Camp, Selena was checking her little sister-in-law out. She would be needing new blood now in the strike leadership. And she wondered how Gloria was taking the loss of her husband. She seemed to be taking it okay. But how was one to know? It occurred to Selena that she hadn't taken the time to get to know this person, Gloria, her own *cuñada*, her sister-in-law, that she hadn't even *looked* at her yet very closely.

Gloria was a dumpy little olive-skinned peroxide blond of about twenty-five. But she looked years older. She had skinny varicose legs, huge pendulous breasts, and a soft flapping belly that had never recovered from the child she bore five years ago. She wore only the shabbiest synthetic clothes, which she bought secondhand at the Saint Vincent de Paul's thrift shop in Calmento. At the moment she was wearing a black Dacron mourning dress with a hem far too short for decorum on this solemn occasion.

And yet, there was something attractive about Gloria, a certain bouncy energetic quality, Selena believed, a certain cocky good humor in her squinty unlovely face. She thought it a pity that she'd never stopped to notice this about Gloria before. She often failed to look closely at people, or listen to them carefully. She considered it a flaw in her character. But up till now she had excused it on the grounds that it was too late to do anything about it. And besides, if you spent too much time on any one person, you'd have no time for the people as a whole, the *raza*.

Yet, thinking about Gloria now, chatting with her as they rolled up the freeway, Selena discovered that she genuinely liked her.

"Gee, Gloria," she said, turning to smile at her across the cab, "I haven't really got a chance to talk to you yet, have I?"

"Naw," Gloria said, popping her Spearmint, "but, hey, you got more important stuff on your mind, no?"

"Well, I don't know, *cuñada*," she found herself saying, "if I hadn't been on such a damn ego trip all the time . . ." And yet even as she said it Selena knew she was still not really seeing Gloria or appreciating her as an individual, that she was still preoccupied with her own problems. "I mean," she added, quite unintentionally, "when you're involved in a struggle like ours, there's such a fine line between . . . between dedication and self-absorption. You know what I mean?"

" 'Course I do," Gloria said defensively. But Selena wasn't sure.

"I mean," she said, "as leader of a movement like this one, in a situation like this one in Calmento, where your motives are always a little suspect, even by yourself, there is this . . . self-loathing, sort of, that you suffer sometimes."

"Hey," Gloria said, dismissing all further speculation on the subject with an eloquent wave of her hard stubby little unphilosophical hand, "don't let it get to you."

But already it was too late. And a fresh little tendril of self-doubt had wormed its way into her leader's heart.

Selena exited at French Camp. Crossed old Highway 50 and drove up the boulevard of valley oak trees past Juvie Hall and the Honor Farm to the brick monolithic county jail. Her squad car tail turned around and headed back to Calmento.

"Probably figures we're in good hands now, eh, Gloria?" she said, and breathed a sigh of relief. Or rather she exhaled, hoping it would bring relief. But she had already remembered the last time she was here, years ago, when she split with the boss's son, leaving poor little Delano Range to rot in jail, alone and visitless. And the more Selena remembered, the more that malevolent little tendril fed and grew.

Till like some kind of carnivorous beanshoot it wriggled its way into the deepest chambers of her prideful heart.

The guards would only let them see Rudy one at a time. Gloria went first. A fat middle-aged deputy searched her bag and let her in. Selena stood behind the barred glass door and watched. The visiting room was long and narrow, with a very low fluorescent-lit ceiling. Exposed electrical wiring and steam fittings ran up and down the brick walls. Down the middle of the room two lines of thirty metal fold-up chairs faced each other through a bulletproof glass panel that went all the way to the ceiling. The prisoners sat on the left side of the panel. On the right sat their visitors, who were mostly female, mostly Mexican and black, with a sprinkling of slick-looking Anglo lawyers. They conversed via telephones that hung on the panel. Just behind the fold-up chairs, on either side of the panel, stood two bull-necked guards with folded arms.

Gloria went down the line in her frumpy wrinkled black mourning dress, took a seat at the end of the room, pulled out a fresh pack of chewing gum, and stuffed the entire contents in her mouth.

Then they let Rudy in. He came bouncing across the room in black platform shoes and a white denim jailhouse jumpsuit, sat down, picked up his telephone, and immediately started cracking jokes, making Gloria laugh and slap her knee. Because of the partition between them, they had automatically begun punctuating their phone conversation with exaggerated gestures. The effect of this pantomime was to give them an even more comic aspect and diminish their already limited appearance of dignity: There they were, this greasy-looking little ferret-faced pachuco with his out-of-date ducktail and pimp curl, and his cheap little gum-popping *chola* wife.

Selena could not hear a word of what they were saying, of course. But suddenly they seemed so . . . gallant to her: Adversity apparently had no effect on them; self-pity apparently was unknown to them.

And she started getting all bleary-eyed and sentimental again, remembering her brother when he was a little boy and all the kids used to laugh at him, exclude him from their games. Even herself. "La Rata! La Rata!" she would yell, right along with the others.

Up till now Selena's recognition of her brother's brave and selfless act, and her indignation at the injustice of his imprisonment, had given her strength to carry on. She had avoided the painful reality of his plight by sending him effusive messages of congratulation: "The tyrant is dead! Long live the heroic avenger of Aguilar!" She had avoided unpleasant feelings of guilt by reviling the system: "How vile the system," she had written to him, "in which a rich gringo can walk out of the cop station scot-free ten minutes after having committed premeditated murder, and for the same offense a poor Chicano gets clapped in the slammer."

But none of this kind of political shit would work for her now. None of it even seemed relevant. The only relevant facts seemed to be that her brother was going back into the Joint again, after only a pitifully few months on the street. And this time it was definitely not gonna be some cheap two-bit beef, but a truly heavy number, one that might well see him into the grave.

Rudy's life was over. His wife was a widow. His kid was an orphan. And for what, really, when you thought about it? For what? And who was to blame? And for what exactly had Aguilar given his life? And who was to blame for that?

Desperately now Selena sought some way out of her dangerous predicament. She tried mythologizing the situation, in her habitual way, telling it as a story in her mind: *And forevermore this difficult period in her life would be known as "Selena's Moment of Weakness," her moment of greatest peril. . . .*

But this didn't work either. Nothing worked. And at last she came to understand that her guilt was real and tangible and justly earned and would be suffered alone and to its fullest extent with no free transfers and no second chances and no saved by the bells.

Twenty minutes later Gloria came out of the visiting room and Selena went in. She crossed the room slowly, awkwardly in her unfamiliar high-heel shoes, suffering the lecherous looks of the skin-headed deputies, the ogling of the long-haired inmates behind their barrier. Her linen mourning dress was uncomfortably warm. Her black nylon pantyhose made her perspire between the legs. She sat down, took one look at that ugly weak-chinned little Mexican man across from her, her own brother Rudycito with whom she had slept and bathed and played as a child, and she broke down and started bawling in front of him for the first time since she was ten years old.

Rudy appeared to accept it as an honor and was greatly moved.

"Selenita, Selenita," he called softly, scratching the window with his tiny grayish fingernails, "don't cry, don't cry, please. . . ."

"You oughta get a medal," she exploded through her tears, "for offing that motherfucker!"

"Ay! Now that is more like it, *carnala*," he said, beaming with pleasure, while the fat-faced guards glared at them with the utmost hostility.

But then too quickly Selena gave in to her sorrow again. "It's all my fault, all my fault, Rudy," she sobbed, "I never stopped to think . . ."

"Hey, sis, you gotta stop it now," he pleaded, his voice breaking, all his honorific pleasure suddenly at an end. And he cast about frantically for something that would firm her up, abolish the regrets that enfeebled her. His little beady rodent's eyes darted here and there. What should he tell her? What should he say? Selena read it all on his face. "*Oye, carnala*, lemme tell you something," he whispered. "Don't say nothing to Gloria, but confidentially, you know, I don't really mind it too much in the Joint. It's like the army, sort of. Everything's taken care of. You know what I mean?"

Nervous, shifty-eyed, with an insipid little grin, her brother said this, anxious to please. What he accomplished in fact was something quite different. There was just enough truth in what he said to achieve the irrevocable breaking of his sister's heart, and the sealing of her tragic fate.

Now that Selena had opened the door to self-doubts, they came flooding in on her like waves, inundating her, extinguishing her fires. All the way home to Calmento she cried. Inconsolable, she cried, as her mother would cry when she came this way tomorrow. Cried so hard she could no longer drive the pickup truck and had to turn the wheel over to Gloria.

Gloria stopped at a boat launch liquor store under the San Joaquin River bridge and bought her a half-pint of brandy, hoping it would soothe her, calm her down. But all it did was make things worse. Selena drank the whole bottle down before they hit the World's Largest Truck Stop. Got all boozy and maudlin and started bawling all the harder, pissing and moaning about what a mean selfish-ass bitch she was.

"*Basta ya*," Gloria said, as they drove up East Eleventh Street in Calmento. "Now just *cálmate*, Selenita; we be home in no time."

"I don't want to go home," she moaned. "Take me back to the wake!"

"No way," said Gloria firmly, chewing her gum.

By the time they reached CCAC headquarters it was already late afternoon, and most of the strikers had come in from the field. Their dusty vintage automobiles were parked all along Fourth Street and up on the railroad embankment.

Gloria parked in the rubbish-strewn vacant lot on the corner and ordered Selena out of the truck. She refused. Exasperated, Gloria ran inside for help.

As soon as she was gone, Selena keeled over on the ripped seat cover and passed out. Or she pretended to pass out. Actually, it was difficult to pass out because the scent of her stepfather's body was overwhelmingly alive beneath her nose.

What she was really after was sympathy.

She wanted Range to come down and rescue her.

It would be the third time he had rescued her recently. Or would it be the fourth? He had rescued her from Bruno. And he had helped her to escape from the packing shed grounds. And out in the middle of Corral Hollow Road, he had rescued her then too, hadn't he? Yes. Gently he had picked her up, just when she was on the verge of breaking down, and carried her away to his car, murmuring things into her ear, sweet solicitous things that he probably wished he'd never said, confessing his love, his devotion to her *causa* . . . even, in his state of shock, and if she had not been mistaken in what she heard, proposing *marriage*, of all things. . . .

And now quite suddenly Selena's wish was granted. Range's dark head, long-haired, bearded, with a brown beret perched cockily over his ear, appeared outside the pickup window. The door opened at her feet and he started anxiously shaking her legs.

"Selena, Selena," he said, "what's wrong? What's wrong?"

To Selena the scene had all the deepest and most soul-satisfying elements of classic domestic drama. She continued to pretend to be passed out; he saw through the deception; yet, it inspired in him a degree of tenderness that a merely genuine indisposition could never have achieved.

Gathering her up in his arms now, uttering little soothing sounds, pressing her against the rough texture of his army fatigue shirt, he carried her out of the truck, into the CCAC building past gawking whispering office workers, and up the stairs to the loft. Then, panting with his effort, he laid her on the bed and said, "Now, you just take it easy for a while. Okay?"

"What for?" she asked suddenly, fluttering her eyes open. She was feeling almost capricious, now that they were alone. "Why should I take it easy? Maybe I don't want to."

"Oh no?" he said, seating himself on the mattress beside her, reaching out to touch her hair. "Gloria said you were feeling kind of . . . 'under the weather' I think is the way she phrased it."

The sun was low in the sky. It was shining in through the westside windows of the loft and a ray of light was striking Range on his right arm. It was a very tan and hard and wiry arm. Its bristly plentiful hair was bleached all golden from the sun. The first time they made love, Selena remembered, she had looked down at his thin nervous hairy body with its sharply defined bikini lines across its narrow loins and flanks and she had said, "Hey, how'd you get such a tan in prison?" And he had said, "I worked as a gardener for my counselor, the last month or so. She let me sun myself on her deck every day." And Selena had said, "I'll *bet* she did!" And then she had fallen upon him hungrily, tickling him, biting him, making him laugh, kissing him down his bony chest, bumpy muscular belly, and on down.

At the moment, however, she was not in the least bit tempted to taste his delights. She kept telling herself that what she needed was not a lover but a daddy. Yet she wasn't sure that even a daddy was enough. She thought perhaps she needed something even more than that.

"What do you want, then?" he asked.

"Not that."

"Not what?"

"What *you* want," she said. "What you can't have."

"Oh," he said, as if he apprehended her meaning exactly, as if in fact he apprehended it better than Selena did herself. "I want more than that, Selena."

"Look," she said, "if you'd really like to do something for me, you know what you could do? You could tell me something very truthfully."

"What's that?"

"Do you like me? I mean really. As a person."

"I love you," he said.

"That isn't what I asked."

"Sometimes I like you," he said. "Other times not."

"When not?" she demanded. She really wanted to know. At the same time she found herself obligingly attempting to project herself and Range into the future, a future in which he still apparently believed. She tried to imagine them together as lovers a few years hence . . . a tough husband-and-wife team of union organizers, rabble rousers, agitators, Reds, traveling from one dusty little one-horse valley town to another, fighting one little dubious battle after another. But when she looked into the future it was empty of herself. She could definitely see Range in that role, an idealized role she had created for him. But he was alone on the set. Or with some other pretty Chicana.

Selena was merely the inventor of the scene. She was not meant to exist within it.

"When am I not very likable?" she insisted.

"When you get all caught up in your own act."

"Well, we all have our little acts, don't we?"

"What do you mean by that?"

"Look at yourself," she said. "Look at this little Che Guevara number you've been flaunting for the last week or so. Not that I don't approve. It suits you a whole lot better than the old jive-talking hipster act, or the cynical jailhouse crap. But what exactly is it supposed to signify, Del? I mean, it doesn't say much for your sense of self, does it? Who are you, anyway? I wonder if you even know. Are you one of us now? One of us chilebeans, us greasers? If so, why be so blatant about it? Huh? We got the message already. You know what I mean?"

"But it's true," he said. "It's real." And his sincerity was not something she could cope with as easily as his duplicity.

"Delano, don't get hung up on me, it wouldn't pay."

"It wouldn't have to," he said.

"Go on," she said, "go on and get out of here."

He stationed himself at the top of the stairs where he could intercept any well-wishers who might disturb her. And for the next hour or so she would hear him and Gloria loyally fending them off.

". . . Come on, you guys, we gotta leave her alone for a while. . . . Everything just came down on her all at once. . . . Who wouldn't be feeling down? . . . Would have happened to anybody else a long time ago. . . . Things just finally caught up with her, that's all. . . . She'll be okay tomorrow, you'll see. . . ."

Selena enjoyed hearing them discuss her plight while she lay helpless on the bed. Their sickroom clichés lulled her, comforted her. Everything was out of her hands now. She lay back, shut her eyes tight, and tried to recharge her batteries. Each great surge of inspiration had consumed enormous funds of her energy. She had no illusions about how long the next surge would last.

Already she was considering her possible successor.

Outside her window now she could hear the campesinos laughing and joking in the backyard. She could smell the goatmeat they were barbecuing over open fires. The backyard was full of tents now, she recalled, tents where they slept with their wives and children. And all of her wild yellow oats were trampled into a soft straw mat under their bare brown feet.

A shame that she had to recall what her own backyard looked like anymore. She got so wound up in grand strategy sometimes that the little things evaded her. She had this truly lamentable tendency to forget the important people, she believed, the humble ones, the invisible ones, the light-footed sombreroed ones with the bent backs.

Nearly every backyard in the barrio had tents now, she remembered. And the abandoned Chinese grocery store on Mount Diablo Avenue had become a dormitory for two hundred men. Southside was like an armed camp now, full of smoking campfires and field kitchens and flapping battle flags and milling soldiers of the *huelga*. The only gringos who dared venture across the SP tracks were cops; and even they were afraid to come with less than two squad cars. No more would vandals deface Selena's murals with impunity. No more would prowlers come stealing down her back alley in the middle of the night.

Or would they? On her night table now as she peered from beneath her lead-weighted eyelids she caught a glimpse of another nefarious letter from the Posse (Pussy) Vigilantus. It had been lying there for three days, half-opened, half-read:

DEAR KREAM KUNT:

We does hearwith AFFART our unnatcheral DEEZIRES to POLEAX yor cute little KRACK from KUIM to tailbone and stuff yor precious KUIVER, yor little KLEO TORRES (rimes with KLITORIS, git it?) up yor BLOWHOLE like the curly head of a sow and then . . .

Crude ugly handwriting, writing disguised to hide the correspondent's identity, familiar writing, suspicious writing (was the Posse really so foolish as to identify itself as the author of such an incriminating message as this?), writing like a thick frayed cable, writing that uncoiled now, leapt off the page and overwhelmed her, tied her down to the bed, bound her up in frailty and infirmity and all kinds of paranoid suspicions and suppositions that she'd never had before.

Trembling with fright, and masochistic delight, she thought of Jay Jay Vanducci as the man with the poison pen.

And this one little hint of possible weakness in the Vanducci camp, this one stinky kinky little scrap of hope, picked up her spirits for a moment. And she lay there listening to the campesinos out back, tearing down her abandoned chicken pen for firewood, whacking at it with hammers, kicking at it with their workboots, jumping on it, cracking the old seasoned one-by-fours into little pieces, laughing about nothing in particular, "Ho ho ho!" like Aguilar used to do.

And others she could hear, shouting encouragement. And others conversing loudly in Spanish. And others singing, playing their out-of-tune guitars.

"*Esperanza, esperanza . . .*" one of them sang now in the backyard of the bathhouse next door, singing of hope, in a raw untutored Norteño tenor.

"The sky is clouding up," she heard another one say, in the Americanized dialect of northern Sonora.

"Gonna rain outa season, *compañeros*," someone hollered from just beneath her window, "and the *jitomates* gonna rot on the vine! *Ai ai ai!*" Selena believed that she could detect just the slightest tinge of irony in his voice, an irony that perhaps he didn't even know was there.

"*Quién tiene dudas en la victoria última de nuestra causa?*" a woman yelled from somewhere across the alleyway. "Who has doubts in the ultimate victory of our cause?" in the languorous drawling accent of Chihuahua, echoing the well-worn phrase of her leader. And again it seemed to Selena that she could hear just the finest edge of mockery in the woman's voice, a mockery that almost had its own life, that existed in spite of the woman's obvious sincerity.

"*Ninguno!*" the campesinos shouted from the yard next door. "No one!" And the next yard. And the next. Till it resounded from all over the barrio. "*Ninguno! Ninguno! Ninguno!*" they chanted, with an exaggerated energy and volume that, it seemed to Selena, was an instinctive method of assuaging their own doubts and fears and flagging enthusiasm.

Demoralization had set in. After years of experience in the field there was no mistaking it. It was the first sign, but indisputable.

Quién tiene dudas?

No one but the Campesinita herself would admit to any doubts . . . the former Campesinita, Palomita, La Niña Reina Chicana, the Little Dove of Southside, Selena the ex-and-never-queen of Calmento, who could now feel her strength seeping out of her body and onto the sweaty sheet beneath her like egg yolk. She knew the feeling well. She even saw the fetus. He looked like a jumbo prawn, deep-fried. Then she flushed him down the toilet and one of his little feelers broke free and it looked like he was waving good-bye. "Bye bye, little Jay Jay, bye bye!" she called out vengefully, as the little bastard gurgled down the Tijuana sewer drain.

Selena came to a decision while she lay there on the bed. She slipped the high-heeled shoes from her feet, rolled off the bed, and padded across the loft to her bathroom. There she sat down at her dressing table, pulled a pencil and a piece of paper from the drawer, and set about composing an open letter to the membership of the CCAC. Very carefully she wrote it out, erasing words, rewriting sentences, till she was quite satisfied with the result. Then she dragged herself back to her cubbyhole behind the black and red Mexican blanket, fell on the bed, and slept drunkenly, exhaustedly, till she was awakened by Range's voice an hour later.

"Come on, Connie, let her get some rest, for Christ's sake!" he was saying.

"No!" Selena called out sleepily. "Let her in. I want to show her something. And you too, Del. Gloria, please just stay there at the head of the stairs and don't let anyone in!"

"What is it?" Connie wanted to know when she'd arrived at the foot of Selena's bed.

"Here," Selena said. And Connie took the letter and read it out loud, while Range stood beside her, reading it over her shoulder:

> H.Q. CCAC
> Calmento, CA.
>
> August 7, 1970
>
> Dear *Compañeros:*
> My first impulse was to make this confession at an assembly of our entire union membership. But I discarded that option on the ground that it would be only another ploy, another self-deception on my part, an emotional plea to you for reassurance and reaffirmation, rather than a sincere expression of regret and repentance.
>
> Therefore, *compañeros,* I would like to admit to you now very briefly something that perhaps you have already guessed. My commitment to your struggle here in Calmento has been a sham from the very beginning. I have never truly been interested in you as farm workers, or in the justice of this strike for your rights, or in your *causa* in general. I have exploited you selfishly out of my own private motives of revenge against one of the growers.
>
> Call the membership together and elect a new leader. I am going away. You will hear from me no more. From this day on, *compañeros,* the greatest favor you could do for me is to think of me as dead.
>
> Sincerely,
>
> Selena Cruz

"Well," Connie said, when she had finished reading the letter, "I think this is probably a good idea, Selena. It's more or less what I've been trying to tell you all along. The only trouble is, I'm not sure you really mean it."

"What do you think, Del?" Selena asked.

"Oh," he said, "I'll tell you the truth, Selena. I just can't take this seriously. I don't think you're feeling yourself. A good night's sleep and you'll probably want to tear it up."

Range hesitated. He was waiting for some response from Selena. He was trying to guess what she wanted to hear.

"Well," he said, when she had indicated with a nod that he might go on, "and then there's all this shit about 'motives' and 'revenge' in the letter. I don't see what it has to do with the strike. I mean, what's wrong with revenge if the fucker earned it? Anyway, it seems to me that you got yourself into this spot, Selena, 'cause you kind of lost touch with the strike. And believe me, I'm out there every day and I can tell you, the strikers feel it too. You know, when Selena Cruz isn't out there, in the flesh, a whole lot of fight goes out of those people. But, hell, all you got to do is show up out on the picket line and they'll be rarin' to go again. And you'll be surprised, you'll pick up on their excitement, and it'll make you feel better too."

"'Rarin' to go,' " Connie said sarcastically.

"I'm not kidding," Range said.

"It's a no-win situation out there, Range. And the strikers know it. The miracle is that they've stuck with us this long."

"Well, I tell you what, Connie," Range said, in a mildly declamatory tone that he had recently acquired, apparently from listening to Selena's speeches. Other things about his style seemed familiar: He appeared to be imitating her gestures and movements to some extent. If she was not mistaken there was a slight Mexican accent creeping into his voice. Though she had kidded him about his Sierra Maestra costume, she approved of these developments wholeheartedly. She had even added his name to her list of possible successors. "This kind of attitude of yours," Range said, "is just about our biggest problem at the moment. And it's just the sort of thing that has put Selena in the situation where you see her now."

"Oh, really? Tell me. What situation is she in right now?" Connie said, with her chin thrust out, hands on hips, feet spread apart. And yet it seemed to Selena that there was something curiously fragile in her cousin's stance by the bed. It was so aggressively assumed that it appeared to throw her off balance; and it looked like you could knock her over with a feather if you wanted.

"Selena?" Range said, incredulously. "Why, she can't even raise her head up off the pillow. Look at her."

"I'm looking," Connie said.

"That's what I mean."

"What do you mean?"

"It's your attitude," Range said. "As far as I can see, Connie, all you've been doing right from the start is just trying to tear her down."

"Some people set themselves up too high," Connie said. "It blinds them to certain important facts, about themselves, and about what's happening around them. They lose their sense of perspective. Not to mention their mercy and compassion."

"Well, I don't know about all that," Range said, shaking his head slowly, stolidly. Yet it seemed to Selena that he was not so simple or stolid as he pretended. "But one thing I do know. Selena is the strike. The strike is Selena. The minute she stops believing in herself," he said, making a slitting motion with his forefinger across his throat, "—that's all."

"Maybe we'd all be a lot better off if this strike had never happened in the first place," Connie said. "I mean it, Selena," she said, turning toward her cousin, her voice suddenly breaking, tears welling up in her dark little Indian eyes. "Look what you did to the campesinos," she said. "How are they going to feed their kids this winter? And if you have no pity on them, then look at your own family. Look," she said, starting to shake, and then heaving up great wracking sobs, "look at what you did to Aguilar. And Rudy. And your mother. And if that isn't enough, then look at your own little sisters, the innocent ones. Who's going to take care of them, *chingada*, when you throw your life away on this chickenshit little fucking teenage vendetta with Jay Jay Vanducci? Tell me that. Tell me!"

"Hold on now, Connie. Easy down, easy down," Range said, reaching across the bed to pat her on the arm. "Listen, I tell you what. Why don't we just kind of cool it for a minute. You know what I mean? Why should we stand here wasting our time trying to figure out who's responsible for things that are already over and done with? I mean, if we really want to lay the blame on somebody, why don't we lay it on the Vanduccis, who are the cause of it all?"

"I don't give a damn about the Vanduccis!" Connie exploded tearfully. "I don't care if they live or die. Don't you see, Selena? They just aren't worth it. Don't you see?"

"Not worth it?" Range said, "Are you serious? They're the most powerful growers in the northern San Joaquin Valley. And you tell me they're not worth it. I just can't believe you mean what you're saying. . . . Anyway, I guess there's no point in arguing about it. The way I see this thing, Connie, if you don't believe in the strike, then maybe you ought to just drop out, go back and work with Cesar Chavez or something."

"Sure," Connie said, wiping the tears angrily from her eyes. "If Selena comes with me. If she really means what she said in her letter."

"That letter don't mean shit," Range said. "Selena ain't going nowhere. She just made that stuff up 'cause she was feeling so down. She didn't mean it 'cause it just ain't true."

"You sure of that, *cabrón?*"

"You *bet* I am!" Range said, with a confidence that defied reality, created its own logic, toppled the laws of chance, and won his weak and wayward leader back to her *causa* one last time.

"Well, Connie," Selena said, startling even herself with the triumph in her tone. "What do you thing about that, eh?"

"I'll put it this way," Connie said, with some dignity, raising herself up to her full five feet two. "I'm walking out of here right now. And I'm not coming back. Now, Selena, if your letter isn't total bullshit, you will come with me. If you stay, then it's *adiós muchacha.* I won't have any other choice," she said huskily, clearing her throat, "because I just won't have any respect for you anymore. I won't be able to trust your word."

"Well," Selena said, "if that's the way you want it, Connie."

"Huh?" she said. She seemed quite surprised.

"I changed my mind," Selena said. "Range has convinced me that my first duty is here with the strike."

"I don't get it."

"Sure you do," Selena said cruelly, feeling her transcendent powers grow with each blow at her sacrificial victim's unprotected ego. "We won't be seeing you around anymore, Connie."

Twenty-two

JAY JAY SPENT THE MORNING after his father's funeral going through his private papers in the Vanducci packing shed office. With one exception, everything was just as he'd imagined it would be. The exception was a half-completed poison pen letter to Selena Cruz, plus a wall safe full of xeroxed poison pen letters to the same person, dated at various intervals in the past few weeks. It seemed utterly astounding and ridiculous to Jay Jay that his rough, simple, tomato-growing father had written these vicious and concupiscent letters. He found it difficult to believe that Bruno had even had enough imagination to create such improbable obscenities. And he had gone to such an incredible lot of trouble to compose them! He must have spent hours and hours on them, disguising his neat small handwriting to make it crude and ugly, misspelling words on purpose, employing a vulgar vocabulary that was not his own. . . . What had ever driven him to do such a thing? And what had he hoped to achieve by it? Had he written the letters solely out of perversity? Or had he told himself he was "just trying to scare her off?" And what about Angie? Had she suspected the truth? Or had she known of the letters' existence all along? Maybe she had. Maybe she had even instigated them. That was a definite possibility, Jay Jay thought. And it explained the imaginative part of the puzzle. . . . The more Jay Jay reflected on the situation, the more disgusting and absurd yet mysterious it seemed.

He would never know why his father had written the letters.

He had never known his own parents. Never had the remotest idea who they were or what made them tick. The idea was horrifying to Jay Jay. But even more horrifying to him was the notion that these poison pen letters might be only the tip of the iceberg, that there were perhaps other things about his parents, worse things, nastier things, things that Bruno had taken to the grave with him, that Jay Jay would never guess, never even suspect or imagine.

A shudder ran through his body. He thought of his mother, and his wife, and his kids. He saw them sitting out on the patio at the big house, as he had left them this morning, all of them tan and healthy and full of life, taking their recent bereavement amazingly well, all of them talking at once, talking about the new baby who would soon be here, trying to think up a name for that thing that was growing in Rose Mary's overripe belly, just about to drop. . . . *"Bruno? Tony? John? Joseph? Or Carmine for Rose Mary's dad?"* At the moment "Bruno" seemed to have the inside track. It was only logical. Even Jay Jay saw its logic and its irony. Death and life, life and death, off and on, on and off, and the world keeps turning round. . . . Anyway, he saw his family in his mind's eye. They were sitting out there by the pool this morning, having breakfast around the lawn table, with the sunlight playing in their curly well-cared-for hair; such a decent, honest, fine-looking, all-American family they seemed to be! And with a terrible lonely feeling in his heart Jay Jay realized that there were many, many things that he would never know about them, any of them. Just as there was a whole world of things, shameful secret things, like his seamy adventures at Crash City, that they would never know about him. And all of them would go through their lives furtively, hiding shameful little secrets from the world, things that no one would ever suspect or imagine about them. And then they would grow old and die. And none of it would make any difference anyhow.

He was sure that Range had fucked his mother.

He had even heard, or thought he heard and tried to shut it out of his mind, the sound of her coins plinking into Range's tin flower box. Yet suddenly the affair seemed so trivial to him, such a silly bedroom farce, especially now that the cuckolded husband was in his grave . . .

He would never know whether his mother instigated the letters or his father dreamed them up on his own.

And what did it matter, either way?

Jay Jay burst out laughing. Laughing, he took Bruno's forged poison pen letters out back and burnt them up in the packing shed's big industrial incinerator. While he was at it, he packed up all the rest of his father's personal papers—letters from old girl friends and wartime buddies, high school yearbooks from '38, '39, and '40, a 4-H citation from the year 1936, snapshots of little Bruno with his prize bull, Bruno with his first tractor, Bruno as a young GI in Italy, Bruno with a beautiful eighteen-year-old Angela Mazzini out in front of Modesto Junior College—and he burnt them up too. Then he went back into the office, sat down at the desk in the rear, under the picture of A. P. Giannini shaking hands with Grandpa Tony, put his workboots up on the clean green ink blotter, lit up one of Bruno's finest cigars, poured himself a brimming glassful of Sambuca Romana, picked up the telephone, and dialed Selena Cruz.

Only then did he admit to himself he was glad his dad was dead. And swore silently as the phone buzzed at the other end of the line that he would never be anything like him.

Only then did he think of that other trunk, the one where the soul of his family was buried, under the olive tree, by the stone wall, across the sea. And vowed he would go to Sicily someday and dig it all up and bring it home to Calmento.

Now two hours later on his way to CCAC headquarters in his pickup truck, with his own tomato fields stretching out through the windshield before him green and fertile for miles around, and the enormous expanse of sky above him cloudless and milky white, and even the unseasonable rain that had threatened his crops all week gone far off over the distant thundering Sierras, Jay Jay remembered those dancing blue and yellow flames in the industrial incinerator and he laughed again. Laughed his fool head off all the way into Southside. For, now that the Vanducci ranch was at last in his hands, he could conceive of absolutely no earthly reason to feel unhappy or angry or guilty or fucked-up or vengeful or bad. Life was too short. Why fight it? Nothing mattered, nothing lasted, nothing counted, everything was absurd, so why not just relax and go with the flow? Maybe they had something over there in the Haight-Ashbury: *Make Love, Not War*. At the moment Jay Jay felt like making love to the whole world, the whole human race. His heart, he felt, was big enough for the entire San Joaquin, and all of its peoples— white, black, red, and brown; past, present, and future. Deep down in his lower regions somewhere he felt this crazy mixed-up wonderful trembling inchoate sensation of excitement and anticipation and warmth and compassion and generosity and tolerance and love. But most of all he felt love. He loved his wife and his kids and his wayward mother and his relatives and his ancestors in Sicily and all the Vanducci gen- erations to come. He even loved his father, now that he was dead and gone. He even loved the townspeople of Calmento, the grower's traditional enemy. He even loved the Chicanos of Southside Calmento, who worked so long and hard in the fields and sheds. And now as he pulled up in front of CCAC headquarters and parked his truck and waved at the young incompetent Calmento cops in their patrol car he even believed that he loved Selena Cruz and would one day count her among his most respected union adversaries. And he smiled at the campesinos lounging under their sombreros on the front steps of the old wooden building and he made his way smiling through their ranks and he let himself into the CCAC office still smiling cheerily at the startled faces of young picket captains, organizers, telephonists, typists, poster artists, and mimeograph operators and he made his way smiling up the stairway and he reached the top of the stairs and he was just about to move into the loft when someone stuck out a hairy arm and barred his way.

It was Delano Range, in a "Chicano Power" T-shirt and a brown beret. He was feeling good, looking good in his longer hair and beard, bouncing up and down on the rubber tire soles of his huarache sandals, exuding nervous energy.

"Talk to me, bro," he said.

"Hi, Del."

"Where you headed, man?"

"Going in here to visit Selena."

"You're tripping out, *cabrón*." *Treeping out*, Range pronounced it. There were other things about him too. Selena had been working overtime on this one, you could tell.

And yet, despite Range's rather combative stance at the head of the stairs and the phony aspects of this new Latino image he was projecting, Jay Jay responded to his old friend with a genuine affection and understanding.

I have no intention of revoking his parole, unless he pushes me too far.

And remembered the times when they were high school kids and used to drive over to Stockton and pick up girls taking the drag on Pacific Avenue. Sometimes the girls would tease Del and ask him where he got his dark curly locks and Latin good looks. And Del would never cop to a drop of Mexican blood in his veins. What he would do was, he would get this panic-stricken little shifty-eyed desperate look on his face, a pleading look, a look that frankly begged the listener's indulgence, and then he would simply lie through his teeth, say he was pure WASP, say he was part Cherokee, part Portagee, Armenian, Assyrian, even Italian, though he knew Jay Jay would never permit *that* and would call him on it for sure.

Now from his perspective as a grown man, a landowner with children of his own, Jay Jay wished he had not been so often cruel to his little foster brother. And he could not understand whatever possessed him to be such a pig.

"No, really, Del," he said gently. "I have an appointment with her. But say, I'm glad I got a chance to see you anyway, 'cause . . ."

"Sure."

"Naw," he said, "seriously, Del. I wanted to tell you something. Wanted to say, no hard feelings, huh?"

"About what?"

"Oh, everything," Jay Jay said. "I mean, I forgive you, Del. That's what I'm trying to say."

"Don't do me no favors," Range said.

"I guess I'm phrasing this kind of clumsily," Jay Jay said. "What I mean to say is, I understand why you . . . why you . . ."

"Do you, man?" Range said, scratching the back of his neck. "Say, that's funny. 'Cause I ain't figured that one out for myself, yet."

"Guess maybe we had it coming, Delano."

"Oh, you got more than that coming, boy," Range said. "You ain't gonna get off that easy." Then he turned and yelled, "*Oye*, Selena! *Quieres a ver este gabacho rubio?*"

"*Qué sí!*" she called out from somewhere inside the loft. "Send him in, Del. Then leave us alone up here. Okay?"

Range let his arm slide down the wood paneling of the stairway and flop to his side. Only then did he flash a grin at his old friend.

"Just one more thing, Del," Jay Jay said, grinning back at him.

"What's that?"

"Now tell me the truth," Jay Jay said; he was unable to prevent himself from saying it. "Were you in this with Selena from the start? Or did she turn you?"

"You're not playing with a full deck, bro, if you ain't figured that one out yet," Range said, and bounced down the stairs to the office.

Selena was awaiting her visitor behind a curtain made of some heavy red and black Mexican fabric. She was sitting barefoot and cross-legged on her sleeping mat, on a white terry-cloth bedspread and a pile of big red pillows. She was wearing a pair of faded denim hiphuggers, a navy blue tank top, and a choker made of little white shells and brown trade beads. And she looked absolutely terrible. Jay Jay was shocked by her appearance. Frail and thin and pale and cloudy-eyed, she seemed to him completely drained by the effort of the strike, demoralized by the tragedy that had befallen her family.

Suddenly he felt an aching pity for Selena, and a deep and heartfelt remorse for the role he had played in reducing her to the state in which he saw her now. He felt a bitter-sweet nostalgia for the past they had shared together, and for what might have been. And, strange as it might seem, he actually felt indignant with her people for allowing her to suffer so, in their place, for draining her energy with their endless demands. He thought of Range, looking so bright-eyed and full of beans. And he couldn't help thinking that Range had been cannibalizing her, in some subtle way, feeding off her life forces, growing sleek and strong at her expense.

Yet, quite at the same time, Jay Jay could not suppress a brutal little thrill of triumph that Selena had fallen so low.

Her infirmity at once aroused his sympathy and a desire to see her utterly defeated.

These conflicting emotions came over him in waves, each erasing the effects of the previous wave. Every time he felt himself warming toward Selena, he was overcome with guilt for betraying his family. And then every time he felt proud of defending his family, he was overwhelmed with remorse for hurting Selena.

The whole thing seemed suddenly so fateful and abysmal that Jay Jay could barely retain his balance. He pushed through Selena's curtain and stood teetering above her, trying to recover his poise, unsure of where to put himself in this tiny makeshift space.

She offered him no help in deciding.

"I . . . I heard you were ill," he began.

"Did you come to gloat?" she asked.

"I came to talk," he said, reestablishing his equilibrium at last.

"Talk?" she said, as if she could not possibly imagine what they might have to talk about.

"Selena," he said, sighing, speaking as honestly as he could, "I've come to make peace."

"Peace?" she said, pronouncing it like a dirty word. "What does that mean?"

"It means," he said sincerely, "that I'm sorry about Aguilar, and with all my heart I regret his death. It means that I am a very different kind of person from my old man. It means that I would like us to forgive each other and forget the past. It means I want to negotiate an end to this strike before anyone else gets hurt."

Jay Jay paused now, waiting for some kind of response. But all she did was frown, shake her head, and change her position on the mattress: uncrossed her long legs, extended her bare brown feet out casually over the edge, and leaned back on her hands.

"Listen, Selena," he went on, "I've thought a lot about this strike. And I've come up with what I think is a fair compromise. Now let me just—"

"Don't bother," she said.

"What?"

"I'm not interested."

"Now, wait a minute."

"I have nothing further to say, unless you're willing to sign the contract we outlined for you in your father's office."

"But Selena, that contract is no good. It could never be a basis of agreement between us. The other growers would never accept it. And if I signed it on my own, they'd just hire some more cheap foreign labor and undercut my prices. Run me right out of business. Can't you see that?"

"I don't want to discuss it," she said. "Now, leave me alone."

"You gotta be kidding."

"I'm not kidding."

"Who are you to answer for the entire membership of your union? What are you, some kind of dictator? Why don't you listen to my terms and then put it to a vote? I don't believe your braceros would turn me down, if they gave me a fair hearing. I'm prepared to offer very generous terms."

"Get out of here," she said very calmly, barely even breathing, it seemed. Her apparent tranquillity was the worst kind of scorn. It mocked him, belittled his manhood, he felt.

"You can't treat me like this."

"Oh, no?" she said, smiling up at him. "Why not?"

"Selena, Selena," he said, taking a deep breath, trying to hold his temper in check, "can't you see what you're doing? You're just deliberately trying to antagonize me. Now, this just doesn't make any sense, holding grudges from the past. Why don't we look to the future," he said, moving toward her, stretching his hand out toward her.

"Can't you see that I'm willing to do almost anything, bend over back-wards, to come to an understanding with you? Can't you see that? Now please . . ." He was standing almost directly over her now. His pantleg was touching her bare foot, her little brown toes that wiggled at him now derisively.

All of a sudden he was overcome with this nearly irresistible urge to reach out and touch one of her toes, her big toe, as it flicked back and forth against her second toe. In order to control and contain his urge, he permitted a righteous anger to stir and grow within himself. He had done his part, goddamnit. He had gone more than halfway. If that's the way she wanted it . . .

"Selena," he said, very sternly, "did you know something? Did you know that I have it in my power right now to crush your strike in a matter of hours? Did you know that? And did you know I have held back from crushing it simply out of the goodness of my heart? Did you know that?"

. . . And yet still he could not keep his eyes off that toe: slender coppery-colored toe, with neutral polish on its longish nail. He knew it so well, remembered it so well. He had even sucked it once. . . .

"And did you know," he said, getting angrier and angrier all the time, "that right now in my desk I have a letter from the governor of this state authorizing me on the grounds of 'crop emergency' to import as many braceros from Mexico as I see fit? Did you know that? And did you know that my labor contractor is at this moment down in Juarez, where there is no shortage of wetback labor, and he is signing up a thousand green-card braceros who will be sitting out there in my field on Monday morning, if I want? Did you know that?"

. . . Jay Jay remembered sucking that toe so well. It was out in the back seat of his mother's Lincoln Continental on a Saturday night, after a double feature at the Hi-Way Drive-In movie. They were parked under the Southern Pacific overpass, on the dirt levee of the Banta Canal. And other things happened with that toe, as he recalled it. Once, a few weeks later, Selena even playfully wiggled it up his ass. . . .

"And did you know," he said, positively fuming now, beating his shirt pocket violently, "that right now, right here in my pocket, I have a court order signed by Judge Benetti that requires you, Selena, by name, to 'cease and desist all picketing, agitation, conspiracy and incite-ment' on or near my property on pain of contempt? Did you know that? You think I'm kidding? Here, look. You see? I bet you didn't know that, did you? Did you?"

. . . Jay Jay was still looking down at that toe. Yet she continued to wiggle it at him, flaunt it right in his face. He broke out in a cold sweat. He felt his face start to tingle and go red. And . . . he reached out slowly, against his will, and . . .

"And did you know," he shouted, "did you fucking know, goddamnit, that the sheriff of this county, and the sheriff of Stanislaus County, and the sheriff of Merced County, have made me a firm commitment of three hundred deputies specially trained in riot control to be made available to me on an hour's notice—to back me up with all the force at the law's command? Did you know that?"

. . . And she did not move her toe away, did not change that cool disdainful expression on her face. . . .

"And did you know," he said, "did you know that isn't even the half of it, Selena? Did you know that? Did you know that I could right now, today, through any number of different means, legal and otherwise, *destroy* you? Did you know that? Huh?"

He reached out and touched her big toe. Just couldn't stop himself. Figured it this way: Time means nothing; if he had touched her toe in the past, even sucked it, then why couldn't he do it again? And then softly, ever so softly and slow, he began to fondle it. She made no attempt to slip it out from between his trembling fingers. Her face was a scornful mask. . . .

"Did you know, Selena, did you have any idea who you were dealing with here in Calmento? Did you? Do you really understand who I am, and exactly what I represent? I bet you don't. Hell, I didn't even know myself till I started talking to all the lawyers and reading through the legal papers. Did you know what I'm worth, now that I've inherited the ranch? Did you know that the list of my possessions, my land, my crops and buildings and equipment goes on for over a hundred pages? Did you know that? Did you know, for example, that aside from the five thousand acres of prime bottomland that I own here in Calmento, I have many other holdings scattered all up and down the state of California? Did you know that? Did you know that I own another two thousand acres of top rice-growing land up in Yolo County? And did you know that I . . ."

The little brown toe had turned white in Jay Jay's grip. Without realizing it he had clamped down on it, pressing it between his thumb and forefinger to emphasize his various points. And then, ever so slowly, he had begun to twist it and let it go, press down hard on it and then stroke it softly, hurt it and soothe it. Now it was just Jay Jay and that little toe in the whole world, and he was talking only to it. He even imagined a little face painted on its nail: Selena's face. And it was alternately grimacing in pain and smiling in pleasure.

"And did you know," he said, his voice very low and intense now, "did you know that I could . . . could break this toe right now? Did you know that? Did you know that I could twist it clean off your foot before anyone got up those stairs? Did you know that? Did you?"

Jay Jay had no idea why he was doing this thing. He understood that it was fatal to his plans for peace in the field. Somewhere in the back of his head he knew he was proceeding in the wrong direction, leading himself into danger. Yet there seemed to be no way he could change his course.

Her distress had aroused his perversity like her arrogance never could.

He twisted her toe again, harder. Then he let it go, toyed with it between his fingers, caressed it. Watching her braless breasts as they rose and fell, watching her naked belly button and her creamy brown hips where the tank top had become untucked. Whispering all the time, "Did you know that? Did you? Huh? Did you?"

But still he could not get her to say anything, or change that serenely scornful expression on her pretty face.

Their intimacy was total, though they were yet estranged. Their emotion was profound, though they had yet to define it. They were the only two people in the world. Selena's cubbyhole in the corner of the CCAC loft was the only place in existence.

And it came to him suddenly that this was the way she had planned it.

He could even visualize the little scene that she had created in her mind: Selena silent, disdainful, coldly attractive . . . Jay Jay loud, brutal, horny. Her "weakness" was feigned, perhaps, just another part of her grand design. And then the rape. The tearing of her clothes. Pulling her blue jeans and panties down with one hand and holding his hand over her mouth with the other. Or over her throat, even. And then the forcible penetration. And the discovery that she was dry as the skinned pelt of a dead animal inside. And then the remorse afterwards. The self-flagellation. The begging for mercy and forgiveness. "*I'll do anything to make it up to you, Selena, anything!*" he cries out. "*Oh, yeah?*" she says, whipping out a contract of her own. "*Okay, just sign here on the dotted line. . . .*" Or blackmail, even; maybe that's what she had in mind.

The instant that Jay Jay understood, or believed he understood, what Selena had in mind, he let her toe go. And he was just about to turn around and walk through the curtain and out of the loft when something held him back.

He was afraid she might have figured out where the poison pen letters came from. He was afraid she would accuse him of being a pervert, like his old man. He felt he would be unable to defend himself against her charge because he would be unwilling to dishonor his father's name, even to save his own.

"And did you know, Selena," he began again, hastily, as if nothing had happened, a propos of nothing save a sudden frantic desire to prove himself a respectable citizen of Calmento, "did you know that I own a thousand acres of land over in Stanislaus County? I bet you didn't know that! And did you know that it has just been incorporated into the city limits of Modesto, zoned for single-dwelling construction? Did you know that? And then there's the fifteen hundred acres of grazing land up in the Diablos. The wheat and barley up in Redding. The cotton down in Bakersfield. Hell, I even own eight hundred acres of timberland up in the Trinity Alps. . . ."

On and on Jay Jay went with this litany of his possessions. It was enormously long and complicated and impressive and . . . incantatory. He could hear his voice deepening and quickening and becoming more resonant as he continued to speak. Even Selena seemed impressed. Quietly and almost respectfully she heard him out. And gave pause at the end to reflect upon its relevance to her own fate, and its ultimate meaning to her *causa* here in Calmento, California.

When Jay Jay was done he felt invulnerable to her influence for the first time since he was a teenage boy. It was like . . . in essence Selena was a kind of filmy, romantic notion; and Jay Jay's hard facts and figures, they just cut right through her. It was like . . . all of a sudden he could not see her anymore, not as a physical reality, not as something that could affect his behavior. It was like . . . she was only a memory.

And what is a memory but just something in your head, an idea?

An idea you could deal with. An idea was not an entity. An idea could not intimidate. An idea was anything you wanted it to be. Jay Jay wanted Selena as his opponent in a game for the highest stakes. Already he was scheming up ways to outguess and outmaneuver the wily Chicana. Already he was developing his own clever scenarios, and encouraging a latent Sicilian dramatic talent of his own. An idea was not a fact. An idea was not even a presence. An idea could not fight back, save to the extent the imagination allowed. An idea was something you could plow right under, if you wanted. Without compunction you could, with a feeling of righteous indignation even, something bright and pure and awe-inspiring, something intrinsic to the God-given rights of land and home and family. An idea you could bury, if you wanted, plant it right back down in the dark soil where it came from. An idea you could forget.

When Jay Jay got back out to his pickup truck the radiotelephone on the dashboard was buzzing frantically.

It was Rose Mary, calling from the ranch.

"Someone wants to talk to you," she said. "It's important."

"Put him on," he said.

"It ain't a he," she said.

And the next thing he knew he was talking to Connie Pescadero.

"Heard you had a fight with your boss," he said.

"How'd you find that out?"

"Whole town's talking about it; you been together a long time."

"Yeah," she said. "Listen, Jay Jay, I want to tell you something . . . in confidence."

"What's that?"

"Selena . . . she has finally gone off the deep end."

"Hey," Jay Jay said, "you ain't telling me nothing I hadn't already figured out for myself. I was just talking to her. Up in that cubbyhole of hers."

". . . Things go much further and she's gonna get herself killed."

"I know," he said, sympathetically. "I know. Look, why don't we do something about it?"

"That's the reason I called," she said. "I'm worried sick. I'd do anything. . . ."

"You got a minute?"

"Sure."

"Connie, let me tell you something. The next time she comes up against me, I'm gonna break her ass. That strike is just going to collapse all around her. Her people are going to desert her in droves. And where do you think that's going to leave Selena? Is she going to see reason at last? Throw in the towel? Pack her bags and leave town? Uh-uh. No way. 'Cause what she really wants out of this thing is to see me in the grave. So, what she's gonna do is . . . she's gonna sit down and rack her brains trying to figure out some new way to get at me. Only this time she's gonna go a step further. Do something crazy. Something violent. . . . Am I right, or not?"

"You know you're right," Connie said. "I wouldn't be talking to you, otherwise."

"Okay then," he said. "Now, I might be jumping the gun on this, Connie. But there is nothing wrong with planning ahead. So, I'll tell you what I'd like to do. Once the strike is over, I'd like to set her up."

"It can't be done," Connie said.

"Don't be so sure about that. Listen, here's what I'd like you to do. As soon as the strike falls apart, I want you to go back to her. I want you to beg her forgiveness or whatever it takes to get back in with her. Then I want you to let me know what her next move is gonna be. If my guess is right, she's gonna try to burn me out. Or maybe she'll try to flood me out. Open up one of the main sluices on the Delta-Mendota Canal, or something. Anyway, whatever she does, we'll have the sheriff waiting for her. He'll catch her in the act and cart her off to jail, and we'll leave her in there a couple of months till she cools off. It's the only way we're gonna get her out of this thing in one piece, Connie, believe me. At least that's my opinion. But what do you think? Tell me. I mean, really. Are you willing to go along with me on this?"

"Jay Jay, there is nothing I wouldn't stoop to, absolutely nothing in the world," she said, "even treachery, even betrayal, to save Selena from herself."

Instead, Connie saved Vanducci & Son a whole shitload of trouble and expense, and confirmed the new Dootch in a resolution he had made the moment he left the cubbyhole in the CCAC loft: This strike was gonna be a damn sight shorter and sweeter than the ambition of Selena Cruz.

Twenty-three

AN HOUR BEFORE DAWN. A tomato field on the outskirts of town, surrounded and defined by the town: a mile-square perimeter of bright lights and bustling harvest time industry.

Range was standing in a long line of bored, sleepy, cigarette-smoking Mexican strikers at the south end of the field, with his back to the Banta Canal. Across the road he faced an equally long line of glowing cigarettes and cigars belonging to members of the San Joaquin County, Stanislaus County, and Merced County sheriff's departments.

"Viva la huelga!" Range or Selena or Corky DeJesus or Gloria Cruz or Jovita or Nacho or Lita or Fulgencio or Enrique Mendoza or one of the three Apaches would cry out, every once in a while. But their hearts weren't in it. Not even Range's. Not even Selena's. It was too early in the morning. And the strike had been going on too long. Defeatism was all around them in the air like the wind.

The wind blew out of the northwest, harder than usual, even for this windy little town. And colder than usual, for this season. The first bad breath of autumn, it hissed through the sunflowers and wild oats by the side of the road, banged at the tin door of the irrigation district pump house, whipped up a storm of dust that stung the eyes and rippled the water of the canal, making it shimmer in the lights from the edge of town.

Range let his eyes move around, following the lights. Off to his left, past the gray humped backs of sheriff's department paddy wagons and patrol cars, he could see the flood-lit redbrick H. J. Heinz "57 Varieties" tomato cannery. Its parking lot was full of black crawling trucks and semi-trailers loaded with bright red tomatoes. Its tin roof was bristling with banks of floodlights, conveyor towers, and smokestacks that belched out puffy clouds of steam. Its mile-long blacktop backyard was crowded with gigantic yellow storage tanks and high stacks of tomato lugs that stretched out all the way up to the Grantline Canal.

To Range's north, out over the hulking shadows of the sheriff's deputies, and a dark screen of sunflowers behind them, and the flat black incongruous emptiness of the tomato field, Grantline Road cut across the horizon, distinguished by a long string of yellow city street-lights, five spot-lit grain elevators, the DiSavio Trucking Company main lot (also under bright lights—everything was under bright lights), the Jiffy Ready-Mix Concrete plant, and the Shell Oil Company substation at the corner of Grantline and Range roads.

Then turning eastward, he could see the shadows of two abandoned farms (Old Tony had bought out their pioneer Anglo proprietors years before), each surrounded by broken-down wooden outbuildings—barns and water towers and chickenhouses and windmills. Still turning to his right, he could see the high rectangular shadow of the Hi-Way Drive-In movie, its screen ringed in red and blue neon.

Swinging around to the southeast now, he could see the small shadow of an irrigation district pump house on the canal. And then, beyond that, the shiny black rails of the Southern Pacific mainline, and the telegraph and telephone lines that ran alongside it. Then, all the way across and above his rear, and forming a kind of frame for his rearward view, the Highway 50 overpass soared through the air. It swooped up just to the east of the tomato cannery, rose a hundred feet above the railroad tracks, the Banta Canal, the white dirt farmroad, an inhabited farmhouse (complete with tin-roofed barn, wooden water tower, a long stack of yellow bales of hay, an orange pickup truck parked in its weedy front yard), and alighted near the western end of the Hi-Way Drive-In movie.

Through this arching frame of bridge, Range could see the whole eastern section of the Calmento rail yard. It was cluttered up with freight cars and switch engines, some of them moving, others standing still, all of them caught in the gleam of white floodlights a hundred and fifty feet high.

Then looking upward, toward the top of the frame, he could see the lights of cars and trucks speeding across the bridge, and the enormously high steel legs of lit-up road signs directed at the traffic on Highway 50:

GORDO'S POOL CITY
Doughboy Swimming Pools
Jacuzzi Jets and Spas
Hot Tubs

10¢ Coffee
FREE REFILLS
(In S.J. County Only)
McDONALD'S

VOTE FOR
SHERIFF JIM HARTER
"Tough on Crime, Easy on Law and Order"

HI-WAY 50 MOTEL
Cabins, kitchenettes
Handwriting analysis by
"Anna"
Character Readings

SUNBLAST BAR AND GRILL
Topless Dancers

And looking down from the top of the frame, he could see the glowing coals of campfires where the bridge squeezed together with the littered ground at its western end. Low-roofed, protected from the prevailing winds, and convenient to the rail yard, it had traditionally been the home of bums, hoboes, and fruit tramps passing through Calmento. As a matter of fact, Range and Jay Jay and Dirty Harry and Big John Ammiratti and Prettyboy Pombo (who, by the sound of his rasping whisper, happened to be standing now almost directly across from Range in the police line) and Sammy Dog and others used to come down here in a pickup truck and hunt bums for sport. Used to load up the truckbed with bad-ass old boys armed with slingshots and BB guns and attack the poor vagabonds in the middle of the night. Roust them out of their bedrolls. Knock over their cardboard homes. Kick over their cans of coffee and beans. Get them madder than hell. Then make tracks in the pickup truck as fast as they could.

Range remembered the time that Jay Jay ran off and abandoned him to the pissed-off bums as the hairiest moment in a life fraught with hair-raising escapes. They trapped him between the concrete pillars, eight or ten of them, foul-breathed, obscene. He climbed up in the cross-stays and tried to evade them with gymnastic derring-do, kips and tucks and rolls and clever leaps from stay to stay. But they brought him down with rocks and clods and cut-off two-by-fours with nails sticking out of them. Dragged him over to their destroyed campsite. Stripped him naked by the fire and, after they got tired of stubbing cigarettes out on his bare skin, held him down on the ground with his ass sticking up in the air and his legs forced apart. Then, grunting and giggling to each other, they exposed themselves. The instant that Range perceived their intentions, he became possessed of an inhuman strength. He broke their grip on him, sprang to his feet, and ran like the wind for a passing freight train. Old Jay Jay and Prettyboy and Big John, they never stopped laughing about how they found him hours later, wandering naked and alone on the western outskirts of town, crying like a baby.

Under the bridge it smelled of refuse and mustiness and used rubbers and human waste and birdshit.

Pigeons lived up under the concrete crossbraces and metal stays, Range remembered. They were fugitives from the city who had ridden into town on flatcars, it was said. And they had been roosting up under the overpass now for many generations, for as long as anyone in Calmento could remember, leaving their white droppings on the white rocky dirt below them. Funny thing about those pigeons was, even though twenty to thirty trains passed under them every day, they still spooked at the first sign that one was approaching. Took off by the hundreds through the columns and out over the field. And they would not come back to roost till the train was long gone.

That time Range ran away from the bums, the birds took off flying then too, he remembered, flapping their wings madly, filling the air with their feathers, battering their heads against the roadbed of the bridge. Some of them even knocked themselves out apparently, and fell limply to the garbage-strewn ground where the bums stopped to pick them up as compensation, ingredients for their pigeon stew.

An unsavory area, to say the least. Whenever a body was found in Calmento (and several were found every year, usually in summer), it was found here. How many had been found here over the years Range could not exactly recall, but there had been many. Usually the victims were identified as transients: Mexicans, Negroes, Okies, hoboes. But every once in a while a reputable citizen of the town would end up here, done in by his wife for his insurance money, or a jealous lover, or a business adversary with an old score to settle, or by hired assassins for unknown reasons.

Murderers came from as far away as Oakland and Madera to drop their bodies here.

Calmento was the crossroads of the west.

One time when Range was in high school some acquaintances of his picked up a couple of girls who were hitchhiking through town and brought them out here and got them drunk on rye whiskey and gang-raped them. Then, when the girls threatened to go to the police, they hit them over the head with a tire iron, tied them down under the wheels of their car, and ran over them repeatedly. Even "got a little rubber on them," as it came out later in the trial. Then, after they figured they'd destroyed all the evidence, they went home to bed in Calmento. Yet, incredible as it might seem, one of the girls survived. She survived for three days without food or water in the muddy rut where she'd been smashed down with her sister in the road under the bridge; she survived till one of the hoboes finally got up the nerve to report the crime to the police; she survived long enough to testify against her murderers and send them up to Folsom for life. Then she died. She was fifteen years old.

A highly unlikely place for a tomato field. If people back east only knew where some of their salad ingredients came from, Range reflected, they'd probably do without the vitamins and minerals.

From where he stood now by the side of the field the noise was deafening, even at this early hour of the morning. Cars and trucks roared by on the overpass. The roadbed groaned and protested. The bridge columns creaked. Switch engines hooted and howled and ground metal against metal in the rail yard. Empty boxcars and tank cars banged into each other, echoing hollowly. Fast freight trains for Frisco came rumbling over the main line, stirring the pigeons, waking them out of their restless sleep, sending them flying out from under the bridge, smacking the air with their wings. Whistles shrieked in the cannery. Tomato trucks revved in the parking lot. Conveyor belts and heavy machinery squawked and croaked and screamed.

To Range the omens were looking gloomier all the time.

The strikers were hemmed in, physically and psychologically, from every side. An orderly retreat under these conditions would prove difficult if not impossible.

It occurred to him that this was the way Selena wanted it. This was the way she had thought it out. Now that she had been forced to fight, the issue would be decided right here and now, she figured, in this place and no other.

But the fucking place wasn't even meant to be a tomato field, Range thought. It was not meant to be a fertile place where you grew food that people would eat. Or at least, it hadn't been meant for that kind of thing for many years. It was meant to be a graveyard or another rail yard or cannery or a ready-mix concrete works or a development of tract homes.

For years, he remembered, the Vanduccis had been refusing to sell this plot of land, despite numerous generous offers. Figured the town would grow out in this direction and they'd make a pile on speculation. They were right, as usual. If they owned this piece of land and no other, their future would be assured.

It was definitely not a very congenial place for Del to be at the moment.

According to information available at the Weber Museum in Stockton and the San Joaquin County Bureau of Public Records and other sources that Range had researched years ago through the mails while still doing his first bit at Preston, this was the site of the original Range adobe, constructed by old Randall Range in the year 1840, and long since turned to dust. Before that, of course, it had belonged to the MiWuk Indians, and Range's great-great-great-greatgrandma Astera Chacón.

The irony of this confrontation on the land of his ancestors was not lost on Delano. Nor was its connection to the lifelong struggle in his own soul between white and dark, gringo and Mex. He would have preferred a showdown with Jay Jay almost anywhere else.

That it would be a showdown, at least in Range's case, there could be no doubt. He had already enjoyed a lengthier period of grace than he'd ever expected. Every time he walked into the parole office, he was sure that Mrs. Jones would take him back into custody on the grounds that he'd lost his 'Ducci job. But all she did was just smile, engage in a little banter, sign him in, and send him on his way back to Calmento.

Jay Jay's munificence in not revoking his parole was puzzling, to say the least. For days Range had been trying to figure it out. At first he had decided that the Wop was just teasing him, toying with his fate. Then, it seemed to be going on too long for a mere game of cat and mouse. Finally he came to the conclusion that Jay Jay, in his new role of third Dootch of Calmento, was being . . . chivalrous. There could be no other possible explanation for his behavior.

It was Jay Jay's way of squaring any debts that might remain between them. So, when the time came to close Range out, he could do it without any qualms or messy feelings of regret.

Down the road now, from the direction of the cannery, Range could see headlights coming. And he could hear a pickup truck bouncing over the ruts, its tailgate chain clattering. And the sound of several big diesels—bus engines, probably, following along behind.

Also from the direction of the cannery, carried on the wind, he could smell hot tomato sauce. A strong, tart, garlicky scent it was, reminiscent of Italian cooking: enticing perhaps in the evening, over wine, but most unpleasant in the A.M.

Range turned to Selena beside him and, remembering the plentiful quantities of hot oily marinara sauce that Angie Vanducci used to splash over their green spinach pasta just before their morning summer school classes, he remarked: "Only a Wop would eat spaghetti for breakfast."

Selena laughed sharply, bitterly in the wind. And the wind blew the sound round the pump house and quickly away to the southeast.

She had barely heard what he said. Apparently she had not even heard the caravan of motors approaching. She was listening to other things, Range thought, voices in her own head, or something. This was the way she concentrated.

Selena still had great powers of concentration. But the appearance of her concentration had changed. To Range it no longer seemed so sure, so serene, so . . . sovereign. Though she continued to expend prodigious amounts of energy to achieve it, and the air beside him was fairly humming with her present exertions, the result seemed much less impressive than in the past, much more anxious and erratic and . . . fallible: *She shoulda heard them fucking motors by now.*

Fortunately, Range's self-possession seemed to have increased at a rate inversely proportionate to Selena's anxiety. In fact, for the very first time in his life he actually felt confident enough to worry about someone else besides himself.

He was worried about Selena.

In the days since her interview with Jay Jay she had confounded all Range's hopes and expectations by continuing to sit back on her laurels and let all the initiative pass over to the enemy. Consequently the strike had never regained the momentum it had lost during Connie's lax and indifferent leadership. Without momentum, without a centrifugal force to hold it together, the strike was starting to cave in under its own inertia. Every day now they were losing two or three local supporters; every day they were losing eight or ten irreplaceable picketers. The barrio people were going back to their TV sets and their welfare rolls. The young Chicano volunteers were going back to their CETA jobs and to preregistration activities and preseason football practice at Stockton College and Modesto J. C. and Calmento High School. The field workers were leaving town, heading for the melon season down in Hanford, and over to King City for the lettuce. And the tomato packers were going back to Jay Jay Vanducci. Already he had his packing shed running again. Soon, Range believed, it was all gonna be over but the crying.

Whenever he called Selena's attention to her rapidly deteriorating position in Calmento, she just laughed and said, "*Siempre de improviso* . . . Jay Jay expects me to come out fighting. Instead, I let him sweat it out. Let him wonder what I'm up to, where I'm gonna strike next."

"He ain't sweating nothing," Range said. "All he's doing is just using the time to consolidate his position."

But he wasn't sure she listened to him. He wasn't even sure she was being altogether frank about her motives for laying low. She'd been acting very very spacy lately, he thought. Ever since she kicked her cousin out of the CCAC her moods had been oscillating wildly. One minute she'd seem almost elated, the next she'd be in a black depression. She seemed lost, anchorless, unable to commit herself to any course of action. Other things were weird about her too. She had mysteriously sprained the big toe on her left foot, for example. And she went around limping on it all the time. But when Del asked her how it happened, she said she couldn't remember. Then, when he pressed her for an answer, she denied it was hurt at all.

The truth was she was half out of her mind with fright. She was evading her responsibilities as strike leader, Range believed, because she was afraid she might fail. And yet, ironically, she was failing because she was afraid. As once she had magically communicated her self-confidence to the strikers, so now she communicated her fears and self-doubts to them, and contributed to their further demoralization.

She was trapped in a quandary of her own unintentional design. If she did not confront Jay Jay soon, he would win the strike by default. If she did not win a victory soon, her effort would collapse. Yet victory was impossible. Or at least, the odds against it seemed astronomical to Range, and monstrously intimidating.

Jay Jay was leading six big busloads of fresh Juarez braceros up the dirt road at this very moment, for Christ's sake. They'd be here any second now. He also had a court order in his possession that prohibited all picketing or agitating on or near his property. Not to mention the one hundred and ten beefy deputies from three counties who were lined up across the road now just waiting to back it up with everything they had. And they had a lot. They had gas, guns, clubs, dogs, masks, shields, helmets, walkie-talkies, paddywagons. . . .

Selena had two hundred tired, grungy, ragged, hungry Mexicans whose militancy was evaporating as swiftly as their illusions: They were beginning to wonder, not without reason, how in the fuck they were going to feed and clothe their children this winter, now that earning time in the agro-industry was drawing to a close.

It was this certainty of defeat, this reality of failure (yet another failure, and worse than the one down in Fresno County), this debt of blood guilt to her family, her *raza*, that Selena was seeking so frantically to evade.

She was right to be scared. It was smart to be scared. Range also was scared. Anyone in his right mind would be scared. But Selena was *too* scared. She was scared shitless, scared witless; she was goddamn hysterical; she was out of her fucking tree.

Last night just after dark, and without a word of explanation, the crazy Chicana had dragged Range's ass down here to this same spot. Shoved him out of Aguilar's pickup truck with trembling feverish hands. Pushed him roughly, impatiently, excitedly across the canal bridge and eleven rows out into the furrows.

"Why? Why?" he kept asking.

"Shhhhhh, shhhhhh," she kept panting, as she limped and stumbled over the rows, "come, come, come, come . . ."

She was in some kind of trance.

Range was afraid of what might happen if he broke the spell.

Besides, it turned him on.

Suddenly she spun around in the furrow, dropped to her knees in the mud, jerked his pants down round his knees and gave him head, head like no fucking head he'd ever been given before. When he came, he came great curdsy gobs which she spat into the furrow. His knees went weak and he fell over frontwards, forcing her down beneath him. Then, with the greeny vegetable smell of truck garden and the bleachy Clorox smell of immortality rising up all around them and Selena's dark hair spreading out under her head like black tangled worms on the fertilized soil he fucked her again in the mouth and turned around and ate her for love and squalor and despair among the bitter tomato plants till they were both surfeited, exhausted, cast together in clay.

"But why?" Range kept asking her, when finally he could talk again. "Why? Why? Why?" he hollered, in total disbelief, rolling up and down in the furrow, screaming with laughter.

"Long before the white man came to this valley," Selena said, in deadly earnest, with her eyes staring straight up at the starry skies, unblinking, "there were women who made love to their men on the field of tomorrow's battle. They said it would bring them luck."

"Well," he said, "I guess we better do it again, Selena, 'cause we are gonna need all the luck we can get."

For over an hour Range and the strikers stood out there by the side of the road, waiting for something to happen. Then, when it did happen, it happened with amazing swiftness and changed everything. And when it was over he was left feeling shocked and empty and used and trying to figure out how it went down so fast.

Jay Jay did not bring his labor buses abreast of the strikers and cops.

He stopped them a couple of hundred yards down the road, near the patrol cars and paddywagons, and came ahead in his pickup alone. He halted in the middle of the road between the two lines of adversaries and switched off his lights. Then he got out, slammed the door, climbed up on the roof, and hollered, "GIMME SOME LIGHT!" And all at once the vehicles down the road switched on their high beams, illuminating him in a brilliant sheet of white light. For an instant Range was blinded, along with everyone else. Then, when he was able to get his eyes open again, he could see Jay Jay standing up there on the roof of his dusty Ford pickup with a portable loudspeaker in his hand.

He was dressed very carefully in a white straw Stetson hat, horn-rimmed glasses, a tan western shirt with pearl buttons, a Levi jacket and jeans, and a tan rawhide belt with a pair of pointy-toed cowboy boots to match.

Looking at him up there, Range thought the Wop looked like he'd lost a little weight here lately. The strike had evidently taken a lot out of him too. *But on him it looked good.* And, though Jay Jay was still by no means a slender specimen, he did cut quite a fine figure, up there above the crowd. He seemed to understand this about himself instinctively, like back in the days when he used to wheel his grand-daddy's Fergy Forklift so gloriously round the packing shed, setting all the Chicana girls aglow. And he exuded a cool, quiet self-confidence now as he began to speak. He moved gracefully as he spoke, in the way of certain very large men, adjusting the brim of his Stetson hat every so often, and kicking his boots out like a country and western music star clearing an invisible microphone cord.

And yet Range remembered him as one of the clumsiest guys at Calmento High, always stumbling over his own big feet.

He spoke without preamble, and in a mild, reasonable, intimate tone of voice, as if he'd just returned to a conversation he'd left off a few moments ago. The Mexicans were at first so astonished by his low-key performance that no one thought to interrupt him.

It was a technique he had learned from Selena.

Now he used it to devastating effect against her.

"I STOPPED THOSE BUSES DOWN THERE FOR A REASON," he said, in the small tenor voice that was so startling in a man of his size, a voice that, amplified through the little battery-charged loudspeaker, seemed at once very near and very far away. "I WANTED TO IMPRESS YOU PEOPLE IN THE CCAC WITH THE FACT THAT I HAVE TWO CHOICES OUT HERE THIS MORNING.

"I CAN DRIVE THOSE BUSES UP HERE AND LET THOSE BRACEROS GO TO WORK AND THAT WILL BE THE END OF YOUR STRIKE BECAUSE THERE IS NO POWER ON EARTH THAT IS GONNA GET YOU THROUGH THAT POLICE LINE.

"OR, IF I WANT, I CAN TURN THOSE BUSES AROUND
AND SEND THEM OUT TO MY BROTHER-IN-LAW OR ANY
NUMBER OF OTHER GROWERS WHO COULD USE THEIR
HELP RIGHT NOW VERY NICELY ON ACCOUNT OF THE
LABOR SHORTAGE.

"NOW, OF COURSE, I CAN'T BE GIVING AWAY GOOD
HELP UNLESS I GOT SOMEBODY ELSE TO WORK MY
FIELD. AND THAT'S WHERE YOU COME IN. YOU KNOW,
I BELIEVE, AND I AM SURE THAT YOU ARE BEGINNING
TO BELIEVE, THAT THIS DAMN STRIKE HAS JUST BEEN
GOING ON TOO LONG. WHY DON'T WE JUST SETTLE OUR
DIFFERENCES RIGHT HERE AND NOW AND GET BACK
TO WORK?"

"I'll tell you why!" Selena yelled.

"Come on!" Corky DeJesus shouted back at her. "Let him finish what
he got to say!"

"Right on!" hollered one of the three Apaches.

"*Qué sí, qué sí!*" others in the line confirmed.

Selena let herself get shouted down.

And Jay Jay continued, very calmly, "IF YOU PEOPLE WILL
DROP ALL YOUR *HUELGA* SIGNS INTO THE BACK OF MY
PICKUP RIGHT NOW, AND IF YOU ARE WILLING TO AC-
CEPT MY TERMS, WHICH I AM SURE YOU WILL FIND
VERY GENEROUS, THEN THERE IS NOTHING STOPPING
YOU FROM WALKING RIGHT OUT IN THAT FIELD THIS
MORNING AND EARNING A FULL DAY'S WAGES.

"NOW, LET ME OUTLINE JUST BRIEFLY WHAT I AM
PREPARED TO OFFER YOU . . ."

"You don't offer shit!" Selena yelled. "We take!"

"Shut up!" Corky DeJesus cried. "We already heard that before, too
many times."

"Shut up! *Qué te calles!*" others shouted down the line, people Range
could not see in the darkness.

Again Selena let herself get shouted down. It was the first time she'd
ever been treated this way. Range felt sorry for her. He turned to pat
her on the arm and comfort her. But she flung his hand away angrily.

"I AM WILLING TO DRAW A LINE RIGHT DOWN THE
MIDDLE," Jay Jay said, slicing the light beams with the flat of his
hand. "I AM WILLING TO COMPROMISE WITH YOUR
WAGE DEMANDS. IN OTHER WORDS, WHEN YOU WALK
OUT THERE IN THAT FIELD TODAY, YOU WILL BE EARN-
ING TWENTY-FIVE CENTS AN HOUR MORE—UN AU-
MENTO DE VEINTE CINCO CENTAVOS LA HORA—" he said,
having done his homework in Spanish, "THAN WHEN YOU
STARTED THIS STRIKE. NOW," he said, surveying his audience
with some satisfaction, "IS THAT FAIR OR NOT?"

His speech was masterful in its simplicity. He was even smart enough to leave out all the accusations and recriminations he could have aimed at Selena. After all, the campesinos were still completely in the dark as to her role in getting them fired off the job. They had no idea that she had libeled them to their boss, accusing them of being disloyal, or that she had lied to them later when she blamed the 'Duccis for all of their troubles. Jay Jay could have easily called their attention to these things, in addition to the fact that she had done them quite cynically, to further her own political ends. He could have devastated her, right then and there, stripped her naked in front of her people. But apparently this wasn't part of his strategy.

He gave her nothing, not even credit for her own duplicity.

In this way he offered the campesinos no central idea or figure around which they could rally in defense. He pretended that they were all simply one big association of free agents, a body democratic, leaderless, anarchic, and perfectly capable of making their decisions by consensus, on the spot.

And it worked.

He disdained the emotional. Logic was his only weapon. And it was irrefutable. Especially from the standpoint of the campesinos, who would soon be facing hunger.

"*Tiene razón!*" Corky shouted. "He's right!"

"*Tiene razón! Tiene razón!*" the campesinos repeated, in tones of wonder, as if they could not believe that there was actually a possibility that they might eat this winter. They were like children, Range thought. The Children of the Fifth Sun, Selena called them. Like children they had rallied around her in the beginning, quickly, thoughtlessly, without a glance back. So now would they abandon her.

"But what about all the rest of our demands?" Range shouted, in a desperate attempt to stem the tide of defection.

He had felt it was Selena's place to bring up this particular point, since she was the author of the demands. But when he had turned to call it to her attention, he had been astounded to find her gazing up at Jay Jay as enrapt by his performance as any of the most benighted and gullible campesinos.

And he remembered the way she used to look up at Jay Jay when he showed off on his grandpa's new red forklift, forty-four lifetimes ago, and he felt a painful stab of jealousy, something like he'd never felt since he was in his teens.

"That's only one of our demands!" he shouted again, stoutly. "What about all the rest?"

"Fuck the rest!" Corky DeJesus piped up. "Let's go back to work. *A trabajar! A trabajar!*"

"*A trabajar! A trabajar!*" cried the campesinos, with the fat little traitorous Corky at their lead. "*A trabajar! A trabajar!*"

And then one of them started to sing. A monotonous little ditty that

Aguilar used to sing when he was working in the field. *"Trabajar . . .
trabajar . . ."* the campesino sang, accompanying himself on a battered guitar. *"Trabajar . . . trabajar . . ."* a popular Mexican song.
And Selena did nothing, and Range could do nothing to prevent the
refrain from picking up and spreading up and down the line, getting
louder and louder and more and more rebellious and exuberant.

"Trabajar . . . trabajar . . ." they sang, ecstatic in their deliverance,
laughing, shouting, dancing around in circles, throwing their sombreros
into the air.

"Ai ai ai aiiiiiiiii qué viva trabajo!"

"Qué vamos a trabajar!"

Long live work. For work was all they wanted. All they did. All they
were. Work was their reason, their will, their way. Work was where they
were at. Why they were here on the planet. Like Aguilar used to say,
work was their middle name.

It was something that Selena had forgotten.

And Jay Jay had remembered.

And then like a dam, first in the middle where Corky DeJesus had
made the first crack, and then pouring inward toward the gap, the line
broke and flowed out to surround the tall smiling Italian cowboy on
the roof of the pickup truck in a single great singing deafening wave
of loving reconciliation.

And Selena was left standing alone by the side of the road with only
Range and her immediate *familia* to accompany her in her disgrace.

Twenty-four

"WHERE'S THE DOOR?" he said.

"Right there in front of you, Del."

"I can't see it."

"In the weeds, there," Selena said.

"Here?"

"I think so."

"That's not it."

"*Seguro?*"

"Naw," Range said. "How'd you find out about this cellar, anyway?"

"Belongs to my aunt."

"Which aunt?"

"Connie's mama."

"Where's she at now?"

"My aunt? Why, she's in the house sleeping, I guess," Selena said. "Mama and Rio are staying with her now, you know."

"No," Range said. "I didn't know."

"Yeah."

"How's she doing, now?"

"Mama?" Selena said, in a curiously offhanded tone. "Oh, she's still in deepest mourning. I'm afraid. Won't talk. Won't eat. Only good thing about it is she's losing weight."

For two days now, ever since the debacle under the Highway 50 bridge, Selena had been astonishing Range, and alarming him, with such displays of eerie detachment.

Yet when he acquainted her with his misgivings, she only laughed.

And then when in anger he called her attention to the fact of her disgrace, the fact that her own people had rejected her, she merely said, "Don't take things so hard, Del. This is war. And it's going to be a long one. I've known that all along. Now, it's true that we have lost our first battle. But the war, I assure you, we are going to win."

Confronted with an audacity such as this, a faith as blind as this, Range found himself unable to react, unable to do anything but unwillingly suspend his disbelief.

Then tonight at CCAC headquarters she had stretched his credulity almost to the breaking point.

"I'm through with this place," she had said in a conspiratorial voice, so that Lita, Nacho, Jovita, Gloria Cruz—the humble ones, the invisible ones in straw sombreros and gay-colored bandannas, the last remaining members of her family—could not hear. "We may have to go underground for a while."

"*Underground?*" he had said. He had found it impossible to believe his own ears.

"That's right," she had said. "We don't, boy, and Jay Jay's gonna clap you back in the slammer faster than you say Cristóbal Colón."

But Jay Jay had made no attempt to jail him as yet.

And Selena's motives went deeper than that anyway.

Nevertheless, here Range was now, knee-high in the wild oats behind her Aunt Amalia's house on South "D" Street, searching for a canning cellar in which Selena used to play with her cousin as a little girl.

"Here's the door!" she said at last.

"Jesus," Range said, "this is like some kind of . . ."

"I know," she said, with a glance at the starlit sky, the sliver of moon. "Sort of hard to find in the dark, no?"

". . . All grown over like this."

"Just the way I like it."

"How do you mean?"

"It's safe," she said.

"From what?"

"Whatever," she said. "First thing I did was set it up. Soon as I came back to Calmento."

"But how did you know?"

"You never know," she said.

"But yesterday you said you knew," Range said. "You knew how it would turn out all along." His tone with her was vehement and yet somehow uncertain, wavering in what he felt to be an almost fatherly way between concern over her inconsistent behavior and anger over her carelessness in allowing herself to be put into a position where she might become inconsistent. He loved to hear this tone in his own voice. It was proof that he cared. It was the voice of his conscience; he'd rarely if ever heard it before.

"Between you and me, Range," she said, laughing blithely, "I don't know shit. Or more precisely, I only know what it suits me to know at the moment."

And then the door came creaking open as she swung it upward from the ground. She let it go and it crashed back into the dry wild oats and mustard weed, raising a cloud of dust that blew off quickly around the house. She reached inside and switched on a yellow light, illuminating herself, Range, and the yellow weeds, the chicken coop, the rabbit hutches, the abandoned pup tents of the campesinos, the unpainted picket fence, and Aunt Amalia's laundry flapping madly on the clothesline behind them.

To Range the moment was long and tense and pure, fraught with all the possibilities of the highest drama. And he knew he would remember it always. In his mind's eye he saw it as painted by the hand of an unknown Flemish master, "The Dawn Conspirators," or something. Which is not to say that he wasn't quite aware of its morbid and even farcical aspects.

"Now what happens?"

"Come down inside and find out."

He scrambled around her and down the creaky wooden stairs. *Bam!* she slammed the door shut above him. It echoed tightly in the small enclosed earthen space. The sound of the wind kept whistling in his ears for a second, and then all was quiet.

Then his ears started to ring with the silence.

When he reached the floor of the cellar he found it was heel-shaped, about ten feet wide and fifteen feet long, with five concentric rings of shelves hacked like steps out of the native clay walls. The shelves were lined with Mason jars full of preserved tomatoes and chile peppers. The ceiling of the place was nothing more than the floor of Connie's mother's bedroom, through which Range could faintly hear the sound of her snoring. The wooden ribs of the ceiling were festooned with cobwebs and ragged black wiring. The only light was suspended from a long wire in the middle of the room. Directly below the light stood a rickety green card table and four old pink supermarket lawn chairs. In one of the chairs a large straw shoulder bag was sitting. Range recognized it instantly. It belonged to La Trucha Connie. Spread out on top of the table were a half-empty bottle of Boone's Farm Tickle Pink wine, a battered paperback copy of *The Labyrinth of Solitude*, by Octavio Paz, and the remains of an enchilada. At the other end of the cellar, closing off its curved rear portion, hung a large red and black striped Mexican blanket, much like the one in Selena's cubbyhole in the CCAC loft. Behind it, Range assumed, a bed lay hidden on the floor.

"We got company," he said.

"You didn't think I meant all that stuff seriously, did you?" Selena said, coming up behind him.

"What stuff?"

"All that about kicking Connie out of the union."

"I don't know what I thought," he said. "But I know what Connie thought. She was pretty sure that you meant exactly what you said."

"Well," Selena said, "I straightened her out on that score."

"When?" he said.

"Oh," she said casually, "the other day. See, I thought I might find her down here. She helped me set the place up. When we first hit town."

"To me it is really kind of surprising," Range said, more mildly than his private suspicions would have indicated. He could not figure out why he was willing to walk so blithely with his lover through the valley of the shadow of her own death. *Connie is working for the Dootch.*

"Surprising?" Selena said. "Why's that?"

"I can't figure out why you'd want to trust her, after everything that went down between you two."

"Trust her? Trust her?" Selena said. "She's my own flesh and blood. If I can't trust her, then who can I trust?"

"You can trust me," he said.

Connie will conspire, but Connie will never hurt her.

"How far?"

"All the way," he said.

Jay Jay is the unknown quantity. Even to himself, maybe.

"That remains to be seen."

"Well, anyway," Range said, smiling, peeking behind the curtain to hide his nervousness, "looks like nobody's home at the moment."

"Looks like it," Selena said. "Cheerful down here, huh?"

"Like the grave."

"Don't be so obvious, Delano," she said. "You could get used to it if you had to."

"Let's not get *too* used to it," he said, sniffing, laughing, turning to face her. She was wearing a red, white, and black sequined headband, a patched and faded denim Wrangler jacket, a Brown Power sweat-shirt, bell-bottomed blue jeans, and a pair of charro boots. Her coppery skin glowed with high color. Her waist-length hair shone lustrous and black under the feeble light of the single bulb.

No one wore defeat like Selena Cruz.

When it suited her to.

She knows everything I know, and more.

It was like a passion play, stiff and ritualistic, the characters of which must play their parts through to the end, with the strictest attention to their lines and no deviation from the script. Selena had written the whole thing out in her brain, probably, a long time ago.

"Why not?" she said, approaching him, kissing him on the neck. "Why not?" she said again playfully, drawing away from him quickly when he made a move to grab her. "A little practice never hurt any-one. Right?"

"Personally," Range said, "I don't need any dry runs. Figure I'll have plenty of time to iron out any difficulties."

"Oh," she said, "you can bet on that, Del! All the way to Judgment Day."

"Eternity," he said, correcting her.

"You don't believe in resurrection?"

"I'm a materialist."

"And judgment?"

"Are you kidding? Look around. Look at yourself. The rich get richer and the poor get poorer."

"You told me once you wanted to be judged."

"I did?"

"By your actions, you said."

"That must've been when I was on the other side," he said. "The winning side."

"I thought you might have a few questions you wanted to ask," she said, changing the subject, seating herself at the card table, beckoning him to join her.

"A few," he said, sitting across from her. "Now that you mention it."

"Shoot," she said, reaching into Connie's bag for a prerolled joint.

"All right," he said. "What in the fuck are we doing in this goddamn tomb?"

"Doing the unexpected," she said with an infuriating self-satisfaction, lighting up the joint, inhaling deeply.

"What's so unexpected about this?" Range said. "It's just the kind of mysto number that you would pull."

"That's what you think," she said, toking calmly at the joint.

"What I know."

"You don't know shit."

"You said that before."

"It's as true as ever," she said, handing the cigarette over to Range. Sucking hard, retaining the smoke deep in his lungs, and then exhaling it, he said in a small tight voice, "I know enough to recognize defeat when I see it staring me in the face."

"But not deception?"

"What?" he said, passing the joint back to Selena.

"Never mind."

"No, come on, what do you mean?"

"Maybe it's all part of the plan," she said, puffing hard, sucking air in with it.

"I give up," Range said. "What's the plan?"

"Wait till Vanducci gets cocky," Selena said, reaching out with her calm fingers and depositing the little roach into Range's trembling ones. "Then hit him where he hurts the most."

"Where's that?"

"I'm not going to tell you that, Del," she said, smiling the smile of the high. "Not till you promise me you'll help me do it."

"I never make a promise," Range said, toking at the stub till it burnt his nails, "that I'm not sure I can keep."

"Couldn't you keep this one?"

"That depends."

"On what?"

"On what hurts Jay Jay most," Range said, dropping the roach to the dirt floor, grinding it under his heel, "and on how you want to hit him."

"How would you hit him?"

"While he was down."

"Ho ho."

". . . But unfortunately he's up now," Range said. "Jesus! Could you believe the way that fucker played his audience? If I hadn't seen it with my own eyes, I . . ."

"Don't you think," Selena said, not listening, "that he is most vulnerable in his shed?"

"To what?"

"Fire," she said.

"Hey," Range said, "that's against the law." He had meant it to be taken as a joke. But halfway through his statement he had felt a yawning chasm opening up beneath his feet, and his words came out sounding much more sincere than he had ever intended.

He was zonked out of his fucking gourd. This weed was dyn-o-mite. Already he could feel it bombarding his brain cells, tightening the imaginary rubber band around his head.

And he was afraid he would play his role out exactly as she had written it.

"Fuck the law," Selena said. "We'll burn him out and his tomatoes will rot in the field and all his laws and all his cops and judges and scabs will become extraneous to the fact."

"And the campesinos?"

"You got to take the long view, Range."

"I'm thinking of winter."

"It's going to be tough. But next year they'll come out fighting. . . . Remember when we were kids, Del, and they used to sneak up in the stacks and winter it out in the empty tomato lugs? Remember that?" she said, her eyes clouding over with her vision. "And remember how they used to make little cubbyholes up there, big ones, apartments, almost, right in the middle of the boxes. They used to bring gunnysacks up there and nail them to the ceiling and the walls to keep the wind and rain out. They used to turn over boxes to use as chairs and tables. They even used to rig up electric lights and secondhand electric heaters and sneak down and plug them into the Vanduccis' meter. . . . I remember one place. It was fixed up like a little ship's cabin. Belonged to one of Aguilar's *compadres*. His name was Juan Quintanilla. Used to call him 'Juan Quin Quin' for short. Funny little guy, redheaded, with the longest tongue. He could touch his chin with it. He could even pick his nose with it. A real comedian. And I remember he seemed to be getting by very well up there, with his bottle of wine, his gunnysacks and rags and old clothes he used to pile in the corner to sleep on. His '*chingadera* heaven,' I remember he used to call it," Selena said, smiling warmly at the memory, "for all of the junk and castoffs of the gringo that he used to collect up there. . . . ."

"Why don't you finish the story?" Range said. But Selena blinked at him like she didn't understand. "Why don't you tell what happened to Juan Quin Quin?"

"What happened?" she said. "I don't remember."

"A big wind came up one night and they found him next morning under a ton of boxes."

"You're full of shit," she said, smiling at him.

"You're out of your fucking mind," he said. It was meant as praise.

"Now before we get too stoned," Selena said, "let me just briefly outline my plan for you." She hesitated a moment. Looked over at Range. And when he did not object (and why did he not object? It was something he would wonder about for the rest of his life), continued, "All we need is three good people and a moonless night. We'll park the truck on Lehman Road, a half-mile south of the shed. We'll cross the field carrying a hacksaw and three five-gallon cans of gasoline. We'll climb the back fence, cut through the lock on the rear door, throw the gas onto the tomato lugs that Jay Jay's got stacked up just inside, and split."

"Who are the 'three good people'?"

"You, me, and Connie."

"Connie?" he said. And all of a sudden he started sweating under the arms, under the gonads, up the crack of his ass. Started grinding his jaw, sawing his teeth together, blinking nonstop. His mouth was dry as dust. His heart was firing off like a Kalishnikov gun.

"Sure. She wanted back on my team, she said. 'All right,' I said, 'but you're gonna have to prove yourself to get back on my team!'"

"And she went along with it?"

"Of course she went along with it," Selena said. "Why wouldn't she go along with it?"

"Well, don't you think that firebombing is a little out of her character?"

"Range, if there's one thing I've found out through all of this, it's that *character can be changed,* on a very deep level."

"You are fucking amazing," he said. And then, exercising every last ounce of his willpower, he at last succeeded in swallowing his profound incredulity. "All right, then," he said. "What about the night watchman?"

"Is there a night watchman?"

"You mean you don't *know*?"

"We'll create a diversion."

"I see."

"It just means we'll need four people on the job instead of three," she said. "We'll get Gloria. She'll work out fine. . . . What do you think of the plan?"

"It's . . . *insane,*" he said. And again it was not meant to be uncomplimentary.

" 'In flames it began,' " Selena quoted, from some obscure source, " 'and in flames must it end. . . .' "

"Where'd you get that?"

"I don't remember."

"Maybe you just made it up."

"Want to hear the rest?"

"Naw," he said, shaking his head slowly, dopily, imagining the walls of the cellar suddenly trembling around him, falling inward, crushing him under tons of gray matter. "I must be crazy too," he said. "But I dig you. I can't live without you."

"Take me now," she said, embracing him. "But you'll have to live without me."

Twenty-five

THE DREAM. The dark. The bed. The man. The curtain. The light. The walls of clay. The walls of ancient campfires and petrified clam shells and Indian bones. The table. The chairs. The wine. *The Labyrinth of Solitude.* The concentric circles of Mason jars stuffed with preserved fruit, preserved vegetables, preserved flesh. The body. The hair. The clothes that one wears.

The dirt floor. The stairway hacked out of the earth. The steps crumbling away to dry rot. The lock. The handle. The door creaking open, slamming down. The dust flying. The grave she had thought she might never leave lying open behind her.

And then the night. The moonless light. The meteorites of late August. And cool fresh air. The presence of friends. The familiar faces. The sniffs and shuffles and nervous laughs. Delanito y Consuelita. *El mono y la trucha.* And Gloria waiting in the Chevycita Bonita somewhere out there across this dark little Mexican town where Selena Cruz was born.

The path. The weeds. The wild oats. The empty pup tents and absent campesinos. The clothesline. The laundry swaying. The chicken coop. The rabbit hutch. The pony corral. The picket fence. The squeaky gate. The sandy alleyway between Third Street and Fourth Street. The cats. The rats in overturned garbage cans. The dogs barking. Goats bleating. Horses whinnying over backyard fences. The Johnny Carson show echoing emptily from four different TV sets. The eternal switch engines, humping and hooting and roaring in the no-man's-land between the races. The shouts of drunkards outside the cantinas on South Central Avenue. Mrs. Sanchez's kitchen garden. Mrs. Madrid's tall corn. Mexican music playing softly on her kitchen radio. The backyards where Selena played as a little girl. The high curb on South "B" Street where she sprained her ankle. Mr. Valdivia's tool shed where she once played nasty with a little boy named Greg, who later came home from Viet Nam in a canvas sack. The irrigation ditch on Mount Diablo Avenue where she fell and cut her head on a broken beer bottle and it took six stitches to sew it up and she still bore the scar to this day, under one thick, coarse, long braid of blue-black hair. Mrs. Alvarez's bean patch on South "C" Street. A line of whispering junipers. A barbed-wire fence. A shallow water ditch. The immemorial oleander shrub of her own backyard. The stall where, on a bright summer morning a lifetime ago, a tall dark stranger took a shower and washed off the dirt from his journey north, and Selena peeked. The incinerator where she burned his clothes. The vegetable garden of her mama, Mama Loca, where she picked a fresh salad for his lunch. And the cactus plant where she used to tie her goat. The rose trees gone wild. The peach tree unpicked. The savage scent of gardenias. The sickening scent of carnations.

In darkness and silence and sinfulness and sorrow, therefore, the abandoned Mexican shack where Selena Cruz grew up. The screen door banging in the wind. The splayed TV antenna rustling on the clapboard siding. Pepper tree branches, each as slim as a willow switch, swishing on the tarpaper roof. The Chevycita Bonita idling in the driveway, *for that is what she likes,* with a grinning Gloria Cruz behind the wheel.

And then the white gravel of South "C" Street. The blacktop of Sierra Avenue, and MacArthur Road. The engine droning. The springs protesting. The tailgate chain aclattering. The four *compañeros* squeezed up shoulder to shoulder in the front seat. And now the graveyard at the Schulte Road corner. And the dark fields of harvest time going by. Tomato, alfalfa, millet, barley, beets. And the peach orchard that Selena once traversed in its entirety on bloodied feet. Or was that somewhere else? Wasn't that down in Fresno County? And wasn't it an apricot orchard? *No importa.* For now it was the DANGER—UNDERGROUND CABLE sign, and the high Western Pacific embankment at Valpico Road for the ten thousandth time. And the last. She did have that flash.

And south now, going slow. Lights out. Past the Banta-Carbona Irrigation District office. Past the unlit Vanducci packing shed. Down behind the shed. Riding along the tall eucalyptus trees that lined the Carbona Canal . . .

It was Connie who finally broke the silence.

"I can't go through with this, Selena."

"What are you talking about?" *I knew my most trusted disciple would betray me. . . .*

"I smell a rat."

"Connie, I am just not in the mood for second thoughts at this late stage in the game," Selena said. *I saw the whole thing as clearly as the hand in front of my face. . . .*

"But *prima,* please . . ."

"No buts about it," Selena said angrily. "Come on, Gloria, let us out here."

"Then what?" Gloria said, popping her gum.

"Like I told you before, *cuñada,*" Selena said. "Drive back and park in the peach orchard. Go up to the front gate on foot. Start yelling at the top of your lungs, so the night watchman will come out and investigate. Stand there yelling for ten minutes exactly. Then get back in the truck and pick us up here."

"What do I yell?"

"Yell anything you want. Anything that comes into your head. Yell 'Viva la huelga!' for all I care. That way, if we get into trouble, we can claim we were framed," Selena said laughing, jabbing her sister-in-law in the ribs. "Who in the CCAC would be dumb enough to shout 'Viva la huelga!' Right?"

"Right," Gloria said, in total incomprehension.

"Okay, let's go."

"Selena, wait a second. I want to talk to you alone."

"You are trying my patience, Connie," Selena said. "If you got cold feet then just say so. And Range and I will go it alone." *I knew exactly the way her mind would work. I knew just the pathetic little noises she would make when she realized the possible consequences of her treachery. . . .*

"Right!" said Range loyally. "Ten gallons oughta be enough for the job."

"All right, you win," Connie said, climbing up on the running board, grabbing a can of gas out of the truckbed, "but don't say I didn't warn you."

"You just do like I tell you. And leave the worrying to me," Selena said. Then she sent Gloria on her way in the pickup truck, and led Del and Connie wading across the shallow irrigation ditch and out into the tomato field.

Before Selena had gone ten yards into the tomato field, she realized that she had made a drastic error in her plans. She had failed to take into account the fact that the furrows of the field were laid out from east to west. Instead of trotting along the natural pathways between the rows of plants, she and her *compañeros* had to struggle with their heavy burdens up and down the humped furrows and fight their way through thick knee-high lines of tomato plants. To make things worse, the field had just been irrigated, and the wet clay was treacherous beneath their feet. Especially Selena's feet. For one of her feet was still limping badly from the toe that had been hurting her, killing her, ever since Jay Jay Vanducci twisted it in her cubbyhole in the loft. She told herself it was "just psychological." But it did nothing to diminish the pain.

It was too late to turn back now, however. And there was nothing to do but continue northward, puffing and sweating and cursing, making for the dark metal bulk of the packing shed which they could see a half mile ahead of them across the field. . . . *I knew the enemy lay in wait. . . .*

In order to make the time pass and calm her heart, Selena tried to imagine what this tomato field must look like in the daytime. She tried to imagine her mother, brother, stepfather, and little sisters out there working on their knees, picking fruit. She tried to imagine a white dirt road cutting through the field, and a long-legged little Mexican girl in a short tattered frock ambling down the road with a big mean fighting cock cradled in her arms. And her feet just goin' *plop plop plop* in the dirt, raising little clouds of dust in her track. And cool sand squeezing up between her toes. And she tried to imagine that same little girl walking up to those poor stoop laborers and asking them, "Hey, was it worth it or not?" And, "Will you ever forgive me?" And she tried to imagine their response. But every time it seemed that Selena might hear, the answer blew away in the wind. And at last she had to give up even the attempt. For the going had gotten very rough in the field. And it had become apparent that they would never make it in time.

Long before they reached the halfway mark, Selena could hear Gloria yelling "*Viva la huelga!*" from the other side of the shed, and knew that her only chance lay in a drastic change of plans.

. . . Yet despite all opposition we made it through, and flung our firebombs on the highly combustible tomato lugs. . . .

"Connie," she said, "put your gas can down and run out ahead of us. Take the hacksaw and cut the lock open. Range and I will run along behind you with one can between us. Otherwise we'll never make it in time."

"Selena," Connie said, approaching her, whispering so Range wouldn't hear. "There is really something I got to confess . . ."

"I know all about it, dear. And I've already forgiven you in advance. . . . I know that you only had my best interests at heart. Now, don't worry. Just do like I say. And everything will turn out okay."

Yet still La Trucha hesitated, splashing her feet in the water, squishing around in the mud, swinging her gas can back and forth anxiously, rustling the leaves of the tomato plants. While from the other side of the packing shed Gloria kept calling out "*Viva la huelga! Viva la huelga!*"

"Move your ass!" Selena said. And Connie sighed in resignation, dropped her gas can in the water at her feet, grabbed the hacksaw out of Range's outstretched hand, and took off running over the rows toward the packing shed. While Selena and Delano scurried along behind her as fast as they could go, hauling the one remaining can of gas between them.

. . . The packing shed went up in flames. The ambushers came running out like insects in all directions, screaming and firing indiscriminately in their panic. . . .

"What the fuck was Connie going on about?" Range panted.

"Hell, I don't know."

"You sure about that?"

Selena laughed in the darkness.

"Well, I'll be damned," she said.

"You don't think I'm stupid, do you?"

"Naw," she said. "Well, I guess you really are on our side now. Ain't you, you little bastard?"

"All the way," he said.

"Won't be long now."

"That's what I'm afraid of."

"You afraid?"

"You fucking A John I'm afraid!"

"Then how come you stick around?"

"I figure . . . if you know what you're getting us into, you'll know how to get us out."

"I've given it some thought."

"Glad to hear that."

"But I'm not infallible, you know."

"I hope you're wrong on that score."

"Just in case, Delano," she said, "I want you to promise me something."

"Just in case of what?"

"Just in case something happens to me . . . I want you to promise me that you will carry on our work in the San Joaquin."

"Nothing's gonna happen to you."

"Promise!"

"Okay, I promise," he said, and started pulling her forward with his end of the gas can.

"Promise me in Spanish," she said.

But before he could answer her someone shouted "FREEZE!" over a powerful loudspeaker and they were captured in a brilliant circle of white light.

Selena was blinded for a moment. And in order to contain her trepidation, she imagined . . . *I fled beside my valiant* compañero. *We made for the eucalyptus trees that lined the Carbona Canal.* . . .

"FREEZE!" he shouted again. But his command was redundant. For they had all been frozen in mid-stride ever since the spotlight came on: Range and Selena frozen in the middle of the field with the gasoline can between them, and La Trucha Connie frozen in another circle of light some forty yards farther toward the packing shed, still in the attitude of a runner.

"FREEZE. STAND RIGHT WHERE YOU ARE. YOU ARE UNDER ARREST."

"I tried to tell you, Selena, I tried!" Connie sobbed, starting back across the field toward her cousin.

"FREEZE. DO NOT MOVE ANOTHER STEP."

"Get down, Connie," Range hollered, "get down!"

"STOP OR WE'LL SHOOT!"

Selena thought she recognized the voice on the loudspeaker. It was Prettyboy Pombo, the Portagee undersheriff of the Calmento substation.

"Stop, Connie, stop!" she screamed, and then almost immediately, it seemed, she could see a number of small scattered yellow flashes lighting up the juniper trees at the east end of the field. And she could hear a flurry of rapid little popping sounds.

"Oh?" Connie said, surprised. "Oh?" she said again, as if nothing quite so startling had happened to her in some time. And settled slowly to her knees.

"Connie!" Selena called. But no one answered. So she started off for the place where her cousin had disappeared behind the low wall of foliage. Right away the little yellow flashes and popping noises started up again. And the tomato plants on either side of her began twitching and shaking ominously. But she ignored the commotion, and the shouts through the loudspeaker, and made her way purposefully across the field, shielding her eyes from the spotlight, watching her feet so she wouldn't trip over the vines.

Then something hit her from behind. Violently she was impelled forward. . . . *I got hit in the side. I was losing blood fast. I was afraid I could not go much farther.* . . . And the next thing she knew she was lying flat on her face on a toppled tomato bush, squishing an overripe fruit with her nose. And Range was lying on top of her, pressing her down harder, harder.

"I been hit," she said.

"Bullshit," he said. "I hit you. Now let's get out of here."

"I can't leave Connie."

"Connie's no good to anyone, anymore," he said angrily. "Now come on!" And cuffed her a stinging blow across the neck. Yanked her forward by the hair. Hard. Making her feel it. And started bullying her down the muddy furrow on hands and knees. While overhead, bullets whipped through the spotlit leaves.

He struck out west, making for the eucalyptus trees that lined the Carbona Canal, using the high wall of plants as a screen between him and the law.

"Move, Selena, move!" he kept urging her. But she felt no inclination to hurry. It was true that men were firing off weapons behind her, around her. And some with brutal voices were shouting at each other across the field. And others were beating their way up through the rows with truncheons. But Selena just could not take them at all seriously. She felt she'd been through the whole thing before. And for some reason she got it into her head that there was nothing to be afraid of.

Now she could hear one of them splashing through the mud nearby, switching through the tomato plants. She could see the beams of his powerful flashlight playing on the plants over her head, darting through the leaves, seeking her out. He was a big man, a great heavy man with enormous feet. He was coming closer, closer all the time.

. . . *I allowed my brave* compañero *to outdistance me.* "Go," *I said to myself,* "go, for you are the Quinto Sol!" *And I hid among the vines.* . . .

Just fifty yards from the Carbona Canal and Selena stopped dead. Wouldn't budge an inch, though Range slapped her and cursed her and pulled her hair and jerked her arm nearly out of its socket.

"Come on, damn you!"

"No," she said, "once is enough."

"You're gonna get caught," he said, tears tracking down his dirty face, shining in the light of the oncoming electric torch.

"There's just this one last thing I can do."

"If you don't go," said Delano, "I don't go."

"*Vaya!*" she said, with irresistible authority, and stood up with her hands in the air. "You got me, mister, I give up!"

And Range slithered off down the furrow to fling himself down the precipitous concrete bank and into the swift-running waters of the Carbona Canal.

. . . My pursuer discovered me a moment later, and brought me trembling to my feet. I fell toward him in the furrow. He dropped his rifle and his light. He caught me in his arms and . . .

Tripping over tomato plants, slipping and sliding in the mud, panting heavily, Selena's great pursuer caught up with her at last. His light blinded her. She could not see his face. But she knew him anyway. She knew him by his silence, and the smell of his sweat. He appeared to her as a young lover, with smooth strong muscles and a white moonface.

He approached to within ten feet of her and then hesitated, trying to catch his breath, trying to keep his balance on the unsteady clay.

He seemed unsure as to what to do with her, now that he'd finally got her. Anything, *anything* was possible. This was California. . . .

And on the impulse of a moment, he . . .

"You win," she said, smiling up at him meekly, "I've had it."

Still he would not reveal himself. He was very very jumpy behind his light. And he could not seem to get his wind back.

Selena read danger in his symptoms.

Yet, what had he to be frightened of but himself, and one small-boned Mexican girl?

"Go ahead, do whatever you want," she said, in what she thought to be a reassuring tone. "I'm tired of scheming."

And fell toward him in the furrow.

He grunted and leapt aside, raising his shotgun as if to defend himself.

A sunburst of light. And Selena was falling backwards even before she heard the blast. She twisted as she fell and landed with her lips pressed to the warm fragrant clay. The dark Virgin came down from the Diablos and carried her away. And in the brain of the body she left behind, her myth slowly wound to an end.

. . . On the impulse of a moment Vanducci abandoned his farm and his family for the love of Selena Cruz. While the indestructible Range, rising from the ashes of defeat to seize the advantage from the leaderless opposition forces, led his people to victory in the field. . . .

Ernest Brawley lives in Rome with his wife Chiara Coletti and his daughter Lucia. At present he is working on another novel. He says of himself: "My family is Anglo-Indio-Hispanic in origin, out of Alabama and Chihuahua by way of Tulsa, Tucson and L.A. My father and my uncles went to work as prison guards and I was raised on the grounds of several California penal institutions, including Chino, Lancaster, Vacaville, San Quentin and Tracy. It was in Tracy, a small railroad and farming community in the San Joaquin Valley, that I went to high school and got my first jobs: farmworker, packing shed employee, and switchman on the Southern Pacific Railroad. One morning while I was riding the head end of a diesel engine out of Tracy Yard I saw a remarkably pretty and bright-eyed little Mexican girl walking by the side of the tracks. I saw her for only an instant, but I was sure that I recognized her from somewhere. Since that day in 1959 I have traveled all over the world and I have lived and worked and studied in many places from Buenos Aires to Tokyo to Paris but I have never forgotten that little Chicana. And at last I have found time to write about her.